Demon of Lorr
A Kingdom of Lorr Novel

M.J. Stewart

The Kingdom of Lorr

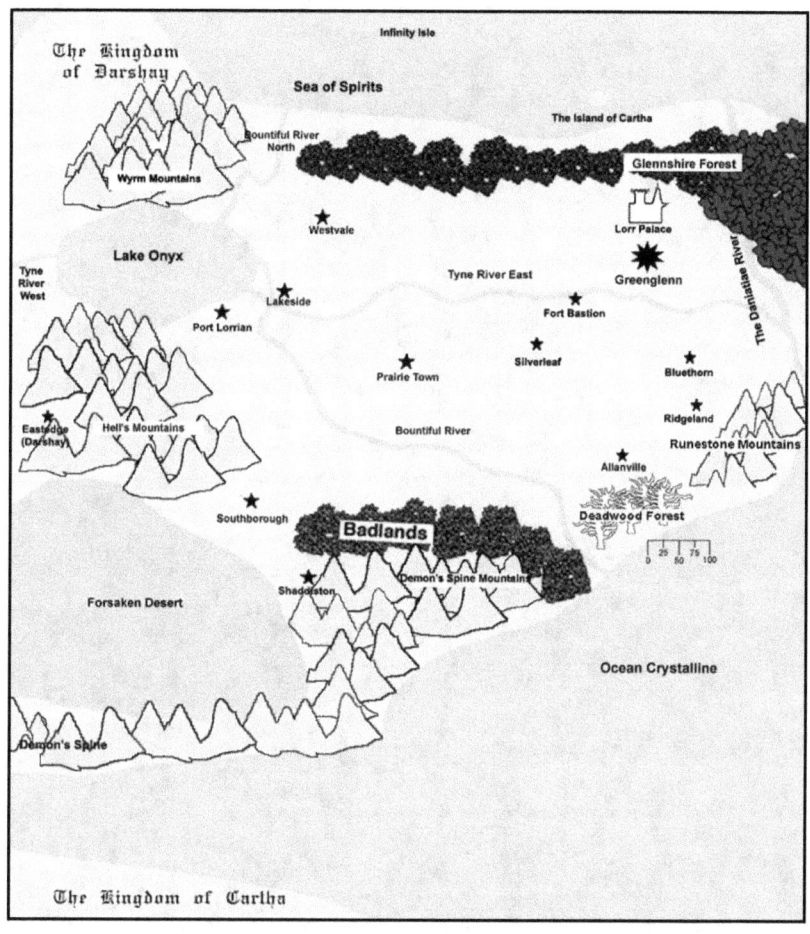

PROLOGUE

Dirk Tauran, Baron of Eastedge, rode his hulking brown warhorse at the head of his entourage in contemplative silence. He was recalling a night three years ago when his life changed, and trying to decide whether it had changed for the better or for the worse.

He had just regained consciousness from the sound thrashing the offworlder Raxe had given him at the foot of WorldHopper's mountain. The three moons shone so bright that the night sky was more gray than black. He could clearly see the corpse of Meldrick Sureblade, High Captain of the Royal Lorrian Home Guard, where it lay in a drying pool of blood. A grin eased across Tauran's bearded face at the sight. Quick the Changeling, however, was gone, which meant the Finder's arrow unfortunately did not kill the boy.

Tauran could also see one of their gryphons in the distance grazing on the sparse grasses sprouting here and there from the rocky valley floor. The omnivorous bird-cat had emerged from where the Legion Midnight mercenaries and the Finder had concealed their mounts so they could ambush Sureblade and the changeling.

One of the two legionnaires that accompanied Tauran still lay unconscious. The other was sitting on the ground, swaying dizzily and whining about his bleeding thigh wound. He had removed his right cuisse and greave to free his leg and had tied a tourniquet around it to slow the bleeding, but judging by the frown on his face and the way his skin appeared pure white in the pale moonlight, he had already lost a lot of blood and had nothing to dull the pain.

"What are you crying about, Fitz?" Tauran asked irritably as he gained his feet. "Your wound

is dressed. You should be thanking the Old Ones for not letting the offworlder amputate the damn leg."

"I'm scared enough to piss," Fitz complained. "I can't walk or sit a gryphon with this wound, and WorldHopper may come down here at any moment to feast on us."

An icy wave a fear washed over Tauran at the mention of the King of the Dragons. The fear, however, was quickly banished when he studied the position of the moons and stars and realized how much time had passed since he was knocked unconscious.

"Don't piss yourself, Fitz. The three of us would hardly make a feast for an adult dragon. Besides, if he were still alive he would've eaten us already. The Finder has surely put an end to him by now."

"But the offworlder went after the Finder," Fitz argued. "What if he stopped the Finder before – by the gods!" Fitz's eyes went wide as he looked up at the mountain.

Tauran looked up in time to see the silhouette of WorldHopper emerging from high up on the mountainside. Even from such a great height, the astounding size of the beast was unmistakable as it emerged from the sheer face of the mountain.

Tauran scrambled to take cover behind a large fallen boulder and prayed the dragon would not notice them. He sighed heavily in relief when the dragon flapped its massive wings one time and proceeded to glide east.

It seemed impossible that a creature so colossal could fly so easily, but fly it did, until it disappeared into the night.

Tauran was about to rise but instead threw himself to the ground again when the shadow of another dragon and then another and yet another detached from the shadows of the surrounding mountainsides, all of them soaring east.

DEMON OF LORR

In less than a minute the sky was so filled with the winged beasts that they completely blocked the moons' light and threw the valley floor into near blackness.

It seemed to take forever for the flying procession of scales, teeth, and claws to finally cease. Tauran waited another few minutes for good measure before he stood.

"Did you see that?" he asked Fitz. "That must've been every dragon in the Wyrm Mountains, and they're all headed east...where the demons are. It's Heaven's War all over again but without the Old Ones!"

There was no answer. He looked over and saw that Fitz's eyes were closed. The wounded man was not dead, though. Tauran could see the rise and fall of the other's torso as he breathed heavily and evenly. Tauran did not know if the man had fallen asleep or passed out from blood loss or fright, and it did not matter to him in the least.

Tauran knew he had to get out of there. It might have been dragon country, but there were other man-eating beasts in the Wyrm Mountains. If they saw all of those dragons leaving they would be emboldened and would eagerly come out into the open to hunt.

The first thing he had to do was find at least one of the gryphons. They were not where he saw them a few minutes earlier. The flight of the dragons had to have spooked them. They were well trained, though, and would not have gone far. As he surveyed the area he turned at the sound of Fitz moaning in his sleep.

"You can't walk or sit a gryphon, eh?" Tauran said at just above a whisper.

He looked at Fitz for a long time and then came to a decision. He looked for and located his discarded broadsword, stepped over quickly to retrieve it, and stepped back just as quickly, but cautiously, to Fitz and then slid the sharp edge of the blade across the sleeping man's throat.

Fitz's eyes opened as wide as they did when he saw WorldHopper. The doomed man tried to cry out and all he could do was gurgle and choke on his own blood.

As Fitz lay dying Tauran stepped to the unconscious Legionnaire and stared at his unprotected neck. "Sorry Chad," he apologized insincerely. "But I'll need all the provisions I can get if I have to walk out of here."

Chad stirred at the sound of Tauran's voice and opened his eyes just in time to see the blade falling toward his neck. "And if I'm able to find two of the gryphons," Tauran continued after the deed was done, "I'll need an extra gryphon and as many extra saddlebags as it can carry. The dragons have gone to fight demons, after all, leaving all of their hoarded treasure behind."

Tauran thought the Lord Ascendant and His Old Ones had finally smiled upon him after years of neglect. He thought wrong. Only one of the gryphons was found. All he could do was fly home. Things seemed to happen impossibly fast after that.

The dark wizard came to him one night when he was staggering home from a night of drunken brawling at a local tavern. The dark wizard knew about what happen that night, the things that no one but the two dead Legionnaires could know, and they certainly could not have told anyone.

For reasons that Tauran could never guess, the dark wizard gifted him with the biggest gryphon he had ever seen. The bird-cat was black from its feathered head to its furry lion's legs. Even its wicked beak was as black as pitch. The only things about it that were not black were its eyes, which were tiny marbles of crimson that seemed to glow in the shadows of the night.

DEMON OF LORR

A saddle rested upon the gryphon's broad back. From that saddle hung a great leather broadsword sheath, and in that great sheath rested Dragon-fang, the Finder's fabled greatsword. The only reason it fit in the sheath was because it had been broken in the Finder's battle against the Child of the Old Ones called Raxe. Even broken, it was still nearly as long as a broadsword. Its jagged broken edge and poisoned surface made it twice as deadly.

The wizard said the black gryphon and the Finder's broken greatsword were gifts from his master. A master he refused to name. All the wizard would say was that the gryphon would fly him safely to and the Wyrm Mountains, to the empty lair of one of the dragons felled by demons during the epic Battle of the Tyne River. He also assured Tauran that the massive bird-cat would be able to carry as much treasure as Tauran could load upon it.

The dark wizard was true to his word. Not only did he and his master help Tauran acquire the treasure, they advised him on how to spend it. With their counsel, Tauran rose to the status of Baron in the barony of Eastedge on the eastern border of the Kingdom of Darshay. In return, the wizard warned, Tauran would be called upon to assist in certain tasks over the years. Some of those tasks were far worse than others, yet Tauran never refused. He treasured his newfound wealth and power and would do anything to keep it.

He *had* done anything to keep it. The pinnacle of their dark requests was the sacrificing of an infant to power an insidious spell.

Tauran had recently begun to tire of their foul requests. He had grown exceedingly comfortable with his station and so confident that he could maintain it without their help that he started to refuse the dark wizard's requests. So when the dark wizard's master sent the beautiful Shara Dune, Queen of the Forsaken Desert in the wizard's stead to inform him of this current task, he had almost refused out of hand.

However, once the Desert Queen had given him the details – and threatened his manhood in a most convincing fashion – Tauran eagerly agreed.

He allowed Shara to think it was her long, sharp fingernails digging into his scrotum that changed his mind. In reality, all the threat did was strengthen his resolve to disappear with his treasure the moment she left. But once he was given the details and assured that it would be his last task for this mysterious master, Tauran decided to accept this final mission.

And this *would* be the final mission. Once it was done, he would take care of a bit of unfinished business and then disappear with his treasure.

Tauran decided that as long as he would never again have to jump at Shara and the dark wizard's beck and call, the change in his life had indeed been for the better.

"I wore my Legion Midnight armor for *this*?" Tauran asked as he, his *Ken d'Zanir* attendant and his cronies watched the descent of the flock of scythe wings.

They had been watching expectantly ever since the giant birds appeared from the east over the high peaks of the Hell's. There were fewer birds than usual, Tauran noticed. There were far fewer birds. It meant this most recent expedition had more fight in it than the first two.

But if the scrawny specimen the birds were delivering was an example of what Tauran and his men were up against, his full gear might have been overkill. Tauran wore every piece of his enchanted crimson armor, assigned to him when he was a member of the Legion Midnight, in anticipation of confronting another Child of the Old Ones.

The visor on his bascinet helmet was pulled down to protect his face and head. A cuirass and spaulders protected his torso; faulders covered his hips. Gauntlets, rerebraces and vambraces covered his hands, upper arms and forearms. His legs were completely protected. Even his boots were plated with the dwarf-forged metal. He had not worn his full suit of armor since fighting in the Legion Midnight during the Cursed Opening.

It took what felt like an eternity to don his full suit of arms. It would be a damnable shame if all of that effort had been for nothing.

DEMON OF LORR

The ever-present Dragon-fang hung at his hip, ready to be pulled free at any moment. The armor and the blade were impenetrable to any physical blow with the exception of Demonsbane, Raxe's blasted enchanted battleaxe. The wide jagged-edged end of the otherwise unbreakable Dragon-fang was ample evidence of Demonsbane's power.

This Child, however, was not Raxe. And even though he had been told that this Child was potentially more dangerous than Raxe or even the Head Mage Rionn Lorr, the Baron had been given the key to this Child's domination. A thrill of excitement and a tinge of fear ran through his bones at the thought of getting the best of a Child of the Old Ones.

But when the captive finally came into view Tauran was thoroughly underwhelmed. There was nothing at all visibly impressive about the man. He was average or less than in every way. His brown skin was similar to Raxe or Jon the Firemaster, though not as dark as either. If he stood to his full height he would still be a head shorter than Tauran. The man's close-cropped coarse hair was dark brown, appearing black from a distance. He was thin and barely muscled with a hint of a paunch, as if he had never seen a real day's labor. The offworlder and the Head Mage were not particularly visually intimidating either, but at least they were lean and fit. This offworlder had the build of a spoiled nobleman. It was hard to believe he was in the least bit dangerous.

Tauran's men wore unimpressive collections of scavenged chain mail, leather-lashed breastplates, visors, gauntlets and pauldrons that paled in comparison to their leader's gleaming blood-red armor. Their deflated expressions at the sight of their approaching captive revealed to Tauran that they found the offworlder just as unimpressive as their armor.

The only member of his party not wearing traditional armor was the exotic warrior that stood taller than Tauran. Even without armor he looked twice as dangerous as the others. The span of his chiseled shoulders was almost as broad as Tauran's armored shoulders. He was dressed in earth tones that blended in almost seamlessly with the terrain.

The hood on his cloak was down and the cloak itself was pulled back to reveal a sleeveless tunic that exposed his long, muscular arms. His weapons belt held a sheath that contained a wide short-sword and was studded with knives of various sizes. The weapons belt held up loose-fitting breaches tucked into ankle-high boots made of thick animal hide.

His name was T'Cheln. He was an elite *Ken d'Zanir* warrior of the *S'Zan Rho* race from an unincorporated coastal region of the distant kingdom of S'Zan. With his stature, weapons and his cold stare, he did not appear to be afraid of anything.

The flock of deadly giant birds circled above them. Their feathers were dull brown, their shades varying slightly. The bird carrying the offworlder broke away and descended in a slow spiral. A few of the men surrounding Tauran were terrified. Those were the ones well traveled enough to have seen the birds before and unlucky enough to have seen them in action.

The other men had heard stories yet still thought of them as merely huge birds and nothing to be afraid of. They all had experience with sky sleighs and the avicaws that towed them. Large avians were nothing new to them.

Their impression changed, however, as the descending scythe wing fell nearer. While smaller than an avicaw, it was sleeker and more muscular, making it look wilder and hungrier than an avicaw. Worst of all, there was a mad, ravenous look in its eyes that betrayed its feral nature despite its peaceful posture. Those beady predatory eyes darted from one man to another, undoubtedly fantasizing about how it and its kin would eagerly ravage them if not for the controlling magic of Tauran's whistle.

When the descending scythe wing was a bit lower than ten feet above ground, its disproportionately massive talons opened to release its captive. By the time the unconscious man hit the ground the predatory bird was already halfway back to its circling flock. A moment later it was indistinguishable from the other birds as they whirled overhead like a dark, angry cloud.

DEMON OF LORR

Tauran lifted the whistle, which hung from a thin chain wrapped tightly around his wrist. He put the slotted mouthpiece between his lips and fixed the silent command in his mind. It was the same command as always. The massive birds were to return to their roost in the highest peaks of Hells Mountains until the next time the whistle was used. That time would be when the King and Head Mage of Lorr were foolish enough to send another sky sleigh expedition this way.

Sky sleighs were uncommon in general. They were available only to royalty and the richest citizens. Travel over or even near the Hells was virtually nonexistent because few humans were foolhardy enough to enter the inhospitable mountain range. All of this made the chances very slim that anyone would happen upon the deadly hawks by accident.

However, if some unfortunate fools did find themselves too close to the scythe wings' roost, there would be no stopping them from attacking. Until then, the spell would keep them bound to the heights of the high mountain ranges, lest their natural behavior drive them to terrorize the earth and skies for hundreds upon hundreds of square miles. They would have to be content to feed on the multitude of big cats, wolves, nimble mountain herbivores, and large reptiles that dwelled in the shadows just below the mountaintops while awaiting Tauran's next command to bring down a royal sky sleigh attempting to take this route to get to the Demon's Spine Mountains further south.

There had been three such attempts. The first resulted in the death of the entire crew. The scythe wings devoured the sleigh birds and the majority of the men and women aboard the sleigh. Those who were not eaten in the sky fell to their deaths, where insects, flesh and bone-eating scavengers, and the harsh winds that scoured the higher elevations of the Hells made short work of any evidence of their passing.

The second attempt yielded only one survivor, a wizard in the employ of the Head Mage that managed to escape the onslaught. It did him little good, though. The survived the air attack only to find his end at the bottom of Hargathall's Cleft, the late Mar-dah's personal killing ground and human refuse disposal. This time, though, Tauran's benefactor had informed him that two vessels were coming.

The doomed sky sleighs would contain Children of the Old Ones and members of the Keeper's Hounds. The command to the scythe wings was to bring this particular Child and kill everyone else, so Tauran could only hope that the Sureblade whelp had perished in the assault. The boy escaped the jagged edge of Dragon-fang only days earlier when he and the rest of the Keeper's Hounds tried to stop Tauran and his men as they assisted with the unleashing of the dark wizard's foul spell.

But Tauran had no time to concern himself with that unpleasant memory. His concern was for the fallen Child lying several yards away. He and his men trudged over to the prostrate offworlder. His men scowled at the helpless, hapless man as Tauran used his crimson metal boot to kick him over onto his back. He wondered if the scythe wings had brought him the wrong man.

"Is this him?" asked one of the Baron's cronies.

"It can't be, Heath." Tauran was incredulous.

Leesil, Baron Tauran's second in command, scoffed and said, "We could've sent the retrievers after him and saved ourselves a trip."

"I wanted him in one piece," Tauran reminded. "The retrievers don't return quarry, at least not breathing and with all of their body parts. But this *can't* be the person we seek. So, Heath, kill him for me."

"With pleasure," Heath answered with a bloodthirsty grin. He pulled his straight sword from the sheath at his hip and jabbed downward at the unconscious man.

The offworlder's left hand shot up so swiftly that it was a blur. It swept the plunging blade aside. Heath's forward momentum and the unexpected shift of his sword caused him to stumble forward, falling toward the suddenly mobile body of the captive. The same hand that knocked the sword away came back across Heath's midsection, slinging the would-be killer violently away with a spray of blood.

DEMON OF LORR

The men around Tauran gasped, all save T'Cheln.

"It seems that this *is* the one we seek," Tauran grinned.

The offworlder's eyes were open, a milky white glaze shrouding his irises and pupils. His face was a blank, impassive mask.

Tauran's men backed away when the stranger's eyelids began to flutter, blinking away the milky residue that covered his normal dark brown eyes. A frown of confusion twisted his features and then his eyes widened with dread as he looked down at his left hand and arm, which were drenched in crimson gore from fingertips to elbow. He scrambled to his feet in horror at the sight of the gutted man twitching on the dry gravelly earth several yards away.

Tauran's men, with the exception of T'Cheln, shuffled backward in fright at the movement. Heath's murder happened so fast that only the keen-eyed *Ken* warrior saw that the stranger's fingertips had been fused into a wicked blade of sharp bone when he killed Heath. To the others it appeared as if the captive had torn through Heath's chain mail, thick leather, flesh and innards with only one bare hand. The lightning quick slaughter had shaken them all and none of them wanted to be the next victim. Tauran was just as shaken but managed to hide it.

"Leesil, subdue the offworlder," Tauran called to his tall, long-limbed friend.

Leesil wore a leather vest over a soft cotton shirt and fitted tanned breeches tucked neatly into gleaming, shin-high, black leather riding boots. His hair was tied back and held fast by a dark red bandana made of thinly folded silk cloth. His brown locks were twisted into a smart braid that hung down to the top of his shoulders.

Leesil pulled his hand away from the pommel of the long scimitar hanging at his hip and held it up in an apologetic gesture. "I apologize, my captain," he began. "But it is not my wish to end up like Heath."

"Cowards," Tauran growled, trying to conceal his own fear. The man who had seemed so weak and harmless only a moment ago had shown himself to be anything but.

And then Tauran remembered the secret to besting this particular Child.

While his men cowered, Tauran stepped forward with exaggerated confidence. The *S'Zan Rho* folded his arms and watched curiously. He could see the fear in his employer's posture while the others could not. He could see the hesitation in Tauran's step where the others saw only foolish but seemingly admirable bravery.

"Your blade," Leesil called. "You may want to draw your blade, man."

"I've no need of it," Tauran boasted as he stepped closer to the offworlder. "Do I, Joel?"

Joel tried to hide his surprise at the mention of his name. He looked at the men before him and then he looked beyond them to see their horses nibbling at the sparse tufts of vegetation emerging sporadically along the ground. He knew he could not get away from his captors on foot. If he knew how to ride a horse he would have tried to get to them, but he was a city boy from Chicago.

It was all he could do to keep his knees from shaking, let alone run. The memory of the harrowing trip in the scythe wings' painful grip continued to send icy waves of fear from head to toe. His back, hips, and ribs throbbed in residual pain from the pressure of the hawks' powerful talons. He was light headed from the loss of blood drawn by their needlepoint claws as the giant hawks traded him among the flock as if they were toying with their food.

Since running was not an option, he tried another tactic.

"Back off!" he warned, feigning confidence as well as Tauran. "Don't come any closer unless you want to end up like your boy over there." Joel had no memory of what had happened to the gutted man before him, but the gore on his arm gave hi a pretty good idea.

His captors seemed as freaked out as he felt. Why not use the situation to his advantage? While trying to hold down his bile, he flicked some blood and bits of gut at the big man stepping toward him. The blood was almost the same color as the leader's armor.

DEMON OF LORR

Tauran could see the fear in Joel's eyes as clearly as the *S'Zan Rho* could see Tauran's own trepidation. The sight emboldened Tauran further as he stepped to within arms reach of the captive.

"You bluff, offworlder."

"Try me," Joel dared as he raised his fists.

Tauran tried him. He took a long, roundhouse swing of a gauntleted fist at Joel's head. Joel was not a fighter but he was not completely defenseless. He ducked the slow punch, stepped forward and jabbed Tauran in the jaw with his bloody left fist. Tauran laughed as he brought up his other hand to snatch Joel's wrist.

Joel tried to pull away, realizing too late that the slow roundhouse punch had been a ploy to bring him in close. A swift kick to the ribs, taught to Tauran by his *Ken d'Zanir* retainer, put the offworlder to his knees. Tauran knew he had to be careful with his armored boots.

He had to be sure to kick the offworlder hard enough to immobilize him but not hard enough to threaten his life. Finally, a hard jab to the point of the chin knocked the offworlder unconscious.

The Baron's men dropped their jaws in awe, amazed that their leader could so quickly overcome a Child of the Old Ones that had so easily dispatched a veteran mercenary of Heath's caliber. Their respect for him and their fear of him elevated several notches.

The *S'Zan Rho*, on the other hand, was not quite as impressed. He suspected some kind of trickery. He had trained Tauran well, as he had been paid to do, but not *that* well. The arrogant easterner would not have been able to best such a power without some kind of secret advantage.

Joel was lying face down on the dusty earth. Pain lanced through him from the wounds caused by the sharp claws of the scythe wings. The blows he had just suffered at the hands and feet of the red-armored clown had his jaw throbbing and his head aching. He could feel warm sticky blood on his face but he dared not wipe it.

He would not even open his eyes for fear of being pounded further. He tried to listen to the strangers' conversation but the sound faded in and out as pain and fatigue overcame him. In a moment, Joel knew, he would not have to feign unconsciousness, so he strained to hear what they were saying before he passed out again. All he could make out was the voice of the red armored brute.

"Bind him and bring him to the dungeons. We have much to learn from this one."

PART I

PRISONERS

Chapter 1: Forced Detour

1.1

Colonel Rheingold Strong watched the fully armed and armored company of Gryphon Ryders approach from the gray southern skies and wondered if this was overkill. His superiors sent only a squad a few days earlier when the colonel led his battalion against the horrible walking dead. This time they sent a full company. Strong could make out one platoon of lance, one of longbow, one of spear, and one of crossbow. He knew they pursued a formidable foe, but his mounted battalion already more than doubled the number of men they were pursuing.

The company of Ryders glided down smoothly in a tight arrowhead formation of ten columns of ten Ryders. They flew almost wingtip-to-wingtip in a wide, staggered pattern. The head of the two middle columns flew a length and a half ahead of the column leaders to the left and right and a full three lengths ahead of the Ryders just behind them. That pattern continued along the span of the company's lines to form a flying wedge or chevron. The bird-cats were in perfect synchronicity, flapping their huge wings in unison, wings that spanned anywhere from fifteen to twenty feet. The large bird-cats canted at the same angles at the same time, effortlessly maintaining the same distance from their flock mates no matter what maneuver they performed.

Just ahead of the two middle columns, the colonel noticed two men wearing wizard's robes. Long staffs hung from both of their saddles. One of the robed men wore the dark brown of an Echelon One mage and the other, a younger man, wore the lighter tan robe of an Echelon Two mage. Mentor and student. As they descended, the tan robed mage and his gryphon turned west and darted away. Strong assumed the younger wizard had gone ahead to scout.

Colonel Strong tallied the head count. High General Ramos had already dispatched Strong's mounted light battalion of five hundred, which consisted of five companies: one hundred sword and shield one hundred full arms, one

1

hundred lance, one hundred spear and ninety eight archers, with Strong and his second to lead them. The Minister of War decided to fortify Strong's battalion with a company of Gryphon Ryders one hundred strong and two powerful Echelon wizards. How could all of this be needed to subdue fewer than two hundred mortal men that did not even employ magic?

Lieutenant Colonel Caleb Godson sat upon his steed a few feet to the colonel's left. He paid no mind to the impressive spectacle descending from the sky. His attention was focused in the opposite direction. He studied the ground curiously. Strong knew the longtime soldier well enough to recognize that he was searching for something.

"Let me know what you find, Caleb," Strong said before turning his attention to the Ryders, who were now earthbound.

With their oversized eagle's wings folded in against their flanks, the gryphons' wide padded cat's paws and muscular feline legs carried them across the sparsely grassed terrain as smoothly as their wings carried them across the skies. The colonel recognized the commanding officer riding at the head of the middle right column.

"Captain Zedek!" Strong called.

The captain heeled his mount to a stop right next to the right flank of Strong's cavalry horse. The two men locked wrists.

"It's been three years, yes?" Captain Zedek greeted.

"Yes," Strong confirmed. "The Cursed Opening."

"Aye," the captain nodded. "We only see each other in dire times." The captain nodded toward the brown-robed mage. "This is Mage Gilder Raynard, an Echelon One mage sent by Rionn Lorr himself."

The mage and colonel nodded and grasped forearms. "Well met," they said to each other.

"'T'is good to see you, Strong," Zedek continued. "But these bein' the only circumstances when that happens, I'd rather not see you at all."

"I have to say I wasn't expecting to see you," Strong admitted. "They only sent us a mere squad of Ryders when we faced those walking dead back east. Now we're pursuing a company of only two hundred normal human men. Does this seem a bit much to you?"

"I hope it *is* a bit much," Zedek said. "That way we'd be done with this all the quicker so that we can go back east to help defend against those walking dead monsters."

"I would not be in such a rush to face those creatures if I were you," Strong advised. "We've just come from there, and as taxing as it was to have been called back across the kingdom when we were less than two days away from Ridgeland, I was more than relieved to hear a regiment had been stationed there. That meant we could come west to fight men instead of those walking dead…things."

"Surely they were no worse than the demons we faced during the Cursed Opening?" Zedek asked.

"Not in might, no," Strong agreed.

He thought about the poor soldier that spotted his son traveling with the walking dead. Strong could still remember, more clearly than he would have liked, the fear and confusion and heartbreaking sadness burned into the soldier's eyes when his own child attacked him. He could still hear the savage screams of rage and anguish of the men under his command as they were attacked and then transformed into the dreadful creatures.

"But in other ways," the colonel concluded, "they were much worse than the demons."

Mage Gilder leaned forward. "Do not underestimate the men we pursue," he warned. "They are *S'Zan Rho* and *Ken d'Zanir*. With their fighting prowess it would take every last man in your battalion to give you a slim chance to best one company of *Ken* in traditional combat. But the *Ken* are not engaging us in traditional combat. We fear they may have some… assistance."

"Since you and your junior Echelon mage are here, I assume they have assistance of a magical nature," Strong said. The confrontation suddenly became less appealing.

"Something like that," the mage muttered.

"What the bloody hell does that mean?" Strong demanded.

"We fear they have found a way to block magic," the mage said.

Strong thought about that for a moment and frowned. "Then what good are you and your protégé going to be?"

Zedek chuckled darkly. "I asked the same question, my friend."

"We don't have to engage them directly," the Echelon One mage began. "With our magic, we can scout much further and faster than your men. As we speak, Mage Kenth is off to cast probes to pinpoint their location."

Strong nodded. "Of course it would be an advantage to know their exact location at all times. But we already know they are running from us and in what direction." The wily soldier raised an eyebrow. "What would be really nice would be if you wizards could use your magic to transport us right on top of them."

Mage Gilder scoffed. "If only it were that easy."

"Then all we can do is follow their trail," Strong said. "From what I've heard of their lizard mounts, we won't run them down. By all accounts those land dragons can run almost as fast as gryphons can fly. But their trail is clearly heading west, where they will have to either enter the Hells to cross into Darshay or meet a ship somewhere on Lake Onyx to ferry them west."

Zedek nodded and added: "It would be foolish for them to travel south, for it would take too long to flee the kingdom. If they do continue south we will have a regiment circling around to wait for them, will we not? All we would have to do is trail them and cut off their retreat."

"You assume they are running," the mage pointed out. "What if they are not?"

"They may be tough," Strong said. "But surely they are not stupid. They must know a superior force would have been sent after them."

"Yes," the mage agreed. "But they are *Ken*. It is not in their nature to flee unless there is no other alternative. Their

4

extra assistance could very well be providing them more than just the ability to block magic, and they are formidable enough without assistance."

"Aye," said Zedek. "I've not seen them fight, but I've heard tales of them when I've visited the western regions of Derr'Shan. If they be as tough as they're made to sound, I'd not expect them to turn tail and run."

"When Mage Kenth casts his probes," Mage Gilder added, "he will spot any ambush the *Ken* may have set. If at any time the probe is snuffed against his will from their ability to neutralize magic, he will immediately know their general location and then pull back to send word to me."

Lieutenant Colonel Godson rode to them at a brisk trot from further along the *Ken d'Zanir*'s trail. The colonel saw the hard set of his Lieutenant Colonel's square jaw, the dark look in his eyes, and knew something was bothering him.

"What is it, Lieutenant Colonel?" Colonel Strong asked as Godson approached.

Godson shook his head with uncertainty. "There is something strange about these tracks, sir. It's been bothering me since we found their abandoned camp north of Port Lorrian. It appears that they are all staying near the shoreline as they head west."

"What do you mean it 'appears' they're staying along the shoreline?" asked the colonel. "Their tracks are easy enough to follow."

"Yes," Godson conceded. "And if these were hoof prints I would have spotted it earlier. These oversized, six-legged lizard tracks are a bit harder to read. But I'm convinced now that there are nowhere near two hundred sets of tracks. At the most, there is half that amount."

Without a word, Mage Raynard gave a small tug to his mount's reins. The mage and the gryphon shot into the sky, racing eastward and parallel to the battalion's path. The two warriors watched the wizard and gryphon shrink out of view as they sped away.

1.2

Mage Paulus Kenth sat astride his gryphon at the top of a steep rise and looked west. He would have preferred to go east. The horror that was making its way to the Bluethorn and Ridgeland region was a much greater threat to the Kingdom of Lorr than a fleeing enemy. However, the Head Mage Rionn Lorr had ordered them to go west. Kenth would fulfill his duty as thoroughly and quickly as possible.

He was no fool, though. Mage Kenth knew he was sent here because he was an inexperienced Echelon Two mage. This threat was the less dangerous of the two. Kenth had distinguished himself during the excavation of Infinity Isle. He was an Echelon Three mage at the time, but his ability to locate even the smallest enchanted talismans and artifacts had impressed Master Mage Delthar enough to recommend his promotion to the Head Mage. Upon his promotion, the Master Mage requested that Kenth be a part of the team that monitored Soullustre's Eye for the presence of demons in the Known Lands. As the second-ranking conjurer in the Kingdom of Lorr, behind only the Head Mage, Delthar's recommendation was highly sought by all Echelon mages.

Kenth appreciated the endorsement. It was a prestigious and important assignment that would have put him in regular communication with the Mage Delthar, but Kenth preferred a more mobile assignment. The Head Mage granted his request and sent him on this mission. Even though it was little more than a dull scouting expedition, it was better than sitting in a dark room staring at tiny yellow lights in a big ruby ball for hours on end.

His sharp eyes followed the curve of the great lake until it disappeared behind the rising foothills of the Northern Hells and then he whispered a spell to summon his farsight. The spell caused a stirring of energy behind his eyes. Into that compressed swirl of magic he lent a bit of his sight, his hearing, his senses of smell and touch.

When the swirling magic was properly saturated with his senses, he pushed down from behind his eyes and moved it through his neck and left shoulder, down his left arm and into his open palm.

A more conservative wizard would have sent it down his right arm and through the long, straight, tapered staff clutched in his right fist. The staff was carved from hard pale wood and was nearly as long as the mage was tall. Runes were carved neatly, if sporadically, along its polished surface and a loop was cut into the wide, broader high end of the staff. Within the loop was secured a large, clear crystal. The staff would have helped to focus and filter the magic, to expend it more efficiently than releasing it through flesh, but Mage Kenth did not want to focus his magic this time. He wanted the broad, unfocused burst that rushed warmly from his left hand because it would cover a wider area.

His magic filled the earth, sky and the southern edge of Lake Onyx as it rushed westward. It moved like the wind, searching nearly thirty square miles for any scent, sight, or sound to relay back to its master. It eventually picked up the familiar sounds of an armed march. The rhythmic sound of heavy footfalls – not the sharp *thump-thump thump-thump* of hoof beats and more like the muffled *whumph* of wide paws – was clear enough to let him know that there were many large animals on the move. Mage Kenth's magic relayed to him the vibration of the earth in time with the sound. He could hear the clink of metal upon metal. Through his magic, he gauged the sound had traveled nearly a half mile before reaching his extended hearing. Although he could not yet see them, he had a good idea why.

There was a small dale just beyond the higher elevation of the foothills, the north edge of which ended at the steep cliffs of Hell's Bluff. His extended sight had not quite reached the bluffs and could not yet see down into the dale. He was sure the enemy was crossing through the dale at that moment. Mage Kenth eagerly anticipated the visual. He had never seen a land dragon, the fabled and fierce lizard that served as the *Ken d'Zanir*'s steeds. He was eager to do so.

But the magical breeze dissipated just shy of Hell's Bluff. Mage Kenth suspected it would, knowing that thirty miles was just about the range of that particular spell when dissipated in so wide a pattern. The Echelon mage whispered the spell once more and sent the magic down his right arm and into his staff this time. The broad casting of his sight gave him their general location. He could now focus on them.

Using the staff to concentrate the breeze of magic, he held it high to cast a horizontal beam of power that followed the same general path as the broader instance of his farsight. He had a general idea of where they were, but he wanted to be sure. The compressed beam would allow his extended sight to travel nearly three times as far so that he could get a visual confirmation of their precise location. The magic would also convey the exact distance.

The magic beam cut west for a time and then, to the Echelon mage's dismay, it ended abruptly.

This time, though, it ended well shy of the bluffs.

"They're coming back this way," he realized aloud.

Mage Kenth whipped the reins and gave a couple of short tugs to his right, compelling his gryphon to dart into the sky, dip its right wing and bank around sharply clockwise until it was flying back east the way they had come. The wizard leaned in close and dug his heels into the bristly fur on the bird cat's leonine flanks. Its feathered head and neck dipped lower and its long cat ears folded back as they gained speed and altitude.

As the mighty wings beat furiously, the mage tossed one more concentrated farsight spell from his staff. This time it was a sheet of magic that would linger and give him an idea of how fast the enemy was approaching. The blanket of magic ended sharply less than fifteen miles away and shrank back toward him with frightening speed.

A wave of what Mage Kenth could only describe as nothingness swept eastward. It was like a hungrily expanding void that devoured his extended senses and threatened to devour him as well.

He knew of the land dragons' renowned speed, and instantly regretted not having mastered the *myst* spell, which created a cloud-like mist on which the spell's caster could ride through the air at incredible speeds.

DEMON OF LORR

Only Echelon One mages, Master Mages, and the most adroit sorcerers were powerful enough to cast the spell and maintain it for great distances.

But he knew that he and his gryphon had enough of a head start to beat them back to royal battalion. From the sounds of the approaching enemy that floated to his magic just ahead of the ravenous void, Mage Kenth estimated the distance from the edge of the void to the Ken was roughly a half-mile.

Not nearly far enough for the Echelon Two Mage.

As the minutes passed and the gryphon streaked across the sky, Mage Kenth closed his eyes and concentrated, calling upon his magic to form a mental warning that he sent out ahead of him to his mentor. An instant later he tossed yet another blanket farsight spell behind him.

The magic detected a host of loud and horribly familiar *thwack*ing sounds just before his magic came racing back at him. The void rushed eastward even faster than before, *much* faster. So fast, in fact, that Mage Kenth was compelled to look over his shoulder with his normal vision.

A host of large, sharp wooden bolts, as thick as an average-sized man's arm, tore through the sky and came right for him. There was a moment of confusion as he recognized the bolts as smaller versions of the ammunition used in bolt-firing ballistae mounted on seafaring warships. That was why the sound was so familiar.

He got over his confusion quickly and yanked the reins down while kicking his left heel into the gryphon's flank. The command sent his mount into a sharp bank that caused the lead bolt – which for some reason was wobbling as it flew toward him – to sail just to the right and above the bird-cat and rider at the apex of its arc.

Mage Kenth mentally recited a spell to cast a protective barrier around him and his mount.

But there was no longer any magic within him.

With a frightened start, he whipped the gryphon into a steep dive that he hoped would take him below the path of the whistling bolts. He hoped in vain.

One bolt ripped through the gryphon's left wing. The bird-cat let loose an ear piercing screech and went into a spiraling plummet that threw his rider from the saddle.

The wizard desperately recited every spell he could think of as he fell. He had to recite them mentally because the rushing air around him sucked his voice away. He waved his hands frantically in an attempt to weave a web of magic that would use the very air to stop his fall, or at least slow his descent to a non-lethal speed.

But there was no more magic to weave. Not a trace of it remained within him or without.

As he fell, a strange serenity overcame him. He knew he was about to die and there was nothing he could do about it.

Echelon Two Mage Paulus Kenth closed his eyes, let the wind roar past his ears, and took the time to wonder just how the magic-devouring void had been able to catch up to him so quickly.

He recalled the wobbling lead bolt that he had barely managed to avoid. He thought it strange that the missile had a small, dark red ribbon attached its flat end. And then he realized why it had flown so erratically. There was something strapped to it...a dark fist-sized object that he vaguely remembered seeing somewhere else.

Before he could remember where he had seen that object before, he struck the earth with a deadly jolt and was no more.

1.3

Raxe stood only inches away from the edge of a high cliff among the vast and barren mountain range, anger clouding his thoughts. He knew he should have been traveling with the rest of his team, which was made up of him, the six surviving members of the sky sleigh crew, Quick, Ethan and Raxe's daughter, Azh.

More importantly, though, he knew he would be no good to any of them until he could get his temper under control. An irrational anger smoldered inside of him and he was having a hard time dampening it.

Joel was gone, stolen away by a swarming flock of scythe wings. Even though Joel's power was unpredictable and uncontrollable, it had proven to be impressive. They needed that power for this mission. Joel was finally starting to open up, too. Just when he had begun to move past the fear and worry that distracted him to the point of being more of a liability than an asset, he was torn away from the group. That sparked frustration within Raxe that was almost too much for him to bear.

It had been years since he had been so angry that he thought he might lose control. In fact, it had not happened since his pre-teen years just after his mother died. It took a while, but to his grandfather's great relief, Raxe finally learned to control his anger. He first taught himself to become numb to it. And then he found a way to transform it into the calm, cold resolve that made him such an effective soldier and assassin.

His anger had been mastered, or so he thought, so he was surprised when it began to erode his calm and resolve. Why would it happen now after so many years of effectively controlling it? Joel was barely related to him, a cousin almost as distant as Shanderah and Rionn Lorr. In fact, until a few days ago Joel was a complete stranger to him. Raxe would not expect Joel's loss to have such a profound effect on him. Did he feel a greater love and sense of duty for the Kingdom of Lorr than he realized?

If anything, that should have strengthened his calm and

resolve the way it had on his first visit to Lorr, when the sorceress Shanderah died and he made up his mind to confront the King of the Dragons for the first time. But now he was anything but calm and resolved. All he wanted was smash something, to use his enchanted battleaxe to tear into the mountain until he reached the other side or died trying.

He knew he would not be any good to his team in this psychological state, so he sent them on without him with the promise that he would catch up with them when he felt he was ready. Azh was much more hesitant to leave without him than the others but he eventually convinced his daughter to leave with the rest of them.

If he bothered to look down he would have been able to see the group making its way carefully down the steep, rocky, switchback trail on the face of the mountain. His attention, however, was directed skyward. He peered over the peaks of Hell's Mountains into the western skies, frustration causing his hands to clinch into tight fists.

Raxe was not accustomed to failure. Every mission he had ever undertaken – whether it was with the Air Force, Special Forces, the Cutters, or the organization – ended in success. He had experienced setbacks on countless occasions but outright failure was something with which he had very little experience...until he lost Joel.

The Head Mage believed Joel was not only the key to this mission to retrieve the Hell Key; he believed Joel was the key to their primary goal of defeating the Dierglyorr. The demon apparently believed the same thing. It had pursued Joel in two worlds before it finally got to him.

And it got to him on Raxe's watch.

The image of the giant birds swarming Joel and carrying him into the western skies was still agonizingly sharp in his mind. That image served to add fuel to his anger and once again Raxe had to struggle to keep it together for the sake of their primary objective. If for no other reason than revenge, he had to press on and make this mission a success no matter how unlikely success might be after the all of their losses.

But there were plenty of other reasons to press on, not the

least of which was his grandfather's safety. The demon continued to hunt his grandfather and Lisa on the other side of the WorldGate. Stopping the Dierglyorr on this side of the WorldGate would go a long way toward ensuring their safety. Another reason to complete his mission was the safety of both this world and his. As badly as the Dierglyorr wanted to destroy the Children of the Old Ones, that was merely the first step in its overall goal of dominating all of mankind on both sides of the WorldGate.

And then there was the promise he made to Ethan's mother. Raxe vowed to Annastace that he would do everything within his power to return her first born home to her safely. Raxe had to keep it together to keep his promise to her. He thought about Annastace's hazel eyes and the way they so earnestly reflected her emotions. The look in her eyes at her fallen husband's memorial three years earlier had almost brought tears to his eyes when he had not cried since his mother's funeral nearly twenty years before.

Meldrick Sureblade had been on a mission with Raxe when he was struck down, and now Meldrick and Annastace's son was accompanying Raxe on a mission. He knew that he could not bear to see Annastace's eyes filled with that sadness again.

Raxe's frustration eased a bit at the thought of Annastace. The anger that sought to overtake him shrank away like some supernatural nocturnal beast slinking away from the dawning sun. His resolve began to solidify and he started to feel more like himself. The anger and frustration were still there, but their intensity finally receded to a more manageable level.

A glance down the mountainside revealed that the team was several hundred feet almost directly below him. They had reached a part of the mountain that was not as steep and treacherous as the stretch of the mountain face they had to negotiate moments earlier. They were only a few dozen yards from the foot of the mountain. Raxe was about to follow their path when he thought better of taking the same route that they had taken.

It took more than two hours for them reach their current location. In the interest of time and relieving a little more frustration, Raxe decided to take a different route.

He backed away from the ledge about thirty feet. He checked to make sure the strap holding his small travel pack to his side was tight and that the strap that held Questblade within its sheath was secure. After a deep breath he broke into a sprint. He ran to the edge of the cliff and leapt, sailing in a long arc that abruptly turned into an intimidating drop.

The rest of the team saw him jump. All of them, with the exception of Azhju'lestra, started to panic. Their first thought was that the frustrated offworlder had gone mad and decided to take his own life. The little girl simply watched her father and smiled.

As Raxe tucked himself into a tight ball and plummeted to the base of the mountain, the others recalled that he had survived a much higher fall just hours earlier. He was a Child of the Old Ones, after all, a descendant of fabled god-like beings. He wore the enchanted armor of his divine ancestor and namesake. By the time he landed with a loud crash of stone and metal, the rest of the group was chuckling at their fearful reactions.

Raxe stood up and stepped out of the dust cloud caused by his impact, shaking dirt from his long dreadlocks and brushing it from the brown skin of his exposed biceps and elbows. Quick, Ethan, and the surviving sky sleigh crew approached him warily. While he did not look as maniacally outraged as he had a couple of hours ago, frustration was still clearly etched into his face.

Azhju'lestra ignored his expression and walked over quickly to resume her usual place at his right hand. A strange instinct tempted him to put his arm around the adorable youngster's small shoulders but he stopped short. It was still too awkward for such shows of fatherly affection.

They had not spent enough time in each other's presence for him to develop any kind of genuine paternal feelings for the girl. If not for the fact that he could feel their familial bond through her aura and their shared heritage as Children of the Old Ones, Raxe would never have believed she was his daughter.

14

DEMON OF LORR

Kids made him uncomfortable. There was no room in his violent world for children. They were too fragile and unpredictable. On top of everything else, Azhju'lestra was just plain weird.

She looked six or seven years old even though she was barely three. She rarely talked and she showed virtually no emotion except for a flash of excitement when she leapt from the doomed sky sleigh with the rest of the crew and passengers. Raxe was not sure if she stayed so close to him out of affection or because her mother, a water faerie even more mysterious than Azhju'lestra, ordered her to. Until Raxe had a better idea of her feelings about him he thought it best to hold back on showing even a small bit of affection.

Quick saw the uneasy expression and lingering anger on Raxe's countenance and hesitated for a moment. But what he had to say was too important. He risked a step toward the offworlder.

"About Joel…" Quick began. "I saw no – " he stopped short of saying "pieces" and sought a better word. "I saw no evidence that the scythe wings had savaged him. He may yet live. Can you not you feel his presence through the connection shared by the Children of the Old Ones?"

"No," Raxe said. His damaged, deep, sandpaper voice rumbled. "But I never could feel Joel's aura. Neither can Rionn Lorr or Gramps."

"Should we not try to discover evidence of Joel's fate, whatever it may be?" Quick asked.

"No!" came a familiar voice from around a large outcropping. All heads turned as the Ranger Elf Rell Kallen stepped into the open. His long braided hair was windblown but otherwise the elf was none the worse for wear.

Raxe rasped, "If my bones weren't still rattling I'd break your legs." His rough, gravelly voice took on a sinister tone. The site of the relatively unscathed Ranger Elf brought the irrational anger creeping back. He took a deep breath and managed to keep it at bay.

As everyone else who had escaped from the sky sleigh battled the deadly scythe wings, the Ranger Elf was whisked to safety by a flaming winged creature that streaked through the sky almost too fast for the human eye to follow.

"That little trick of yours comes in real handy for a coward," Raxe growled.

"It was magic, not a trick," Rell corrected. "But then I would not expect an ignorant offworlder to know the difference."

"You have a Phoenix stone," Quick observed. "Not exactly standard gear for a Ranger Elf, is it?"

"This is not a standard mission," Rell returned. "My queen has charged me with the retrieval of the Hell Key and I mean to fulfill that charge. That is something I cannot do from the afterlife." He raised an eyebrow. "You know of the Phoenix stone? You're rather learned for such a young one."

Quick's pride urged him to boast of his training at the Kingdom of Lorr's *Chronichai Tul Myst* academy of magic. His instinct urged against it. Instinct won out. He changed the topic of discussion back to the matter at hand.

"How should we find out what happened to Joel?" Quick asked Raxe.

"We *don't*," Rell interjected. "If he survived he'll live or die by his own wits. The Hell Key must remain our priority."

"Rionn didn't bring him here to die," Raxe reminded. "I know he hasn't been much help but we'll need him before this is over. There's a good chance he's alive. Back at Port Lorrian, when the *Ken* attacked, they tied him up but tried to kill everyone else. That could mean the demon needs him and I damn sure don't wanna find out why. If he's not dead we have to get him back."

It was at that moment that Raxe realized why Rionn Lorr brought Joel to the Kingdom of Lorr, even if the Head Mage himself did not know exactly why at the time. Joel's power was not affected by whatever it was that neutralized the others' magic at Port Lorrian.

While everyone else was powerless, Joel managed to kill two fierce land dragons with his bare hands...or what passed for his hands at the time. If Joel's power could not be dampened, he could be an invaluable weapon for their cause.

But then again, Raxe knew, Joel could be just as

dangerous a weapon *against* their cause if the Dierglyorr found a way to use Joel against them.

"And if he *is* dead?" Rell challenged. "How long do we search? The demon won't wait for us to find his corpse. It will do what it must to gain control of the Hell Key. We must do the same."

"The Ranger Elf has a point," Ethan mumbled, his head hung low.

Raxe was surprised Ethan was talking at all. He had been brooding silently since the sky sleighs were brought down, and with good reason. The young tracker lost his fellow Keeper's Hounds in that attack, including a couple that he held in particularly high regard. Ethan was no stranger to combat, but he was still only sixteen years old. Raxe wondered if Ethan was really that strong or if he was just a damn good actor.

"There is no doubt that Rionn Lorr brought Joel here for good reasons," Ethan continued. "However, we all are charged with the task of retrieving the Hell Key. I think we should locate Mar-dah's keep as soon as possible."

"I know a talisman as powerful as the Hell Key should never be in the possession of a demon," Quick agreed. "But even if the Dierglyorr does find it first, it can't use it. The WorldGate and Hell Keys can only be used by Children of the Old Ones."

"If I must," Rell added impatiently, "I will continue on to Hargathall's Cleft alone. If there are any clues there to the location of Mar-dah's keep, who's to say the demon won't find them if we dally?"

The surviving sky sleigh crew looked on with keen interest while the elf, offworlder, changeling and Keeper's Hound considered their options. They also wondered what their role would be now that the sky sleighs were gone.

Raxe was the leader of this expedition and he could command all save the elf to do as he wished, and what he wished was to go after Joel. Rionn Lorr had earned Raxe's trust, which was not an easy thing to do.

It seemed to him that Rionn's efforts to bring them both across the WorldGate would be wasted if they did not at least try to find the other offworlder.

At the same time, however, he could not discount the concerns of the elf and the young Sureblade. What would they do if the demon found Mar-dah's keep and the Hell Key within it while they searched for Joel? That could not be allowed. Quick was right in his assertion that the Keys could only be used by Children of the Old Ones. However, Rionn Lorr and Raxe knew something the others did not, not even the crafty Ranger Elf.

There was another Child of the Old Ones out there.

The Child was likely the offspring of Mar-dah and the desert witch Shara Dune. They knew of the Child's presence but had been unable to pinpoint his or her location, nor Shara Dune's, for that matter. If the Dierglyorr, an ancient and immensely powerful sixth level demon, gained possession of both the Hell Key and the hidden Child, it would have complete control of the gates of hell.

With an army of demons at its command, its ability to cross the WorldGate at will, and its knowledge of magic long forgotten by any other living being save the King of the Dragons, it could do far more damage than Mar-dah had during the Cursed Opening. But then again, what would happen if they abandoned Joel? They could later find themselves in another situation where their magic failed. Joel would be the only one that could help them. Without Joel's help, or even worse, if the demon found a way to use Joel, they might not find the Hell Key anyway.

On a whim, Raxe turned to Azhju'lestra. The little half-water faerie girl tugged on a long aqua-blue lock of her silky hair. Raxe squatted down so that his eyes were level with his daughter's.

He marveled yet again at her resemblance to his mother. Only her hair, complexion and eyes resembled Sabrina's. The sparkling of those multi-hued coral-colored eyes in the fading sunlight, along with her tiny, curious smile, extinguished the last bits of frustration still smoldering within him.

"What do you think, Azh?" Raxe asked playfully.

"Ask Questblade," she answered without hesitation.

She said it as if it were the most obvious thing in the world. Raxe wondered how she even knew what Questblade was, and then remembered that the enchanted short sword was one of many topics of conversation he had with Quick on the sky sleigh before everything went wrong. He had to chuckle at his absent-mindedness. Even though magic was no longer brand new to him, it was far from second nature.

His own internal magic was involuntary so he never had to think about it to invoke it. He knew the enchanted short sword was on his hip but it never occurred to him to use it. Azh, on the other hand, to whom magic was as common as breathing, probably thought her father was a dunce.

"Good thinking, girl," Raxe said. He gave her a quick kiss on the forehead without even thinking about it. Azh flashed a surprised smile at the peck.

So much for not showing affection, Raxe thought.

He unsheathed Questblade and held it with the blade resting on his open left palm and the pommel gripped firmly in his right hand, just as his grandfather showed him. Clearing his mind of everything but the question, he thought:

What path should I take?

Having used the enchanted blade before, it was easier for him to invoke its magic a second time. The people standing around were silent. He could not even hear them breathing and he wondered briefly if they were holding their breath. A moment later he forgot about them altogether. He forgot about the warming blade in his hands. He forgot about everything else. There was only the question.

What path should I take?

And then there was the heat pulsing through his bones and muscles like warm blood through veins and arteries. White light filled his mind for a moment before it shrank into a vision of his grandfather's short sword floating against an ocean of black, pointing toward the heavens.

Quick could have sworn he saw a flash of light. It was so fleeting that he could not be sure if it was real or imagined. He did, however, feel the magic.

A glance at the curious expressions on the faces of the Ranger Elf and Azhju'lestra revealed that their sensitivity to magic had picked up something as well. Ethan and the sky sleigh crew, while very interested, did not show any signs that they had noticed the burst of magic.

A moment later Raxe was placing the short sword, pommel down, onto the rough sloping earth.

Amazingly, the sword stood straight up the flat base of its otherwise spherical pommel, impossibly balancing on the sloping and uneven ground. *This* drew the attention of Ethan and the crewmembers. They now wore the expressions that Quick and the other two magic folk wore when they felt the magic of Questblade as it pulsed from Raxe.

The blade stood for a moment longer before dropping onto its flat side. The tip of the short sword pointed southeast.

"South," Rell Kallen said with a smug half-smile. "The blade points in the direction of the Demon's Spine and Hargathall's Cleft. It is settled, then. The magic of the Children of the Old Ones has spoken."

Raxe caught the sarcasm in that last part but he knew he could not argue. The magic of Questblade *had* spoken. While it did point towards the Demon's Spine, Raxe knew he could not abandon Joel. His gut told him if there was any chance his fellow offworlder was alive, they had to find him.

"Questblade speaks only for me," Raxe declared. "It doesn't speak for the rest of you. The blade says *I* go south. The elf chooses to go south. The rest of you don't have to."

"Of course we will," Ethan assured. "We are warriors charged by the King and the Head Mage to accompany you on this quest, not frightened children seeking an excuse to abandon the mission."

"We will follow you into the heart of Mar-dah's dark stronghold and beyond, if need be," Quick added.

"No, you won't," Raxe returned.

He looked at the mountaintops. The cool shadow of Hell's Mountains had fallen over the group. The wicked peaks of the foreboding mountain range seemed to devour the setting suns. Raxe turned back to Ethan.

"Tonight, we rest," Raxe began. "In the morning you and

Quick will go west into the mountains, into Darshay if you have to, and find out what happened to Joel.

"When you find him, do whatever you have to do to bring him back and meet us at Hargathall's Cleft." Raxe paused as he considered the alternative. "If you find evidence that he's dead, catch up with us as fast as you can."

The offworlder turned a cold warning glance to the Ranger Elf and continued. "Azh, Rell Kallen and I will go to Southborough with the sky sleigh crew. We'll re-supply and arrange transportation for the crew to get back to Greenglenn. From there we'll continue on to the Demon's Spine."

Rell Kallen said nothing and nodded his agreement. The elf was fully prepared to go after the Hell Key alone but he could not deny that Raxe's presence could be useful.

Ethan started to protest. The set of Raxe's jaw, however, and the seriousness of his glare silenced the young soldier before he uttered a word. The expression of hurt on the young man's face said more than any words could.

Raxe knew how dedicated Ethan was to completing the mission assigned to him. He also knew how proud the young Sureblade was to follow in his father's footsteps by defending his kingdom alongside a Child of the Old Ones.

Though Ethan made a valiant effort of hiding it, he was crushed by the fate of the other Keeper's Hounds. The loss of his follow demon hunters made him even more determined to see this mission through to the end. But they had to find Joel...or at least find out if he was dead, even if Questblade told him to do otherwise.

Ordinarily, the fact that he had been named leader of this expedition would compel his charges to follow his orders without him having to offer any explanations. Raxe, however, had to be sure that Ethan would perform his task without the distraction of constantly wishing he were a part of the search for the Hell Key.

The young man needed to be encouraged. Ethan needed to be challenged if he was going to put forth maximum effort to find the other offworlder.

"If you trust the Head Mage," Raxe began, "trust me. He named me leader for a reason." He placed his right hand on

Ethan's shoulder. "Don't think I'm just sending you two away to protect you. I'd be better off with all of the swords and magic I can get, and those scythe wings are probably just the beginning of the danger we'll all face.

"But Joel is as important to this mission as I am. Rionn understood that. You have to understand how important it is for you to find him. Both of our worlds could depend on it."

Ethan felt a warm blush of shame for his momentary doubt. His resolve solidified as he lifted his chin and his shoulders.

"Then we *will* find him," Ethan Sureblade vowed.

Raxe almost felt guilty for not being completely honest with the teen. In truth, he believed Ethan would be much safer searching for Joel than he would be searching for the Hell Key. He had been uneasy about bringing Ethan in the first place and only did so at the insistence of Rionn Lorr. Raxe did not care if Ethan did have his father's lasso, crossbow, javelin and broadsword – as well as what the Head Mage had called the Gifted Sight. Sixteen was too freaking young for a job this dangerous. This was Raxe's chance to keep his promise to Ethan's mother. He was afraid that if he missed this opportunity he might not get another.

1.4

Lieutenant Colonel Caleb Godson was the first to spot the return of the Echelon One mage. Gilder Raynard streaked high through the air atop a thick cloud of mist, which not only puzzled but also worried the Lieutenant Colonel. He reached over to grasp the shoulder of his superior officer, who was engaged in a discussion of strategy with one of his captains. Colonel Strong looked up at the Lieutenant Colonel and then looked to where Godson was pointing. Strong's steel-gray eyes narrowed to watch the mage approach at great speed, as if he were an arrow shot from the golden bow of the Old One Lorr Himself.

"Why is he returning on a myst and not his gryphon?" the Lieutenant Colonel asked.

"His myst is faster," Strong noted grimly.

Less than two seconds later the thick, white, mist swirling around the wizard's legs and feet settled him gently to the ground and then dissolved into nothingness. The grim set of the wizard's thin lips and narrow jaw, along with the cold dread in his dark blue eyes, worried Colonel Strong. Before he could ask what was wrong, the Echelon One mage began shouting commands.

"Shields to the front, Strong! Quickly! Bring both the front and rear in to me as tightly as they can manage! And prepare to ride north!"

"North?" Strong asked. "There's nothing north of here but Lake Onyx!" He had to call out the last part because the wizard was already streaking to the great lake on his myst.

The Colonel turned to his Lieutenant Colonel, who looked just as confused as Strong felt. He paused for only the briefest moment.

"You heard the man!" Strong barked. Echelon One mages were both powerful and battle tested. Strong may not have understood their art but he respected their abilities and he trusted them. "Shields to the front!" The Colonel looked north at the quickly shrinking form of the wizard as men scrambled and orders were shouted.

A shadow fell over the hazy sky. Strong turned quickly,

his back to the lake, and looked left to see the eastern skies blocked from view by a thick hail of sharpened black bolts flying at them in a high, horribly slow-moving arc. His eyes widened and he quickly looked to his right.

To his horror, against the faint glow of the two suns through overcast skies above the peaks of the Northern Hells, another hail of deadly bolts sailed skyward toward them in the same inexorable arc.

Both of the assaults spanned too wide a distance for the battalion to clear if they tried to ride south to avoid them. And Strong was certain that their enemy was prepared for – and likely counting on – just such a reaction.

The sounds of startled swears could be heard among the rising volume of shouted orders, heavy hoof beats, the clanging of metal, and the sound of heavy wings beating as the Gryphon Ryders launched into the air. Every sound was strained with urgency. They moved with fear-fueled haste yet well-rehearsed precision. As the wizard had commanded, all of the shield men settled in at the front, overlapping and locking their shields to form a steel wall over the western edge of their broad column.

Strong started when he thought about the soldiers at the rear, where there were no shields to protect them from the bolts sailing in from the east. Even while afraid, the seasoned warrior was calm and calculating, estimating how far the bolts would penetrate into his battalion.

The bolts approaching from the east would arrive first. From the trajectory of the deadly missiles and the speed at which his men funneled inward at a tight northwestern angle, the bolts would land almost a quarter of the way inside of the back end of the retreating column.

The Colonel looked to the west and calculated that the hail of bolts would cut just slightly less deep into the front lines, just beyond the three rows of shield men that protected it. He held his breath as the deadly sharp blackwood bolts falling from the east began their downward arc, picking up speed as they descended.

All his men could do was hasten their already frenetic

pace. Some looked over their shoulders as they spurred their mounts to breakneck speeds. Others dared not look, leaning just above bobbing manes and keeping their faces rigidly forward, pushing their cavalry horses with both shouted commands and heels to muscle-sheathed ribs.

Colonel Strong said a prayer for his soldiers as the bolts were nearly upon them. He wanted to turn away but he refused to, believing that turning away would be a betrayal of the men about to die for him and their kingdom.

But the lead bolts abruptly changed direction, and so did all of the rest, as if hitting an impenetrable wall. And when Strong squinted, he could indeed see the faintest glimmer of light, an almost invisible red glow at the tip of the bolts just as they bounced astray and flipped away end over end in every direction but straight down.

It was as if the bolts were hitting an invisible roof and then sliding down the sides until they fell safely away, eventually either tumbling out into Lake Onyx or landing just outside the lines of the southernmost edge of their collapsing column. Strong looked north again and saw the wizard more than a dozen yards out in the suddenly churning lake water.

Mage Gilder's face was a mask of fierce determination and focus. His plain, long, dark brown staff – which resembled a straight bow staff – was held high in his right hand while his left was thrust beneath the dark surface of the lake. The great flock of gryphons, with their massive wings beating and gliding in turn, cast dark silhouettes behind the mage as they circled the stark gray skies in the distance. The staff glowed the same pale magenta as the transparent glimmer that turned away the hard blackwood bolts.

"The wizard is shielding the rear lines," Strong breathed. "Thanks be to the old ones."

"Colonel!" Godson called as he rode back to Strong's side, pulling the commander's attention away. "The wizard would have our men ride out into the lake? That isn't a shallow river we can ford. They'll drown if they go out there. We outnumber the attackers. We should stand and fight!"

The Colonel felt the same way, but despite his doubt, he trusted the wizard. When he turned north yet again and noticed that the pace of the churning water surrounding Mage Gilder was beginning to slow, and when he saw light ribbons of vapor wafting up from the water's surface, his doubt turned into confidence.

He had seen that phenomenon before. It was just south of the capital city of Greenglenn at the Tyne River when the Head Mage had performed the same enchantment to allow them to cross the swollen river. He wanted to sigh in relief but he did not have time.

"To the lake!" Strong roared, his deep voice booming above the din. "As quickly as your mounts can carry you! Don't stop running until your horses are swimming!"

Without hesitation, but with more than a few curious glances, his soldiers launched their steeds toward the lakeshore. Lieutenant Colonel Godson threw a stunned glare at his superior and opened his mouth to object, but he stopped cold when he saw Strong's dark glare of warning.

"There's a reason they sent a battalion and two Echelon mages against a company of mere men," Rheingold Strong said in an intensely even tone. "I trust Mage Gilder, and even if you don't, you *will* follow orders."

The colonel looked over at the mass of bolts falling from the western skies. The front had retreated, but not enough. Strong narrowed his sharp eyes again as he looked for the faint glow of the magical shield being cast by the Echelon mage. When he found it, he was anything but relieved.

The shield was beyond where the bolts would strike, and to his dismay, it was shrinking all the time, retreating almost as if it was fleeing from the threat it was created to counter.

And then it was completely gone.

Strong cringed when the heavy bolts poured violently down onto the front line. The deep clang of the hard wooden bolts striking steel boomed across the foothills like thunder. The sound of screams from men and horses followed closely behind as the lead bolts extended just beyond the shield line, far too many of them finding flesh and bone.

The weight and force and sheer number of the arm-length bolts drove the shield men to their knees. Other bolts found their way through the seams in the wall of shields. As shield men fell to the onslaught, the wall collapsed inward in quick and disciplined movements to close the gaps and keep the wall as solid as possible. The wall shrank quickly but drifted steadily backward, and after a few agonizingly long seconds the battalion was finally out of range.

But in their wake was a horrific scene. Dozens of impaled bodies, both human and equine, were pinned to ground in grizzly positions. As the last bolt fell, a small army of fiercely muscled, leather-armored warriors riding monstrous, six-legged reptilian mounts came pouring over the foothills from the east and west. Both groups fanned out as they came on, prepared to intercept any attempt to flee to the south.

The strategy was fully expected, but the nightmarish sight of the snarling, slavering, snapping land dragons still caught the colonel utterly unprepared. The beasts' terrible size and speed, their rows of needle-pointed teeth, and their crowns of horn clusters gave them look of a horde loosed from the very depths of hell. Even Lieutenant Colonel Godson, so eager to fight, was momentarily struck dumb at the sight.

The monstrous steeds and their intimidating masters closed on the front line at a fearful pace. The colonel was prepared to give the order for the battalion to reverse their retreat and attack their pursuers in full force, knowing in his heart that they could not win but preferring to die in battle, not dying while fleeing. But he changed his mind when he turned his worried gaze north once more to check the wizard's progress.

The muddy shoreline had been transformed into white slush. The frontrunners of his retreating battalion leapt over the slush and landed not in the lake, but on it. A rectangular sheet of ice expanded along the surface of the water, forming a white island almost a half-mile in area. Strong was reminded of the battle of Silverleaf, the opening skirmish in what would become the short but ruinous campaign known as the Cursed Opening.

The Head Mage created a bridge of ice across the Tyne when Glynhalla the Rainmaker, a rain elemental and agent of the evil Child Mar-dah, flooded it. And like that ice bridge,

27

this island of ice was not smooth and slippery, which would have been a hazard to their cavalry horses. It was rough and slushy, firm enough to hold them but giving just enough to grant secure purchase to the hooves of the charging steeds.

He thanked the Lord Ascendant that the wizard was able to finish his work before their enemy's mysterious magic vacuum finished its work.

Colonel Rheingold Strong changed his command.

"Arc Thorndevil formation, soldiers! To the south! Archers' Greeting and Raxe's Anvil! Hold those *Ken* bastards! Everyone else, keep moving to the lake!"

Within a matter of seconds the remaining shield men formed another wall, this one curved and bowed outward toward the onrushing *Ken*. This time they left just enough space between their shields to allow their wall of steel to be complimented by the company of lance men, who fitted their pointed polearms between the seams.

The formation resembled the long side of a thorndevil, a heavily muscled, three-foot long weasel-like animal found in the Badlands and southern regions of the continent. The animal had a thick hide and was armed with strong needle pointed quills that it used for defense against larger predators and offense against its prey.

The companies of archers and spears swiftly lined up just behind them along the length of the front, their spears and crossbows and longbows leveled. Raxe's Anvil – a formation named for the Old One Raxe who, like his father, was both warrior and blacksmith to his fellow Old Ones – fell in behind the archers.

Raxe's Anvil was comprised of the full arms company, strong and fierce warriors wearing the heaviest armor they could while still riding in relative comfort atop their massive warhorses. They carried oversized war hammers, spiked clubs, bronze maces, long-handled battleaxes, spiked flails and two-handed greatswords.

The five companies easily outnumbered the attacking warriors but the lizard-riders came on without pause, shouting war cries sounding eerily like the collective roar of a pride of enraged tygras. The instant the formations were complete, the archers and spearmen greeted their attackers with a devastating volley of crossbow bolts and longbow arrows and spears. Another volley darted in from overhead as the Gryphon Ryders swooped in to assist.

Many of the *Ken d'Zanir* fell from blows to vital areas, but not nearly enough of them. Far more were able to protect their vital areas with shields, buckles, and the broad-headed heavy weapons that they hoisted with such ease.

The arrows that got through to pierce their muscular arms, legs and even outer pectorals were brushed away with little or no regard as the warriors charged on. Most of the land dragon steeds completely ignored the bolts that bounced off of their green-scaled hides and the bony horn clusters atop their heads. A few missiles brought a very small number of the great beasts down when they were lucky enough to find their eyes or the back of a throat when they found an open pair of jaws that could not snap shut fast enough.

The *Ken d'Zanir* was on them before the archers could launch a second volley. The archers retreated as the *Ken* crashed into the front line with an explosion of metal almost as thunderous as the arrival of the hail of blackwood bolts. This explosion, however, was not accompanied by only the screams and roars of men and horses. It was made even more terrible by the shrieking and hissing of the monsters upon which the *Ken d'Zanir* rode.

Colonel Strong and his lieutenant colonel looked on in dismay while soldiers continued to race pass them on their way to the frozen island on the lake. Strong felt helpless as the front line crumbled under the assault of the *Ken*. In less than a minute they had torn through the Thorndevil Arc and were met by Raxe's Anvil. Surprisingly, the *Ken* actually dismounted and charged the full-arms company on foot. It was then that Godson fully understood why his commander had called for a retreat.

The *Ken*, impossibly nimble and quick for their size, dodged the furious hooves and snapping teeth of the royal army's warhorses to snatch soldiers from their mounts. The huge men from the western fringes of the Westin Continent, the western edge of the Known Lands, were easily equal to at least two of the Kingdom of Lorr's elite warriors. The difference between the Lorrian soldiers' and the *Ken*'s size, strength, quickness and fighting skill brought to the Lieutenant Colonel's mind the image of a group of seasoned warriors fighting against green adolescents.

And as if the *Ken* themselves were not bad enough, their steeds were exponentially worse.

The smallest of land dragons were longer and heavier than the biggest warhorses. They were lower to the ground, which gave them even more of an advantage. The sleek, six-legged reptiles savagely attacked the horses and the soldiers with their long curved claws and rows of razor-sharp teeth. The beasts' speed was incredible. Their long bodies had the flexibility of a snake. And they did not die easily.

It took several soldiers to bring down one of the land dragons and most of them died in the effort. Tooth and claw bit through holes in chain mail and penetrated leather and weak points in metal armor. The sheer weight and strength of the monstrous lizards broke necks and backs.

The Gryphon Ryders lent support where they could. They shot arrows and launched wicked javelins down into the *Ken*. Many of them even swooped down to strike at them with blades and polearms. But the *Ken* also had bows, slings, and javelins. Both gryphons and Ryders fell from the sky. High-leaping land dragons brought down Ryders who dared to swoop too low.

Lieutenant Colonel Godson looked on as the number of defending soldiers diminished with frightening speed and almost missed Strong's order for retreat. He wheeled his mount around and sent it dashing for the lake. He did not look back until he was more than two-dozen yards onto the island of ice.

When he did look back, he swore aloud.

Nearly a quarter of the attacking company had already penetrated Raxe's Anvil and was bearing down on the retreating, mounted archers. The archers turned and fired as their cavalry horses charged onto the frozen lake. The leading

Ken warriors fell to the hail of concentrated arrows and crossbow bolts but their steeds continued on, pointed tongues lolling hungrily as they closed the distance between them even faster without their riders' weight to slow them down.

The rider-less land dragons were the first of the enemy to leap easily across the slushy shoreline onto the wide sheet of ice. Their weight and the force with which they landed sent a shudder through the sheet of ice, causing it to tilt. Colonel Strong, who had retreated as far back as he could on the crowded ice island, looked on in horror.

They were trapped. There was nothing to slow the approach of the *Ken* and their steeds and there was nowhere left to go.

"What now, Mage?" he called over to Mage Gilder, who stood a few yards away and looked to the west across the Great Lake Onyx. The mage turned and raised a hand for patience, looking much too untroubled in Strong's opinion.

Strong was about to lay into the mage when he heard a loud rumble and then an explosive crack coming from the direction of the shore. To his slight relief, the island had broken almost straight across the quarter-mile wide sheet of ice, about ten yards away from the shore. The momentum of the rushing land dragons pushed the frigid island further out into the lake. The chasm between the sheets of ice only grew as more land dragons, many with riders and many without, leapt across the water from the smaller piece of ice to the larger one.

Within the span of ten seconds, the larger island was too far away for even the powerful bounds of the land dragons to clear the distance. But by then there were more than enough of them on the island to do a considerable amount of damage.

The Colonel would minimize their opportunity.

"Into the lake with these bloody whoresons!" Strong cried. "Attack! Attack! Attack!"

The royal battalion was only too happy to obey. They swarmed the stranded *Ken* and their mounts. This time their numbers was too great for even the awesome warriors and land dragons. The Lorrian forces savagely struck down both man and beast while driving them to, and over, the edge of the island and into the ice-chilled lake water.

The heavy land dragons were obviously not amphibious reptiles. This was evident in the way they immediately flailed and then sank after falling into the deep water. The men, as powerful and confident as they were, were not stupid enough to attempt to regain the drifting sheet of ice and swam for the shore. More than a few of the royal soldiers died during the assault, but with assistance from the Gryphon Ryders it did not take long to clear their little frosted island of the enemy.

"Colonel!" Lieutenant Colonel Godson cried in alarm as the last sounds of battle faded to silence. "Look to the shore!"

The slight relief Strong felt when the small island broke away was dismissed by yet more concern.

"I was waiting for this," he growled.

Back at the shoreline, long rows of land dragons came trotting over the foothills hauling what initially appeared to be wagons carrying large mechanical devices. But Strong knew they were not wagons. They were small wheel-mounted ballistae, the projectile war machines reminiscent of giant crossbows. Those were the devices that had launched the deadly blackwood bolts to start this one-sided battle.

As the land dragons were steered into several lines just beyond the shore, the *Ken* warriors hastily loaded and aimed the oversized slings.

"The battalion is an easy target," Godson whispered.

"May the Old Ones protect us," Strong prayed.

"Not the Old Ones," came Mage Gilder's strong voice from the colonel's right. "An Elemental, maybe."

Strong looked further into the distance to his right and saw a wave approaching from the western waters of the great lake. He knitted his brow in curiosity and wonder at the sight. The natural tide came in and out of this side of Lake Onyx from the north and south.

How in the seven hells could the steadily growing wave come in from the west?

The leading ripples of the oncoming wave slowly spun the ice island and carried it even further away from shore, but not quickly enough to take them out of the range of the ballistae's sharpened blackwood shafts. The ice island began to turn even faster as the growing wave approached, so fast, in fact, that the horses and the men had to brace themselves. The horses widened their four-legged stance while the men sat on their haunches. Those who carried long polearms jabbed them into the icy surface and held tight. Strong spun nimbly in the opposite direction to keep the *Ken* in sight.

The *Ken d'Zanir* saw the wave approaching and realized that it grew exponentially as it came on. Many of them retreated as far away and as swiftly as they could from the shoreline. The ballista operators, though, stubbornly continued their work. Before they could trigger their several rows of ballistae, the wave roared onto the shore at its weird angle and completely engulfed the machines, men and animals that were not quick enough to escape.

By the time the water settled, the ice island had spun over a half-mile out into the lake. Only stray pieces of water-soaked wood and metal remained on the shore. There was no sign of the *Ken d'Zanir* who manned the ballista. Mage Gilder's last remark finally registered with the colonel.

"An Elemental," he echoed. "The Sea Mistress is here?"

His answer was a stirring of water in the distance out west. He caught a glimpse of beautiful flowing hair as the stunning Sabrina, Mistress of the Sea of Spirits, disappeared beneath the surface of the Great Lake Onyx.

"How could she help us?" Strong asked. "Is she immune to the *Ken's* ability to neutralize magic?"

"She's beyond the circumference of the *Ken*'s void," the Echelon One mage explained. "Once she used her magic to set the wave in motion from beyond their reach, the physical properties of wave took over. Like pushing a cart down a hill, after the initial push, gravity does the rest."

"What do we do about the *Ken*?" Godson asked.

"Their projectile weapons were either destroyed or swept out into the lake," Strong answered. "I don't expect they will try to wait us out. They will surely understand that the Sea Mistress can attack them from a distance."

"Their weapons," Lieutenant Colonel Godson said uneasily. "They were hauling wheeled ballista weapons. How

33

could they have accomplished that without us seeing the telltale tracks?"

Strong stroked his wide, stubbly chin. "The ballista had to be waiting for them out west," he surmised. "And the group that hid so well from us and then attacked from the east after we passed had to have had the ballistae delivered to them."

"Yes," Mage Gilder agreed. "The question is who delivered it to them, and who placed them there for the *Ken* who attacked from the west?"

"And another critical question," Strong began, "Where are the *Ken* going now?"

"I fear their destination is south," Mage Gilder answered. "They were never fleeing from us. This was a planned attack. If not for Mage Kenth's warning to me, their attack could very well have wiped us all out."

"Mage Kenth?" Strong had almost forgotten about the lower ranking mage. "Where is he?"

The grave look on the mage's face was answer enough.

After a brief moment of silence, Lieutenant Colonel Caleb Godson spoke. "Why would the *Ken* be going south?"

"From what the Head Mage has told us," Mage Gilder explained, "their primary mission is to stop the Child Raxe and his party from recovering the Hell Key from the Demon's Spine Mountains. The *Ken* will follow them until they catch them and kill them. Attacking us was a bonus. The *Ken* will resume their pursuit of the Child. They'll keep to the eastern fringes of the Hells in order to remain concealed as they make their way south."

A dark look fell over the colonel's face. "And *we* will follow the *Ken* until we catch and kill *them*."

"Yes!" added Captain Zedek with fierce determination as he settled his gryphon down alongside Mage Gilder. "All we need to do is send for more men. Just one more battalion would – "

"Take too long to arrive," Mage Gilder finished. "We must track them ourselves."

"I appreciate your ferocity, mage," Strong admitted. "But

that would be a fool's errand. We'll be lucky to have half of our original number, and we obviously did not have enough men to begin with. What's worse, you'll have no magic to use against them."

"But we will have the element of surprise," Mage Gilder returned, a devious gleam in his dark blue eyes. "They will not expect us to hunt them after this loss. And though my magic will not work against them directly, there is much I can do with my magic in preparation for our next meeting. They are not the only warriors who can use trickery."

Colonel Strong turned a questioning gaze to Godson. The grim determination he saw in the faces of his Lieutenant Colonel and the captain of the diminished Gryphon Ryder company encouraged him. All of them knew it was virtually suicide to pursue the *Ken*. They were all soldiers, though, fierce and proud. They were all hungry to redeem themselves after such a crushing defeat. The only question was how.

"Wizard Gilder, I'll need you to contact the palace to send for reinforcements," Strong said. "You wizards can communicate much faster than we can using scouts or pigeons, if had pigeons. We will follow the *Ken* at a safe distance while we make our preparations. We may or may not engage them. Whether or not we do will depend on how ready I think we are. If nothing else, we should be able to provide a clearer trail for our reinforcements to follow.

"But if at any time I feel we have an advantage," the colonel concluded, "we will attack with even more savagery than they displayed when they ambushed us."

1.5

Two of the *Ken d'Zanir* stood atop a grassy rise overlooking the shores of Lake Onyx. They were just under a hundred yards out of reach of the wave that had swept away the ballistae, the land dragons that transported them, and the men that worked them.

Both men, like the rest of the *Ken d'Zanir,* were well over six feet tall, broad of shoulder and narrow of waist, their long limbs lean and chiseled with muscle. The taller of the two was taller by roughly three inches, which made him close to seven feet tall. The top of his large head was adorned with a coiled headdress made of short, stubbly, azure-furred tygra hide. The hide was wrapped several times around his head with tightly braided strips trailing down his back.

They stood among a litter of blackwood bolts that protruded from the earth, many of them still pinning dead and dying men and horses to the ground. The taller warrior snatched one of the bolts from the ground. The bolt had a small red ribbon bound to its flat end. After pulling it out of the ground he flipped it so that the pointed end was facing up.

A dark fist-sized object was bound securely to the staff a few inches from its deadly point. The object had a rough surface that was such a dark reddish-brown it could easily be mistaken for black. It was somewhat round but not a perfect sphere. It was tied to the staff by a thin but tough leather thong that was fitted through a small hole drilled through the object. The *Ken's* long, thick fingers worked on the knot for a few seconds until it was undone. He handed the bolt to his companion and then tied the ends of the thong around his broad neck.

All the while, both men looked out at the ice island as it continued to float slowly out onto the great lake. The shorter of the two spoke first.

"It was the water witch, High *Ken* Lonos. I saw her just as she submerged."

"Of *course* it was the water witch, *Ken* L'Atir," replied

High *Ken* Rkam Lonos in an irritated tone.

He did not see the Mistress of the Sea as his second had and he had no idea where the wave had come from, but as commander of this detachment of *S'Zan Rho* warriors, he would never admit it to an underling.

"I smelled her foul presence well before I saw her," Rkam Lonos lied. "These weak easterners could never have survived an assault from the *Ken d'Zanir* without the help of foul magic."

"Do you think she was successful by mere chance?" L'Atir asked. "Or do you think she knows the limits of our ability to extinguish magic?"

The *Ken* commander gave a dismissive wave with a big hand. "It matters not. She will not interfere again. Our benefactor has declared that she will be dealt with in short order, as will the rest of the unholy magic wielders in these eastern lands...especially the so-called Children of the Old Ones. Our *truly* divine assistance will assure their fate."

L'Atir smiled deviously. "Yes, for the Leader God S'Zan guides us."

"As always," Rkam Lonos agreed. "For now we will resume our pursuit of those who seek the Hell Key. On the way, we will pass through Port Lorrian to re-supply and sate our appetites. *All* of our appetites. And upon our exit we will tear that cursed city and its denizens to the ground. No one will be spared."

L'Atir's sly smiled faltered for a moment. "No one?" He asked. "Including the women and children? Prince T'Cheln may greatly object to such mass slaughter."

"T'Cheln is *not* the commander of this unit," Lonos reminded. "*I* am. As long as he is babysitting that ridiculous baron while we do the real work of imposing the will of the grim God S'Zan on these accursed easterners, his opinion and his parentage mean nothing to me. And you would do well to *never* question my judgment again."

The shorter man nodded and gave a quick bow of acquiescence. "Of course, commander. I apologize for my insolence. It would be my great pleasure to strike three fingers from my right hand for my indiscretion."

"No need for that," Rkam Lonos said, apparently satisfied with the offer. He stood tall and surveyed his force.

"We lost three men at Port Lorrian," he continued, "and several more here. We will make the entire city of Port Lorrian pay for our losses. Our benefactors want us to make a 'grand statement' of our faith in the course of hunting the Child Raxe, and we will do just that.

"The people in this kingdom are followers of the weakling gods Lorr and the Ascendant One. It will be an honor for them to fall by our hands. And then we will make the Child Raxe pay just as dearly. Gather our men, L'Atir. We ride to Port Lorrian. No man, woman, or child will be left alive when we leave!"

Chapter 2: Captives

2.1

Raxe, on first watch while the others slept, pulled his cloak tighter around him against the rapidly dropping temperature. The sharp, cold wind at his back whistled its way west to shock away some of the fatigue of their earlier ordeals and helped him stay alert. As welcome as the chill was this evening he was still anxious to get out of the cold of the high elevations.

He knew, however, that he would soon miss the consistent cold when they skirted the edge of the Forsaken Desert. He was all too familiar with the opposite and extreme night and day temperature shifts of that area from his short stay in Southborough three years earlier.

The thought of their relatively close proximity to the Forsaken Desert brought to mind the image of Shara Dune's sand creatures. A glance at the rest of their small party made him more uncomfortable, especially when his gaze passed over Ethan Sureblade.

The teen had no business here.

Quick had changeling magic, which made him the most formidable threat among them when there were no demons around. Raxe would never admit it aloud, but he knew the Ranger Elf Rell Kallen's elven nature made him stronger, quicker and more agile.

Those natural advantages coupled with a lifetime of training made the elf more than a match for Raxe in both hand-to-hand and weapons combat – again – as long as there were no demons around.

Even his daughter, as dainty and frail as the pretty little girl appeared, was much more than she appeared. Both the Head Mage and her mother, The Mistress of the Sea of Spirits, warned Raxe that the unprecedented combination of magic in Azhju'lestra's blood could very well make her more powerful than anyone could predict.

Raxe knew better than to question either of them in

matters of magic.

But he did question the Head Mage Rionn Lorr about Ethan's involvement. At least the survivors of the sky sleigh crew were adults. Ethan was a kid. He was highly skilled with all of his weapons, especially his broadsword, but he was a kid just the same, a kid that had just suffered a tragedy that no one so young should have to face.

The other sky sleigh that was brought down by the scythe wings contained every member of the Keeper's Hounds except Ethan. They had all been friends to the teen, and one of them, a young woman only a couple of years older than him, was more than a friend. Their loss was clearly a distraction to Ethan. Raxe feared it was a distraction that would eventually put the boy in jeopardy. He would not be able to live with himself if he broke his promise to Annastace and failed to return her son safely home.

Ethan's presence may not have bothered Raxe so much had it not been for an experience on one of his few Cutter missions. He had been escorting Dr. James Stewart, the elite team's computer hacker, into the compound of a ruthless Southeast Asian warlord when they were fired upon by a detachment of paramilitary guards that had stumbled upon their trail. Raxe – codename Axe at the time – ended up fatally shooting three of their pursuers.

When he checked the bodies to make sure they were dead or to finish them off if they were still alive, he saw that one of his victims had been a young boy no older than Ethan. The kill haunted him for years before he was finally able to put it behind him. Ethan's presence on this mission brought all of that back.

Raxe's head snapped up when he thought he saw a furtive movement of shadow low to the ground within the surrounding brush. With the image of the sand creatures still in his mind, he quickly snatched up Demonsbane and jumped to his feet. He peered into the shadows, holding his enchanted battleaxe at the ready, waiting for the movement to repeat itself.

He slowed his breathing and let his body relax, preparing

to respond to any threat. But then he realized that Demonsbane was not glowing. Since he could not feel his magic stirring within him, he dismissed the possibility of the four-tentacled demon-spawn creatures being in the vicinity. But then he remembered how the *S'Zan Rho* had somehow managed to suppress everyone's magic back at Port Lorrian and wondered if it could be happening again.

Had Shara Dune gained access to whatever the *S'Zan Rho* used back then and given it to her warriors? If so, there very well could be sand creatures out there. They were definitely close enough to the Forsaken Desert for a hunting or scouting party to be in the area.

Without his or Quick's magic they would not stand a chance if the sand demons attacked. Not even the powerful Ranger Elf could stand against more than one of the fierce warrior-monsters.

Stealth, however, was not their style. If sand creatures were indeed out there they would have attacked by now. Besides that, Raxe could still sense the magic around him. He detected magical auras visually as white, transparent motes of energy jumping off of their owners like tiny droplets of liquid. Had his magic been squelched, he would not be able to see the faint traces of magic radiating from the life surrounding him.

Raxe watched and waited. Nothing happened. He reminded himself that the movement he saw was close to the ground. Sand creatures would have cast a much larger shadow. It had to be an animal, something more frightened of them than he was of it. What's more, the elf and changeling were usually the first ones to detect danger. If there was a threat out there the two of them would have awakened.

Raxe scanned the area for a few minutes more just to be sure. He crept out to where he thought he saw the movement. There was nothing but silence and shadows interspersed with dim silver shafts of moons' light. When nothing happened he decided it was just a small forest creature passing by their small camp.

He relaxed, if only just a bit, and went back into the clearing.

Still keeping an eye out for any movement, he sat back down at his bedroll, facing in the direction where he thought he saw the movement. After a few more wary minutes of watching and waiting he decided that it was safe to contact the Head Mage.

Raxe opened his pack and felt around until he found the palm-sized box. He pulled it out and made himself as comfortable as he could on the cold, hard ground. He shook the box four times, as directed by the Head Mage, before snapping it open.

The small wooden stylus, as always, sat atop the smoothed out reflection sand instead of being buried beneath it, as it should have been after being shaken. He picked up the stylus and carefully drew the symbol the Head Mage had shown him. When the drawing was complete he waited several seconds and then used his index finger to stir the sand and wipe away the symbol.

He watched in amazement as the sand continued to stir even after he removed his finger. After a few seconds the stirring slowed almost to a stop. The only portion that still moved was at the upper left hand corner of the rectangular box. The moving portion of sand parted slightly to form letters, and then words, and then a sentence.

Not difficult after all?

"Wow," Raxe whispered, careful not to wake the others. He smoothed out the sand with a finger before using the stylus to write a response.

No, he wrote in the reflection sand before smoothing it out once more. After a couple of seconds, the sand moved.

How fares the quest? Rionn Lorr wrote in his own box of reflection sand hundreds of miles away.

Ryan frowned. *Not well.* He scratched. *We lost both sky sleighs, the entire crew from* Sundance *and most of the crew from* Cloud Chaser. *Joel has been taken. He was alive when I last saw him.* Raxe went on to write their location and the names of the survivors.

When he was finished, more than a few breaths passed before the sand moved again.

DEMON OF LORR

May the fallen find peace with the Lord Ascendant. Rionn Lorr returned. *In what kind of shape are the survivors?*

Pissed. Really pissed. And determined to find Joel and the Hell Key.

Good. The Head Mage returned. He was not familiar with the term 'pissed,' but from the context and his familiarity with Raxe's euphemisms, he correctly assumed they were angry. *Located a text this morning.* He continued. *Found a passage that might prove useful. Time enough to convey?*

Not sure, Raxe wrote as he glanced once more at the surrounding shadows. He was not entirely convinced that they were alone but he did not have enough evidence to prove otherwise.

Besides, he needed to see that passage. If there was the slightest chance that the passage could evoke something useful from the memories that Shanderah had implanted in Raxe's mind before she died, he had to try. The ancient sorceress's memories could contain information to help them defeat the walking dead or at least find out why the demon was sending them east.

He smoothed the sand again. *Write fast*, he scratched.

The reply came an instant later.

> *The world wept when Daniatiae Lorr, the first Head Mage of the Kingdom of Lorr, fell to the Leaders at the Runestone Mountains.*
>
> *Beneath the bejeweled bosom of the Lady, where Her precious stones look defiantly to the realm of shadows, spans an artery through which Her flaming lifeblood flows.*
>
> *There, where only the pure or the tainted may pass, they would be welcomed into Her embrace.*
>
> *And it was there where those whom She accepted would rupture that artery to expose her flaws and exploit Her imperfections in order to hew a wedge from the heart of the Lady, so that the wedge could be devoured for all eternity by the shimmering giver and taker*

of life.

*Daniatiae Lorr battled the pure and the
tainted alike to stay this horror. In the end,
Daniatiae Lorr did Herself fall to those whom
She accepted.*

Raxe had to smooth the sand several times because the
message, as small the letters were, was too long for the box
to hold all at once. He made a point to commit each word to
memory before wiping them clear. He was skilled at
memorizing details. It had been an important part of his job
as an assassin for the organization and he took pride in his
adeptness at that particular skill.

After the message was complete he stared at the last two
sentences filling the small box of sand while replaying the
rest of the message in his head. He cleared his mind of
everything except the message, hoping that the words would
spark one of Shanderah's transferred memories. He took a
deep breath to clear his mind and find his center. It was
easier to do now than it had been in the recent past. He had
done it so many times over the last few years that it had
almost become second nature.

It did not happen instantaneously, but within several
heartbeats, Raxe had peeled away all sound, smell, and
thought. He could no longer feel the chill wind that blew
through the clearing. All he could see in his mind's eye was
the little box of sand, elongated in order to display the full
message. The sand was then swept away so that only the
words remained, dark gray words on a stark white
background.

He willed the words into a beacon for Shanderah's
memories but nothing happened.

"Shit."

He sighed in frustration but made sure to turn his head to
keep from blowing away any of the reflection sand. Finally,
he smoothed the sand to write his response:

Nothing familiar, Raxe wrote. *But questions. Why the
change of tense in the passage? Why the lack of consistency*

in references to Daniatiae?

Explain. Rionn wrote.

Raxe thought for a moment before writing. He wanted to be certain to write exactly what he meant. He started to write a couple of times but immediately cleared the writing when he noticed he was not phrasing his thoughts effectively. On the third try, he wrote continuously.

1st sentence past tense, 2nd present tense, 3rd and 4th either past or future tense or probabilities from use of "would" and "could." 5th sentence past tense again.

It took a little longer for a response this time. Raxe assumed Rionn Lorr was considering his reply. And then the sand moved again.

Observant, Rionn Lorr complimented. *Could be literary license? Tendency of the author?*

Possible, Raxe responded. *But it bothers me.*

Bears consideration. Think on it. Rionn advised. *I will do the same. What about references to Daniatiae?*

Referred to as "Daniatiae Lorr" in beginning and end, but as "Lady," "Her," and "She" everywhere else.

Again, Rionn wrote, *Literary license?*

Possible, Raxe wrote again. *But is it an accurate historical record or work of literature?*

Both?

Possible, Raxe repeated. *But questionable.*

He thought he saw a subtle rustle in the shadows again. He strained his eyes but saw nothing. The elf and changeling still slept soundly and that eased Raxe's tensions somewhat. Their senses, even in sleep, were far sharper than his. If anything was out there he was sure they would have heard or smelled it. He shrugged away his nervousness and returned his attention to the box of reflection sand.

Interesting, but doesn't explain significance of Bluethorn or north Runestones. Theories? Rionn asked.

Not now. Soon. Will keep in touch.

The wind shifted, stroking Raxe's face with a cold hand. He had to snap the lid closed quickly to keep the sand from blowing out of the box. Quick and Rell Kallen snapped up to seated positions immediately, each grabbing their weapons.

Raxe was surprised the small sound of the lid being closed would startle them so, but the fierce looks on their faces as they glared into the darkness of the surrounding brush told Raxe that the box of reflection sand was not their concern. The offworlder reached for Demonsbane just as a dark form broke silently away from the shadows.

The squat, broad shadow appeared to Raxe to be a crouching, creeping man attempting to take them by surprise. But he had been spotted, so why would he continue to crouch and creep?

And then Raxe noticed the magic. Twice the amount of energy poured from the newcomer than from the average human and almost as much as from the Ranger Elf. Raxe wondered what it could be if it was neither human nor elf. When he saw the silhouette of raised weapons taking shape, rising from the low, wide shadow that crept ever closer to the edge of their campfire's light, he knew he would get his answer very soon.

The Ranger Elf rose smoothly and quickly to his feet, his long sword poised and his sharply canted eyes wide and alert, his knees slightly bent, ready to move. Raxe stood straight, moved his legs a bit farther apart, and let his battleaxe hang from the handle's leather strap in his right hand. Quick was on his feet as well, looking expectantly out at the approaching shadow figure.

But then the changeling sheathed his weapon.

"You know something we don't, kid?" Raxe rasped as softly as his damaged vocal cords would allow.

A smile spread across the teen's face. "Bartok!" he called. "It's Quick, the changeling. We mean you no harm."

"We know who ye are," returned a voice almost as gravelly as Raxe's and twice as deep. "We know not yer friends. From the looks of 'em *they* mean us great harm."

The owner of the intimidating voice stepped into the firelight and Raxe recognized his features as dwarven.

The point of the dwarf's peaked helmet rose as high as the top of Raxe's chest. Dots of firelight gleamed in the beady eyes that were otherwise hooded in the shadow of the bascinet helmet's raised visor.

Long and braided red whiskers streaked through with gray hung down from below a knobby nose and a wide, strong jaw. As relatively short as the dwarf was, he was nearly as wide.

Broad-ringed chain mail was draped over the rough-hewn, thick leather vest that covered the dwarf's massive torso. Thicker leather straps were sewn with heavy stitching to the shoulders of the vest to form spaulders that shielded his wide shoulders.

The dwarf's bare upper arms were bigger around than some tree trunks Raxe had seen. His heavy biceps, triceps and bulky forearms were taut as his meaty fists gripped the thick shaft of a long-handled, double bladed war axe. The war axe blades were not crescent-shaped polished silver like the blades of Demonsbane. The dwarf's war axe blades were wicked, worn wedges of sharpened dark grey iron. Where Demonsbane was made for precision maneuvering and slicing, the dwarf's war axe was a weapon made for brute force, hacking and chopping and crushing.

"Elf," Bartok growled at Rell Kallen before leveling his fearsome glare on Raxe. He took a moment to inspect Raxe's unique armor and battleaxe before continuing. "And ye, stranger. Ye trespass on our land and have the gall to greet us with raised weapons? Lower them or die."

"I do not think we will, dwarf," the Ranger Elf defied. "We had no idea you were here or that this was your land. We only wish to pass through peacefully. I've heard of your kind's strength and skill in battle, but there is only one of you and we are no slouches. You lower *your* weapon and let us be off or we will be forced to hurt you."

"We?" the dwarf asked mockingly. "What 'we'?"

The telltale soft chime of the jewel at the head of Raxe's battleaxe touching the metal ring of his axe frog echoed through the night.

Rell Kallen turned to see Raxe with raised, empty hands and Demonsbane hanging from his hip. Raxe turned to the elf and shrugged. Rell Kallen looked over at Ethan and saw that the youngster was not holding any of his beloved weapons.

And then the elf's pointed ears detected the sound of movement in the darkness around them...a *lot* of movement. A quick glance revealed a number of squat dwarven shadows in the surrounding brush.

With a frustrated sigh, the Ranger Elf sheathed his long sword.

2.2

Head Mage Rionn Lorr's loose brown cloak and long, dark blonde hair billowed out behind him as his thoroughbred steed, Ebony, carried him at a full gallop. They chased their shadows across the grassy plains as the two suns were still continuing their climb into the eastern skies.

Cavalry horses carrying a small squad of elite cavalrymen trailed Ebony by fifty yards or more. In most circumstances the squad leader would insist that their charge ride while surrounded by soldiers. In most circumstances, though, they would not be accompanying the Head Mage, who could and would do more to protect them than they could ever do to protect him.

But one thing struck the squad leader as odd. He had not seen the Child of the Old Ones often, but on the few occasions he did, he never saw him armed with anything other than his long, crooked staff. Now, though, a long broadsword rested in a leather sheath at the wizard's hip.

The reason the sword was there made him slightly uneasy about the Head Mage riding out so far ahead of them, but there was not much he could do about it. Ebony could easily outrun and outlast the cavalry's larger horses. They could not catch up with the Head Mage unless he wanted them to.

The message Rionn Lorr received had been dire, but as the damage had been done by the time word reached him, he saw no need to expend the energy it would take to fly to Port Lorrian upon his myst. That did not mean he would dally. Ordinarily he would have sent his highest-ranking wizard within the Conjurer's Alliance, Master Mage Delthar, or another master mage to investigate this occurrence. Mage Delthar, however, was riding east to join Echelon One Mage Jonathan Markus to intercept the army of walking dead that was slowly making its way toward the city of Ridgeland.

There were other Master Mages and high-ranking members of the Conjurer's Alliance Rionn could have sent, but the he wanted to see this for himself. Even though his wife, Catherine, had admonished him on more than one occasion for feeling responsible for the Kingdom's current predicament, Rionn could not help second guessing himself.

If he had executed Mar-dah instead of banishing him years ago, as many of his advisors and friends suggested, the wizard would never have had the opportunity to free the demons in the first place. And while Rionn had not admitted this to anyone, not even his wife, he feared the escape of the demon Dierglyorr was his fault, as well.

Most assumed the demon slipped out of the sixth level of hell because of Mar-dah's careless use of the Hell Key. Rionn was certain that was not the case, at least not entirely.

His evil distant cousin had only opened the first through fifth levels. At the battle against those demons at the Tyne River during the Cursed Opening, Rionn had depleted his inner reservoirs of magic but the horde of demons kept coming. As a result, he had to pull magical energies from Nature in order to hold the demons at bay and buy time for the king's valiant warriors to escape.

Rionn knew that the drain on Nature's energy in addition to the general unbalance caused by Mar-dah's use of the Hell Key would weaken the barrier between this world and the seven hells for the briefest instant, only a fraction of a second. But even that instant, shorter than one flicker of a hummingbird's wing, may have been enough. It could have been more than enough to allow a creature as powerful and clever as the Dierglyorr a miniscule window to escape. Rionn was thankful that a *seventh* level demon had not slipped through, but he felt no less responsible for the damage wrought by the sixth level demon that did.

For the last several days he had been overseeing healers, alchemists, and other mages as they sought desperately to find a cure for the plague that caused the dead to rise from their graves. For not only did the demon-slain casualties of the Cursed Opening awaken from death, the wounded victims of the evil Child Mar-dah's loosed demons were transformed into creatures very much like the walking dead.

The infected were impervious to pain and possessed inhuman savagery and strength. To make matters worse, they were spreading the plague to non-military citizens. Thus, the army of walking dead now included civilian men, women and children.

The defenders of the kingdom found that inflicting enough physical damage could immobilize them. The danger of direct confrontation, however, was too great for the king's warriors. It had already been demonstrated that the plague could too easily spread.

The soldiers would have to battle fallen comrades-in-arms and, in some cases, infected family members. As valiant as they were, such terrible confrontations could very easily make them hesitant at best and distracted at worst. In the end, sending men against the plague-stricken legions could only serve to increase their number.

Even though a squad of Master and Echelon One Mages could quickly wash the cursed army away with a surge of their devastating whitefyre, Rionn could not allow the obliteration of so many innocents. He had to find a way to cure them.

But he had grown claustrophobic and restless in the alchemists' chambers. He had grown frustrated with their – and his – inability to find a cure that would return the wounded to normal and put the dead to rest. He needed this temporary distraction to clear his mind and refocus, no matter how potentially dangerous it was.

The thought of the danger caused him to look down and to his right at the staff strapped to his saddle. The rough surface had never been smooth. The living bark covering the hard wood had always been pitted and lined. It had always resembled weathered oak bark. But from the time he had cured it and made it his wizard's staff, it had never been cut.

The surface of the staff might have resembled the bark of an oak, but it was far from it. The staff had been a relatively young branch of an ancient enchanted tree called a *Hecyinthir*, found on a nameless uncharted island at the southeastern fringes of the Known Lands. The island was the closest landmass to the searing climate of the eastern extreme of the Ocean Crystalline and was barely habitable.

When he was a young man, Rionn Lorr's final trial to earn his inheritance as the Head Mage was to brave the sweltering, treacherous island and battle the *Hecyinthir* for one of its young limbs. That was the closest the Head Mage had ever been to death, but he won the limb and it had been at his side for over forty years.

Most wizards' staves had runes that were carved or painted or bejeweled to help them focus and control magical energies. His staff needed none of that. The power within the tree lived on within the staff even after its separation from its host to make it a powerful focuser and augmenter of Rionn's already considerable magic. That power made the stave impenetrable to any type of physical or supernatural force…until Rionn's previous visit to Port Lorrian.

Over the years the staff had absorbed or deflected the deadly points and razor sharp edges of all manner of weaponry without yielding so much as a scratch. White-hot flames had licked the surface of the staff on more than one occasion, as had boiling oil, dragon fire, and lightening. None of which left even the slightest sear upon the *Hecyinthir* bark.

But the *Ken d'Zanir*, however, with their mysterious ability to banish magic, managed to scar the staff during their failed assassination attempt.

He looked at the broadsword at his left hip. He may have been the Head Mage but he was no stranger to swordplay. Weapons training had long been a part of the overall training of young wizards attending the *Chronicai Tul Myst*. The academy of magic trained wizards to serve and protect the Kingdom of Lorr and the founders of the revered school believed that their students should be skilled in the use of magic *and* the blade. All of their students received at least some weapons training at the Royal Military Academy. Rionn was nowhere near as adept in swordplay as he was in the use of magic, but he was skilled.

Some of the finest swordsmen in the kingdom had trained him throughout his childhood and well into his early adult years. Those who were old enough might remember the time that a young Rionn Lorr carried a broadsword at all times.

Before his trial of the *Hecyinthir*, the broadsword at his side was the only instrument he carried. It had served the same purpose as his staff. The blade and grip and egg-shaped pommel were engraved with runes etched in an ancient language to assist him in the wielding of his magic. The weapon had served him well.

This time it would serve a different purpose. Should his magic fail as it did the last time he was in this town, he would be much better prepared to defend himself. He might not be a match for the elite fighters of the *S'Zan Rho* warrior nation without his magic, but he would last longer with a formidable blade with a crooked wooden staff as his only weapon.

Rionn was pulled out of his reverie by a haze of dark smoke hovering over Port Lorrian like the shadow of a crouching titan. The scent of scorched wood assaulted his nose as he entered the city limits along Port Lorrian's main road. The further in he rode the stronger the scent became, accompanied by slowly blossoming fear and anger deep in his gut. Within minutes the scent grew so strong that he could taste it on the back of his tongue.

To his relief, the outlying homes were untouched. That relief turned to despair when the nauseating scent of charred flesh joined the smell and taste of burnt wood. Within minutes he came upon the first visible signs of destruction.

The main thoroughfare was lined with scorched buildings, homes and small business establishments. Many of them were still smoldering. When Rionn looked down the intersecting roads he saw slaughtered livestock and pack animals littering the cobblestone streets.

And then he saw the people.

First he saw the men. Most of the first wave of corpses wore the badges and sashes of the town's law enforcement. Rionn knew Port Lorrian's militia boasted a total of over three hundred officers. They were well trained and well armed, and apparently, completely routed.

He estimated there were well over two hundred bodies along the main road and its first two intersections. Only a half dozen of those bodies were *Ken d'Zanir*. It was a certainty that the nearby parallel roads that he could not see contained more of the same.

The bodies of Port Lorrian's official defenders soon gave way to the bodies of civilian defenders. Young, middle aged, and even a few elderly males were sprawled haphazardly all over the street in pools of drying blood. They lay beside modest swords of differing types or crude clubs or bladed farm tools. Even the town smithy, a huge, bearded man still clad in his forging apron and armed with a broadsword in one hand and a heavy forging hammer in the other, lay dead in middle of the street with a massive gash in his head. Two *Ken d'Zanir* lay dead to either side of him. Those two were the only other dead *Ken* he saw for the rest of his harrowing visit to Port Lorrian.

To someone unfamiliar with the *S'Zan Rho* warriors, it would seem impossible that fewer than two hundred men could do so much damage to a town of this size with such an ample defense. The Head Mage, however, was all too familiar with them. He knew how physically superior the *S'Zan Rho* people were to most other humans. He knew firsthand how skilled they were at combat, and he had seen the fierce creatures that served as both their steeds and attack animals. Local law enforcement, heads of households and local farmers probably in town bartering for supplies, all of them fought against the elite warriors and died.

After three blocks of this carnage the scene grew worse. Three columns of corpses lined the thoroughfare. It was obvious that the people had been lined up to be neatly and summarily executed. Every person had one deep, bloody scar to a critical area and each mark evidenced a different a type of weapon. There were headless corpses, deeply sliced throats, crushed skulls, and deep puncture wounds to the chest. Some of the bodies were cloven nearly in half either vertically or horizontally.

DEMON OF LORR

As the grisly line extended toward the center of town, bodies began to be found in more random positions in addition to the orderly columns.

Those people had not died the quick death from powerful blade cuts or single, fatal blows from blunt and spiked weapons. They were savagely torn, with teeth and claw marks apparent even through the heavy spatters of blood coating the bodies. In many cases, body parts were completely missing. The Head Mage immediately thought about the fierce land dragons that served as the *Ken's* steeds. He could visualize them running down and savaging the people who did not willingly stand or kneel to allow themselves to be cut down.

By the time he reached the center of town, Rionn Lorr was filled with violent anger and deep sorrow, all of which only increased when he reached the town square. The town square was a large courtyard roughly one hundred yards long on each side. On the east side of the square was Center Market. Its shops were smashed and small fires blazed here and there amid the debris. The remains of slaughtered livestock lay carelessly discarded in pools of blood.

On the north adjacent side of the Center Market was City Hall. Dark smoke wafted out of every window of the three-story brick building. The street level walls were pocked with deep, foot-wide craters, damage that could only be done by war hammers. The columns that framed the once majestic entryway had been smashed into large chunks of mortar. The balcony that they once supported was now a ragged pile of wood, stone and metal. It, like everything else, was spattered with blood and gore.

On the south adjacent side of Center Market, the remnants of the open-air theater lay in smoldering ruins. Soot covered everything. The stage was reduced to a mess of splintered, broken planks of wood. The benches and chairs had been reduced to so much tinder, ashen kindling feeding the fire within the theater.

The town church faced Center Market from across the quadrangle. The church was dedicated to the Lord Ascendant and had once been a beautiful construction. Rionn Lorr had spoken there several times. He was not an ordained priest, but as both a Child of the Old Ones and the Head Mage, he was occasionally asked to conduct services as an honorary clergyman. It had been a while since he did so, but this was one of his favorite places to speak.

The church was a modest, yet elegant complex. The only tower the structure boasted was the bell tower, and it had been toppled. The only other grand feature, before being smashed into a hill of rubble, was the high stone stairway that spanned twenty-five yards perfectly centered at the front of the complex.

The lack of adornment was a dedication to the teachings of the Church of the Lord Ascendant. Function was considered more important than form. The Lord Ascendant judged one's faith not by how fervently one praised Him, but how fervently one served and respected all mankind. For that reason, the complex was as much a school and library as it was a temple of worship. And now only one wall remained completely intact. And it was obvious that the only reason it had been spared was because of the message written on the wall in blood:

> *The Old One S'Zan became the One True God when the Lord Ascendant forsook this world. Believe, blasphemers, or suffer the same fate as this city of sinners.*

The town square was two blocks east of the inn where Rionn stayed only a few nights earlier; where he, Raxe and Joel, Quick the changeling, Ethan Sureblade, and the Ranger Elf Rell Kallen were attacked by the *S'zan Rho Ken d'Zanir* assassins. As much as the Head Mage disliked and distrusted Rell Kallen, he had to admit that had it not been for the presence of the Ranger Elf, all of them would have been killed that night.

And it was indeed a painful admission. Before Rionn Lorr met Catherine, the half-human-half-elf beauty who would become his wife, she was to become the Ranger Elf's betrothed. It was an arranged marriage to which Catherine was opposed.

DEMON OF LORR

Catherine was opposed to many of the elven traditions, primarily because those traditions led to the execution of her elven mother and human father for their forbidden union.

Catherine was spared only because her maternal grandmother was the queen of the Elf Land's Thâlstrën Kingdom. When Catherine and Rionn Lorr met and quickly fell in love, Catherine eagerly shunned tradition and spurned Rell Kallen, who genuinely loved her even though that love was not returned, to run away with Rionn Lorr.

The Ranger Elf hated Rionn Lorr for it and the elven queen was not too fond of him either. Rell Kallen made no secret about his desire to take Catherine back, even – or preferably – over Rionn Lorr's dead body.

Such a course of action was not to be. Rionn Lorr was a Child of the Ones and a wizard, which bestowed upon him a legacy of magic more powerful than any other mortal being. He was also the Head Mage of the most dominant human kingdom in the Known Lands. These factors stayed any retaliation by the elven queen. She did not want to start a potentially devastating war against the humans to retrieve a willful half-breed granddaughter that had no desire to return to her homeland, anyway.

Rionn wondered how much it galled the Ranger Elf Rell Kallen to be ordered to the Kingdom of Lorr to assist the man he felt stole away his future bride. Then again, Rionn was sure that it would please Rell Kallen to no end to help with the retrieval of the Hell Key and then steal it back to the Thâlstrën Kingdom. That would be a small measure of revenge for both the Ranger Elf and the queen who felt the Hell Key would be safer under elven guard than under humans' protection. They felt it was particularly dangerous to allow a Child of the Old Ones to possess it, for only a Child could use the Key to open the gates of the seven hells.

Rell's presence that night of the assignation attempt turned out to be a blessing. It only took four of the *Ken* warriors to kill ten elite royal guards.

They nearly killed all three Children of the Old Ones, the formidable changeling, and the young but talented Ethan Sureblade. Had the elf not been there to shift the odds when the *Ken d'Zanir* attacked in the dead of night, the *Ken's* ability to extinguish magic and their devastating fighting ability would have made short work of them all.

This time nearly two hundred of the *Ken* assassins attacked the entire town of Port Lorrian. Its citizens and defenders never stood a chance.

Rionn Lorr detected the dreaded and familiar coppery scent before he saw it. The water in the large, ornate fountain in the middle of the square was tainted dark red, saturated with the blood of men, women, and children. The ground all around the fountain was covered with a sticky film of crimson. Soldiers were removing the last of the bodies from the fountain as Rionn looked on with equal amounts of despair and rage in his dark blue eyes.

When he came upon what was left of Colonel Rheingold Strong's battalion, he saw his own despair and anger mirrored in their eyes and their body language. He found the colonel, Echelon One Mage Gilder Raynard, and the commander of the Gryphon Ryder Company Captain Zedek standing a few feet away from their steeds: a cavalry horse and two gryphons. He reined Ebony to a stop a few yards away from them and dismounted. They all turned to look at him and shook their heads sadly.

"I deeply regret the loss of your pupil," Rionn Lorr said sincerely to Mage Raynard as he tried not to look at the bodies piled up around the fountain. "Mage Kenth was a promising young wizard. The Conjurer's Alliance has been weakened by his loss."

"Thank you," the Echelon One Mage returned. He looked at the horror around him and bristled. "At least he was an agent of the Kingdom of Lorr and knew the attendant risks, as did the fallen warriors under Colonel Rheingold Strong's command and Port Lorrian's defenders.

"But these poor people... They were innocent civilians. The bastards slaughtered them, Master Lorr. What madness is this?"

"War is what this is," the colonel growled, his face flushed with rage. "This is an open declaration of war."

DEMON OF LORR

"One crisis at a time, commander," Rionn Lorr cautioned.

The Head Mage cast a broad glance around the square. The squad that accompanied him was dismounting and surveying the carnage with shock and loathing. The haggard remains of Strong's battalion, who had been attacked and diminished by the same warriors who had savaged this town, were occupied with several tasks. They searched among the bodies for survivors, restocked their supplies and gathered and stacked lumber, tools, and varying metal works.

Several Gryphon Ryders circled the skies above them. Several more stood beside their winged mounts while the bird cats grazed the few unsullied patches of grass they could find. And then the Head Mage noticed there were fewer Ryders than there should have been.

"Captain Zedek," Rionn said, "where is the rest of your company?"

"Scouting ahead," Captain Zedek answered. "Keeping track of the *Ken*'s progress and position."

"Do you think that's wise considering their earlier ambush?" Rionn Lorr asked.

"They are staying well back of the enemy," the captain assured. "From the skies, with their spy glasses, they can keep watch of them from a safe distance."

"Is it really worth the risk?" Rionn questioned. "A regiment has been mobilized to pursue the *Ken* and engage them. They'll be only a couple of days behind you. Your Ryders and Strong's battalion have suffered enough losses. Between your confrontations with the walking dead and the *S'Zan Rho* elite *Ken*, you have more than done your duty to the Kingdom of Lorr. Minister of War Geoffrey has given the order for you to wait here until the regiment can come and relieve you."

"It *is* worth the risk," the colonel insisted. "Our men were eager to hunt these killers down after our defeat at Lake Onyx and they are twice as determined after seeing this cowardly display. Not a one of them would go home now."

"We have a plan," Echelon One mage Raynard added. "The Gryphon Ryders will stay close enough to keep track of the *Ken* while staying far enough away to escape to safety should the *Ken* spot them and attempt to attack with their wheel-mounted ballistae. We have to know their position before we pounce, should we decide to do so."

The Head Mage's eyes narrowed. "I'm sure you have an excellent plan. But it is not their wheel-mounted ballistae that concern me."

Rionn Lorr took a deep breath and focused. With very little effort, he cast his farsight with a wide field of perception, following the general path of the Bountiful River. It took only a few seconds to locate the Gryphon Ryder scout team nearly seventy-five miles south, but he searched beyond them. He sent his farsight farther south, wider to the east and west, spanning from the ground to miles above the earth, higher even than the clouds.

And then he saw them.

His suspicion and fear proved well founded. Above the clouds, moving swiftly and purposefully, came the swarm of the same deadly scythe wings that brought down the two sky sleighs ferrying Raxe and his team south to search for Mardah's mountain.

The smallest of the scythe wings, so named because of their wickedly curved and pointed beaks, were three times the size of the largest gryphon. There were larger birds but scythe wings were like a flying pack of wolves. They hunted in large groups. They were known to wear down larger prey to eventually swarm and rend their unfortunate quarry to pieces either in mid flight or, in some cases, on the ground. Rionn counted at least sixty of them in this flock.

The flock's tight formation and their broad wingspans combined to block the sunlight below, casting a stark, massive, arrow-head shadow as they burst through the clouds and fell upon the nine-Ryder scout team. The gryphons sensed the approach of the flock moments before the deadly birds attacked and their response was to scatter madly in every direction.

The men and women riding the gryphons could only hold tightly to their reins and dig in their heels. The experienced Ryders leaned in close and tilted their bodies in unison with their familiar mounts, riding them smoothly despite their startled movements.

The Head Mage divided his focus, continuing to will his farsight ahead while readying a teleportation spell. He knew this spell alone would not work in time. It was difficult enough to lock on to multiple subjects to teleport when they were still. When those subjects were moving in such random patterns it was next to impossible for even an accomplished mage.

But Rionn Lorr was much more than an accomplished mage. He would have been able to do it quickly if he was not already concentrating on casting his farsight at such a great distance and width. With the extra time it would take to lock in on nine panicked gryphons hundreds of yards apart and flying swiftly in different directions, all while keeping his farsight focused, the swarming scythe wings would have them, so the Child of the Ones made them fly in unison.

He sent out a strong suggestion to the large bird cats, calling to them all to turn in the same direction and move into a tighter formation. It was a simple spell that did not require much time or concentration. The birds resisted at first because their natural instinct was to scatter to escape predators. The Head Mage had to will an extra surge of power into his command to overwhelm their instinct.

The Gryphon Ryders were in a near panic. They could not control their mounts and now they were flying in a way that would make it easier to kill all of them in one concentrated attack. The Ryders leaned in even closer, hugging the bird-cats' wide, muscular, feathered necks as the scythe wings closed in with frightening speed.

Rionn Lorr cast one more spell with the speed of thought, a blunt conjuring of a wide blanket of power that manifested itself as a transparent, oval-shaped, silvery shimmer in mid air. It appeared just ahead of the fleeing Gryphon Ryders.

The bird cats and their Ryder's, had no idea what the shimmer was and had no desire to come into contact with it. Rionn Lorr, however, gave a powerful mental tug that could not be resisted.

The swiftest gryphon and Ryder hit the disk of energy first and disappeared. It took yet another strong pull of will and magic for the Head Mage to compel the others to follow.

Colonel Strong, Captain Zedek and all of their men started, some even gasped, when the Gryphon Ryders popped out of nowhere into the skies above them. First one, then two, then five popped into view as though flying through an invisible window. Rionn terminated the spell when the last Ryder appeared, but not before one exceptionally swift scythe wing flew through the transparent portal.

It nipped at the tip of the gryphon's leonine tail, the snapping of its curved and pointed beak audible even from the ground. The Ryder sent the bird cat into a sharp dive. The scythe wing overshot its prey and looped around. The giant bird hesitated for a moment when it realized it was separated from its flock and then resumed the chase. Its massive wings brought it closer to its prey with every stroke.

By the time the monstrous hawk closed on the Gryphon Ryder, they were within crossbow range of the airborne Ryder archers that had stayed behind. The marksmen wasted no time. They expertly avoided their comrades as they peppered the giant hawk with bolts.

Its head, back and wings pierced, the scythe wing plummeted to the ground. The Ryder it was chasing steered her gryphon out the dead bird's way, letting it crash to the ground near the fountain in the middle of the square. Men, horses, and gryphons scattered to avoid it.

"Well done!" Strong bellowed. "Who knows how to pluck a giant bird? Looks like roasted hawk for supper!"

His exclamation was met with guffaws and cheers. Hooves thundered as the cavalrymen raced to the fallen bird to make certain it was dead.

"Good job, as always, Head Mage!" Captain Zedek called as he and Strong jogged over to the get a closer look at the scythe wing.

Rionn Lorr barely heard him. Echelon One Mage Gilder Raynard stayed behind and watched the Child of the Old Ones, who was still preoccupied with his farsight.

DEMON OF LORR

No longer having to maintain the teleportal, Rionn was able to cast his farsight after the speedily retreating scythe wings with much more intensity.

Not only did he see, hear, smell, and even feel with his five natural senses, he extended his supernatural perceptions. In a few moments he was able to detect the spell influencing the predatory flock. Their prey having mysteriously vanished, the giant hawks turned back south and angled west, back toward the peaks of Hell's Mountains with purposeful speed.

Rionn Lorr got a sense of the magic that compelled them. It was an effective spell, masterful in its simplicity and efficiency. It gave a slight push to the massive birds' already ferocious instinct to harry and devour while directing their choice of hunting and roosting area, which the giant birds were infamous for protecting with a frenzied urgency.

Rionn tried to get a sense of the person who cast the spell. Every spell carried the signature of its conjurer, a hint of his or her life force that served as the foundation for any conjuring. Only the most capable wizards could detect it. That was, of course, assuming that the spell was actually cast by a conjurer. Apparently no conjurer had cast this one. There was an utter lack of life force. That usually meant that a talisman of some sort, created by a now-deceased conjurer, was the source of the spell.

The flock veered more sharply west while Rionn Lorr widened his scope of perception in order to continue searching south while following the scythe wings. A deeper probe of the magic influencing them was suddenly rendered impossible when his farsight ran into a wall of blackness.

Rionn felt himself shudder at the sudden psychic impact and quickly pulled back. He noted the distance and direction in which his farsight travelled before encountering the now-familiar void.

"What happened, Master Lorr," Mage Raynard asked.

"I found the *Ken*," the Head Mage answered. "Just over one hundred miles south, somewhere between the Bountiful River and the Hells, but closer to the Hells. They're moving south, toward the Demon's Spine."

"What are scythe wings doing in Lorr?" Raynard asked. "They occupy the far western coasts of the Westin Continent, thousands of miles away." And then his eyes widened. "And the *S'zan Rho* are from that region as well," he realized. "Do they have the magic to control the giant hawks?"

"Doubtful," Rionn Lorr said. "The people on the Westin Continent shun magic. The *S'zan Rho* despise it most of all. That's what makes it so fittingly ironic that they have found a way to squelch it."

Gilder frowned. "*Fittingly* ironic? I don't understand."

"Is not the power to extinguish magic but another form of magic?" Rionn posited. "It's unlikely they would seek out any type of magic on their own, but the ability to neutralize it is something that they'd eagerly accept if offered to them."

"Yes..." Gilder said thoughtfully.

"It is no coincidence that the *Ken* and the scythe wings are here in the Kingdom of Lorr at the same time," Rionn continued. "The demon Dierglyorr chose its pawns carefully. So, Mage Gilder, are you sure you want to continue to pursue them without the support of the regiment?"

"I can only speak for myself, Master Lorr," the Echelon One mage began. "But I'm fairly certain the colonel and the captain will agree with me to carry on the chase. Now that we know about the scythe wings we can stay earthbound. The gryphons travel as well on the ground as they do in the sky, though not as quickly.

"If the regiment catches up to us before we catch the *Ken*, then all the better. If they do not, we will be sure to hold the savage bastards until the regiment arrives to finish them."

"Are you sure that is what the others want?" Rionn Lorr pressed.

"Of course he is!" Strong roared from behind them.

The two wizards turned to see the cavalry commander and the Gryphon Ryder captain approaching. Strong was a tall, wide man with broad square shoulders. He was dressed in light steel plate armor on his torso and thick woolen breeches tucked into riding boots.

He had close-cropped salt-and-pepper colored hair that stood up in disciplined spikes. He walked next to the shorter, thinner Gryphon Ryder, who was dressed in a light mail hauberk over a leather tunic and loose fitting cloth riding breeches. His long brown hair was tied back with a bandana. Despite the differences in their dress and size, they shared the same grim determination in their eyes.

"Yes," Captain Zedek agreed. "The mage *does* speak for all of us."

The Head Mage was impressed with their conviction but he had not made up his mind as to whether they were brave or crazy. He was especially confused when he considered the Echelon One mage, and he said as much.

"What will *you* do, Mage Raynard, when you face the *Ken* and they take away your magic?"

"I intend to put my magic to good use to help us prepare for the *Ken* before we engage them," the lower-ranking wizard assured. "I can use my magic to treat injures. Also, I was a carpenter's apprentice before I came to magic, so some of the first spells I learned were spells that helped my father and I in our trade. I can use my magic to speed the process of building war machines." A dangerous glint came to his eyes. "And even without magic, I'm fairly skilled with both pike and sword.

"You are welcome to come with us, Head Mage," Mage Raynard offered. "I've seen you practice with that broadsword of yours. Magic or no, we all would be proud to stand by your side in battle."

"Would that I could," the Head Mage sighed. "But I have to get back to the palace. Now that I have a better idea of the scope of the demon's plot, I realize even more how important it is to stop the dreaded walking dead army in the east." He turned so that the Echelon One Mage and the two commanders stood before him.

"I trust the three of you," Rionn continued. "If you say you have a workable plan, I will take you at your word. But I feel I must implore you to be careful with this foe. Take care not to let anger and vengeance cloud your judgment."

The three men put their right fists to their hearts and nodded in salute."

"For the honor of the Kingdom of Lorr," Rheingold Strong declared. "We will proceed with caution and, only if a favorable opportunity presents itself, strike with measured ferocity."

"For the honor of the Kingdom of Lorr," Rionn echoed, returning their salute. "God's speed to you all."

While they were talking, Ebony eased over to them with silent hoof falls. Rionn Lorr swung himself onto her saddle and gave a nod before reining the beautiful black horse around and riding over to his squad leader. Four squad members joined them as they rode out of town.

*   *   *

A pair of soldiers had been standing within earshot of the two commanders and two wizards. Once the commanders and the Echelon One mage had dispersed and they lost sight of the Head Mage beyond the crowd of soldiers, one of the soldiers turned to the other.

"One could almost make the argument that the *S'Zan Rho* have a point," he began at just above a whisper.

The other turned to him quickly, a scowl twisting his features. "Surely I did not hear you correctly," the soldier growled.

"I don't mean *this*," the first soldier said, gesturing at the carnage around them. "I mean about their disdain for magic."

"*This* has nothing to do with magic, fool," the other snapped. "Just the opposite, in fact."

"But they are pawns of a demon, a creature of the foulest magic," the first soldier argued defensively. "And it is free only because of the magic of the Children of the Old Ones."

"And it is the magic of a Child who will bring us through this," the other returned. "And I'll suffer no more of this inane chatter." He dropped a calloused hand to the pommel of the short sword at his hip.

The other raised his hands defensively. "I said '*almost* make the argument.' I want justice for these citizens as much as anyone."

"I expect you to prove it when we catch those sons of whores," the other warned before turning and stalking away.

Lieutenant Colonel Caleb Godson stepped up to the soldier's side.

"I understand your sentiment," the Lieutenant Colonel said in a confidential tone. "But you must be *very* careful about sharing that sentiment." He thought about his conversation with the colonel days earlier after their confrontation with the army of walking dead before giving a last word of caution. "Some may consider such words treasonous."

"I speak only against magic," the soldier argued, "not the crown."

"To some, there is little to no distinction between the crown and the Child of the Old Ones behind it."

"I don't know if that is a good thing or a bad thing," the soldier mused.

"I suppose it depends on one's perspective," Godson surmised. "Unless you can read minds, that's all the more reason to keep such doubts to yourself. You can never know the true intentions of those to whom you speak. And you never know who may be listening. Magic workers have ways of hearing things that are not meant for them to hear."

2.3

Joel heard his wife call his name. He was looking down in puzzlement at a dead man lying a few feet away from where he was standing. Fat flakes of snow drifted lazily down to settle peacefully on the corpse. The dead man was lying on the pavement, the right side of his face in the snow, a small red dot in his temple and a puddle of blood slowly pooling out in every direction under his head. Blood and brain matter was spattered on the inside of the open car door.

Joel craned his neck to look over on the other side of the car, where another dead man lay with the same wound in the middle of his forehead.

Whoever shot these two was a great freaking shot, he thought, just before he got a whiff of a recently fired gun – which was odd because he had no idea how he knew how a recently fired gun smelled – and felt something cold and heavy in his right hand. He looked down and saw the gun in his hand.

Lisa called his name again and he turned. Instead of seeing his wife, he saw a large circle filled with absolute nothingness, like a black hole without the vacuum, the circumference of which was a little wider than he was tall. A rope of silver flame flickered around the edges, its movement both intriguing and frightening at the same time. The wonder of the phenomenon piqued his curiosity. The unknown of what waited inside that black infinity terrified him.

Lisa called his name a third time and Joel realized her voice was coming from the sliver-flame-rimmed void. His fear turned into elation and his curiosity into longing. He dove into the unfathomable darkness without hesitation, expecting to see his wife on the other side.

His expectation was dashed immediately. When the darkness engulfed him he was summarily reminded that Chicago, Illinois, and his beloved wife were quite literally a world away.

He became aware of a dull and consistent ache in his arms and realized without looking that they were stretched out taut and somehow fastened to a hard, cold, damp surface. The entire environment, in fact, was heavy with humidity. But unlike the surface against which he was fastened, the air around him was almost swelteringly hot. The thick moisture mixed with his own sweat and made his clothes cling to him uncomfortably.

As consciousness continued to creep slowly back he realized that he was hanging by his arms and his legs were bent. His knees hovered a few inches above the floor while his feet and shins were tucked under his body so that the top of his bare feet scraped the gritty, slimy floor beneath him.

He started to gather his feet under him to stand, knowing the damp floor would probably feel worse on the bottom of his feet than on the top, and quickly changed his mind. He was conscious, but he decided not to lift his head or open his eyes for a couple of reasons. The smells assaulting his nose threatened to gag him and he dreaded to see what would cause such a stench. In addition to that, the throbbing pain in his chin and side reminded him that he might receive another beating if his captives were there, watching and waiting for him to wake up.

His captors. As much as he wanted to convince himself that he was dreaming, he knew this was his nightmarish reality. Now he understood how foolish he had been to allow Rionn Lorr and Ryan Franklin to talk him into crossing the WorldGate.

He had been in this world less than two days, riding in a sky sleigh, which was just a big wedge of wood and steel towed by giant birds, for God's sake, when a swarm of other giant birds slaughtered the sleigh birds, tore the sleigh to pieces, and delivered him to the men who eventually brought him to this dungeon. At least he assumed it was a dungeon. His eyes were closed so he had no idea if there were windows or not, but there was a chill in the air and a stifling sensation of closeness, a claustrophobic feeling of unseen walls pressing in on him, that made him fairly certain that he was somewhere deep underground.

The scratches and bruises from his rough handling at the claws of the scythe wings still pulsed across his arms and torso. The thrashing he received at the hands of the deadly birds' master angered him as much it pained him. Worst of all, he had no idea why this was happening to him.

He kept his eyes closed and listened as intently as he could. He could hear the echo of distant, muffled footsteps. Voices, as distant as the footsteps and too vague to be understood, floated to him as well. As he continued to listen Joel heard something else, something closer. It was a rhythmic and vaguely familiar sound that he could not quite place, so he focused on it until he could.

The other sounds began slowly fade into the background of his awareness and he could finally tell what it was he was hearing. It was the repetitive sound of breathing. The slow, undisturbed, deep breaths sounded to Joel like the breathing of someone to his left who was sleeping. Satisfied that he had identified at least one person near him, and that that person was sleeping, he resumed his auditory survey.

"You may open your eyes, now," came a hoarse but clearly feminine voice. The sudden sound caused Joel to jump in spite of his efforts to remain still.

Knowing his façade had been shattered, he slowly gathered his feet beneath him, stood up, lifted his eyelids and turned his head to see the owner of the unfamiliar voice.

A woman dangled from the wall adjacent to the one from which he hung. Her hands were bound high above her head with her wrists crossed, shackled with thick iron manacles attached to taut, rusty chains that ran up the wall and disappeared into a small hole cut into the stone. Her bare feet were pulled roughly two feet apart and her ankles were held fast to the stone wall by iron braces that were secured to the wall by heavy bolts and thick screws. A glance over his head showed him that the chains suspending him also fed into a neatly drilled hole in the wall. He turned his attention back to his cellmate.

In different circumstances, *vastly* different circumstances, she would have been stunning. Even through the grime and dark bruises that covered the honey-brown skin of her face, exposed arms and feet, Joel saw her striking features.

70

DEMON OF LORR

Thick black eyebrows with a soft natural arch knitted over long-lashed eyelids. Those eyelids hooded tired but sharp hazel eyes that fixed on him with a suspicious glare. Rounded cheekbones curved softly into a delicate jaw and tiny chin. Her full lips were curved downward at the corners to form an exhausted frown. A filthy cloth, which was nothing more than a big sack made of a burlap-type material with the bottom seam cut out, covered her from her neckline to the top of her calves. Her arms and calves had the muscle tone of a track runner.

She did not have the gaunt frame and sallow skin tone that evidenced the onset of malnourishment. While she was obviously beaten and tired, her weary eyes still possessed a defiant spark. Joel surmised that, unless they fed her very well and allowed her regular exercise, both of which were highly unlikely for a prisoner bound as she was, she could not have been captive in this dungeon for a very long time.

"How did you know I was conscious?" Joel asked.

"I saw the change in the rhythm of your breathing," she explained. "I saw your eyes moving behind your eyelids. They went from the random movements of sleep to more deliberate motions. I could see them move in response to sounds."

"Observant," Joel said.

"Yes, it is," the woman agreed. She was silent for a moment as she studied him. "You're not very good at this."

"At what?" Joel asked.

Her suspicious gaze intensified. "As if you did not know."

Joel sighed. The effort sent a shock of pain through his ribs that made him wince. He decided not to argue and changed the subject.

"Where are we?"

Her answer was an incredulous look that lingered for long seconds before she turned to watch the door and simply ignored him.

"Look," Joel went on. "I was unconscious when they brought me here. And even if I'd been conscious I still wouldn't know where the hell I am. I'm not from here, you understand, so if you could just tell me what *city* we're in, I'd appreciate it."

Her answer was silence.

"Well," Joel said in a defeated tone. "I'm Joel. Could you at least tell me your name so I'll know who's ignoring me?"

More silence.

Joel shrugged as much as he could manage with his hands bound the way they were and turned his attention to their cell. The stuffy chamber looked to be roughly ten by eight feet, and was lit by a torch in the corner across the room on Joel's right hand side. The torch was small but just strong enough to cast the room in a dim, yellow-orange gloom that left much of the floor and the far corner of the room in shadow.

A small vertical slit roughly five and a half feet high was cut into the heavy wooden door directly across from Joel. The same yellow-orange torchlight bled weakly through the slit from the outside of the cell. There were no windows in the walls so there was no natural light of any kind.

His watch had been taken from him. That had been his only means of telling time in this world where he had yet to see any type of timepiece and everyone seemed to judge time by the position of the sun. No, he reminded himself: the position of the *suns*. Other than the blue jeans he wore, his watch had been his only physical link to his home. In this rank, sweltering cell without windows he would have no way of telling day from night.

How long would he have to be here before he was found? Would Rionn and Ryan find him at all? How long had he been here already?

Joel's heart rate quickened and he furrowed his brow.

"How long have I been here?" he asked nervously.

The woman captive gave him a curious sidelong glance.

"You're serious, are you not?"

Joel's fear-fueled irritation made him snap: "Hell yeah, I'm serious!"

"Calm yourself," she said sternly. "Of course I, like you, have no way telling day from night in this place." Her tired eyes cast an accusatory stare at the walls around her. "But I think I can roughly figure out how the days go by. By my reckoning you have been here about a day."

"A day?" Joel could not believe he had been out for so long. His worry intensified. "If you can't tell day from night down here," he questioned nervously, "How do you figure I've been here a day?"

The woman gave him a brief, suspicious look. "I'll let you figure it out for yourself, stranger."

"Whatever," Joel said as he returned to his survey of the cell. He looked back at the slot in the door and let his gaze trail downward. His eyes were starting to adjust to the dim light and the pools of shadow became more distinguishable. A small, closed slot was cut into the bottom center of the cell door. A metal frame so rusty it almost blended in with the brown wood of the door outlined the slot. He guessed it was a retractable panel so their captors could slide trays of food into the cell.

The thought of food made him aware of his empty stomach. The dull ache of hunger slowly intensified into an acute pang that caused him to inhale sharply. The sharp inhalation caused another jolt of pain to race up and down his ribcage, which in turn caused his breath to catch in his throat and sent him into a coughing fit.

The coughing led to yet more pain and the pain to yet more coughing until he was gagging and struggling for air. It took nearly a minute for him to catch his breath, and when he did, the familiar and dreaded tightness seized his lungs.

"Oh no," he gasped.

The woman raised an eyebrow as she listened to him wheeze and watched his eyes widen and dart from side to side in obvious worry. She could see panic rising in him as his chest began to heave. Suspicion gave way to curiosity when she concluded that his growing struggle to breathe was genuine.

"Constriction?" she asked.

Joel nodded. "The coughing," he huffed, "triggered an asthma attack."

He fell silent, having to conserve his breath and concentrating on what, if anything, he could do. His albuterol emergency inhaler was long gone. His other medications were lost when the sky sleigh was attacked, and in any case, those meds were not for sudden attacks. Against his hip in his right side pocket he could feel the bulge of the small cloth pouch full of chewable herbs that had worked so well for his asthma back at Port Lorrian and again on the sky sleigh. It was odd to him that they took everything else, his shoes, socks, shirt, everything except his tattered blue jeans and the medicine in his pocket.

Did they not know what the herbs were and simply ignored them? Did they know exactly what they were and decided to taunt him? What could be worse than having the cure or treatment for a deadly ailment at his hip that he could not reach because his arms were bound? That must have been what it was, he decided. This was some sort of psychological torture. And it was working. He had to fight against the panic creeping steadily upon him so that he could focus on keeping his breathing even.

The woman watched as the strange newcomer closed his eyes and took slow deep breaths. He was obviously trying to control his breathing, but the continuing wheeze and the worried bunching of his deep brow over his tightly closed eyes made it clear that the constriction was getting worse. With each breath his chest and shoulders heaved higher and his frown deepened.

As the minutes passed, the wheezes grew into strangled gasps. And then Joel began to pull against the chains that bound him to the wall. He strained so hard that veins popped out in his forehead, neck and every other part of his body where his skin was exposed.

The woman captive's heartbeat quickened when she realized the man was really suffocating. His brown skin, only slightly lighter in tone than her own, turned ashen before her eyes. His thick lips went from dark pink to a dull shade of purple as his breaths grew shorter and ever more rapid.

DEMON OF LORR

In less than a minute, his breathing was barely audible, only rapid, stunted puffs, even though his chest heaved more forcefully than ever and his legs twitched. He opened his eyes wide and turned to her, casting a worried, pleading look her way as his eyes glazed over and closed. His head dropped and hung limp, and after a few more desperate attempts at gulping air, his body went still.

"So you really *were* a prisoner," the woman said. She felt a slight tinge of pity and then she counted him lucky. He would not have to endure the suffering that their captors had been inflicting upon her and the other unfortunate souls imprisoned elsewhere in these dungeons.

"Well, stranger," she said to the still body. "These bastards are not the type to take prisoners, unless they want something from them, that is. I don't know what they wanted from you but I am happy you died before giving it to them." She studied the body a moment longer as a disturbing thought came to her.

"I mean no offense, but I hope they get you out of here before you start to smell. There was a dead prisoner somewhere on this hall when they first brought me here, the stench almost…"

She stopped when she realized she was talking to a corpse. "You've been here too long, Dayna," she said to herself. "Now you're talking to-"

Her words turned into a yelp of surprise and fear when Joel's head snapped up and his eyes opened wide. He turned dead, milky eyes to her disbelieving stare for a moment and then he turned away. Without making a sound, he thrust his arms forward against the broad iron chains.

She heard a clanging snap from somewhere deep inside the wall and then Joel's chains went completely slack. Joel dropped his hands to his sides, causing several yards of both long chains to slide from the hole in the wall and fall to the floor in a coiling pile on either side of Joel's feet. The coil rose almost as high as his knees. The manacles still clung to his wrists but the heavy chains dragged loosely from the bulky braces as Joel reached into his pocket and retrieved a small pouch.

Dayna had not noticed anything unusual about his fingers before he broke free, but the digits that reached into the pouch were elongated and pointed like avian talons. She looked quickly back up at his eyes, which were once again staring at her. Unlike a moment earlier, his brown eyes were normal and trained on hers. The blank expression had turned into a questioning one.

Joel gasped as the constriction returned. He glanced around swiftly as if he did not know where he was and then looked down in surprise at the pouch in his hand. His arms trembled violently as he strained against the heavy manacles and chains to lift a pinch of the herbs into his mouth, but once he did, it took only a few seconds of chewing before the wheezing began to dissipate.

When his breathing was under control, he struggled to secure the drawstring on the strap before finally letting the chains and manacles pull his arms back down so heavily that he dropped to his knees. He looked back up at Dayna.

"What happened?" he asked.

"*I* should be asking *you* that question," she answered, noticing that the fingers that brought the herbs to his lips were, like his eyes, normal once again.

"Oh," Joel said as he realized what had happened. To him, it seemed like time had jumped. However, he did not remember the red-rimmed vision that usually preceded his transformations. He guessed he had lost consciousness from lack of oxygen before the change came upon him.

"I don't know how you did that, stranger," Dayna began, her face brightening with hope, "but please do it once more, this time for me!"

"I can't," Joel admitted.

Dayna's expression quickly darkened to its previous scowl. "You *are* a spy," she accused. "You offer a false exchange, then? Do you expect me to trade information for my freedom? I will not. Have your handlers do their worst. They will get no cooperation from me."

"Lady, I don't know what the hell you're talking about," Joel said. "Whatever you just saw is something I have no control over. I can't even remember it, much less repeat it."

"You lie," she snapped.

"Believe what you want," Joel snapped back. "I don't give a damn."

He looked at the thick iron bands around his wrists and the coiled piles of chains to either side of him.

"What am I doing here?" he asked no one in particular. "I never should have come to this messed up place. I should be with my wife." A tear escaped from each eye. "And my baby…"

Dayna thought he was going to sob but he did not. He just sat there in a defeated posture, his shoulders slumped and his chin buried in his chest.

With the exception of the two tears slowly trailing down his face, however, he was outwardly emotionless. She had seen that look before, and did not think anyone could act this well. This was no spy, she concluded. This was a man bereft of hope.

"If you cannot willingly repeat that feat of strength, stranger, I suggest you either find a way to re-bind yourself or find the wherewithal to devise an escape attempt in the next few moments. By my reckoning, our meals will be here very shortly and I doubt they will react kindly to your newfound relative freedom."

Joel barely heard her. He was lost in disturbing thoughts about his wife. He wondered where Lisa was, what she was going through, if she was still alive. In his mind it was a foregone conclusion that he would never see her again. There was no way he was getting out of this alive.

He was trapped, separated from the people who brought him into this world. For all he knew the scythe wings finished everyone on both sky sleighs. He held no false hope that he would emerge from this dungeon alive. All he could do was pray for his wife's survival.

Not only did he barely notice the suspicious woman's warning, he almost missed the darkening of the upper slot of the cell door. He looked up at the slot to find a pair of wide eyes staring at him.

"The offworlder is free!" came a nearly panicked voice from the other side of the thick door. "Sound the alarm," his voice faded along with the sound of his rapidly thudding footfalls as the man ran down the hall. "The offworlder has broken loose!"

The startled guard's voice became mingled with other voices as men shouted all up and down the corridor. Swift footfalls echoed through the halls but Joel paid them no mind. He was still lost in despair and did not believe his situation could get any worse.

His melancholy was so deep that he barely acknowledged the bright torchlight spilling into the cell as the heavy door flew open and slammed against the wall with a crash. Joel looked up just as a dozen men armed with short clubs or heavy fists rushed him and began pummeling him with hard punches and vicious kicks.

Even as he slid across the rough floor from a particularly violent kick, even as his body jolted from sharp and blunt blows to his back, arms, and legs, he thought it strange that no one struck his head or face. A stray blow would glance off of his chin, jaw or ear on its way to his shoulders and chest, but no real attempt was made to strike him above his shoulders.

Even still, the pain was tremendous. All he could do was close his eyes and roll into a tight ball as he was struck over and over and over. Soon the pain went away and his body went numb. Exhaustion and hunger overcame the pain and unconsciousness finally, and blessedly, claimed him.

2.4

"I still do not understand why we surrendered so easily," grumbled Ranger Elf Rell Kallen, absently kicking a loose stone across the hard-packed earth as he paced back and forth like a caged lion. "We could have fought our way out of this."

He cast an irritated glance around the underground chamber. Dim, pale, cyan light emanated from small glowing stones set into the top of shelves of rock protruding from all four walls about six feet above the floor. As dim as the light was, it covered the entire room, leaving no area in shadow. The chamber was just large enough to keep the group from feeling claustrophobic. Solidly crafted wooden chairs and settees were placed around the room, each one with a small table set in front. The chamber resembled some sort of waiting area.

"Do not underestimate the dwarves," Quick advised. The changeling stood a few feet away from the door, leaning comfortably against the wall. His travelling tunic and breeches hung loosely off of his long, spare, adolescent frame. His brown hide riding boots rested beside his bare feet. "They are fierce and cunning warriors and we are in their territory. They have all manner of surprises for trespassers."

"I have more than a few surprises of my own," assured the Ranger Elf. "And we have no time to waste sitting idly in this cave cell while the demon seeks the Hell Key."

"This isn't a cell," corrected Quick. "And we are not prisoners."

"What are we, then?" asked Rell Kallen. "Are we guests? That heavy wooden door may be open but there are armed guards just outside. And they have our weapons, boy. All except the offworlder's, that is. Though they are polite for the moment, we are captives nonetheless."

"Captives are bound," Quick pointed out. "They are locked in a cell. We are neither."

"So naïve," Rell Kallen scoffed. He turned to Raxe, who was sitting on one of the settees seemingly lost in thought. "What say you, offworlder?"

Raxe scratched his scalp beneath one of his long brown dreadlocks, subconsciously noting how much work they needed. The cyan glow from the light stones reflected softly off of his enchanted silver armor, including the open-topped visor resting on the bench next to him, as he reflected on how they ended up being held by the hidden dwarven nation within and beneath Hell's Mountains.

He thought back to how he and his grandfather discovered the existence of Joel, seemingly another Child of the Old Ones, who was being hunted by the demon Dierglyorr in the guise of a high-ranking organization agent back in Chicago. He recalled how the Head Mage had crossed the WorldGate to bring Raxe and Joel from their world to his. And finally, how two sky sleighs ferrying him, Joel, and the Keeper's Hounds south were brought down by a flock of giant hawks just over Hell's Mountains.

"We did the right thing," Raxe finally answered in his deep, damaged voice that sounded a lot like two rough stones being rubbed together. "If they wanted to hurt us they would've tried by now. It *would* be nice, though, if someone would come talk to us. All they told us was 'wait' when we got here last night. We've been cooling our heels for at least twenty-four hours. But I agree with you on one point, elf: We're wasting too much time here."

Rell Kallen turned a suspicious eye to Quick.

"Changeling," he began. "You know more about these dwarves than the rest of us. You weren't surprised when they crept upon us on the surface and you are familiar with them when no one else even knew a nation of elves existed under Hell's Mountains."

Even Quick's best friend, Ethan, was puzzled. Ethan had been silent since the dwarves captured them, brooding over the loss of his Keeper's Hounds teammates. Though even in his losing fight to overcome his dark depression, he found himself curious.

"Yes, Quick," the young Sureblade added, absently fingering his empty weapons belt and lamenting the confiscation of his beloved weapons passed down to him from his father. "How long have you known about the dwarves? Why would you keep the information a secret?"

All eyes turned to Quick. He met each gaze in turn and then answered.

"I've known about them nearly my entire life," the young changeling admitted. "They were the first non-animal race with whom I had ever lived. Before then I had lived only among animals, going from one species to another. I was never able to live among them for long because they all sensed that I was different and eventually shunned me.

"I had been living among a group of cave raccoons in the Hells. They had just chased me away when I wandered upon a small hunting party of dwarves. I placed myself in their path and transformed into a dwarf. Because I was so young, they initially mistook me for an orphan or a lost child from their nation and adopted me as one of their own.

"I lived with them for eight years before the elders and mages realized how different I was. They wanted to kill me immediately, fearing that one day I would leave and reveal their existence. But King Grimhammer stopped them. Like Rionn, he believed that I was trustworthy and that my abilities would make me a valuable ally. He made me vow to keep their secret but I still had to leave. There were those among them who would plot to end my life even against the king's wishes. I have kept my word. Not even Rionn knows they are here."

"Why are they so secretive?" Ethan asked.

"For years I had no idea. No one ever spoke to me of why they remained hidden. I do know that during the time of the Old Ones they were known as the Stonehammer Nation and they lived in the Demon's Spine Mountains. They sided with the Protectors in Heaven's War, and the Leaders all but wiped them out. Their few survivors escaped and secretly made a new home beneath the Hells."

The Ranger Elf cocked an eyebrow. "I notice you said 'For years' you had no idea. So you *do* have an idea now?"

"So do I," said Raxe. "Quick followed the Finder here when the Finder stole the Hell and WorldGate Keys. He trailed the Finder from here to the Badlands, where Quick took the WorldGate Key from him. The dwarves had to keep their existence a secret because they were both hiding and guarding the Keys."

"Yes," Quick confirmed. "When I lived here, I did not even know the Keys were in the dwarves' possession."

"Odd," Rell Kallen said. "If the dwarves and the Keys were so well hidden, how is it that the Finder was able to steal them?"

"That's why he was called the Finder," Raxe rumbled. His gravelly voice was a constant reminder of how dangerous and ruthless the Finder was. It was the Finder who threw the dagger that pierced Raxe's neck and permanently damaged his vocal chords. It was the Finder that made possible all of the chaos caused by Mar-dah in the Cursed Opening.

"I don't think we are in danger," Quick assured. "But I *do* wonder why they revealed themselves to the rest of you. People have passed through this territory for years without ever detecting any hint of the presence of the Stonehammer Nation. The dwarves could have just as easily remained hidden and let us pass through."

"Because the last ye were here," a deep, booming voice returned from the hall just outside the chamber, "the Old Ones' Keys were pilfered by yer companion."

A moment later, five dwarfs came through the open door. The one in the middle, at least an inch taller and more than an inch wider than the others, led the quintet. Just to his right and a half-step behind him was General Bartok. To his left was a dwarf that was clad in a very similar fashion as Bartok, from his peaked bascinet helm to his heavy chain mail.

The only difference Raxe could immediately discern between the two was the long stave the other carried. It looked to be made from a jointed ash tree branch as thick as the dwarf's broad wrists. His fist was shoulder-high as it clutched the stave right at the joint where the shorter upper part of the staff bent a little over one hundred degrees from the longer section. Runes carved into the length of the staff marked it a magic wielder's instrument.

The leader's flowing, gold-trimmed black cloak was pulled back to reveal a gleaming breastplate etched with the crest of the Stonehammer Nation: two ornate war hammers, crossing, heads up, to form an "X" set within a wide decorative shield.

Hairy, muscular deltoids bulged from the sides of the breastplates. His huge arms were bare except for thick leather bracers, studded and reinforced with big iron rings for added defensive protection and offensive damage. Matching greaves protected the bearded dwarf's thick shins below the leather breaches covering his tree-trunk thighs.

He did not wear a helmet like the four men flanking him. His wide head and thick, straight, rust-colored hair were ringed with a thin golden band that, along with his ornate cloak, made his station obvious.

"Jax Grimhammer of the Grimhammer Clan, King of the Stonehammer Nation," Quick greeted, tapping his right fist to his right breast and then his left. He held his fist there until the dwarven king responded with a single tap to his right breast and nodded. "General Bartok and Mage Listwhin the Wise," Quick continued. "It is good to see you all. And with all due respect, your majesty, the Finder was certainly *not* my companion. Had I known where he was going and why, I would have beaten him here to warn you.

"When he went into the Hells I didn't know he was coming for the Keys. I didn't follow him into the mountains because I wasn't sure if he was aware of my presence. He could have easily used the ample cover within the mountains to ambush me. I had no way no of knowing that he knew of your existence. And, of course, I did not know the Keys were here. It was not until he emerged with them that I became aware of the nature of his quest."

King Grimhammer studied the changeling for the span of several breaths. The sovereign dwarf's dark green gimlet stare, made even darker in the shadow of his deep brow and bushy, wiry eyebrows, bore into the young changeling. Even though the top of Grimhammer's head barely reached the bottom of the adolescent changeling's chest, his bearing made him seem twice the other's size. To Quick's credit, though, he did not shrink from the intimidating glare. He stood his ground and faced the dwarf king with confident yet respectful self-assurance.

The dwarf king turned an appraising gaze to the offworlder. "Ye think ye be the descendant of the Old One Raxe?"

Raxe shrugged. "That's what people keep telling me."

"The thief we came to know as the Finder made the same claim when he came among us," Bartok said. "He even presented a battleaxe that bore such a strong resemblance to the real Demonsbane that even we, the descendants of the proud Stonehammer dwarves that assisted the Gatekeeper and the original Raxe with the enchanted weapon's very creation, were momentarily deceived."

"And in that moment of deception," the king growled, his baritone voice even deeper than before, "he attacked. Before we could put him to the tests to prove his identity he slew several of our best warriors and two of our Guardians with that cursed and poisonous Dragon-fang broadsword. And then he made off with the Keys. Another Guardian was sent after him to retrieve them. She never returned."

Bartok concluded the tale. "We found out – far too late, mind ye – that the Child Mar-dah lent the thief a bit of foul magic to disguise Dragon-fang as Demonsbane."

"And that is why," King Grimhammer said, turning his gimlet gaze onto the offworlder, "ye must surrender ye battleaxe and short sword."

A hush fell over the room. Bartok and the other dwarves tensed, preparing to take the weapon if it came to that. The survivors of the sky sleigh tensed as well, not knowing what to expect. Raxe looked over at the young changeling.

"What do you think, Quick?"

Quick nodded. "I think you should do as the king asks."

"Ok," Raxe said. "Here you go." He slipped Demonsbane from its frog and held its handle out to the dwarf king.

"Do ye think me a fool?" Grimhammer huffed. "I'm not yet knowin' if ye are a Child or not, but damn sure'n I ain't findin' out thataway!"

Behind the king, both General Bartok and Mage Listwhin chuckled. The offworlder was clearly conducting his own test to see if the dwarves really knew of the properties of the enchanted battleaxe. The king indeed knew that one of its properties was the fatal surge of power that would kill anyone that touched it if that person was not a direct descendant of the Gatekeeper. It was the Gatekeeper and his son, the first Raxe, that forged the battleaxe Demonsbane, and the two Old Ones made sure that only someone in their bloodline could wield it.

The dwarf king looked over at Listwhin, who then turned to the soldiers behind him. "Bring the sack," he ordered.

Two of the dwarves at the rear of the small group stepped forward. The one on the right held a large leather sack, which he held open before Raxe. The offworlder placed Demonsbane in the sack and took care not to drop it. The harder than diamond, razor sharp crescent axe blades would easily cut through the leather if it were dropped. He did the same with Questblade.

It took both of the compact, powerful dwarves to carry the weapons without dragging the sack. Demonsbane was so heavy that every muscle and tendon in their powerful arms, shoulders and necks bulged from the effort of keeping the enchanted battleaxe barely suspended above the coarse stone floor. They took quick shuffling strides as they hauled Demonsbane and Questblade through the doorway.

Raxe smirked as he watched them hustle from the room. He turned to King Grimhammer. "So, your majesty," the offworlder began. "With all due respect, if I may ask, what is it you want from us?"

"Only ye," the king grunted. "We'll be testin' ye, finding out if ye truly are the descendant of your namesake."

"What kind of test?" Raxe asked suspiciously.

"Ye'll be finding out soon enough," Listwhin the Wise said as he followed King Grimhammer and his entourage out of the waiting area.

"They have a test which requires you to relinquish your weapons..." Ethan said needlessly.

"Yeah," Raxe said. He turned to Quick and gave the changeling a grave look. "You'd *better* be right about this, kid."

2.5

CARTHAN PALACE, KINGDOM OF CARTHA

King Vergoth and Queen Lairen sat silently in their small, private conference chamber. It was the only room in their expansive palace that could be considered small. The wall-to-wall carpeting was deep and plush, perfect for absorbing sound. The walls were of the thickest stone. The door was crafted from layers of dense wood. An iron knocker had to be specially made for both sides of the door so that their guards could alert them by knocking from the outside and they could get the guards' attention from within.

The room was made for the sharing of secrets.

The sovereigns of the Kingdom of Cartha sipped on the finest wines in the Known Lands. The king sipped a robust red, the queen, an elegant white. The two of them were as different as their preference in wines, but their dichotomy served them well.

Lairen was the picture of intelligence, calm and patience. That façade effectively hid how shrewd and opportunistic she truly was. She was a stunning beauty in her youth, and though she was born to a peasant family, she and everyone close to her knew she would use her looks, intelligence, and ambition to rise to a high station.

She deftly worked her way up through every social circle until she met a young prince. There were plenty of rivals for his affections, all of them from prominent families. In the beginning it seemed almost foolish for her to even think about competing for the prince's favor against such highborn ladies. Lairen was not in the least bit deterred.

Most of her rivals fell victim to various scandals and a few to tragic and untimely deaths. In the end, Lairen was the last one standing. There were some who were suspicious of Lairen, but none of the misfortune that befell her rivals could be traced back to her. For the most part, the prejudice and air of superiority of the average highborn citizen worked to her great advantage – as she knew it would.

Most aristocrats in the Kingdom of Cartha summarily dismissed the possibility that a lowborn girl could possess the resources or intelligence for treachery of such magnitude. And if any thought she did, they would never admit it aloud for fear of encouraging other lowborns to reach beyond their station. As a result, very little suspicion fell upon Lairen, at least publicly.

Vergoth, on the other hand, had always been quick-tempered and impulsive. He was not dim-witted in the least but he was unimaginative and blunt to the point of rudeness. Had he not been born the eldest son of a king, his highest station in life would likely have been a laborer. He was handsome, tall, strong and skilled with a sword, so perhaps he would have been a career mercenary.

His personality, on the surface, was magnetic. He could draw people to him and hold them, unless they were astute enough to eventually see how shallow he truly was. Had he chosen the path of a thief he would likely have spent his life in and out of prison. Or he would have lived a short life that ended at the end of a rope after stealing some nobleman's gold or laying with his woman. But he was born the eldest son of a king and thus the ideal mate for Lairen.

There was no love in their relationship and there never had been. In private, neither of them made any pretense that there ever was. He was attracted to her physically, and most importantly – because physical beauty always faded with time – her cunning. She was attracted to his station. It was the perfect match.

The one thing they did have in common was ambition. Though Vergoth could not match his wife's intelligence, he was smart enough to realize that she could expertly guide him to the greatest heights. Because of her, the Royal Crest of the Carthan Kingdom was engraved in the Table of Sovereigns just to the right of Seat of Power. Even though their kingdom was one of the smallest, both geographically and in population, together they made it the second most powerful kingdom in the Known Lands, second only to the Kingdom of Lorr.

That, however, was not enough for either of them. They wanted to be the *most* powerful kingdom. They would be recognized as such only if their crest supplanted Lorr's at the Table of Sovereigns Seat of Power. To Vergoth and Lairen it was not a question of *if*, but *when* this would happen.

Once that goal was achieved they would go on to consolidate and advance their power by doing something that had not been accomplished in the Known Lands since before Heaven's War. They would conquer and then incorporate enough of their neighboring kingdoms to not only crush but completely discourage any challengers.

Vergoth began to drum his fingers impatiently on the heavy oak conference table. The table was so thick that the sound was almost completely absorbed into the highly polished wood. Lairen was the one to finally break the long silence. She made a show checking the small timepiece connected to a gilded chain wrapped securely around her wrist.

"They are not late, Verg," she informed. "Why do you fidget so?"

The king shot an irritated glance at his wife, prodded, as always, by the sobriquet he so disliked. "They know I hate to wait. They know I am *always* early to my appointments. They should be here by now."

"*We* are always early to *our* appointments," Lairen corrected. "Except, of course, when the appointment is the Council of Sovereigns."

The king sighed heavily. "Are we to have this tedious conversation yet again?"

Lairen smiled prettily. "You know how persistent I am."

"I also know how eidetic you are, my *love*," Vergoth answered tiredly. "You know why you cannot join me at the Council of Sovereigns. None of the rulers' spouses are allowed to come."

"Several queens attend," Lairen countered.

"But those are the queens who are in the bloodline of the monarchy," Vergoth responded in a bored monotone.

This was a verbal dance of which he was sorely tired. He endured it for no other reason than to annoy his wife.

"Is there any rule that says they cannot bring their spouses? Or is it only the common practice?"

"It is tradition, Lairen. Who am I to break it?"

"You are the Liege Gregor Vergoth *tul* Cartha," she reminded him, using his full name and honorific to emphasize her point. "I am your Queen: Lairen Stefania Vergoth *tul* Cartha. We rule this land *together*, unlike other sovereign spouses who are merely glorified valets or handmaidens or concubines. I will not be treated as such."

Vergoth paused for a beat. Now this was something new. She never missed an opportunity to tweak him with the use of the "Verg" nickname and subtle barbs. Her other taunts were usually so subtle that he sometimes did not even realize he had been mocked until much later; and he was sure there were many that he missed altogether. This time, though, she was being openly defiant. It was something she had never done before.

He wondered if this was a new tactic. Had she really changed? Or was she trying to get his infamous temper to flare? Perhaps she was attempting to distract him before the upcoming meeting, knowing that in an angered state he would be even more dependent on her to be the voice of reason and navigate the path of the impending conversation.

If that had indeed been her goal, Vergoth mused, she would be sorely disappointed. She may have indeed changed but she was not the only one. Instead of reacting with his usual fire and volume, his reply was an indulgent smile.

"Of course, my Queen," he said in a sanguine tone that was completely out of character. "When we have gained the Seat of Power, I will have the proper standing to break with implied tradition. It will be an honor for you to join me at the Table of Sovereigns."

"And it will certainly be an honor to be at your side, my king." Lairen answered without pause. She was far too shrewd and self-aware to pause the way Vergoth just had, but he was adept at reading other's emotions no matter how well they hid them. And he certainly knew his wife well enough to notice that she was as taken aback at his subdued response as he had been at her open defiance.

The tense situation was interrupted by a soft, muffled knock at the outside of the door. The queen glanced at her timepiece and smiled.

"A full five minutes, early," she noted.

"Indeed," Vergoth said as he rose and walked to the heavy door. When his back was to his wife, he added, "I wonder if they will have any news that my independent sources have not already relayed."

"My" independent sources, Lairen mused. *Again he uses the singular pronoun.* She was under the impression that he shared with her all of his covert independent resources. Had he merely misspoken or had it been a truly revealing slip of the tongue? *No matter. I, too, have my own independent sources of which he is completely ignorant.*

The king released the six latches and locks on the door and then gave several hard raps with the knocker. The noise resounded loudly within the small chamber, but to the guards on the outside the sound was as soft and muffled as theirs had sounded to the king and queen. That was their signal to two of the six guards stationed in the hall to push the door open. King Vergoth stepped clear as the door swung slowly inward to admit Head Mage Samuel Tilsworth, his First High Advisor, Mage Michael Roderick, and the Second High Advisor, Mage Stratham Glund.

King Vergoth frowned as the robed trio of powerful wizards stepped into the room. In the past he would never have allowed three such accomplished conjurers to enter his chamber simultaneously. His suspicious nature and sense of self-preservation simply would never allow it. Should they decide to turn against him, there would be little or nothing he or his guards could do about it. But things were different, now. Instead of fear or anger, he only felt mild curiosity.

"I don't think I've ever seen you three in the same place at the same time. Is your news so convoluted that it requires the three of you to relay?"

Wizard Tilsworth bowed reverently. "Not convoluted, sire, but there is certainly much to tell. I thought it best that you hear each report from the one directly responsible."

"Let's have it, then," the king commanded. "I want a summary from each of you first, and then I would hear the necessary details."

Stratham Glund stepped forward and bowed. "The royal sky sleigh has been brought down in the same manner as the previous two. A thorough search was performed but no survivors were found. The scythe wings devoured those who were able to evacuate in their uniwings."

The king was not satisfied. "No survivors were found, you say, but that does not necessarily mean that there are no survivors. Have we any tangible evidence that all of the Children are dead?"

"Not as yet, my king," Glund admitted.

"Scythe wings do not eat bones, wizard," Vergoth pointed out. "They do not consume steel. Until Raxe's invulnerable armor and battleaxe are found, you must assume he is alive. The same can be said for the Ranger Elf's longsword and bow. Weapons of elven make are easily distinguishable from common weapons."

Glund inclined his again. "Of course, sire. I bow to your wisdom. The search will continue until more definitive evidence can be found."

"Spare me the false flattery, wizard," Vergoth warned. "That is less wisdom than common sense, which seems to be lacking of late. What is your plan for the likelihood that they have survived?"

The second high advisor to the Carthan Head Mage thought for a moment before answering. "We know that their search for the Hell Key will take them into the Demon's Spine. If they are alive to continue their quest, they will have to resupply. It is likely that they will require a guide.

"To that end, it is almost a certainty that they will have to acquire what they need in either Southborough or Shaddiston, the border towns closest to the Demon's Spine. We already have agents in that region spreading the anti-Children of the Old Ones sentiment, and very effectively, might I add.

"I placed a mage in that region some years ago. He has been doing an excellent job representing our interests. He and the local authorities there would be more than happy to delay anyone sent by the king to venture into those mountains."

Vergoth nodded. "See that they do. Is that all of your summary?"

"No, sire," Glund returned. "There is also the desert witch. She has been dispatched with the means to kill the Mistress of the Sea. Sabrina's meddling on behalf of the Kingdom of Lorr and the Children of the Old Ones is nearing its end."

King Vergoth made a steeple of his fingers as he listened. "Sabrina is a powerful elemental," he reminded. "Perhaps the most powerful in the Known Lands. Are you certain Shara Dune is up to the task?"

"Indeed, my king," Glund assured. "The very same dark wizard responsible for unleashing the plague of the walking dead is providing the resources needed to destroy her."

The queen cleared her throat conspicuously. When all heads turned to her, she asked, "Mage Glund, my husband is quite right in his assessment of Sabrina's might. Are you willing to risk your rank, your freedom and quite possibly your life on this 'dark wizard' in which you've invested so much trust?"

"Indeed," Glund repeated. "Under our Head Mage's expert direction, of course. And none of his actions can be traced to our good Kingdom."

"If they do trace his actions to us," the king warned with ice in his voice, "know that you will be sacrificed in the fashion of the mad Wizard Drake."

The mad Wizard Drake, they all knew, was an overly ambitious mage who sought to use dragons' blood to bolster his power several years earlier.

His efforts threatened to start a second Dragon War, but King William and Rionn Lorr prevented the war by apprehending the Wizard Drake and handing him over to WorldHopper for his justice.

King Vergoth wanted badly to go to war with the Kingdom of Lorr but the time was not yet right, and his timetable would not be rushed. Vergoth wanted to make sure his wizards understood that he would claim ignorance and Glund would take all of the blame if his efforts were traced back to the Kingdom of Cartha.

When King Vergoth was satisfied that his threat was properly received, he turned to the First High Advisor. "And what do you have for me, Mage Roderick?"

Roderick took a step forward and bowed. "My king, all goes as planned in regard to the *S'Zan Rho Ken d'Zanir*. They have effectively diverted and all but decimated a sizable battalion from the Lorrian ground forces. Lorr's navy has located the barge used to transport the *Ken* and their ballistae to outflank the hapless men, but there is no evidence on the barge that can tie it to us."

"William will send a larger force after them," Vergoth said. "Have you accounted for that certainty?"

"Yes, Your Grace," Roderick assured. "Lorr's military is quite preoccupied by the chaos in the east. That alone will delay their efforts to marshal a force significant enough to challenge the *Ken d'Zanir* company. Once they do, it will take days for them to overtake the *Ken.* By then, the *Ken* will have caught and dispatched any unlikely survivors from the sky sleighs. As formidable as the Raxe Child and Ranger Elf may be, they cannot hope to overcome a company of elite *Ken* warriors."

The king turned his attention to his Head Mage. "Wizard Tilsworth?"

Tilsworth nodded to his second advisor and turned his attention to his king. "Our mole in the Kingdom of Lorr reports that all goes as planned, and in many ways, even better. Dissension is being sown effectively not only in the southern regions of Lorr, but also in the military itself.

"Their Conjurer's Alliance and military are as predictable as the rising of the suns. And they are as clueless as they are predictable.

"As long as our sovereign allies continue to do their part…which is to do nothing, your objectives will be achieved in short order."

DEMON OF LORR

"My husband," the Queen interceded again. "What of the one monarch that chose not to attend your clandestine meeting of sovereigns opposed to the Kingdom of Lorr?"

Vergoth scoffed. "They are so small and insignificant that they may as well not exist. In fact, once we have achieved our goals, I'll see to it that they cease to exist."

Head Mage Tilsworth spoke again, as respectfully as he could. "Sire, I must ask. Are you not fearful of the possible consequences of collaborating with the other kingdoms to plot the downfall of Lorr? I trust your wisdom in all things, but as your closest counsel outside of the Queen, it behooves me to mention that you may be skirting dangerously close to breaking the First Great Directive."

King Vergoth leveled a cold stare at his Head Mage. It took quite an effort to quell the rage stoked by the audacity of the wizard Tilsworth. How *dare* he question his sovereign?

"Might I remind you, Tilsworth," the king began, "that the First Great Directive forbids the joining of kingdoms in waging war upon another kingdom. *I* am not waging war against the Kingdom of Lorr. The *S'Zan Rho* is not affiliated with any of the ten kingdoms of the Known Lands and they are not fighting under our banner. The other kingdoms are not joining forces with me, either. As you said yourself only a moment ago, they are not doing *anything* as we move freely through their lands to fulfill our own directives. Is that not correct?"

"Yes, sire, but I only – "

"You will *only* do as I command, wizard!" Vergoth snapped, at the end of his patience. "And my command is for you and your subordinates to now provide me with the details of your respective tasks."

Queen Lairen raised a perfectly arched eyebrow. The king had surprised her several times this day. The first shock was when he did not rise to the bait when she openly defied him. The next was his allowing his kingdom's three most powerful wizards into his private chambers at the same. And then he disrespected and berated the most powerful of the three, the master of the other two, in their presence, while his elite guards stood on the other side of a soundproof wall.

They could not possibly come to their king and queen's aid in time if the wizards decided to turn on them.

Even with his explosive temper, Vergoth's usual innate sense of self-preservation would preclude him from making such an outburst while at such an obvious disadvantage.

The queen knew what that meant: he did not consider himself to be at a disadvantage. That meant her husband had either completely lost his mind or he felt he had some advantage of which she was unaware. That meant, in turn, that she had some investigating to do, because either possibility was utterly unacceptable.

Chapter 3: The Test

3.1

"Damn, that's an ugly dog," said the driver of the dark blue sedan speeding down the highway.

"So stop looking at him," said the passenger, running his manicured fingers through his short blonde hair in exasperation. "You're driving me crazy saying that every five minutes."

"His big head is taking up half the damn rear-view mirror," the driver said. "I could swear it's bigger than it was yesterday. I can't keep myself from looking at it."

"So let me drive for a while," the passenger said. "Take a nod for a couple of hours or something."

"No way. I'm the driver. That's what I do. Besides, I couldn't sleep with that thing in the car if I wanted to."

"So what do I do until we find the old guy and the looker?" asked the passenger.

"You baby-sit little Chi-Chi back there."

The passenger chuckled. "Chi-Chi? So you've named it? What is that, short for Chihuahua?"

The driver shrugged. "That's what it looks like, a Chihuahua with a touch of acromegaly. Well…more than a touch." He glanced at the animal again and stifled a shudder. "So what do you think? Indianapolis?"

"What the hell kind of name is that for a dog – oh, you mean the targets. It's probably not their last stop but it's a good place for them to stop and stock up. Maybe switch vehicles."

"We can stop, too, ask around a little," the driver suggested.

"If you have to take a crap just say so," the passenger ribbed. "Or we can hit a drive-through if you're hungry. Otherwise we don't stop. We don't have to ask around. We've got *Chi-Chi* back there. If they've stopped in Indy, he'll know."

"You really think that dog is tracking them?" the driver asked incredulously. "From the car?"

"I don't care," the passenger admitted. "The boss told us to follow the dog's lead so that's what we're doing. He seemed pretty certain to me back in Chicago."

The man in the passenger seat glanced back at the dog, taking care not to let his gaze linger. Though he would never admit it, the weird animal disturbed him as much as it bothered his partner. The oversized and proportionately broader Chihuahua-like head stared past them and straight ahead. The wide-set eyes glowed faintly lavender and barely noticeable in the daylight, but both men knew the glow was there. Those weird eyes shone brighter and sharper the night before and every time the shadows deepened inside the car when they passed through tunnels or under viaducts.

And the driver was right, the passenger noted. The animal's broad shoulders, chest and ribcage, along with its head and short, thick hind legs did seem slightly larger than before. Its upper and lower fangs peeked further out from the animal's thin black lips. Even its whiskers seemed thicker, like dangerous spikes.

The passenger almost jumped when his cell phone buzzed. He snatched it from its charger and flipped it open.

"Shepherd, here," he said.

The driver saw the "Unknown" ID on the cell's display before his partner grabbed it and knew it was the supervisor.

* * *

"What've you got?" supervisor Johnson asked Shepherd from the back seat of the limousine. An olive-skinned, dark haired man sat across from him, leaning forward expectantly.

They're still going south on I-65, came Shepherd's voice through the cell phone's speaker.

"How far are you behind them?"

Just a few hours, the passenger said confidently. *I think we can overtake them in less than a day.*

"How do you know?" the supervisor asked.

There was a pause before the agent spoke.

DEMON OF LORR

We've picked up reports of a couple of stolen cars along I-65. Eyewitness reports mention an old man and young woman. The specific descriptions varied: hair color, eye color, skin complexion. The general descriptions, though, like height and approximate age, are consistent.

"Good. Keep me informed."

With that, the supervisor snapped his cell phone closed and looked up at his companion.

"It won't be much longer, Marco," the supervisor promised. "When we get the wife and the old man, Axe won't be far behind."

"How are the traffic light camera upgrades going?" Marco asked with his usual, poorly hidden anxiety.

"Well," Johnson returned.

"Are you sure they're going to work?" Marco worried.

"Are you questioning our technology?" Johnson asked irritably. "Their disguises won't fool the thermal scopes. They *will* see through any prosthetics and capture the true facial characteristics and bone structure. We've got super-servers and satellites dedicated to capturing and transmitting every image and comparing them to our sample. I've ordered the upgrades installed from Bloomington all the way back to Chicago. If they stay on or anywhere near 65, and they will, we'll get them soon."

Marco nodded. He leaned forward and gave Johnson a look that was supposed to be intimidating. Johnson found it almost comical. He kept his face impassive as Marco finally said what was on his mind.

"Ok, Johnson, I get that you're going to kill Axe, the guy who was contracted to kill me. That's what I'm paying you for. But what's to stop your organization from sending someone else after me?" Marco demanded. "You guys don't seem to be the kind of outfit that would give up so easily."

"New intel," Johnson lied. "I've strategically planted information that will make you an asset instead of a target. You'll be seen as a conduit to lead them to higher priority targets. Political targets."

"Cool," said Marco as he fished a cigarette out of his pocket and lit it. "D'you mind?"

"Go ahead," Johnson said, deftly hiding the disgust he felt. The cigarette smoke did not bother him in the least. But the gall of this fool to light the cancer stick *before* asking permission was an unforgivable oversight to a man like Johnson. He had men killed for less.

But Marco was a means to an end. He had value at the moment. Once that value had been exhausted, though, things would definitely change.

*   *   *

"Why'd you lie?" asked the driver. "We heard a few stolen car reports over the police band but no descriptions. Like you said, all we're doing is following the dog's lead."

"He was testing us, Hunter. Don't you remember? The last time we talked he told us to never mention the dog over the phone. He doesn't want *his* boss to know he's using this freaking monster. I had to tell him something."

"Do you really think we're just a couple of hours behind them?" Hunter asked.

"I have no idea," Shepherd admitted. "But I do know this dog is panting harder than last night and his eyes seem a little brighter. I'm pretty sure that means something."

"Yeah," Hunter agreed. "It means he's a weird freaking animal. I can't wait to get this job done so we can cut him loose."

Neither wanted to say it aloud, even though they both knew there was a branch of their organization dedicated to this type of thing. This dog, this "retriever" that their supervisor had ordered them to bring along to track their targets was some kind of supernatural creature, and neither of them wanted anything to do with it.

3.2

At a gas station just south of Indianapolis, Indiana, a stooped old man shuffled his way slowly from the station's convenience store to a waiting full-sized SUV. He had a friendly smile and nod for everyone he passed as he inched across the pavement, leaning heavily on his quad cane and being careful not to slip on the cold, slick pavement. A much younger woman stood near the rear of the SUV, pumping gas into the vehicle and waiting patiently for the telltale click of the nozzle to tell her the tank was full.

One could tell at a glance that the two were closely related. The younger woman had to be a daughter or at least a niece. Their noses, straight with slightly wide nostrils, were nearly identical, as was their light brown skin complexions.

What one could *not* tell from a glance was that the kindly old man was memorizing every face at which he smiled. He took note of every stride and gait so he would recognize them if he ever saw them again. Faces could be easily changed. He was living proof of that. Sometimes, though, even experienced agents forgot to change the way they walked. That was especially true when they underestimated their target. And even after the way he took out a would-be robber and crooked desk clerk back at that seedy hotel in Chicago, Dan was pretty sure the organization was still underestimating him.

Only the young woman at the waiting SUV knew that the hobbled old man had at least three guns hidden beneath his heavy woolen overcoat. She watched him, knowing he was taking even more time than usual. At first she thought he might actually be tiring. It was a very convincing act. But when she looked into his brown eyes she could tell how alert he was. She noticed that he moved slower on purpose, as if he were looking for something. When the old man's gaze locked on a couple of city maintenance workers operating on the traffic light camera in the intersection, he did not tear his gaze away until he arrived at the car.

"What is it, *Dad*?" she asked just as the nozzle clicked.

The old man looked worried. "Get in the car, baby girl."

She replaced the nozzle and did as she was asked, and the old man quickly joined her.

The woman started the car and pulled out into the street before she turned to the old man.

"Dan, what's wrong?" she asked. "Are you starting to get as nervous as I am about riding around in a stolen SUV?"

"We've talked about this," Dan said with a slightly annoyed edge to his voice. "After the incident at that seedy hotel we *had* to switch vehicles and we didn't have time to go through legal channels. I loved that damn van, but they would've been able to track us."

"Incident?" Lisa challenged. "You ripped a man's throat out and blew another man's head off. I think that's a bit more than an incident."

"If I hadn't done those things you would've been raped, robbed and killed," Dan said bluntly. "So don't expect me to feel guilty or nervous about them or this SUV."

"Then what's got you so worried?" Lisa pressed. "You're not your usual flirty, smart-ass self today."

"Something's coming, Lisa," the old man said. "I don't know what, but something's coming. And there's something about those maintenance workers that's bothering me."

"What?" Lisa asked, giving the men a look in her rear view mirror. "They work on those things all the time."

"I've seen several crews within the last couple of miles, and several more this morning as we drove through Indianapolis."

"Are you afraid they might be upgrading them? Improving the resolution?" Lisa asked.

"There are too many of them. Most cities don't work like this," Dan explained. "There's an unusual sense of...I don't know...urgency about it."

"You think the organization is behind it?" Lisa asked. "Even if they are upgrading them, we still have these disguises."

"If it's the organization, they'll be doing more than just improving the resolution," Dan said. "Let's just get the hell outta here…quickly but not *too* quickly. Fast, but not fast enough to get stopped by the cops. Just —"

"Got it, Dan," Lisa assured. "I won't call attention to us."

"I'm sorry, Lisa. I'm just a little on edge right now."

"I know," Lisa said with a smile. "Don't worry about it."

They rode in silence for a time. During that silence, Lisa glanced over at Dan several times. She wanted to ask him questions. She had so many of them, but in his preoccupied state she was not sure that he wanted to talk. He did not seem to notice the times she opened her mouth to speak and then closed it with a sigh. His gaze moved constantly from the sky through the windshield to the passenger side rear-view mirror, through the side window to the skies of the western horizon. And then the cycle started again.

Lisa was still trying to digest the fact that this man was at or more than two hundred years of age.

"You can feel something coming," Lisa decided to say. It was not the question she really wanted to ask, but she was curious about this, too. "Is it magic?"

"It *could* be," Dan said. "But it could just be an old man's extreme paranoia and worry building up."

"So let's explore the magic thing, first," Lisa suggested. "If you can't rule it out, try to narrow it down."

"Spoken like a doctor," Dan noted.

"It comes naturally," Lisa said matter-of-factly. There was no ego or bluster, only a statement of fact. "When you're trying to diagnose a sick pet, you start with what you know and rule out everything that doesn't fit."

Dan nodded. "Have you ever just known a storm was coming without really knowing *how* you knew?" He began. "Sometimes you can smell it on the wind. Sometimes you can see it in the clouds. But sometimes, even without any of those conscious predictors, you just *know*."

"I think so," Lisa said after a thoughtful pause.

"That's how I feel now," Dan said. "Only I don't feel a storm coming from the sky. It's very faint. I can usually feel magic more definitively than this.

"People who are sensitive to magic experience it in different ways. For me it's like a soft breeze. I feel it in gusts.

The strength varies, the temperature might vary, but it comes in gusts for me.

"But now," Dan continued. "It's hard to explain. It's almost like I keep hearing the breeze whistling in the distance and it's coming this way, but I never actually *feel* it."

"Is it good magic or bad magic?" Lisa asked, still finding it hard to believe she was actually talking about magic.

This was not their first conversation on the subject and she had even seen it in practice, but it did not yet seem real to her. She did not know what it would take to make it seem real. Considering they were being pursued by a demon posing as a high-ranking official of a powerful spy organization, she was not anxious to find out what it would take to make magic seem real.

"Magic is neither good nor evil," Dan explained. "Sometimes the intent or the nature of its wielder permeates the magic to make it feel good or evil and sometimes it doesn't. In this case I can't feel any intent. I can't feel any good or ill will."

Just longing, Dan thought. *Like hunger.* He did not say it out loud for fear of making Lisa even more frightened than she already was.

"Have you been thinking about your magic?" Dan asked. He was eager to change the subject.

Lisa sighed in relief. That was exactly what she wanted to ask Dan about.

"I have," she said. "I'm pretty sure if I actually *had* magic, according to your logic, it would have something to do with healing."

Dan leaned toward her with a curious arch of a gray eyebrow. He was impressed that she remembered what he said about a person's magic manifesting itself in something they enjoyed or something to which they had an affinity.

"What makes you think so?"

"Before I was a vet I wanted to be a nurse, like my mom, and her mom. It runs in the family, sort of like yours and Ryan's magic."

"Healing?" Dan asked distractedly. "I sure hope so. That could come in pretty handy."

Lisa looked over at him. He rolled down the window and stuck his head out into the cold air to stare intently into the southwestern skies.

"What's wrong?" Lisa asked. "What do you see?"

"Nothing yet," Dan said. "But I hear a chopper."

"Really?" Lisa said before falling silent to listen for herself. It took almost a minute, but she finally heard the faint *whup-whup-whup* of a distant helicopter.

"Ok, I hear it now. How did you hear it before I did?"

Dan looked over at her. "You think your hearing should be better than mine because I'm so old?" he challenged.

"Well...I..." Lisa stammered.

"Just messin' with you, girl. Your hearing probably is better than mine. I just know what to listen for."

Lisa gave him a light swat on the shoulder before continuing. "Couldn't it be a traffic or news chopper?"

"Those choppers don't sound like this," Dan said. "Check your rear-view mirror."

Lisa did, and then she gasped. She went light-headed for the briefest moment and her heart rate began to soar.

"There are about three cars coming up fast," she said, fighting panic. Her right hand went to her forehead and she rubbed feverishly.

"Both hands on the steering wheel, ten and two o'clock," Dan said calmly. "And don't panic."

"You should drive," Lisa declared.

"We don't have time to swap seats," Dan explained, his voice calm and even. "I'll have to talk you through this."

Lisa shook her head vigorously even as she accelerated. "Dan, I'm sorry, I can't do –"

"You can't do anything but drive," Dan interrupted. His voice was a little more forceful but still calm. "Nothing else matters right now but the sound of my voice, OK?"

Lisa took a deep breath and nodded once. "OK."

"Good," Dan said. "Floor it to the next exit. It's less than a mile up."

Lisa put the pedal to the floor and had to stifle a yelp when the eight-cylinder SUV leapt from 75 mph to 95 in about three seconds. She held onto the steering wheel tightly enough to hurt her hand as she guided the SUV to the exit.

The three dark sedans sped up to chase her. When she merged with the feeder road Dan instructed her to turn right at the next intersection. She fully intended to, but when she reached the intersection she looked to her left and saw another black sedan racing toward her. In a panic, she floored the gas pedal and shot straight through the intersection, through a red light, causing oncoming traffic to brake frantically and honk their horns.

"What are you doing?" Dan asked, careful to keep his voice even.

"I *don't know* what I'm doing!" Lisa cried. "There's another car coming! I didn't know what to do!"

By then, four pursuing cars had weaved their way through the intersection and were coming on fast. Dan looked out of the window and up into the sky and saw a helicopter bearing down on them, as well.

"OK, Lisa," Dan said with almost annoying calm. "You see that building up ahead?"

"Yes," Lisa said worriedly, noting the unfinished structure less than a quarter of a mile down the feeder road and roughly twenty yards away from the right side of the road. The metal frame of the two-story structure had only one completed wall that faced the highway. Unmanned cranes, excavators, dump trucks, and cement mixer trucks sat all around the skeletal frame like sleeping metal giants.

Dan glanced out at the chopper again. It had passed the pursuing sedans and was almost on top of them.

"That's a Defender," he said. "I can fly that."

"What does that have to do with anything?" Lisa asked in a near panic.

"Pull into the construction site and stop right by the wall," he ordered.

"You want me to *stop?*" Lisa asked.

"We can't outrun them, girl. Just do it!"

DEMON OF LORR

The deafening sound of gunfire roared from the chopper. Lisa screamed as large chunks of pavement detonated around the SUV from the high-caliber ammunition pouring down on them like explosive rain. She snatched the steering wheel to the right and pressed the gas pedal again, pulling off the feeder road several yards before the start of the paved driveway to the construction site. Dan held on for dear life as the SUV soared over a ditch on the side of the road and crashed onto the brown grass.

The SUV tipped over to the right onto two wheels, then rocked back to the left and was on the other two wheels before finally crashing back to all four. By that time they had jumped the curb of the driveway and were rocketing toward a resting front-end loader.

Lisa screamed again, hit the brakes hard and veered to the left, scraping the passenger side of the SUV against the loader with a loud screech. Dan leaned away as far as he could to avoid the jolt and said a quick, silent prayer of thanks, knowing the scrape could have been much worse.

But then they were rolling head-on towards a parked crawler crane. Lisa tried to scream again but her voice had gone hoarse. She braked and went right, narrowly missing a head-on collision with the crane. This time she was not able to regain control of the SUV. They went into an uncontrollable spin during which the SUV once again began to rock onto two wheels to the left and right.

The entire time, stuttering fire from the chopper peppered the ground and construction vehicles around them, ricocheting off of the metal behemoths and sending gravel and bullets flying in every direction like shrapnel.

The SUV finally came to rest ten yards away from the front wall of the unfinished construction and a few feet away from a large crane. Lisa sat there silently, staring straight ahead with eyes wide and mouth agape, still gripping the steering wheel with violently trembling hands. Dan gave one more silent quick thanks when he noticed that the crane truck was acting as an effective shield between them and the chopper...for the briefest of moments, at least.

He reached into the back seat with his left hand to get the enchanted shield and used his right to firmly grasp Lisa's shoulder. She jumped at his touch, still dazed. When she looked at him she noticed he had his crazy rifle slung over his shoulder. She had been so focused on driving that she did not even notice him retrieving it.

"Slide out on my side," Dan said, pulling her firmly.

She let him pull her out of the SUV through the passenger side door. The moment her feet touched the gravelly ground, she released yet another hoarse scream because the chopper opened fire again, blowing gaping holes into the roof of the SUV and blowing out the windows. Dan snatched Lisa to his side and threw up the shield just in time to deflect more gunfire from the hovering chopper. Blinding ripples of white light bloomed around them when the high caliber shells struck the magical barrier. The force of the blows almost buckled Dan's knees but he managed to stand firm.

The four sedans screeched to a stop and two men dashed out of each one. They immediately positioned themselves around the construction site in places that provided clear lines of fire around the crane. In a moment they had joined the chopper in firing on the targets.

Dan and Lisa ran, shoulder to shoulder, towards the unfinished building with Dan holding his magical shield like an umbrella. He had to tilt it just a bit so that the angle of the shield's dome-like barrier protected them from the airborne and earthbound shooters.

The smaller caliber weapons caused barely noticeable undulations of energy in the otherwise invisible shield, but each powerful blast from the chopper sent shockwaves down Dan's forearm that caused his arm, and therefore the shield, to tremor madly. Lisa marveled at the fact that he was able to keep hold of the enchanted shield.

They made it to the front wall of the building and pressed their backs to it. Dan released Lisa's shoulder and held the shield out with both hands. Concentric circles of white light rippled in front them, just beyond their feet, and on either side of them as the multi-caliber ammunition was stopped short by the magic of the shield. The continuously rolling waves of light, spreading like malevolent ripples of water in a pond, revealed a dome of protective energy that was roughly eight feet in diameter radiating out and around them from the edges of the small round shield.

Lisa would have been amazed if she had not seen it before, and if the circumstances, like the last time she saw the magic of the shield in action, had not been so horrifying.

Dan used it back in Chicago to save her from hundreds of attacking shadow wraiths – handkerchief sized sheets of demonic blackness with razor-sharp edges that attacked with frightening speed. But the sight of the shells exploding against the shimmering magic of the shield just inches in front of them, as well as the large chunks of wall bursting all around them just outside of the protective shield, were too much for her to take. She sunk to her knees and closed her eyes to pray, tears streaming down her face.

Dan looked down at her and knitted his eyebrows in frustration. "No time for that, girl!" he yelled over the deafening hail of gunfire. "You've got some shooting to do! Take the shotgun. You know how it works!"

Lisa's eyes popped open wide. "What?"

"What the hell do you mean, 'What'? I can't hold this shield forever!" He grunted and bucked at another volley from the chopper before continuing. "Even if I could, this thing forms a half-sphere at best. If any of them smarten up and work their way behind us they'll be able blast us right through this wall. We've gotta shoot back, Lisa. Look!" Dan nodded to the right.

Lisa looked over and saw two men easing their way further around, proving Dan's point.

"They're flanking us," Dan cried. "We don't have much time!"

"I can't kill them!" Lisa screamed. "I'll hold the shield!"

"C'mon, then!" Dan snarled. He would take what he could get.

Lisa rose shakily to her feet and stepped to Dan's side. Flinching at each explosion and fighting down panic, she

109

took a deep breath and swore to herself that she was not going to get them killed. She braced herself and reached out for the shield.

"Hold tight," Dan said. "Knees bent, feet spread. Put your shoulder into it."

Lisa followed his directions and replaced one of his hands in the straps of the shield with one of her hands and then the other. The force of the gunfire immediately rocked her back on her heels. She held on to the shield but lost her balance. Dan, thankfully, had anticipated this and was there to catch her. He held her waist firmly while she gathered her feet under her. He leaned in close to her ear.

"You ready?" he asked softly.

When Lisa nodded vigorously, her face a mask of angry and fearful determination, Dan let her go. She flinched but held firm this time, bending at the knee a little deeper and slightly leaning forward against the onslaught. Her body jerked in response to the constant gunfire, especially from the chopper, but she grimaced and held on.

Dan did not need the target locking function of his weapon for what he needed to do. He pointed the bulbous end of the tricked-out shotgun barrel at the men flanking them to his left and squeezed the trigger, holding it down long enough for it to jump into spray mode. The shotgun stuttered twice as it fired ten rounds in two one-second intervals. The bullets flew through the barrier from behind as if it was not there.

Ten rounds hit each man from belly to shoulder, the last few striking them even as they were airborne from the first few hits. Dan knew the men were wearing bulletproof vests beneath their heavy coats, but he also knew his spinning, screw-tipped rounds would drill right through the Kevlar.

The flankers on his right saw Dan's volley and scrambled for cover when the old man turned to level his weird, double-barreled shotgun on them. They dived behind heavy machinery but Dan's deadly rounds tore through the body of a crane and dropped another agent. The last flanking attacker barely escaped the second volley.

"Hit the chopper!" Lisa yelled. "My arms are breaking!"

"I can't," Dan said. "We need it."

"How the hell are you going to get that *uhhnn!*" Lisa's question was cut short by a grunt as she was rocked by another round of fire from the big guns of the chopper.

"Shut up and hold on!" Dan ordered. "I need to concentrate."

This time Dan sank to his knees, letting the shotgun hang at his side from its shoulder strap, and closed his eyes. Lisa was about to bark an admonishment at him but stopped when she noticed his mouth and hands moving.

The chopper had stopped firing for a few seconds. But the shooters on the ground noticed Dan on his knees and opened fire again. Their fire did not bother Lisa, but her heart went cold when she noticed the chopper swinging up and over them, heading behind the wall just like Dan said they eventually would. She knew that a volley from those guns would tear easily through the wall and through them.

She looked down at Dan to scream a warning and saw that he was already looking at her. Before she could say anything, Dan calmly but gravely said:

"Close your eyes. Now."

The moment she did, she felt a soft breeze and her ears suddenly clogged up. Her stomach went queasy for instant and then she felt a strong but painless jolt. It was as if someone snatched a chair from under her and she landed on a firm cushion.

Her ears popped almost painfully. The next thing she heard was the spinning of helicopter propellers. But they were much closer than they were before. And then she heard Dan's voice. But this time he said something odd:

"Jump or die."

Lisa opened her eyes and saw that she was sitting in the cushioned back seat of the chopper, still holding the shield out before her. Dan was sitting in the front left seat holding his modified sawed-off shotgun on the chopper pilot.

The pilot's eyes went wide.

"How the hell did you – "

The shotgun barked once, blasting the pilot out of the open helicopter door with a spray of blood. Lisa yelped at the sound and tried to look away, but her eyes were transfixed on the pilot as he fell and slammed to the gravel-strewn ground of the construction site. The violence of the impact shocked her out of her trance and finally allowed her to tear her eyes away. She looked over at Dan with dread and confusion.

Dan shrugged. "I told him to jump or die. Talking wasn't one of his choices."

"How did we get here?" Lisa forced herself to ask.

"How do you think?" Dan asked.

Lisa was silent as the old man seized the controls on his side and took the chopper above the wall. The five remaining agents stood around, wary and confused, trying to figure out where the hell the couple had gone and how. They did not bother to look up at the helicopter, having no reason to think anyone other than the pilot was controlling it. With their attention on their targets, they did notice the man falling from the sky. They were caught totally unaware when Dan brought the chopper over them and opened fire.

Lisa gasped as their would-be assassins scattered. She knew Dan would kill if he had to but this seemed excessive. Her gasp turned into a sigh of relief when she realized he was actually shooting the sedans. Once the agents were hunkered down behind various construction vehicles, Dan smiled.

"He didn't use the *really* big guns on us because his own guys were too close," he said. "But I don't have that problem. Check this out…"

He fired the chopper's side mounted grenade launchers. The sedans exploded. The cover of the construction vehicles saved the agents' lives from the deadly fire and flying debris. Lisa could feel the wave of heated air buffet them as Dan swung the chopper around to the south and shot away.

"If you weren't here," Dan said confidentially, "I would've turned all of those bastards to blood pudding."

"I'm glad you didn't," she said sincerely. She had already watched her husband kill two men, and counting the pilot, she had watched Dan kill three.

Every death was either in self-defense or defense of her but that did not make the memory of them any easier to bear.

"And good job, by the way," Dan added. "I'm proud of you."

Lisa smiled uneasily. "Thanks." She did not think she did such a good job but she knew it could have been much worse. At least she had not gotten them killed.

She caught a glimpse of a line of state trooper vehicles speeding toward the construction site and wondered what story the surviving assassins would tell them.

And then she wondered how her husband was doing.

3.3

Hunter and Shepherd stood at the side of the road outside of their dark blue sedan. They could see columns of dark smoke rolling into the air and they could hear the sirens. They could hear *all* of the sirens: police, fire department, and ambulance. Traffic was backed up on the highway for miles in both directions from people who stopped their cars on the feeder on both sides of the highway, gawking at the flaming remains of the blasted cars and refusing to drive anywhere near the recent firefight.

Hunter turned to look at their spooky canine passenger. It was sticking its severely oversized, Chihuahua-shaped head out of the back passenger side window and looking south. It was not looking at the aftermath of the battle, though. It was looking over it, staring at the backside of a black helicopter as it grew smaller and smaller in the southern sky.

"That chopper is one of ours, isn't it?" Hunter noted.

Shepherd turned to him and nodded. "Yeah. You think our guys took them out?"

Hunter looked at the dog again and shook his head. "From the way Chi-Chi is staring after that chopper, it looks like the broad and old man are in it. Look at his eyes, they're glowing weaker but they're glowing. And he's still got that English Pointer thing going on in that direction."

Shepherd cocked his head to the side as he noticed. "Maybe our guys took them prisoner."

Hunter shook his head no. "The order is to terminate, not capture. If the targets are in the chopper, it's because they commandeered it."

"You're right," Shepherd agreed. "Look at that noggin of his. It's a little smaller again, about the same size it was when we got him."

Hunter frowned. "If that thing gets bigger and uglier the closer we get, I'd hate to see him when we catch up with those two."

"Yeah," Shepherd agreed. "I don't wanna see that either."

3.4

The dwarves let another day pass before it was time for Raxe to take the "test" that King Grimhammer mentioned. The surviving members of the quest to find the Hell Key were trying to determine whether the dwarves let so much time pass in order to prepare the test or to make Raxe more anxious about what was coming. Raxe did not know or care. All he wanted was to be well rested when the time came.

He slept soundly for a few hours but then began to dream the dream he had been having since he learned the details of their quest. The dream haunted him as frequently as the dreams of his damnation had when he gave in to the magic of Demonsbane years ago, but this new recurring dream did not unnerve him as badly. The dream of going to hell had been a dream of the future. That horrible dream actually came true, if only temporarily, and might well come true again. This dream was of something that happened in the past.

> *He was back in the Southeast Asian jungle, serving as the point man for the three-member infiltration team.*
>
> *Axe, as Raxe was known within the organization, would normally be perched in a tree to serve as lookout and sniper while Terrance Oakley – or Oak, as he was called within the Cutters – joined the infiltration team. Oak was surprisingly stealthy for a man six-feet eight inches tall. This mission, however, called for sneaking through cramped sewers and underground conduits.*
>
> *Oak's size was not at all conducive to such conditions, so Axe took the point while Oak waited in the chopper just over three klicks away with Wings, the chopper pilot, and Arsenal, the Cutters explosive expert.*
>
> *Accompanying Raxe was Dr. James Stewart, aka "Doc," and Min Wah, the infiltration specialist.*

The three of them were clad in black and gray camouflage and outfitted with night-vision goggles, earpiece comm devices and assault weapons. They made their way to the perimeter of the warlord's compound.

Min Wah, also known as Quicksilver, guarded the rear while Doc crept along in between them. As always, Doc could barely contain his nervousness. He was actually half decent at stealth and infiltration and he was a surprisingly good shot. The problem was he hated it. He preferred to stay in the van or the plane and do his hacking from a distance. Unfortunately for him, this job required a more up close and personal touch.

Axe often wondered why Doc stayed on the team for nearly two years. Though he was glad the reluctant agent stuck around as long as he had. Doc had never failed to disable a security system or hack a server for intel, no matter how complex. He was an instrumental part of the team.

Doc reached up and put a hand on Axe's left shoulder, halting the point man in his tracks. When Axe turned, Doc tapped his ear and pointed at the darkness to their left to indicate that he heard something in that direction. Axe nodded to indicate that he heard it, too. But he pointed two fingers at his own goggle-covered eyes and then pointed in the direction they were walking to indicate that they needed to keep moving.

Quicksilver nudged Doc roughly from behind. Doc glanced down at the hand that nudged him, particularly at the set of silver-plated spiked brass knuckles she wore on any mission that allowed for them. Doc grimaced and crept on.

They walked a few more paces and then, without warning, Axe turned a fired off a shot from his suppressed M110 Semi-Automatic Sniper

System rifle. Doc froze for the briefest moment, lifted his M16 semi-automatic and started sighting for targets. He almost squeezed off an errant shot when Quicksilver's thin but strong-as-steel fingers gripped his shoulder. She leaned close to his ear.

"Cover me!" she whispered, pointing in the direction she wanted him to fire.

Without hesitation this time, Doc fired blindly in that direction as Quicksilver melted into the shadows. In less than thirty seconds Axe had only fired three rounds while Doc's supressed M16 stuttered again and again. None of the shots were actually silenced, but the shots were muffled thumps as opposed to loud pops. The night went silent again just before Quicksilver materialized from the darkness around them.

Axe looked down and smiled at the blood dripping from her brass knuckles and fingers.

"Is that all of them?" Doc asked in a low, nervous whisper.

"I think so," Quicksilver said. "I know mine are dead but we'd better confirm Axe's."

"Did I get anyone?" Doc asked uneasily.

"No," Quicksilver answered. Doc sighed in relief as the slim Asian woman continued. "But you kept them pinned down so I could ease in and do them. Thanks."

Doc's sigh ended abruptly and his grimace returned.

"Wait here," Axe said before vanishing into the shadows as smoothly as Quicksilver had. It did not take long for him to confirm that the first two targets were dead, one with a headshot and the other with a shot to the throat.

When Axe got to the third ambusher, he knew just what to expect. He knew he was a dreaming and he knew how to wake himself from most of his bad dreams. But he never roused himself from this dream. It was a form on penitence for the lives he had taken.

He had been having this dream so often of late, though, that he was almost numb to the guilt from re-living the memory of killing the young Asian teen. But he went on nonetheless, stepping softly on the balls of his feet through the thick brush until he got to the prone body lying face down.

This time, though, the close-cropped hair stained with blood and brain matter was not black. It was blonde. Axe's heart rate quickened as he aimed his rifle and kicked the body onto its back. The wide blue eyes staring lifelessly through him were not the brown eyes of the Asian boy that usually haunted this nightmare.

The corpse had Ethan Sureblade's face.

Raxe woke up with a start. Azhju'lestra was there in an instant to give Raxe a reassuring squeeze of the hand.

"Do not worry," she said. "You *are* a Child of the Old Ones. You will easily pass whatever test they have for you."

"I know," Raxe answered with a smile.

Raxe wished the coming test had been what was bothering him. The fact was that had not distressed him at all. There was no doubt he was a descendant of Raxe and the Gatekeeper, so he had no doubt he would pass their test, but his daughter's words brought their predicament to the forefront of his concerns. He was not sure if the test would be as easy as his daughter seemed to assume. That uncertainty, coupled with the new twist to his recurring dream, kept him from getting any more sleep that night.

DEMON OF LORR

3.5

Twelve armored dwarves with various weapons held at the ready marched into the chamber to escort Raxe and the rest of the sky sleigh survivors through a series of tunnels. There was complete silence other than the sound of their footfalls, leaving each of them to their own musings.

At one point Raxe worriedly thought the test would be some kind of literal trial by fire because of the strong scent of molten metal that began to permeate the wide stone corridors. Soon after, the corridors became significantly warmer than the cool tunnels they traversed earlier. As they trudged across an intersecting corridor, they were greeted by the roar of multiple furnaces, loud hissing, the ringing of metal striking metal, and a blast of heat. A glance to the left down the intersecting hall revealed a faint red-orange glow at the end of a corridor that turned sharply to the left. Raxe made a mental note that a smithy lie somewhere around that corner.

After passing the corridor, the heat, smells and sounds of the smithy faded away. The guards ushered them along for a few more minutes until another corridor branched off to the right. At that point, four of the guards led Raxe down that perpendicular tunnel while the remaining eight guards kept the rest of the group moving straight ahead.

Raxe's trek ended in a narrow tunnel that terminated at a four-foot wide iron door. One of the dwarves stepped forward and banged on the door with the pommel of a broadsword that was, from pommel to blade tip, almost as long as the dwarf was tall. The iron door swung slowly into the space beyond with a loud grinding of metal on stone. As soon as the door was open wide enough the escorts ushered Raxe through the doorway with rough shoves.

Raxe turned and faced the iron door as it swung closed with a loud bang. A moment later he turned to see where he was. He stood near the left corner of one of the short sides of a rectangular arena not too different than the Royal arena he visited on his first trip to Lorr.

The most obvious difference was that this arena was in the heart of a mountain...or maybe beneath it. Raxe could no longer tell. They had climbed and descended so many times so randomly that Raxe had absolutely and completely lost his bearings well before arriving at the arena.

The floor of the dusty, rock-strewn field had a rectangular footprint about half the size of a football field. Four high walls defined the field. Wide thresholds dominated the center of each wall in addition to the corner door through which Raxe entered.

Two of the thresholds that faced each other from the shorter sides were about eight feet wide and dark gray, nearly black, and reinforced with studded iron bands that lined the doors' edges and divided them into four panels of equal size. Ten-foot wide wrought iron gates blocked the other two thresholds. Each vertical bar that formed the gates was as thick as big man's forearm. Horizontally oriented crossbars supported the upper and lower ends of the vertical bars.

Broad metal loops imbedded in the rock walls lined much of the wall space between the wide entryways. Thick chains hang from some, worn hemp ropes hung from others. Raxe assumed that those loops, ropes and chains were used as leashes to restrain combatants within the arena.

The high walls rose nearly twenty feet and were topped by the lowest rows of bleachers. Fifteen receding shelves carved into the subterranean stone supported long wooden and metal benches to form the stadium seating. Only one side, the side nearest to Raxe, was occupied. It was packed with adult dwarves of varying ages.

From their dress and gear, Raxe assumed they were ranking military officers. All of them were armed with different types of well-crafted weapons and wore similar clothing: tan tunics under brown hauberks or vests with loose woolen breeches smartly tucked into brown, shin-high, hiking boots. The colors they wore were various shades of tan and brown similar to the earth and stone that formed Hell's Mountains. All of them wore sashes tied around their biceps or looping under their arm and over their shoulders.

Some wore more of them than others. The sashes varied in color, but all were lighter and darker hues of a color from a rainbow. The dwarves were grouped according to the color of their sashes for the most part, perhaps denoting families or individual communities among the underground nation.

The female dwarves were almost indistinguishable from the males to Raxe's eyes with a few exceptions. Their lack of facial hair and the swell of breasts beneath their hauberks and leather vests were the only things that revealed their gender. They looked every bit as fierce as the males. People were milling around the stands, talking and laughing, casting expectant glances and occasionally pointing down at him or one of the massive central doors in the walls. They were clearly looking forward to whatever was about to happen.

An arched ceiling, as high as the stadium was long, curved up from the topmost row of seating. A latticework of metal beams crisscrossed a few feet below the arched ceiling, supporting broad chains that in turn supported massive torch lamps that threw bright light throughout the stadium like giant chandeliers. Smoke rose from the lamps, and when Raxe tilted his head at just the right angle he could see the smoke disappearing within a series of narrow vents cut into the stone ceiling.

A line of window portals were cut into the high walls only a few feet below the first row of stands atop the walls. Some were wider than others. The widest ones were cut in sections so that there appeared to stone bars in the portals. In the spaces between the windows, large torches flared brightly, adding more light to subterranean the stadium. Those lamps also partially illuminated the rooms behind the windows.

Raxe saw Rell Kallen and four of the six surviving members of the sky sleigh crew looking through one of the windows. Through the other, the other two crewmembers along with Ethan and Quick peered nervously down at him. And he could barely make out the top of his daughter's head.

He could see her aqua-hued hair, the soft blues and light greens and wispy strands of white, framing the soft curve of her light bronzed forehead. Her thin eyebrows and wide, oval eyes – so similar to her mother's – just managed to peek at him over the sill of the portal. He saw something in those eyes that he had not seen from the girl before: fear.

They had only known each other for a few days, but in that short amount of time they had already faced harrowing dangers. When they were attacked by the swarm of scythe wings and forced to jump from the doomed sky sleigh, the girl's pretty face reflected excited nervousness and not a trace fear. But she was afraid now.

Raxe took a moment to look inside of himself to find Azh's presence within him. He found it quickly, even among that of the other Children of the Old Ones, including Rionn Lorr and the Head Mage's daughter, the faint presence of his grandfather from across the WorldGate, and the barely discernable presence of the hidden Child. Azh's aura was the closest to his. The sensation of a heartbeat slightly out of rhythm with his own and the whisper of her thoughts like a gentle breeze in the corner of his consciousness were clearly distinguishable from those of the other Children of the Old Ones.

He learned from his grandfather that a Child of the Old Ones could read – and project thoughts into – the mind of a direct offspring, unless that offspring had the knowledge and strength of will to block them. The offspring, on the other hand, could not initiate such communication with a parent or predecessor.

Raxe focused on those whispers that he knew were his daughter's and they instantly gained volume. She knew he was there the moment he focused on her, acknowledging and accepting him without hesitation or the slightest hint of trepidation at his intrusion. He got the sense that she did not consider it an intrusion at all. Her response was a curious daughter responding to a kind of verbal call from her father. It was a welcome call, in fact, a salve for the worry she felt at his predicament.

What's wrong Azh? Raxe asked. *Why are you so afraid?*

I thought the test was something you could easily pass because we are Children of the Old Ones... she responded. *But I am not so certain, now.*

DEMON OF LORR

Raxe tried to mask the growing sense of apprehension resulting from her words. *What's changed your mind?* He asked.

Something approaches, she warned. *The dwarves are bringing your test. I can feel their presence through the water in their bodies. The dwarves bring something I have never sensed before, something large, hungry, and full of malice.*

Thanks for the warning, Azh. But don't worry. Whatever it is, I'll be able to handle it. He tried his best to project calm and reassurance.

He was not in the least bit sure she was buying it.

Raxe broke their connection, fearing she would be able to feel the hammering of his heart whether he wanted her to or not. He turned his attention to the doors and gates around him and wondered what the dwarves had in store for him. He felt safe in assuming he would have to fight. The only question was who or what he would have to fight. Back at the royal stadium he had battled Meldrick Sureblade, Ethan's father. This time he knew he would not get off so easily.

The constant chatter drifting down from the stands suddenly hushed, causing the offworlder to look up at the observers. A moment later King Jax Grimhammer, flanked by General Bartok and Mage Listwhin, stepped to the edge of the first row of seating almost directly above the center iron door. The dwarven King of the Stonehammer Nation turned his back to the field and faced his subjects.

"Stonehammer warriors!" He called in a deep, booming voice that filled every corner of the arena.

"King Jax!" the crowd cried back in unison.

"This human claims t'be the progeny of the Gatekeeper! Even has the nerve t' name 'imself Raxe after the Gatekeeper's own divine son!"

The crowd gave a collected gasp of appalled disbelief. Shouts of "Liar!" and "Blasphemer!" and various profanities rained down.

Raxe wanted to point out that he did not give that name to himself. The Head Mage and old Shanderah gave him that name because his real first name, Ryan, sounded so much like the Head Mage's first name, Rionn. He doubted the enraged crowd would care to listen to that explanation, though.

The king continued, and if Raxe had not been watching and listening in person he would have sworn the dwarf was speaking through a bullhorn.

"We all know what happened when the last outsider arrived and claimed t' have the blood of the Gatekeeper flowing through his veins, do we not?"

This statement was met with a host of boos, hisses, and derisive whistles. Raxe even heard "Let his blood flow across the arena floor!" and "Death to imposters!" screamed out by many in the audience.

3.6

In one of the viewing rooms just below the bottom row of bleachers, Azhju'lestra turned a worry glance to Quick. The armed guards surrounding them flinched at the sudden movement but resumed a calm but alert posture when they realized she posed no threat.

"But father *is not* an imposter," Azh said worriedly. "We are both Children! The Gatekeeper and Raxe *are* our ancestors!"

"Of course," Quick said in a comforting tone. "And soon they will know this to be true."

We will see if his claims are true! The king's voice boomed from below. *If he does NOT have the blood of the Gatekeeper flowing through his veins, his blood will be flowing all over the floor of this arena!*

* * *

A deafening cheer erupted. Even though less than a quarter of the large stadium was occupied, the roar echoed as if it was filled to capacity. The cheer was so raucous that Raxe almost missed the loud clanging sound made by the opening of the wide wrought iron gate on the long wall to his right. And then, as if someone had flipped a switch, the crowd went silent.

Raxe turned just in time to see a horrific creature bound through the opening. Something huge with thick, grayish-brown fur, razor-sharp claws and wickedly long and pointed teeth sailed fifteen feet from the opening and landed lightly, much more lightly than something so large had a right to. The only sound it made when it landed was the clacking of curved claws almost as long as Raxe's forearms when their needle tips hit the ground. The thing looked up at the hushed crowd for a moment before turning its baleful glare on the unfortunate man standing alone near the corner of the arena.

"Oh…shit…" Raxe swore.

* * *

In the viewing room, Quick gasped and his eyes went wide with fear.

"A *guardian*?!"

The young changeling immediately went into a transformation. Within two seconds his body wavered, shrank, and sprouted feathers. Before the changeling sparrow could dart between the bars, a fierce call from one of the dwarven guards stopped him.

"No, changeling!" the brown bearded dwarf warned. "The elf and the girl may be formidable but are ye willin t'bet they be able – or in the elf's case, *willing* – t'protect the humans from us if ye leave?"

The fluttering sparrow paused, retracted its feathers, and began to grow. In the next moment the tall, sandy brown-haired gangly teen stood before them in the same loose brown tunic, tan breaches and hiking boots he had been wearing before he transformed.

He glared angrily at the guard and then turned to look through the window. He leaned closer and lifted both hands to grab the stone bars. He had seen such creatures before. He had watched the Finder kill a guardian in the badlands shortly after the gargantuan, black-armored mercenary stole the Keys from the Stonehammer dwarves. The Finder killed the fierce beast, but he had been wearing his dwarf-forged full suit-of-arms that was almost as impenetrable as Raxe's divine armor.

More importantly, the Finder possessed Dragon-fang. According to legend that massive broadsword was fashioned from an actual dragon's tooth, which imbued it with its own particular magic. A dragon's tooth was virtually unbreakable by anything created by a mortal. The sharp blade of Dragon-fang could cut through something as dense as dragon scales, which were harder than any metal. Worst of all, the blade was poisonous. One cut from its razor's edge would infect and eventually corrode organic material.

The legend of Dragon-fang stated that if its keen edges did not kill, its poisonous bite surely would.

But Raxe's armor did not cover his entire body. It was forged by the gods and completely invulnerable, yes. But his biceps, triceps, elbows, the back of his knees, and most importantly his neck, were not covered. And while Raxe owned Demonsbane, his own enchanted weapon that had broken Dragon-fang in two, he had surrendered it to the dwarven king the previous day. In fact, the offworlder had no weapons at all.

* * *

Back on the arena floor, Raxe was sweating. At first glance the creature reminded him of a tygra cub. Like the young giant cats, this monster had a bulky, muscular, feline body and stood over six feet tall even while crouching. This creature, however, was grayish-brown instead of the tygra's azure. Even more astonishingly, it had the head, ears, and long muzzle of a wolf. Its thin black lips peeled back slowly into a nightmarish snarl while huge canine eyes as black as a coal glowered at him.

The only things Raxe had ever seen that were more frightening than this creature were dragons and demons. The only reason he was sure this creature was not a demon was because his magic did not awaken.

A surge of fear tore through him when he considered the possibility that his power had failed because the dwarves, like the *Ken d'Zanir*, could somehow squelch magic. But then he took note of the pale, nearly transparent glimmer of energy spraying from the creature and knew it was permeated with a great deal of magic.

That was all he had time to think.

The creature attacked with flashing claws and snapping, slavering jaws. Raxe broke to his left and sprinted to evade the beast but he was not nearly fast enough. One powerful thrust of the beast's thick hind legs took it over forty yards in less than two seconds. Instead of landing and skidding on the ground, the thing bounced, instantly changing direction and hurling itself at Raxe with terrible speed.

Raxe was sprinting and knew he would not be able to dodge the creature, so he dropped. He fell face first but caught himself on his open hands as the wolf-cat shot over him. Raxe pushed against the ground and sprung back to his feet to run in a different direction.

He chanced a look over his left shoulder as he righted himself to get a fix on the creature's position and was almost sorry he did. The wolf-cat flew into the stadium wall, but instead of slamming into it and crashing to the hard ground as Raxe hoped, the thing impossibly clung to the wall like an insect, its wicked claws and incredible strength suspending it easily while the creature pivoted.

With a powerful shove of its hind legs the guardian sprung from the wall directly at the offworlder. Raxe dropped again, but the beast was much closer this time. He could not fall quickly enough to clear the reach of the wolf-cat's massive forepaw as it twisted in the air and reached down for a sure grip on its prey.

The forepaw came down forcefully on Raxe's upper back. The needle pointed claws would have punched right through normal armor. On Raxe's impenetrable armor, though, the claws only screeched and sparked as the guardian sailed past.

One claw managed to graze along the flesh of the back of Raxe's exposed neck, just to the left of the hard lump of scar tissue that marked the entry point of the Finder's throwing dagger. The guardian's claw then hooked on the rim of Raxe's open-topped helm. To Raxe's good fortune, the helm slid easily off of his head. A couple of his long, thick locks were snatched painfully out of his scalp in the process, but Raxe knew it could have been much worse. It could have easily been his entire head hooked to that monstrous claw.

The force of the blow drove Raxe hard to the ground. He tried to catch himself as he did a moment earlier but he had been pushed with too much force. His articulated breastplate absorbed the force of the impact on his torso. His arms, though, from his wrists to his triceps, experienced a shocking jolt of pain from his fruitless attempt to break his fall.

Raxe took the briefest moment to right himself and that was all it took for the wolf-cat to catch him. The beast was on him before he could push himself up. It drove him back into the hard-packed earth face first with two powerful paws in Raxe's lower back.

DEMON OF LORR

Raxe turned his head so that the left side of his face smashed into the ground to keep from breaking his nose. The bitter stench of sulfur stung Raxe's nostrils so severely that he wished he *had* broken his nose. That stench, combined with the cloud of dust sending grit up his nose and down his throat, almost made him gag.

He was hopelessly pinned but managed to pull his head up and back so that the back of his head pressed against his armored left shoulder. From this close, the creature's pelt resembled a mess of pointed brown and gray knitting needles. He saw the scythe-like claws on the wolf-cat's rear left paw thrust over an inch deep into the rocky earth. He could also see his discarded headpiece just behind the wide cat's paw and realized just how precarious his situation had become. Raxe strained to turn to the left and looked up out of the corner of his eye. To his dismay, he saw the beast's wide wolfen head filling his vision.

The wolf-cat snuffed and panted while pressing its nose roughly into the ropy locks of hair on Raxe's head. The creature's breath stank of death and each exhalation was a near-blistering hot puff of steam. The canine muzzle slid down the back of his head until it reached his bleeding neck. Raxe cringed at the cold and slimy touch of the wolf-cat's nose. The rough wetness touched the paper-thin, but deep and bloody scratch and stung like rubbing alcohol and salt.

And then things got even worse.

The wolf-cat licked him.

The wide, rough, flat tongue slathered Raxe's jaw with saliva as thick and clingy as syrup and as acrid and sour as bile. Raxe coughed, gagged and spat. Tears ran uninhibited from his eyes, momentarily blinding him and streaming down his face to cut clean streaks across his dust-covered skin.

"Aaarrrrgh!" he cried, unable to hide his revulsion. He assumed the sudden outcry would startle the monster into snapping his head off, which would have been preferable to what was already happening.

But instead of feeling the awful claws and teeth of the beast, the immobilizing weight suddenly lifted. The stench

129

receded. The smell still lingered in his nose and at the back of his throat, but the cloud of that nauseating mixture of scents was no more.

Raxe pushed himself up slowly and raised his head. He was not sure what he would see and was thoroughly shocked when his vision cleared. The massive wolf-cat was a few yards away, lying on its belly and panting. The evil snarl was replaced by benign curiosity and something resembling recognition. Raxe realized that the beast did indeed recognize him. At the very least, it recognized his scent and knew he was a direct descendant of the Gatekeeper.

The beast batted Raxe's headpiece over to him with a flick of its huge left forepaw. Raxe, now on his knees, reached out to retrieve his headpiece with his right hand while wiping the sickening drool away from his face with his left, never taking his eyes off of the wolf-cat.

He finally looked over his shoulder to the crowd. All of them stared in stunned silence. A smile made its way across King Jax Grimhammer's broad, square face.

"Does this mean I passed your nasty ass test?" Raxe called.

The king of the Stonehammer Nation Dwarves laughed. It was a mighty guffaw that sparked a deafening cheer from the crowd of warriors seated behind him.

Chapter 4: Runners

4.1

"You want me to do *what*?" Shara Dune snarled. She writhed serpent-like beneath the soft bed furs, sliding from beneath the long, thin, sweat-slicked arm draped over her bare shoulder.

Mage Stratham Glund, the Second High Adviser to the Head Mage of the Kingdom of Cartha, propped himself up on his elbows, causing the covers to drop halfway down his waist to reveal his square shoulders, lean chest and flat stomach. He looked contrite but he repeated himself.

"You have been asked to travel to the north shores of Lake Onyx to kill the water witch Sabrina."

"The north shores?" Sabrina snapped. "They are at the foot of the Wyrm Mountains. That's dragon country!"

"The dragons have respected the Treaty for decades," Glund reminded.

Sabrina scoffed. "As far as we know. No one can say if they have or haven't plucked a stray traveler or three over the years."

"Our benefactor is well aware of this," Glund said. "You will be provided what is needed to complete this task. And he is more than happy to allow you to renegotiate your fee. Only tell me, and I will relay to him what it is you require."

At that, Shara Dune sat up and let the furs slide down to her hips. She let the mage feast his eyes on her glistening golden skin and more than ample bosom. At the same time, she let her spell of enchantment flow softly enough that the mage would not be able tell his lust from her magic. It was always easy to do at this precise time. The powerful mage always let his guard down with her for a short time after their lovemaking. This was when he was most malleable.

She was not keen on confronting the Mistress of the Sea. The idea of doing so at Lake Onyx, the water witch's home, made the prospect of facing her infinitely less appealing.

As powerful as Shara knew herself to be, she knew that Sabrina, in or near the water, was the most powerful elemental in the Known Lands. Shara would need all of the help their so-called 'benefactor' could provide, which she had no doubt would be significant. He provided that incompetent ass Tauran with the resources to capture a Child of the Old Ones, after all. Surely he could give her what she needed to best a mere elemental.

But that did not mean she would not gouge him for all she could. She took slow, deep breaths as she thought for a moment. The mage's eyes followed the hypnotic rise and fall of her perfect breasts as Shara Dune's subtle spell enveloped him. As a go-between, Shara knew Glund did not make the final decision. She could, though, make sure he pled her case and endorsed her with all of the desperate persuasion he could muster.

"A third of the Kingdom of Lorr," she said, making it sound like a concession. "I want everything from the Bountiful River to Hell's Mountains; from the southern shores of Lake Onyx to the Badlands and the northern edge of the Demon's Spine, to rule as I please without interference. I want an army of men to supplement my army of sand creatures. I ask you, wizard, is our benefactor prepared to pay such a price?"

For the first time since she had known him, Stratham Glund looked uncertain. He brushed away a long, dark brown strand of hair hanging near his eye.

"That is…quite a bit," he said. "I was authorized to pay whatever price you asked but I do not know if such a high price was anticipated."

A small, sly smile curved one corner of her elegant lips. "If you were authorized to pay anything, a price this high *must* have been anticipated. Our benefactor is obviously no fool. He would not have brought me into this campaign if he was not aware of my prowess…or my ambition."

Glund finally pulled his dark gray gaze away from her breasts and to her desert-sand colored eyes.

"But of course you are correct, lovely one. You shall have your third of the Kingdom of Lorr. If I must, I will make sure our benefactor meets your price."

Shara could see that he was completely under her power, more so now than ever. It was time to ask a question she had asked many times before without ever receiving a satisfactory answer.

"Just who *is* our benefactor, Stratham my lover?"

The mage stared longingly into her eyes for a long moment. "I'm sorry, Shara, but I am not certain. I merely take my orders from the First High Advisor to the Head Mage. He takes his orders directly from the Carthan Head Mage, who in turn follows the king's commands. I can only assume our benefactor is one of them, or perhaps someone with deep enough pockets to curry the king's favor."

"Hmmmm," Shara mused thoughtfully. She wondered, and not for the first time, if she should try to move up to the next rung of the ladder.

Had the time come for her to turn her charms and beguiling magic onto the First High Advisor, Mage Michael Roderick?

Perhaps, she thought, *after this mission*. "Tell me, you beautiful man," she purred. "Just how I am to kill the water witch?"

4.2

The MD-500 Defender helicopter sped along somewhere over Kentucky at nearly two hundred miles per hour. The sun had set a half hour earlier and a cloudy winter haze obscured both starlight and moonlight. The black special ops helicopter easily blended into the dark night sky. Dan flew low and stayed over sparsely populated rural areas to minimize the risk of being spotted.

Lisa held the sides of her seat with a white-knuckled grip as Dan piloted the chopper. She had never ridden in a helicopter and the experience was terrifying, especially under these circumstances. It was too dark to tell where they were, and from the air, Lisa doubted she would recognize their location, anyway.

There were lights in the distance that clearly defined a small town, tiny dots of light that stood out in the darkness just beyond a wide black void that stretched out in a lazy, southeastern curve. It reminded her of a giant black snake whose head and tail were hidden within the blackness surrounding the city lights. She did not know if she should be relieved or afraid to be entering a town.

"So tell me about your husband," Dan said suddenly.

The unexpected question startled Lisa. She immediately became defensive. "You met him," she replied.

Dan nodded. "Yeah, under less than ideal circumstances. We were fighting and running for our lives. And I think it's fair to say he wasn't quite…himself at the time. I want to know how he is on a good day, on a normal day."

"Why?" Lisa challenged. "He's…" it felt weird to even utter the words but she did anyway. "He's across the WorldGate."

"Just curious," Dan said. "I'm just wondering what my grandson has to deal with."

He actually wanted to know about Lisa more than Joel, and he knew that she would be less than forthcoming about herself. She was still apprehensive, still unsure how much she should trust him, as she should have been.

134

Dan was hoping that if she started talking about Joel, he could glean something about her from the way she talked about her husband. It was an old trick he learned back when he was an operative. The way a person chose to describe something or someone they cared about usually said as much about them as it did the thing or person they were describing.

In addition to that, the act of talking about a pleasant and familiar subject could put the talker more at ease. They almost always became comfortable enough to talk more about themselves. The technique worked more often than not.

When Lisa asked: "What do you want to know about him?" Dan knew it was about to work again.

"I don't know," Dan said. "His general demeanor."

Lisa shrugged. "He's quiet, I guess. Not brooding or antisocial or anything…just quiet. It takes a while for him to open up to people. And he's very particular about who he opens up to."

"Ok," Dan replied. "Why do you think that is?"

"He came up rough," Lisa answered. "He was an orphan. When he was a toddler he was left at the harbor in Baltimore. A priest visiting from Chicago found him and brought him back there. He grew up in a Catholic group home…saw more of the streets than any kid should see. He was able to stay out of serious trouble but he watched a lot of his friends go the wrong way. That's why he has a problem with trusting people."

"What drew you to him?" Dan wanted to know.

Lisa grinned. "He was cute. Hell, he still is. There's something about his quiet nature that I've always found, I don't know, attractive. I could tell he liked me, too, so I wanted to get him to open up to me. When he did, that was it. He had me and I knew I had him."

Dan nodded. "So you like a challenge, huh?"

"No. I liked *him*."

"And you pursue your interests."

Lisa's eyes narrowed. "I thought you wanted to know about *Joel*."

"I do," Dan insisted.

"Are you sure the organization can't track us?" Lisa asked, abruptly changing the subject.

"Pretty sure," Dan answered, inwardly cursing his luck. Lisa was a clever one.

She frowned. "What do you mean 'pretty' sure?"

"I disabled the GPS and every tracking device I could find," Dan assured. A wince flashed across his face so quickly that Lisa almost missed it. He went silent for a long moment, taking slow, deep breaths. Just when Lisa was about to ask if he was all right, the old man went on.

"There could be more devices that I didn't find. But those guys have access to jets. If they knew where we were they'd have us by now."

Lisa leaned forward to take a closer look at Dan. "Are you OK? You look tired."

"So do you," Dan returned petulantly. "But I'm not complaining."

"We've been flying for hours," Lisa said, ignoring the insult. She knew that the older man had to be exhausted and probably in pain from so much physical exertion. She made an effort to be patient with his unusually surly attitude. "How much fuel does this thing have left? When can you land?"

"When will you go to sleep?" Dan snapped irritably. They were nearly out of fuel, which added to his anxiety. Dan kept that to himself.

"I'm not sleepy," Lisa said with a measured tone. "But I *am* air sick. How long can you fly with the stench of vomit all around you?"

Dan frowned. "That's gross. Not ladylike at all."

"I don't feel ladylike," Lisa grumbled. "I feel sick."

"OK girl," Dan relented. "We're about to land, anyway. Why don't you close your eyes?"

"That might not be a bad idea," Lisa agreed. She closed her eyes and gripped the sides of her seat even harder.

Keeping her eyes closed was indeed a good idea. She could feel their descent, mostly in her stomach, yet she managed to hold down her bile. She knew her queasiness would have been even worse if she had been watching the ground rise up to meet them.

Lisa took a deep breath to calm her stomach and breathed in the strong scent of fresh water. The unexpected smell surprised her into opening her eyes to find the source of the smell. When she saw black waves just below them reflecting the spotlight from the descending helicopter, she had to stifle a scream.

"What the hell, Dan?" she demanded. "Are you dropping us into the Mississippi?"

"I said close your eyes, girl," Dan snapped. "And that's not the Mississippi. It's the Ohio River. We're going to the Kentucky side."

"The Kentucky side? It looks like we're landing right in the middle of the river! Can this thing float on water?"

Dan sighed in poorly concealed irritation. "No. That's the point. We have to ditch this chopper and make sure it takes them a while to find it. Now sling that duffle and hold on to it tight and then close your eyes like I told you."

Lisa did as she was told. As soon as he told her to close her eyes – for the third time that day – she had a pretty good idea what was about to happen. And she was pretty sure it would not help her queasy stomach.

The impact of the chopper on the water was surprisingly mild but Lisa squeezed her eyes tighter when she heard the loud splash. The sound did not last long, though. An instant later her ears were popping and the relatively firm and dry feeling of the bucket seat turned into an uncomfortably wet and spongy sensation on her bottom. She opened her eyes and they bulged when she saw the two of them were sitting on the ground atop a rise on the south bank of the river.

"I'll never get used to that," she said.

"You won't get a chance to," Dan said in a weak, tired voice. "Not for a while, anyway."

"Dan, what's wrong?"

"Just tired, that's all. I'm two hundred years old. Remember? But it's nothing a good night's sleep won't fix."

Lisa watched as the helicopter, with its propellers slowing down but still turning, sank in the middle of the dark river. The slowing propellers threw water onto them and well past them before they finally stopped spinning. The light from the chopper spotlights blinked out and cast them into complete darkness. Lisa realized with alarm that the chopper was their only transportation. They were still several miles north of the city.

"Where are we gonna get a good night's sleep?" Lisa wondered aloud. "Are you going to blink us to a nice warm hotel?"

"I wish," Dan said tiredly. "The magic I used today took a lot outta me, more than I thought it would. It's been a while since I cast this many spells in such a short period of time."

Not to mention all the running and shooting holding that shield against so much firpower, Lisa thought. "So how are we gonna find somewhere to sleep?"

"We're just outside of Paducah." Dan offered with a sly smile. "I've got connections here."

Lisa could easily tell his smile was forced. His eyelids were drooping and the set of his thin, wispy white eyebrows betrayed his discomfort. Dan was tired and most likely in significant pain.

He reached over and gently pulled the duffle bag strap from Lisa's shoulder and slid it to his side. He rummaged through it for a few seconds and retrieved a wide-angle flashlight. He stood the flashlight on its square flat end and turned it on to its lowest setting to give them some light. He used the light to fish out one of the many disposable cell phones he stowed in their large duffle, turned it on and started to dial.

Lisa was too tired and distracted to pay attention to the phone call. The sound of Dan's voice, the lapping of the waves, and the sounds of the city drifting along the winter breeze faded into the background of her consciousness. She stood up and walked closer to the top of the sloping rise and gazed out into the dark sky.

Her mind was still reeling from all that was happening and had happened, but when she started thinking about her husband again, her nervousness started to fade. Instead of worrying about where he was and what he might be doing, she thought about how happy their reunion would be, how she would hug him with all of her strength and kiss his full lips. The memory of his warmth and strength relaxed her, galvanized her, made her forget about everything else and filled her with a sense of harmony that she feared she might never feel again. She knew that everything she was going through would be worth it when she got to see Joel again.

She turned back to Dan with a renewed vigor. And then she noticed a tear on the right shoulder of his wool overcoat. A dark stain surrounded the tear. There was not quite enough light to see the color of the stain but Lisa knew what it was.

"You're bleeding," she said, rushing over and kneeling by his side. "I didn't see it in the helicopter because I was sitting to your left. You should've said something."

"It just started bleeding a few minutes ago," Dan admitted.

"What happened? How did you get cut?"

"Not a cut," Dan said. "It's a bullet-graze."

Lisa stared for several breaths to let the words sink in. Finally she asked: "They were shooting at us hours ago. How the hell are you just now starting to bleed?"

"That's part of why I'm so worn down," Dan explained. "I've been using a spell to keep the wound from bleeding. That and the teleportation spells are getting to me."

"Why not just use a healing spell?" Lisa asked.

Dan shook his head tiredly. "Don't know one. Healing spells are too complex. Shanderah couldn't teach me any real healing spells with our link across the WorldGate. Our communication was only audible, sort of a psychic telephone. A healing spell requires symbols and hand gestures that she couldn't explain verbally."

"Well," Lisa said thoughtfully, "Maybe I could..."

"Try your magic?" Dan asked. "Hell, it's worth a try."

"So how do I do it?" Lisa asked.

"Hell if I know," Dan said. "I just told you I don't know any healing spells."

"You know about magic," Lisa countered. "Is there, maybe, some general way to focus it?"

"It takes years to learn how to feel your own inner magic, Lisa, let alone focus it."

"Why?" Lisa persisted.

Dan found himself so impressed with her curiosity that he overcame his exhaustion and pain-fueled irritability.

"Because it takes a level of concentration that few people have instinctively," Dan began. "You have to be able to clear your mind of everything, if you can. Or at the most, find one thing to concentrate on, something that will allow you to relax your mind, like the cliché of a hypnotist swinging a pendant back and forth. The goal is to open your perceptions to the magical energy within you. The idea is if you can free your mind of all distractions, you'll notice the radiation of magic within the core of your being."

Lisa nodded her understanding. "I can do that."

She had just done it, in fact, when she was thinking about Joel just moments earlier. This time, she would concentrate on Dan's wound. She seated herself comfortably beside Dan and carefully took the torn edges of the rip in his overcoat in each hand, along with the torn cotton sweater beneath it and the thermal long-sleeve shirt that was stuck to his skin by his coagulating blood. A light tug opened each tear enough for her to see the wound in dim glow of the flashlight. It reminded her of a wound she once saw after shaving the fur from the shoulder of a hunting dog that was grazed by a stray round from a careless hunter.

With quite a bit of effort, she managed to block out that memory. She then tuned out the distant noises around her. It was easier the first time because she was thinking about Joel. It was easy to lose herself in his memory. It was a little tougher with this nasty wound but she found a way.

The cold night breeze became non-existent to her, as did the smell of the river. The last sensation she banished was the sound of her breathing. In a matter of minutes her was world became the thin, two-inch long rend in Dan's brown flesh slowly oozing crimson over his skin. Before long she could feel strange warmth close to her heart.

DEMON OF LORR

The warmth throbbed outward and through her body in time to the pulsing of the blood flowing from Dan's injury. Lisa embraced that warmth.

That was when she heard the whispers.

They seemed to be coming from everywhere at once. She heard whispers rising from the ground all around like a slow exhalation of breath, soft chitters floating along distant breezes, murmurs drifting down from the sky.

The sound took on the characteristics of an audience in a packed auditorium. The various mumbling tones were infused with curiosity and excitement, surprise and expectation, as if the audience was as aware of her as she was of it. There were far too many voices for her to distinguish any words. She believed she would be able to hear the words if she tried, to follow a specific conversation if she narrowed her attention to it, but she did not want to.

The sound was not at all cacophonous or distracting. To the contrary, the strange jumble of tones and pitch and cadences all fused into a hypnotically sublime harmony that only fortified the warm energy flowing through her.

She visualized the energy coursing through her arm and to her fingertips before lifting her hands and cupping them over Dan's wound. She closed her eyes, and with the image of that pulsing line of blood and torn flesh frozen in her mind, she visualized the staunching of the blood flow. And then she visualized pink strands of tissue forming and pulling away from the edges of the open wound. Those strands began to slowly intertwine and overlap, stitching themselves together from one end to the other. When they were done, she visualized the bloody tear as a thin, swollen line of scar tissue.

Lisa took a deep breath, released it and then removed her hands. Her heartbeat quickened with expectancy, she peered at the wound.

It was still open and weeping just as it had been before her effort to heal him.

"Damn," she whispered. "Did you feel anything?"

Dan shook his head sympathetically. "Honestly? No, I didn't, at least not in my arm. I felt *something*, though. There was some magic moving but it wasn't anything I could identify. Then again I didn't expect to. Very few people – especially non-wizards – can even feel their magic on their first try. Manipulating it on the first try is almost unheard of."

"*I* felt something, too," Lisa said. "It was almost like a wave of warm water flowing through me. I was able to direct it through my hands."

"I can't confirm or deny what you felt, Lisa. All I can say is I didn't feel anything near my wound. I'm sorry."

Lisa waved her hand dismissively. "Don't worry about it. There's more than one way to hold a cat." She pulled the duffle over and reached inside with both hands.

"That's 'skin' a cat, isn't it?" Dan asked with a smirk.

"I'm a vet," Lisa said. "I heal cats. I don't skin them."

"So you're a cat lady, too, I suppose."

"Damn right," Lisa said absently. "Here we go," she continued, an excited and pretty smile brightened her face when she pulled out two small packets in one hand and a slightly larger packet in the other. "This is alcohol, steel, and polydioxane."

Dan cocked an eyebrow. "If I didn't know better I'd think that was some kind of witches' brew."

Lisa chuckled. "The steel is a little curved needle," she explained, indicating the smallest packet. "The alcohol: these disinfectant swabs; and the polydioxane is the suture. It dissolves as the stitched wound heals. Unfortunately, though, I don't have any anesthetic."

Dan bit his lip more than once when Lisa went to work stitching up his wound. He wished he had packed some whiskey, but he had not had a drink in over three years.

He had that last drink when he was attempting to calm his frayed nerves when Ryan, his only grandchild and only close living relative, went across the WorldGate the first time. Before then it had been almost thirty years between drinks. This would have been a good time for one more sip of the strong stuff.

With no liquor to be had, Dan fell back onto his meditation. He closed his eyes, took deep, steady breaths and thought happy thoughts. Recollections of pleasant times with Cynthia, his only child, and Ethel, Cynthia's mother and Dan's wife of more than fifty years, easily pushed all thoughts of pain to the periphery of Dan's consciousness. He remembered the three of them ice-skating on frozen ponds in rural northern Illinois and every-man-and-woman-for-themselves snowball fights in the wintertime; holding Ethel's hand in one hand and Cynthia's in the other on trips to Lincoln Park Zoo in the summertime.

Any extended thoughts about his deceased wife and daughter, however, no matter how pleasant, always eventually led to melancholy. But Dan would hold on to the pleasant thoughts for as long as he could.

"It's over," Lisa told him. "I'm done."

Dan's eyes popped open in surprise. "That was quick, and not all that painful."

Lisa shrugged. "I get a lot of practice."

"I can see that," Dan returned. He half-smiled as he inspected her work. "I've had a few field-dressed wounds before. This one was by far the quickest and the neatest."

"Almost like magic, huh?" Lisa teased.

"Almost, girl," Dan nodded as Lisa put a long, wide bandage over the stitches. "Almost."

4.3

Dan and Lisa looked to their right at the long, narrow cone of a headlight beam across the river a few hundred yards to the south. They followed it towards its source until the light disappeared behind the tree line that ran parallel to the river about fifty yards behind them. The cone grew narrower and more intense, revealing a small break in the tree line through which a well-worn path emerged.

A mid-size Ford sedan pushed the cone of light ahead of it to cut a swath through the darkness. A bright police style spotlight mounted outside the front driver side window sent another bright beam of light through the darkness. It bounced and swiveled until it eventually found them. The sedan slowed and then turned in their direction.

Lisa turned to the elderly Child of the Old Ones. "You really trust this guy, Dan?"

"Hell no," Dan answered.

"Then why call him?"

"Because he can help us, and we need help. Don't worry. He's a good guy, just like his dad."

Lisa looked puzzled. "But you don't trust him."

"I don't trust anyone," Dan admitted. "Hell, I barely trust my own grandson."

"Who is this guy?"

"His name is Nathaniel Rogers II," Dan told her. "An ex-cop. His dad and I were good friends and did some work together back in the forties. We kept in touch after the war. I came down here a couple of times after he moved in with Nathaniel II here and his wife. Nate died about four years ago. I just found out when I talked to his son earlier tonight."

Dan stood, hefting the big duffle as he did so. He slung it over his shoulder, unzipped the bag, and slipped his left hand into the opening. Lisa heard the telltale click of the arming mechanism on Dan's radically modified shotgun.

A light within the car came on to reveal a middle-aged man with dark brown hair that had gone gray on the sides and back. Dan looked hard at the face within as the car pulled closer. After a slight nod of satisfaction, the disarming click sounded from within the duffle just before the wrinkled brown hand withdrew from the bag.

"That's him," Dan said with a grin. "Same ugly mug as his dad."

As he came nearer Lisa could see more of the driver's features. The corners of Nathaniel's thin lips curved downward in what appeared to be a perpetual frown. His nose was of average length, but it had a bulbous tip and a slight turn as if it had been broken. He had sad, tired eyes with crow's feet almost as deep the much older Dan's. Those eyes turned onto Lisa as he slowed to a stop. He left the headlights burning but angled the car so that they were not shining directly on them. His eyes remained on her in a way that made her slightly uneasy.

"I don't like the way he looks," Lisa declared.

Dan grinned. "You mean you don't like his appearance or you don't like the way he looks at you?"

"I mean both."

Nathaniel stopped staring at Lisa when he climbed out of the car, finally turning his attention to Dan.

"Nathaniel," Dan called with a brief smile that turned quickly into a consoling visage. "It's good to see you. And again, I'm sorry about your dad. He was a great guy."

Instead of the standard appreciative smile and nod, the frown remained. "That would've been nicer to hear at the funeral," Nate called back, making no effort to step closer.

"I know," Dan admitted. "And I'm sorry. The last time I talked to him I knew he was sick. I planned to come down but I had a family emergency, too."

And indeed he did. Dan had talked to Nate two weeks before he had his first clear vision concerning the crisis that had come to be called – as explained by the Head Mage Rionn Lorr when he came across the WorldGate to retrieve Joel and Ryan – the Cursed Opening.

After having that vision, Dan devoted all of his days and nights to communicating with old Shanderah across the WorldGate. Together they made preparations for the ultimately successful campaign.

But how could he tell that to Nathaniel? A "family emergency" sounded incredibly lame even to Dan's ears. The truth, on the other hand, would surely make Nathaniel think he was crazy and ruin any chance of getting the younger man's assistance.

"A family emergency kept you from calling for almost four years?" Nathaniel asked. He sighed and his frown at last turned into a smile. "Look, I'm sorry, Dan." His voice softened as he walked to Dan and extended a hand in greeting. "I shouldn't be like that. I'm glad you finally made it down. You're looking well."

Dan heard the surprise in Nathaniel's voice, as well as a hint of bitterness. Nathaniel was no doubt wondering how Dan could look so well while his father, a younger man, had already succumbed to the ravages of age. Dan was well accustomed to that look. He had seen it more than once over the course of his long life.

Dan took Nathaniel's hand and gave it a firm shake. "Thanks. And thanks for letting me off the hook, kid."

Nathaniel chuckled. "I haven't been a kid for a long time."

"You are compared to me!" Dan boasted.

"Speaking of kids," Nathaniel said, returning his leer to the attractive young African-American woman. "Who's this pretty little thing?"

"This is Lisa," Dan said. "I'm looking out for her for her husband."

Nathaniel grinned wolfishly. "Husband? That's too bad."

Lisa tossed him a quick, forced smile.

"What's going on here?" Nathaniel asked, tearing his gaze away from Lisa. "You call me in the middle of the night asking me to fly you somewhere in my plane. You show up mysteriously in the middle of nowhere, walking, no less. With – what is that, anyway?" Nathaniel indicated the tear in Dan's coat and the stitched wound beneath it. "A patched-up bullet wound?"

"It's a long story. I'll fill you in on the way. And don't worry about the wound. Lisa did a good job sewing me up so there won't be any blood stains in your car."

"That's good," Nathaniel said. He moved a deceptively swift hand into the big hip pocket of his heavy trench coat and pulled out an automatic pistol. "Because she won't be able to tend to it with cuffs on her wrists. Now drop the bag."

"Shit," Dan swore softly.

It was chilly in Paducah but not as cold as it was in Chicago. It definitely was not cold enough for the coat Nathaniel wore. Dan cursed himself for not seeing this coming. Exhaustion and pain were no excuses. If he did not trust anyone, he should have been prepared for this possibility. Dan knew his body was getting too worn down for this type of action but he had always believed his mind was more than sharp enough. Now he had to wonder if he was too old physically and mentally.

A few minutes later the three of them were in the sedan going south on Interstate 24. Dan and Lisa had their hands cuffed tightly and painfully behind their backs with plastic ties. Dan leaned forward.

"Why are you doing this Nathaniel?" Dan implored. "Your dad and I were friends. Good friends. He'd want you to help me."

"I know," Nathaniel affirmed. "You know what he told me just before saying good bye to me and mom? He said: 'If Dan ever needs your help, you help him and don't ask questions.' He made me promise him that on his deathbed.

"You were supposed to be that good of a friend to him and you couldn't make it to the funeral? You couldn't even make a goddamned phone call? Mom was heartbroken over it. I might not know you the way they did, but what I do know, I don't like."

"So you're kidnapping us?" Lisa interjected, her outrage overcoming her fear and common sense.

"That's just one of the reasons," Nathaniel snapped back. "The other reason is a report that went out over the police bands. I still listen to them, you know. It's a hobby. The feds put an APB out on an older man and young woman who stole a chopper, killed some people. They're covering a three hundred mile perimeter from Indianapolis looking for them. And now you two turn up at the riverside?

"Dad never talked about what you two did in the war in detail, but I always knew it was high-level covert stuff. That's the only reason I'm not handing you off to the Paducah PD.

"As soon as I heard your voice on the phone, asking what you were asking, I knew it was you the feds are looking for. It shocks the hell out of me that you're still doing this kind of thing in, what? Your nineties? That's freaking unbelievable. But the way dad used to talk about you, he sure thought it was possible."

That was because Nate the first knew Dan's secret. He was with Dan during their POW extractions. The night before their first mission, Dan warned Nate that he might see some curious things. He refused to give any details, knowing some things simply had to be seen to be believed. Nate scoffed and and dismissed Dan's vague claims as exaggerated bravado.

That was before he actually saw the magic of the Shield of Innocents while taking heavy fire from the enemy.

Dan had to perform a few other feats of magic during their various missions. The people they rescued thought Dan was performing miracles. Dan actually explained his abilities to Nate, but Nate never really believed him. Nate and the others who witnessed Dan's abilities thought he was an avenging angel sent by God Himself.

The only reason they did not tell their superiors was because Dan convinced them that the brass would think they were crazy. He knew they would be Section Eight-ed while Dan was shut down so they could investigate how he convinced so many people that he could work miracles. He always assumed some of them would tell their families. Apparently Nate had spoken very highly of Dan to his wife and children without going into specifics. Nate had always been a smart, practical guy.

"Think about it, Nathaniel," Dan urged. "There's a reason your dad told you not to ask questions. Believe me when I

148

tell you that those weren't the feds we were fighting. That was a different group with a long, dangerous reach. That's why we need you to honor your father's wishes."

"I'm a retired police officer," Nathaniel argued. Dan could hear a twinge of guilt in the younger man's voice. "I still respect the law. You're not even denying that you've done the things they're saying. I can't condone murder. I have to turn you in."

Dan stared hard at Nathaniel through the rear view mirror. "How much is the reward?" he demanded.

Nathaniel would not meet Dan's gaze through the mirror when he answered. "Dad worked his ass off but had almost nothing at the end. Mom is in a hospice. Margaret and I are on a fixed income. Between the funeral, burial, the hospice, and our normal expenses, we can't make ends meet."

Nathaniel's sad, guilty expression suddenly turned angry and he glared back at Dan through the mirror.

"I don't have to justify myself to you, old man," he snarled. "You're the one on the wrong side of this. You've murdered people, for God's sake. I'm doing the right thing and I deserve to be rewarded for it."

"We haven't murdered anyone," Dan argued. "Every life was taken in self-defense. These people don't want to arrest us. They want to kill us."

"I'll let the FBI sort all that out," Nathaniel said.

Dan sighed heavily and sat back. He looked out at the stars slowly moving past in the night sky. He tilted his head back onto the backrest and closed his eyes, his shoulders slumping with the weight of his exhaustion.

Nathaniel looked at Dan through the rear view mirror and knitted his eyebrows and then shifted he eyes to Lisa.

"Is he all right?" Nathaniel asked with genuine concern.

"No," Lisa said quickly. "He's an old man. We've been on the move for days with very little sleep. He's lost a lot of blood from a gunshot wound. Of course he's not all right."

Nathaniel was silent for a time. Lisa, sitting on the passenger side of the back seat, could see a mixture of both anger and concern on Nathaniel's face.

"Maybe we should go to the hospital," Nathaniel offered.

"No," Lisa said. "You may not believe us, but our lives are in danger. They may be watching the local hospitals."

"I'm turning you in, anyway," Nathaniel argued. "I might be pissed at Dan, but I don't want him to die. Why not get him some medical assistance while the feds are en route?"

Lisa's voice lowered with sincere worry. "We're as good as dead once you turn us over to who *you think* is legitimate law enforcement, and probably sooner if you take us to a hospital. His wound isn't serious. He just needs a little time to recover. Please, could you at least let him get a good night's rest before you turn us in?"

There was a long pause before Nathaniel grunted. "I'll let you stay in the shed behind the house overnight. But the feds are going to be there first thing in the morning."

"Thanks," Lisa said. She glanced over at Dan and wished she could rub the worried crease in her brow. Dan was completely still with the exception of the slow rise and fall of his chest. *I hope you have a plan, Dan.*

4.4

Joel was once again greeted by acute pain upon awakening. This time, however, he made it a point not to react to the throbbing in his ribs and legs or to the dull ache in his arms, which was as persistent as ever. His hollow stomach cramped agonizingly but he controlled his breathing and maintained his relaxed posture. While he was not even close to being used to the suffering, the anguish was familiar enough for him to temporarily force it to the back of his mind so that he could once again listen to his surroundings before revealing that he was awake.

None of the sounds were new. He could hear footfalls both near and far, dull moans from other prisoners, the conversations of passing guards as well as the low sounds of discussions by jailers somewhere in the dungeons. Their words were unintelligible at first, distorted by echoes and muffled by distance and closed doors. As he continued to listen, though, he could eventually make out some of the words. His ears were becoming attuned to the low sounds and echoes in the way one's eyes became attuned to darkness. Finally, he listened to his cellmate's slow, even breathing.

"I am Dayna," she said, startling him.

Joel looked up in surprise. "Oh," he said sarcastically. "I had to catch a severe ass-beating for you to trust me enough to finally tell me your name. How did you know I was awake that time?"

"An ass-beating?" Dayna returned. "I do not know what violence against pack animals has to do with anything. I've simply concluded that you are not a spy for that fool Tauran. As for knowing you were awake, you did a good job of keeping your breathing even, but your eyes gave you away. They still shift in reaction to sounds. Eye movements of a dreaming person are more random. Those in a deep sleep have barely any eye movements at all."

"How long was I out this time?"

"Long enough to miss another meal," Dayna answered.

"The cramp in my stomach is testifying to that," he said with a grimace. He looked up at his arms, which were once again suspended above his head. The chains were taught and had been re-fed through the hole in the wall as before.

"Another meal is only a couple of hours away," Dayna continued, "but if they had not force fed you water during your unconscious states you likely would have died of thirst by now."

"I'll remember to thank them," Joel said dryly.

"You're talkative again," Dayna noted, "like you were when you woke up the last time. Will you be falling deaf and dumb again, as well?"

"I was in shock, I guess," Joel explained. "Now I'm resigned."

"To what, Joel?"

"You're pretty talkative yourself all of a sudden," Joel observed. "Why is that?"

"As I have said, I no longer think you are a spy, and I would like to know what you really are. Whether you can control it or not, you have the ability to escape this place. You can be of use to me."

"I can't help you, lady – "

"Dayna," she corrected in an icy tone. "A 'lady' is an aristocratic showpiece, a trophy for fat, greedy lords and politicians. I am Dayna, Joel. Please address me so."

"I can't help you, *Dayna,*" Joel returned with an exaggerated bow of his head that sent shocking pain through his neck and shoulders. After a sharp intake of breath he exhaled slowly and continued. "The ability you're talking about only seems to show up when I'm about to die. That's why I could break those chains when my asthma was killing me but those soldiers could beat me to a pulp."

"They called you 'offworlder' before," Dayna noted. "Is that true?"

"I guess," Joel said with a slightly painful shrug.

"How did you get here?" she pressed.

Joel thought he saw that same spark of hope in her eyes that she showed him when he broke free of his constraints.

He did not want to stoke the flames of that false hope but he was not going to lie to her, either. So he looked at the floor and said nothing.

"Did the Head Mage bring you here with the WorldGate Key?" Dayna pressed. "Did Raxe accompany you to Lorr?"

Joel looked up at her. "How do you know about all that?"

"The Children of the Old Ones are no secret," Dayna told him, "neither is the Hell Key or the WorldGate key. What *is* a secret is why you're here."

"Doesn't matter," Joel said quietly. His chin dropped once again to his chest. "I'm gonna die here."

"You said you were 'resigned' a moment ago," Dayna recalled. "Is that what you are resigned to? Death?"

"What else?" Joel answered. "They're obviously keeping me alive because they want to know something." He shook his head slowly. "But I don't know anything. It won't take them long to realize that, and when they do, I'm dead."

"But you said your power comes to bear when you're about to die. They can't kill you."

"Not directly, I think," Joel agreed. "But who's to say they can't keep me here like this until my body breaks down on its own?"

"You prefer them killing you straightaway to this prolonged torture."

"When the end result is the same either way?" Joel asked, "Yes."

"Then you're a fool," Dayna chided. "As long as you have breath, you have a chance."

Joel frowned. "What's that, some kind of joke about my asthma?"

"It's the truth," Dayna told him. "You're smart enough to realize that they're keeping you alive for a specific purpose, but not smart enough to know that you can use that to your advantage. You do not even try to think of a way to escape. That's foolish."

"If you got any ideas, Dayna, I'm all – "

His sentence was cut short by a piercing female scream that ripped down the outer hall.

"Torture?" Joel asked.

"The worst kind," Dayna sneered. "One of the female prisoners is being raped."

"Damn..."

"Yes!" Dayna snapped. "Damn them all."

Joel looked at the door, his head turned slightly to the left in the direction from which the pitiful sounds came. His hopelessness turned to frustration as the cries, soon accompanied by rough male grunts and taunting laughter, assaulted his ears. A thought occurred to him, causing him to look hesitantly back over to Dayna.

"Yes," she said softly, answering the unspoken question in his eyes. "It has happened to me, as well, although not as often as the other women in these dungeons. The false baron has picked me to be his 'exclusively' and he forbids the others from touching me. Thankfully he spends most of his time away from the dungeons. It is a nightly occurrence for the other women. You've been unconscious more often than not so you have been lucky enough to not notice."

"Who is that poor girl?" Joel asked.

"Someone's daughter, perhaps," Dayna said angrily. "Or someone's mother, someone's wife."

Joel immediately thought of Lisa and the men who had threatened to rape her back on that Illinois highway. What would happen to her if she were captured? He had no confidence that the old man would be able to keep her safe, no matter how much Ryan insisted he could.

Joel tried to dismiss his wife's memory just as quickly as it had popped into his mind. He had too much to worry about already. The last thing he needed was to torture himself with even more troubling thoughts. But the terrible wails down the dark hall would allow him no peace.

"From what I gather," Dayna went on, eager now to talk if for no other reason than to distract them both from the disturbing sounds.

"Most of the prisoners here are former high-ranking officials of the county, their top aides, and members of their families, many of them female family members."

"What happened?" Joel questioned. "Did Tauran take over the town?"

"It would seem so," Dayna confirmed.

"How could the kingdom let this happen?" Joel wondered. "From the little I know of Rionn Lorr, this doesn't seem like something he would condone."

"He and King William would not, if we were in the Kingdom of Lorr," Dayna agreed. "But we are in Eastedge, a barony in the borderlands situated in the southwestern foothills of the Hell's. This is the Darshay side of the mountain range, but this county has only the slightest association with the monarchy.

"The town of Eastedge, or Eastedge proper, as I believe it is called, is the main economic center of the barony. It lies a in a section of the Serpent's Way Valley that's wider by half than the rest of the valley. The Kingdom of Darshay recognizes the Eastedge barony for taxing purposes only. For the most part, Eastedge governs itself."

"So what is this, some sort of outlaw border town that changes leadership all the time?" Joel wanted to know.

"Understand," Dayna replied, "I am not from this region. What I know about the current state of this area is from what I've overheard from conversations among prisoners and guards. What little I know of this area's history is from gossip that floated to my home town from across the Kingdom of Lorr."

Joel shrugged as much as he could manage in his precarious position. "That's a hell of a lot more than what I know. Let's hear it." He, too, was anxious for a distraction from the terrible noises.

"I would have to say that Eastedge was once, when I was but a child, exactly as you assumed," Dayna verified. "The land in this valley is not fertile, water is in short supply. That makes this area inhospitable to farmers, millers, trappers, and hunters. What little work there was could only be found in the rock quarries and iron mines in the surrounding outskirts of the county, and those were slowly being stripped bare.

"It was a hard place to make a living, which meant only the hardest and hardiest could thrive here. The reigns of leadership in this town went to the highest bidder or the most ruthless mercenary.

"More than twenty years ago, it is said that a wealthy old nobleman and his sons from the northern coast of Darshay purchased the county from its mercenary lord for far more than the area was worth. The nobleman became the baron and invested in the land. He funded excavations to expand the quarries. In his efforts, he not only expanded the quarries, he found an underground spring that supplies enough water to supply modest farming and small livestock. They turned Eastedge into a thriving community."

"So what happened?"

"From what I gather," Dayna explained, "A little over two years ago, Tauran led a small army on a siege against the county. The army was made up of low-ranking castaways from the Legion Midnight who had been stripped of their armor by the King of Lorr and subsequently released and exiled because the kingdom did not have the facilities to jail Mar-dah's entire army. They came here and overwhelmed the local authorities."

A voice came from the next cell, startling both Dayna and Joel. "There is far more to the story than that, milady."

"Who in the seven hells are you?" growled Dayna, looking over her shoulder and talking at the wall behind her. That guarded, suspicious look quickly returned to her striking visage.

"This nobleman to whom you refer was not some power hungry opportunist like his predecessors. Saying he turned this region into a thriving community is a gross understatement. He was a businessman who converted this county from a mining region with a few struggling taverns and trading posts into a prosperous mercantile community with a real government."

"Who are you, the county's PR director?" Joel asked.

"I have no idea what a 'PR director' is," the voice answered. "I am Bartholomew Northforest, the nephew of that very nobleman. He and my cousins rescued Eastedge from near ruin and turned it into one of the most important towns in eastern Darshay. And Tauran did far more than lead a simple 'siege' as you put it."

"Do tell," Dayna said sarcastically.

"He took over by bribing three of the lords of the four other estates that comprise this barony. He murdered or kidnapped loved ones of the other two, as well as those of several lords of the smaller houses who had the courage to stand against him.

"He's kept the support of the traitorous barons by collecting fewer taxes from them to pay to the crown. He makes up the difference by taking a larger share from those that opposed him. Under Tauran's incompetent leadership the region has begun to backslide toward its less scrupulous past. But we *will* win Eastedge back, no matter what it takes."

Joel listened to the story and tried his best to care but he could not. These medieval politics had nothing to do with him. It was a welcome but short-lived distraction and he quickly lost interest. He sighed and glanced around yet again at his alien surroundings.

What the hell was he doing here? The longer he stayed in this world, the more he hated it. He tried once more to tell himself that he was doing what he had to do in order to protect his family. But, as it had each time since he awoke in this cell, that idea rang hollow to him. How could he help them from a dungeon in a different world? He had already come to terms with the fact that there was no way he could make it back home. It was stupid to think otherwise.

As hopelessness threatened to engulf him once more, he noticed that the sounds of suffering and perverted amusement had ended. At least God, or the Lord Ascendant, as they said this side of the WorldGate, granted him that small reprieve.

Chapter 5: Decisions and Sacrifices

5.1

The dwarves' attitude toward Raxe and the rest of the group was completely changed after the offworlder passed the test. Their weapons were immediately returned to them. And then, amid incessant complaints from the Ranger Elf Rell Kallen about them wasting precious time, they were treated to a huge banquet. Once again the dwarves escorted them to their destination, this time with jokes of crude dwarven humor instead of threats and shoves.

Within an hour or so, the group was seated around a large dining table waiting for the king and his entourage to arrive. Tankards of mead sat in front of every guest, even the young Azhju'lestra. Raxe requested that her mead be replaced with milk or water. The husky dwarven serving woman gave him a strange look and then burst into laughter. She muttered something about the offworlder having a strange sense of humor as she moved on to serve another guest.

Mounds of roasted potatoes, carrots, and onions were wheeled around and served to the guests just before huge platters of braised meats accompanied with big earthen bowls filled with gravy were proffered. Raxe was not sure what kind of animals the dwarves could hunt or breed for food this far underground. Visions of moles and badgers and ground hogs and snakes danced in his head. But the meat was cut into unrecognizable chunks and smelled heavenly, so it was easy for him to squelch any curiosity about their source.

"We've no time for this foolishness!" the elf barked. "Do you idiots think the Dierglyorr is attending dinner parties?"

"But Bartok says it's the middle of the night, Ranger Kallen," Ethan said. "We may as well get a hearty meal and a night's rest before we set out again."

"Who cares what you think, boy?" the elf snapped.

The young soldier glared at the elf. "I have tried to be respectful of your rank in the Elven Rangers. But you're making it very difficult."

"Who cares what you think, boy?" the elf repeated.

"Ignore him, kid," Raxe advised. He turned to Rell Kallen. "You're free to go, elf," he reminded. "If you can find your way out of here."

The Ranger Elf had become just as baffled as Raxe within and under the Stonehammer Nation's region of Hell's Mountains. He simply sneered at the offworlder.

"I could show him the way out," Ethan offered. "If only to put a stop to his constant whining."

"As if you could, whelp," Rell Kallen taunted.

"But he can," Quick assured. "Even without the enhanced senses of an elf, Ethan is almost as gifted a tracker. And he has a perfect memory when it comes to direction and backtracking."

Based on what Rionn Lorr told him before just before they started their journey, Raxe believed Ethan's directional talent was an aspect of his gifted sight. He kept that information to himself, knowing that the Head Mage wanted to keep Ethan's gift a secret for now...even to Ethan.

"Of course, I could lead you back to the surface as well because I'm familiar with these caverns," Quick continued. "But you would have to say 'please' very convincingly."

The Ranger Elf ignored Quick's taunt and raised a thin eyebrow in response to the first part of the young changeling's statement. He turned his canted green eyes to Ethan for a moment before turning back to his meal. He teased himself with the thought of forcing the boy into leading him out, but to do that he would probably have to kill the offworlder, his daughter and the changeling.

Unfortunately for the elf, he still had need of at least one of the Children of the Old Ones.

"If I may, master Raxe," said a young brown haired woman with dark grey eyes, soft cheekbones and a dimpled chin. Raxe turned to the speaker sitting a few seats to his right. She was one of the surviving sky sleigh crew. They had been so quiet that Raxe had almost forgotten about them more than a few times.

"Please," he said. "What's your name?"

Her thin lips spread in a coy smile. "Morgana, sir."

"Just call me Raxe," he instructed. "I'm not into formalities. What's on your mind?"

"I wonder why they even had to test you at all," she began. "And why they are still in hiding. The Finder stole the Keys three years ago. What else are they safeguarding?"

"Habbit," the Ranger Elf interjected in a condescending tone. "Dwarves are not the most intelligent race in creation."

The dwarven attendants and guards at the door leveled hard stares at the Ranger Elf, but Rell Kallen made it a point to ignore them as he continued.

"They've lived this way for so long they know not what else to do with themselves."

Raxe shook his head. "It might not be a good idea to insult the people serving you your food."

Quick spoke up. "You question their intelligence? They've established a civilization under these mountains. They built ventilation systems to dispel the smoke from a massive forging complex and managed to exist without detection for two thousand years. I'd say such feats take a great deal of intelligence."

"If they are so intelligent," Rell Kallen countered, "why are they still hiding themselves? What are they afraid of?"

"We're afraid of nothing, insolent elf!" King Grimhammer thundered as he barged into the room.

As always, Listwhin and Bartok flanked him on the left and right. The king and his Head Mage stopped at the head of the table while Bartok continued on in Raxe's direction. The dwarven general lifted a leather sack about twice the size of Raxe's fist and set it heavily down in front of the offworlder.

"*This* is what we continue to guard," the general said reverently. "Look inside, offworlder."

Raxe undid the cloth string holding the package closed and opened the sack. He peered in for a few seconds and looked up at Bartok with more than a hint of confusion.

"What's this?" he asked. "Some kind of powder?"

"Tis ore," Bartok said. "Titan's Ore."

The eyes of every non-dwarf in the room, with the exception of the offworlder, went wide with disbelief and wonder. Raxe looked around at the group incredulously.

"Ok," he said. "So everyone knows what it is but me. Could somebody please fill me in?"

Bartok's broad chest rose with pride. "Tis the ore of the very same metal used t'fashion yer armor and weapon," he explained. "Our ancestors helped yer ancestors forge 'em. Once cast, Titan's Ore is impenetrable, as ye already know. T'is a natural property of the metal, but t'is also exceptionally receptive t'spells. It can be infused with magic t'fill any purpose ye choose."

Quick let out a breath. "Titan's Ore was said to be lost during the time of the Heaven's War. The only continent where it could be mined was obliterated."

"The only continent ye knew of," the king informed. "Only the gods knew of the ore under the Hell's, and they entrusted that secret t'the Stonehammer Nation along with the enchanted broadsword Keys."

The Ranger Elf's gaze darkened with suspicion. "And are we to believe that you will simply let us walk away from here with our knowledge of your great secret?"

"Fear not for ye' safety," Listwhin said with a sly smile. "This be the last of the Titan's Ore. The rest was exhausted during the War."

The promise seemed hollow to the Ranger Elf, as he was sure it did to the rest of the guests. He would keep an even closer watch on their hosts.

"Well, thanks, I guess," Raxe began. "I'm good with modifying weapons but I don't know the first thing about blacksmithing. I wouldn't know how to cast it into anything."

"We have master smiths that'd be honored t'assist a Child of the Old Ones," King Grimhammer assured. "The same way we assisted yer ancestors. Do ye' already have an idea of what ye'd want to forge with the Titan's Ore?"

Raxe thought about it for a moment. "I sure do."

5.2

Later that evening Raxe sat alone in his new quarters. The dwarves provided private rooms for every member of Raxe's party. They somehow managed to ventilate the small apartments with cool fresh air, much more pleasant than the stale air that permeated every other place he had been within the dwarfs' habitat. The offworlder was in deep thought about what exactly he would forge with his Titan's Ore when a knock sounded from the wooden door of his quarters.

"Come in," Raxe called.

Ethan opened the door, stepped into the room and then closed the door behind him. His normally bright, steel blue eyes seemed darker, and it was not from the pale torchlight that illuminated the room.

"I have a concern," Ethan began, with an expression that thoroughly underscored his words.

"Oh yeah?" Raxe asked. "What would that be?"

"Do not mistake my words for fear, Raxe, for I am not afraid. But I am concerned."

"There's nothing wrong with fear," Raxe assured. "Kept under control, fear keeps you alert, wary. So are you gonna tell me what you're concerned about?"

Ethan hesitated, not knowing exactly how to say what he was feeling. He decided the best way was to just say it.

"I am without magic," Ethan finally declared. "I have no enchanted weapon or exotic fighting skills. All of the other Hounds have fallen so I do not even have a team to work with." Ethan lowered his head and took a deep breath. Raxe had seen that expression before. It was the look of someone fighting back tears. Once the young Sureblade composed himself, he continued. "I've even lost the shard from Sollustre's Eye. I wonder what use I am to this expedition."

"Are you saying you want out?" Raxe questioned. "I'd understand. You and the other Hounds were meant to help if we faced demons, but since all of the other Hounds are gone…"

"I do not 'want out,' as you say," Ethan corrected. "I wish to stay. But I fear I would be more hindrance than help.

162

I could not even best one *Ken d'Zanir* on my own. If Quick and I face magic or some other great threat, Quick would be too busy keeping me safe to fight effectively."

"Your father didn't have the use of magic," Raxe countered. "But he managed to save my life and Shanderah's life on several occasions."

"And in the end he fell to the Finder," Ethan argued, "a bigger, stronger warrior. Yes, the Finder had dwarf-forged armor and Dragon-fang, but he had no magic. Yet he bested my father without receiving so much as a scratch. How can *I* expect to do half as well against more dangerous opponents?"

"Don't sell Meldrick short," Raxe advised. "And don't sell yourself short. Even without magic of his own, the Finder managed to kill more conjurers and magical creatures over the years than you or I could guess. Your father couldn't beat him, but if he hadn't faced him and slowed him down, the Finder would've killed Worldhopper before I could stop him and Mar-dah would have won. And to be honest with you, kid, I think you have a chance to be a greater warrior than your father."

Ethan shot him an incredulous look. "No offense, Child of the Old Ones, but it seems you engage in false flattery to boost my confidence."

"Meldrick had years of experience on the battlefield and he was a little heavier and stronger than you are now, but those are probably the only advantages he had over you, even at your young age. It might be hard for you to believe, but your quickness, natural fighting instincts and pure skill are as good or better now than your father's were when we worked together."

"So you are saying I should stay with the expedition?" Ethan questioned.

"I'm saying you have to decide for yourself," Raxe answered. "You have to listen to what your heart and head say is best."

"That's the problem," Ethan admitted. "My heart and head are at odds. My head reminds me that I do not possess magic like Quick. It tells me that I do not possess fighting skills approaching yours or the Ranger Elf's, and that I would merely get in everyone else's way. My heart, however, tells me to stay, to fight and sacrifice whatever I must to ensure the safety of my kingdom and her people."

Raxe grinned. "You wanna hear something funny, kid?"

"This seems a strange time for jokes," Ethan returned.

"Not that kind of funny," Raxe amended. "I mean strange. I've been having the same concerns about you since this expedition began. I was thinking about how much of a disadvantage you've been at since you joined us. I wondered if you were sticking around in some silly attempt to live up to your father's reputation.

"I've been trying to decide if your pride was blinding you to the fact that without magic or advanced martial training, you don't stand much of a chance against a lot of the threats you may face."

Ethan frowned in puzzlement. "First you say you would understand if I left. Then you sing my praises. Now you decry my shortcomings. I'm confused."

"I want you to tell me if you want to go back to the safety of Fort Bastion or if you want to stay here and risk your life against unbeatable odds," Raxe said.

Ethan did not hesitate to reply. "I want to help keep my kingdom safe. If that means staying and giving my life, I'll do so happily. If that means leaving so that I am not a distraction to the rest of the group, then that is what I will do, no matter how much it would pain me."

Raxe gave the young Sureblade a long, appraising stare. "I thought you might say that. You are your father's son, no question. That's why I had Stoll light the forge."

"What are you saying, Raxe?" Ethan asked.

"I'm saying courage without caution is foolhardy. Acting out of pride without common sense is just plain stupid. And it's no coincidence that you know the difference. That was the last thing I needed to know."

"Why did you need this knowledge?" Ethan asked. The offworlder's vagueness was starting to worry him.

"To decide whether or not to give you more of an advantage," Raxe revealed. "It's no coincidence that these dwarves had Titan's Ore. It's no coincidence that you're a part of this expedition. Go get your weapons and meet me in the smithy."

"The smithy?" Ethan echoed. He could feel gooseflesh rise on his arms and his heart began to race.

"Yeah," Raxe answered. "Like I said, it's no coincidence that you're here. If we didn't need you on this quest you wouldn't be a part of it. And since you don't have magic or 'exotic fighting skills,' as you put it, I've decided to give you both. I'm going to make a weapon for you."

5.3

To Master Mage Delthar, the scene was something straight out of hell. Sitting tall in his saddle, the bright midday suns revealed to him every morbid detail. This was the third time he had ridden out to scout the dread army that was slowly approaching Ridgeland, and the sight was worse each time. Once again the numbers of the walking dead had increased. He thought he had glimpsed hell at the Tyne River three years earlier. Never would he have believed that a sight more terrible than a legion of demons could exist.

The legion of walking dead was worse.

They meandered along the foothills in a wide, unorganized column with slow but inexorable determination. A reddish-brown, oily slick of dark blood, indistinguishable fluids and the suffocating stench of death and decay marked their passage.

Many of the wretched creatures did not walk at all. Some, whose legs were present but not functional, crawled on all fours like sickly quadrupeds. Others with only one leg or no legs at all dragged themselves along by clawing ruined, bony fingers into the earth.

Of those that could walk, their gaits covered the spectrum from stooped shuffling to drunken shambling to various degrees of limping to walking almost perfectly upright. And even though many walked upright, none of them would be mistaken for normal.

The fairer skinned among them were stricken with sallow complexions etched with thick bluish veins that crept beneath their skin like cracks creeping across damaged marble. The skin of the darker complected victims was ashen and paper-thin. And then there were those that had been in the ground so long that it was impossible to tell what their complexions had been when alive. Their flesh had turned gray with gouts of it sloughing off from various parts of their bodies.

Those with eyes stared blankly ahead with empty expressions. Those with only dark hollows in their eye sockets still managed to move straight ahead purposefully as if they could see precisely where they were going.

Their clothing varied greatly as well. It was easy from the garments of quite a few to tell whether they were reanimated dead or infected living. Burial robes – some yellowed and rotted with age while some newer and relatively fresher – along with the ceremonial leather armor of deceased soldiers, betrayed many of truly dead.

The men and women bearing weapons and dressed in more functional armor, including mail, leather, and steel plate, were soldiers and local law enforcement who were likely killed or wounded in battle against demons three years earlier, or within the last few days against the walking dead.

There were also those dressed in peasant garb. Farmers and millers, smiths and merchants, women in nun's robes and habits as well as men in priest's cloaks were easy to identify. Even housewives, and most dreadfully, more than a few children were among the grisly procession, unfortunate souls who were near the man of the house when three year old wounds transformed them into horrific parodies of humans.

Not long ago, Master Mage Delthar had witnessed such a transformation first hand. Back in Fort Bastion he watched as a decorated veteran of the Royal Army, Captain Johnican, succumbed to the plague. Even before his final transformation, the man had visibly deteriorated. He had gone from a tall, stout man to a lanky mess of skin and bones.

The Master Mage remembered feeling the quickening flutter of magic just before the doomed captain's change was complete. Johnican went insane, attacking Delthar and Geoffrey, the Minister of War. The Master Mage destroyed Johnican's body while retaining the captain's severed head for study. But even after burning the body to ash with a burst of whitefyre, the head lived on.

"What are you musing about, mage?" boomed Minister Geoffrey's baritone voice.

Delthar looked over his shoulder in fleeting surprise. Lost in thought as he was, he had nearly forgotten the Minister of

War and four soldiers of the royal infantry sat astride their horses just behind him.

"I would not call it 'musing,' minister," the Master Mage corrected. "I'd say 'dreading' is a more appropriate word."

"Indeed," Geoffrey concurred. He cupped his big right hand over his mouth and nose in a futile attempt to avoid the stench as he continued. "Their numbers have grown, have they not?"

The Master Mage looked out at the procession, which stretched lazily out to the east for over half a mile.

"Unfortunately, yes," he confirmed.

"It pains me deeply that we weren't able to warn away the defenders from Trader's Parish before they confronted the contingent of walking dead from the north. There were more than one hundred and fifty valiant fighters and less than a quarter of them survived. And now the fallen are part of this foul procession."

"There was nothing we could do," Delthar said. "The trappers attacked before we could inform them that the enemy could not be felled by mundane force of arms. We were lucky to save the few we did."

Both men turned their attention to the slow-moving force, taking care to stay at least fifty yards away. It was bizarre. As horrible as the foul army appeared, they were strangely peaceful. The only noises from the phalanx were the sounds of uneven footfalls and dragging sounds of those that pulled themselves across the earth, the clinking of metal from the soldiers' weapons and armor, and the many other instruments – hoes, spades, smithy hammers, pokers, kitchen knives, and so on – carried by the civilian victims.

All of them wore calm, vacant expressions, but both the Master Mage and the Minister of War knew how misleading those expressions were. While seeming calm and detached when undisturbed, they would explode into berserk savagery should their progress be impeded in any way.

"At this pace, they'll be at the border of Ridgeland in less than two days. How can we stop them?"

"I was just thinking about how we stopped Captain Johnican," Delthar said. The minister cringed just a bit at the mention of the poor soldier as Delthar went on. "If John the Firemaster were here, he could reduce the lot of them to ash."

"Your whitefyre could do the same," Geoffrey noted.

Delthar shook his head. "Their numbers are too great. Even if I had the raw power to unleash enough of it to do the job, the risk of losing control of such a primal, destructive force would be too great. The Head Mage himself would be hard pressed to control that much whitefyre. Jon's elemental magic, on the other hand, would allow him to easily control his conjured flames."

"Has anyone been able to locate the Firemaster?" Geoffrey asked. "It is not like him to be absent during such troubled times."

"No one has heard from him yet," Delthar informed. "And we cannot spare the resources to search for him."

"Hmmm," Geoffrey began, scratching his chin. "But couldn't you and several more Echelon One mages each cast a smaller and easier to control amount of whitefyre to dispose of them safely?"

Delthar nodded thoughtfully. "Ever the strategist, eh? Yes, my friend. I suppose we could."

"Then why don't you?"

Mage Delthar sighed deeply. "There are infected among them like Johnican. There may yet be a way to save them. If there was a way to separate them from the deceased we could destroy the true walking dead and cull their numbers significantly. But with many of them, it is difficult to tell whether or not their wounds were mortal before they turned."

Geoffrey grunted. "As horrible as it would be, wizard, their loss would be merited under the circumstances."

"Maybe," Delthar said. "But the Head Mage believes the infected can be cured."

"What do *you* believe?" Minister Geoffrey asked.

"I believe it is worth trying," Delthar admitted. "There are innocents among them. Children. We have to try. And if anyone can do it I'm sure the Head Mage can. I have been pondering possible solutions, as well, but we must be careful not to take too much time in finding a cure."

Minister Geoffrey tugged lightly at his thick, but neatly trimmed beard before the invading stench forced his hand back over his mouth and nose. "Yes. It would be best to stop them *before* they complete whatever task to which the demon has set them. Not afterwards."

"Yes, it would," Master Mage Delthar said distractedly. The wizard raised a shaggy white eyebrow as he remembered something. "What of the militia approaching from Allanville? Have they been warned?"

"Yes," Geoffrey said. There was an uneasy pause before he went on. "But no warning was needed. They are led by Robinson Stottlemeyer, a retired colonel and presently the Earl of the Allanville Territories."

"I remember him from the Royal Infantry," Delthar said. "The Allanville Territories are among the richest lands in the Kingdom. I'm not surprised King William rewarded Stottlemeyer so well. He has received many awards for outstanding service. As I recall, though, he had to be disciplined almost as often. He was an exceptional soldier but he had a penchant for being hot-headed and brash."

"And quite thorough," Geoffrey added. "Apparently he was aware of the infectious nature of the enemy as well as the most effective way to defeat them. Our scouts have reported that the Allanville militia has encountered several small groups of the walking dead coming north to join the main phalanx. The militia struck them down with overwhelming attacks using fire."

The Master Mage pursed his thin lips, causing his mouth to completely disappear behind his thick mustache. His whiskers twitched irritably.

"My farsight has shown me that the militia is coming this way, Geoffrey. Why are they not veering east to Ridgeland to form up with the battalion there? For that matter, why are they coming at all? You have not summoned them."

A look of confusion darkened the Minister of War's countenance. "When we first discovered that they were approaching, I honestly did not object. We may very well need them in this endeavor. However, after I received the order from the crown, they *were* instructed to march to Ridgeland."

"Well," Delthar said, "by my reckoning, they should be just beyond that line of foothills to the south, less than a quarter of a mile away from our location. They're loaded for bear, with a squad of archers as well as a team of boroughs towing catapults and wheeled-mounted braziers."

"They may be of great assistance if we get the king and Head Mage to give the command to attack," Geoffrey noted. "But I know not why they are coming our way."

"I suppose we can ask them when they arrive," Delthar declared.

He went silent for a time after that. He slumped in his saddle, resting his right elbow on his right thigh and his chin on the heel of his right palm. His hand immediately disappeared inside his long, bushy white beard as he gazed at the enemy. The wizard swept his dark gray gaze thoughtfully along the length of the motley procession.

Minister Geoffrey cut a glance at the Master Mage and raised an eyebrow. "I've seen that look, wizard. What are you planning?"

"Not to destroy them, I assure you," Delthar said. "I only wish to slow them down."

Without warning, the Master Mage spurred his mount to full gallop and rode west, parallel to the southern edge of the march. Minister Geoffrey watched curiously but did not follow. His four subordinates all turned questioning gazes to the Minister but all Geoffrey could give them was a shrug of his broad shoulders.

"I've known old Delthar for thirty-five years," the minister explained, "since the Master Mage was a young Echelon Two mage and I a young Lieutenant."

The old veteran's eyes glinted fiercely as he recalled their youthful exploits. "We served together when the Kingdom of Lorr fought to repel the Kattahn Kingdom's forces when they were foolish enough to attack Lorr while they occupied the northern fringes of Darshay. Our victory crippled the Kattahn enough to allow the Darshayan forces to drive them completely out of their kingdom.

"We became friends then, and have remained so as we've elevated through the ranks of our respective professions. So when he gets that look and follows it with abrupt action, I know it means he's made decision, and one that involves a significant output of magic."

Delthar reined his mount to a stop and turned around to face Geoffrey. "I suggest you and your men move back, minister!" the wizard called. "Thirty yards at least!"

The Minister of War and his aides complied immediately while the Master Mage turned his mount and heeled it to a gallop once more. He rode to the rear of the enemy phalanx and looped around behind them. After dismounting lithely, he pulled his wand from his cloak and slowly lowered himself to his knees. A curious Geoffrey followed his men, taking care to stay the requisite thirty yards away from the edge of the phalanx.

Anyone unfamiliar with the bearded old man would have assumed he was praying. The way he knelt, in his long robes and cloak, with his head bowed, eyes closed and hands clasped tightly together, it was easy to assume the wizard was a priest, praying intently to the Lord Ascendant or one of the Old Ones. And perhaps he was praying, Geoffrey allowed. Perhaps conjurer's incantations were prayers of a sort. Geoffrey was a soldier. What did he know of magic?

If one looked closely, however, they would see the thin wand descending from the long, wrinkled, intertwined fingers and plunging into the grassy earth. They would have noticed the shimmering glow emanating from the wand, barely visible in the bright suns' light.

From thirty yards away, it was difficult for Geoffrey to see the wand at all. He knew it was there, though, and no one could miss the slow tremor that began underfoot.

The tremor grew. The minister's cavalry horse began to snort and shuffle and back away even further from the march of the dead despite its master's attempts to keep it still.

DEMON OF LORR

A confused Geoffrey dismounted. The moment his feet touched the ground he could feel heat rising from the earth through the soles of his riding boots. He could also feel the earth tremor with an intensity that nearly made his teeth chatter.

Geoffrey followed his mount's lead and hustled his tall, husky frame further away. His men followed suit upon their cavalry horses. Geoffrey eventually caught up to his horse and pulled himself up into the saddle again. With a quick tug of the reins, he directed the horse a few more yards away and turned back to face the army of the walking dead. He turned back just as the tremor erupted into an explosion of sound and the ground caved in beneath the enemy.

The booming collapse of earth belched forth a plume of smoke, dust, and...ash? The Minister of War and his soldiers had to shield their eyes and noses against the cloud of white ash, dark smoke, and the smell of scorched earth that gusted past in thick, hot waves. To make matters worse, all of it was accompanied by the nauseating stench of the marching dead.

When the smoke finally cleared, the marching army was gone and the minister was looking out over a large, deep crater less than ten yards in front of him.

The minister started to speak and immediately went into a teary-eyed coughing fit. After a few moments of this he was finally able to speak. "Ho, there, wizard! We backed away a good fifty yards and still were almost swallowed. You said we only needed thirty!"

"I said 'thirty yards *at least,*' old warrior!" The Master Mage called back.

Delthar was already on his horse and riding back to the minister's side. Geoffrey rode to meet him and the two of them turned their mounts toward the crater.

They stopped a few yards away before dismounting and walking carefully over to the edge. Geoffrey looked down into the crater and raised his eyebrows.

"That's over thirty feet deep, wizard," the minister noted.

The fallen marchers were already untangling themselves from one another and climbing clumsily to their feet – those of them that had feet. Those that did not simply righted themselves enough to continue their inexorable crawl.

"It will not stop them," Delthar admitted. "I'm sure they will eventually scale those earthen walls, but it will likely crumble beneath their fingers and feet for a time. It should slow them down quite a bit, buy us another day or two."

"How did you do it, man?" Geoffrey had to know. "That was impressive."

"Whitefyre," Delthar shared. "It has many uses. I burned the earth beneath them to ash. The thin layer of earth remaining beneath their feet was not strong enough to bear their weight. I extinguished the fire before the collapse so there was no danger of incinerating the lot of them."

Minister Geoffrey stroked his beard. "The way they are contained, one more blast of whitefyre, even without the aid of other mages, might just rid us of this threat altogether."

Delthar turned his gaze to his longtime friend. "We have just had this conversation, have we not?"

"You surprise me," Geoffrey said. "I know they *were* people at one time, but now they are naught but walking plagues sent to carry out a powerful demon's plot. You were always one to make the hard choices, to sacrifice the few for the safety of the many."

"Yes," Delthar agreed. "As you well know, I've often thought the Head Mage's compassion and belief in mankind bordered dangerously upon naïveté. His decision to banish Mar-dah instead of calling for his execution particularly disturbed me.

"I disagreed when he insisted upon the imprisonment of the weather witch and Lothar the Lupine. Their allegiance to Mar-dah during the Cursed Opening easily merited a death sentence. Yet he chose to only jail them."

The grizzled old wizard cast another long glance at the clambering, plague stricken marchers at the bottom of the chasm. Someone that did not know Delthar as well as Geoffrey would have missed it, but the minister saw a small hint of pity in those dark gray eyes. "In this, though, I agree with Rionn. If it is at all possible, we *must* save those who can be saved."

"Then let us pray you are correct," Geoffrey declared.

"Why has Stottlemeyer's militia not arrived?" The Master Mage wondered aloud. "They should be here by now."

He went silent and closed his eyes. Geoffrey saw the faint movements of the wizard's whiskers and could hear words whispered too quietly to understand. Delthar's wild eyebrows suddenly knitted angrily and his dark gray eyes opened wide. He turned an intense glare on the Minister of War.

"Apparently, Geoffrey, this militia does not recognize your authority. Look to the southern skies."

With a frown that was equal parts confused and suspicious, Geoffrey did as advised. His confusion turned quickly to anger when he saw a line of small barrels soar into the air from behind the foothills to the south.

The barrels came right at his and Delthar's location. Just as the barrels reached the apex of their flight, a long line of flaming arrows came streaking behind them. Delthar and Geoffrey were very familiar with the assault. The last time they saw it was against the demons at battle of the Tyne River during the Cursed Opening. The barrels were filled with flammable oils, powders, or both.

"What in the name of Hargathall's Greatsword!?" the minister swore. "The fools are attacking!"

"Not for long," Delthar assured.

The wizard raised his hands high and made an exclamation that sounded like a grunt. An instant later bolts of pale blue lightening leapt from his long, wrinkled fingers. All ten bolts cut jaggedly into the air and branched out into countless other forks of lightening that tore into the descending barrels.

Explosions thundered through the midday sky. The powerful concussions from the multiple blasts scattered the approaching arrows, snuffing out the flaming tips and sending them tumbling harmlessly to the ground.

As the smoldering remains of the barrels fell from the sky, the thunder of hooves floated to the Head Mage and the

Minister of War from the south. Both men turned to see armed, mounted men charging hard over the hills followed closely by foot soldiers brandishing swords. Undaunted, the Master Mage and the Minister of War rode out to meet the charge.

It did not take long for the apparent leader of the militia to realize who the two men were. The lead rider in the middle of the line of charging soldiers raised an open hand and reined his horse from a full gallop to a stop. The rest of the riders followed his lead and the foot soldiers halted as well. Once the militia had ceased its charge, the commander and two of his soldiers continued their approach at a slower, non-threatening pace.

Delthar, Geoffrey, and the four soldiers accompanying them never stopped riding. They continued at an easy trot until all nine riders met. The militia commander still wore an expression of mild surprise when they came together.

The commander, a long, lean man who looked to be in his mid to late fifties, along with his militiamen, saluted with a fist to their chests.

"Hail, Minister," the commander greeted.

Minister Geoffrey returned the salute and nodded in greeting. "Hail to you, Commander Stottlemeyer. I'm surprised to see you leading a militia after your retirement from the Royal Infantry."

"Forgive our aggressive approach, Minister Geoffrey," the commander bade. "When we saw our barrels blasted from the sky, we thought the demon had sent a mage to defend his hellish army. I too was surprised to see you and the Master Mage. I would have expected the two of you to be stationed at the palace helping to coordinate the efforts of the military and Conjurer's Alliance respectively, not among the rank and file in the field."

Minister Geoffrey gave the militia commander a stern glare. "We both saw the approach of this dread army and decided to get a closer look at the threat. So, you did not expect us to be here, eh? Is that why you disobeyed the order

I sent via our scouts? You were told to form up with the battalion at Ridgeland."

"With all due respect, sir," the commander explained, "I suspected that order to be a ruse, a trick of the demon to send us away due to our effectiveness in destroying the groups of walking dead from the south that sought to join their fellows here and increase their numbers."

"You thought it a ruse, did you?" The Minister questioned. "You thought it a ruse even though there has been a standing order for days *not* to engage the enemy? I know you have retired from service but you know that any official militia formed is subject to royal command just the same as the enlisted forces."

"Again, with all due respect, minister, we are an organized, respected, and long-standing militia eager to serve and protect. We are not a hastily assembled band of ruffians like those poor souls from Trader's Parish. As you can see," Stottlemeyer swept an arm behind him to indicate his soldiers and archers, as well as the boroughs that were just pulling their catapults over the hill. "We are well prepared to deal with this threat."

Geoffrey's eyes narrowed. "An order is an order, commander. It is not for you to pick and choose which orders to follow and which to ignore. The non-engagement order was given for several reasons. It is your responsibility to follow it."

Stottlemeyer was silent for a long moment. When he finally spoke, his frustration was evident.

"Minister," he began, "I am a decorated veteran. I served the crown faithfully over half of my life. You have known me all that time. You know how I felt about orders that I believed were not truly in the best interest of the kingdom. I followed them grudgingly while in service.

"Things are different now. And this order, I fear, defies logic and common sense. How can these abominations be allowed to go unchallenged while they spread their horrible infection across the kingdom?"

"You forget your place," Geoffrey warned. "Do not think that your distinguished service elevates your militia beyond the authority of the crown."

"Does this order truly come from the crown?" Stottlemeyer challenged suspiciously. "Or does it come from the Head Mage?"

It was the Master Mage's turn to speak. "An order from the Head Mage *is* an order from the crown. It is gross insubordination to attempt to separate the two for your own purposes."

Stottlemeyer turned an accusatory glare on the Master Mage. "I've known you for years, as well, mage. And I know that you have questioned the Head Mage's wisdom on more than one occasion. If you honestly believe in this order, tell me why."

Delthar's gaze went colder than Geoffrey had seen in a very long time. "Because there are innocent civilians among them!" the Master Mage snapped. "There are men, women, and children that we may be able to save, as long as some overzealous fool does not wipe them out!"

The commander's expression softened a bit but he remained as stubborn as ever. "I know of the innocents among them. I know all too well. We encountered them along the way. We took no joy in what we had to do. It breaks my heart to say this, gentlemen, but the slim chance that they might be cured does not even come close to outweighing the threat they pose."

Geoffrey shook his head. "That is not your decision to –"

"That is *common sense*, minister!" Stottlemeyer barked.

"Enough!" roared the Minister of War. "This insubordination will be tolerated no longer. You will take your militia to Ridgeland and await further orders from the crown, and I can assure you that this is no ruse. This is a direct order from the Minister of War!"

"I will happily turn myself in for whatever punishment the crown sees fit after this horror has passed," Stottlemeyer vowed. "But if you want to stop us now you'll have to arrest the lot of us. Even with the powerful Master Mage at your side, I doubt the six of you could accomplish such a task."

With a snap of his reins, Stottlemeyer wheeled his horse around and began riding slowly back toward his militia. His flanking guards followed suit. After riding a few yards, the militia commander called out:

"Catapults at the ready! Adjust for shorter range!" There was a rush of movement as the soldiers led the boroughs into position, unhooked them from the catapults, led the pack animals away and began to adjust the catapults.

"Stottlemeyer!" the Minister roared.

The commander looked over his shoulder. "I suggest you all ride clear, sirs, in case some of the fire falls short." He turned back to his militia. "Load catapults! Archers ready!"

Soldiers went about the task of loading the small barrels into the catapult cups while the archers hurriedly formed a neat line at the braziers to light their arrowheads.

"This is your final warning, Stottlemeyer!" Geoffrey called.

"As this is mine to you, sir," Stottlemeyer called back. "Ride clear or risk the same fate as the army of the damned." The rogue militia commander directed his attention back to his soldiers. "Militia! On my comm—"

Stottlemeyer never finished his sentence. There was an ear-popping clap of thunder as the Master Mage shot a bolt of pale blue lightening from one fingertip. Stottlemeyer went rigid and glowed for the briefest instant before going limp where he sat. A second or two passed – a second or two that seemed like an eternity to the men watching – before Stottlemeyer finally slid from his saddle and fell heavily to the ground.

The pair of militiamen flanking their commander turned in alarm and shock. The rest of the militia froze and looked on in stunned silence.

Even the four soldiers accompanying the Master Mage and the Minister of War looked over at Delthar with disbelieving stares.

"You've killed him!" the militiaman on the left accused, stabbing a finger at the wizard. "You've murdered Commander Stottlemeyer!"

"No," Minister Geoffrey said before Delthar could respond. "Killed, yes, but it was not murder. You were his second. Now the militia is under your command. Will you follow my orders or force us to do what *we* have to do?"

There was a pregnant pause as both sides stared each other down. The Master Mage's expression was hidden behind his thick whiskers but his icy stare betrayed his intensity and determination.

The Minister of War was torn. He felt like a hypocrite for admonishing the militia commander for disobeying an order that he himself did not fully believe in. He wanted to admonish the Master Mage for such a grave action. Stottlemeyer had been a good soldier despite his brashness. He did not deserve such a terrible fate even though he knew it was merited under the circumstances. And despite Delthar's fierce gaze, he knew that deep down inside the Master Mage felt the same way.

"What say you, soldier?" The Master Mage challenged.

The new commander of the militia glared at the Master Mage with contempt and more than a hint of fear before coming to his decision.

"Stand down!" he called to his men, never taking his eyes away from Master Mage Delthar. We ride to Ridgeland!"

Delthar and Geoffrey sat rigid in their saddles and looked on until the militia finished unloading their catapults, extinguished their arrows, and commenced their ride east. When the last of them disappeared behind the foothills, both men slumped heavily and sighed.

"I'm truly sorry I had to do that, minister," Delthar said with grave sincerity.

Minister Geoffrey rode over to the wizard's side and placed a big meaty hand on Delthar's narrow shoulder.

"I regret that you were given no choice, Master Mage. He was a good soldier but his defiance could not be allowed to stand." The minister turned to face his four soldiers. "What

180

say you, men? I give you permission to speak freely. I want to know how you feel about this."

One of the men shrugged uneasily. "His fate was unfortunate, and I'm not quite sure such a drastic response was deserved. But yes, he did bring it upon himself."

Even though the other three nodded in agreement, the Master Mage did not miss the way they looked at him the moment after he struck down the militia commander. He wondered how honest they were being.

"I took no joy in taking Stottlemeyer's life," Delthar assured. "I know not if you speak from your heart or from your sense of duty, but know this: whatever the demon's scheme, you can be sure that part of it is the seeding of discontent and dissension among the kingdom's defenders. That way lies chaos, men, and it is for chaos that the Dierglyorr exists."

Geoffrey nodded. "The Master Mage speaks true," he concurred. "Do not allow yourself to fall victim to that seeding as Commander Stottlemeyer did. That is not a threat, but a plea. It is a dark deed that has been done this day, and it is something we hope to never have to repeat."

"We understand," one of the soldiers returned.

"We'll not be swayed by the demon's treachery," another promised as the other two nodded their agreement.

Even though the words rang true to Delthar's ears, his experienced eye did not miss the apprehension that the soldiers tried their best to conceal.

5.4

Annastace Sureblade brushed a long dark curl from her eye to no avail. The brisk autumn wind merely blew it right back. She pulled her wool cloak tighter around her shoulders and wished she had brought a small scarf to tie back her hair. Catherine Lorr, sitting next to her on the high bench of the horse-drawn carriage and wearing a cloak of died and spun cotton, smiled.

"You should have taken me up on my offer to braid your hair, Anna," she teased. To rib her friend further, she ran her slender fingers along her long, pale blonde plaits. "I've no problem with the wind as you can see."

"What?" Annastace asked with mock surprise. "And have people mistake us for twins?"

Both women chuckled. No one would ever mistake them for twins. Annastace was several inches shorter than Catherine. Both women were shapely, but Catherine was long and willowy while Annastace was more compact and buxom. Catherine's skin complexion was fair. Annastace, on the other hand, had a honey brown complexion.

Catherine had thin and elegant lips, a straight nose, sharp cheekbones and slightly canted, almond-shaped, pale green eyes under thin, high-arching eyebrows only slightly darker than her skin.

Those features were starkly contrasted Annastace's full, sensuous lips, small rounded nose, thick dark eyebrows and wide hazel-brown eyes. In addition to Catherine's canted elven eyes, she also had slightly pointed ears that were much more prominent when her hair was pulled back or braided.

"Twins or not," Catherine said slyly, "I think those gentlemen out there would choose either of us."

She nodded her head in the direction of a group of men in a wheat field chopping and loading stalks into borough-drawn carts. The men worked hard to harvest the season's last wheat crop but they could not stop themselves from continuously glancing up at the two women, both of whom were exotically beautiful in their own unique ways.

"You use the word 'gentlemen' rather loosely," Annastace replied with disinterest. "You'd think they've never seen a woman before."

"They're *men*," Catherine shrugged. "And I'm sure they're not accustomed to seeing their mistress watch over them while they work."

"No, they're not," Annastace agreed. "I cannot tell if they're distracted by our looks or annoyed that I'm observing them personally."

"A little of both, I'm sure," Catherine said.

"It's their own fault," Annastace said firmly. "My inventory has come up short the last two seasons. Since Meldrick died, some of them believe they have license to steal from me.

"Apparently they don't think a woman is intelligent enough to manage her own land. What they don't know is that I always managed the land and the finances. Meldrick was too busy with his military obligations."

"What kept you from observing them in person the last two years?" Catherine asked.

"I did not think I had to," Annastace answered. "Two years ago the Tyne River and its branching irrigation streams had barely recovered from the demons' blood that poisoned them after the Battle of the Tyne, so I expected a significant loss. Even still, I believed my shortfall to be worse than it should have been. When I inquired about it they blamed the Cursed Opening and I gave them the benefit of the doubt because they had always been loyal in the past."

Catherine raised an already sharply arched eyebrow. "And what was their excuse last year?"

"They had none. They simply and adamantly feigned ignorance."

"And yet you did not terminate them?"

"I felt a bit sorry for them," Annastace admitted. "They had not recovered from the losses suffered after the Cursed Opening. Laborers were nearly destitute while widows of fallen soldiers were granted recompense from the crown in honor of our husbands' sacrifices.

"That was the only reason I overlooked last year's

shortfall. They needed the extra crops to either eat or sell. This time, though, I'm going to follow the harvests from the fields to the mill. My charity only goes so far."

"Indeed," Catherine said.

"They at least *pretended* to respect me when Meldrick lived," Annastace went on. "It was only fear of retribution from a Home Guard captain, but it was something. Now I have to deal with this idiocy. They see a successful woman without a husband and grow more resentful each year."

Catherine sneered with disgust. "It seems they would just quit you and find another employer, a male employer, if they hate working for you so."

"We've always paid better than most. With Meldrick's wages as a soldier and now with my recompense from the crown, we could afford to pay more than the average wages. The only people that pay as much or more are other knights with the same or higher rank than Meldrick, and they have all the workers they need."

"They try to cheat you because you're a woman," Catherine observed needlessly. "For too many men, misplaced pride trumps money."

"Especially wounded pride," Annastace added. "A few of them had the nerve to pay court to me shortly after Meldrick passed, thinking they had a chance to possess me as well as my holdings. Meldrick was slated to become a vassal when he retired from military service, you know. The crown has reserved an estate in stewardship to add to our current holdings for that very purpose. The law dictates that I must be married to claim it, though.

"I suppose those suitors thought they could advance from peasants to vassals by winning my favor, nut I'll never wed a man I don't love just to increase my wealth or to keep from being alone. I turned them all away graciously. Most of them were nonetheless stung by my refusal. Now they seek to cheat me at every opportunity."

"Anna, have you told Ethan about these troubles?"

Annastace shook her head. "No. He would quit the military in an instant to come home and look after me…and he would never be happy. As much as I would love for him to leave such a dangerous profession, I know it is in his blood as much as it was in his father's. I love him too much to be that selfish."

Catherine sighed as she regarded her friend. "There is a place for you at the castle, you know. The king's treasurer is in need of able assistants. You can live there and rent out your home at Fort Bastion. You can hire an assistant, a *male* assistant, to oversee your personal business affairs until Ethan is willing or August is old enough to become master of the Sureblade estate."

"I would do just that if I could find someone I trusted," Annastace assured. "I've interviewed several men. It always comes down them wanting my holdings and the stewardship as well as me.

"Unmarried vassals look to increase their holdings to petition the crown for the establishment of a barony. Many of the married men refuse to manage the land for a profit. They want to purchase it outright while taking me as a mistress and they do very little to conceal their interest. The married men that don't want me as a wife or mistress, or at least have sense enough to keep such desires to themselves, are warned away by untrusting wives."

"I worry about you, Anna. If your employees and other men grow bolder as time passes, do you think that concealed dagger you carry will protect you?"

Annastace shrugged. "Perhaps I'll petition the king for men-at-arms."

"That is an excellent idea," Catherine said.

"Although if King William granted my wish, I wonder how long they would want to play chaperone to my children and me."

The Head Mage's wife returned her attention to the men working in the fields until a playful, high-pitched scream arrested her attention. She turned to see her daughter, little Shandie, alternately chasing Annastace's son and daughter. When the little girl turned to pursue August, Arielle would sneak up behind her and tickle her ribs.

The pretty three-year-old girl with the dark blond hair

would jump and squeal with laughter, turn, and chase Arielle. When she did, August would creep up behind her and tickle her ribs, and then the cycle would begin anew.

It was difficult to look at the Sureblade children without being reminded of their parents. Catherine stared at the Sureblade twins, with their mother's curly chestnut brown hair and their brown skin, just a shade lighter than their mother's, and their father's steel blue eyes. She then thought of Ethan, who, with his blonde hair, comparatively fair skin and steel blue eyes, as well – looked so much like his deceased father. She smiled sadly and a pang of sorrow pierced her heart.

"I know it's been three years, Anna," Catherine began, still looking at August and Arielle. "But how are you and the children faring?"

"We're managing. It's still difficult but we don't cry as much as we used to. Sometimes when I see Ethan scowl or laugh, he looks so much like my Meldrick that my heart breaks all over again. He misses his father, so do the twins.

"Meldrick positively doted on them. Having been an orphan, he never knew the love of a mother and father. He made sure his children knew how much he loved them." Annastace took a deep breath before continuing. "From time to time the loneliness is so hard to bear that I have to throw myself into the business of managing our properties to keep from breaking down."

"You do realize that you don't *have* to be lonely, don't you, Anna?"

"Of course, Cathy. I have no shortage of suitors…but as I've said, none of *them* suit me."

"Who does?" Catherine asked, knowing the answer.

"A man I can't have," Annastace answered wistfully. "And you *know* that man is the offworlder. What makes it worse is that I've seen a spark in his eyes for me."

Catherine grinned. "Many men have a spark for you."

"In most cases that spark is merely lust," Annastace countered. "But there is something different in Raxe's eyes. Something more."

Catherine's smile widened. "Do you think it's love?"

"Love?" Anna rolled her eyes. "It's too soon for that."

"I saw that look in Rionn's eyes when we first met," Catherine said. "What Raxe feels may not be love now, but if properly cultivated..."

"And how would that be possible?" Annastace asked. "The only time he comes to this world is when it's in danger. As soon as this danger has passed he'll go back across the WorldGate to his home. There's no time for cultivation."

Catherine fingered her chin thoughtfully. "No time, you think?"

"Oh, stop it, Cathy. Are you half elf or half cupid?"

"You know how connected elves are to nature. Love is merely an aspect of spirit, which is as much a part of nature as the earth, water, fire, and air."

Annastace's proud and defiant posture slumped for a moment as she turned toward Catherine. "Tell me, Cathy. How do you do it?"

"Do what?"

"How do you deal with being the wife of the Head Mage? He is away risking his life as much as if not more than Meldrick was. I was terribly lonely and frightened that he would never return. And then, when he did not return..." she paused to sniff and fight back tears. "And now my first-born son has followed in his footsteps."

Catherine put a slender but strong arm around Annastace and smiled sadly. "I deal with it the same way you do, Anna. I stay as strong and positive as I can. Sometimes, though, when he's away and no one else is around, I do cry a little."

"I just pray Raxe can keep Ethan safe," Annastace said. "I asked Raxe to promise to bring him back safely. I know it was terribly unfair of me to do that. I honestly did not expect him to make the promise."

"But he did, did he not?" Catherine asked.

"Yes," Annastace confirmed with a small smile. "He did. And he was sincere."

"Raxe is a good man, better than he realizes," Catherine assured. "Ethan is in good hands."

Annastace smiled wider. "Thank you for spending the

day with me."

She was about to say more when she noticed one of the field laborers walking their way. He literally had his hat in his hands and his mouth was set in a nervous frown. But as he approached, both women could see a hint of suppressed indignation in his dark brown eyes. Annastace straightened up and replaced her sad countenance with a blank expression. Catherine removed her arm in response to her friend's sudden change in posture.

"This is Louis approaching," Annastace whispered to Catherine. "Be wary of his wandering eyes."

Catherine, with her sharp vision, had already noticed. Despite the worried scowl and the resentment simmering just below the surface of his ingratiating demeanor, she could see his eyes roving over both women hungrily as if he could see right through their clothing.

"Is everything all right, Louis?" Annastace asked when her employee was several yards away from their carriage.

"All goes well," Louis answered hesitantly with a nod. "But the men are wondering if they will be paid today."

"Why would they wonder that?" Annastace asked. "They are always paid after a full day's work."

"Yes, milady," Louis answered with a forced smile. "They only wonder because they are not accustomed to you personally overseeing us. There is a concern that you are displeased with our work, that you may withhold payment until the harvest is complete at week's end."

As he spoke, he made a half-hearted attempt to keep his gaze focused on her eyes, but they still flickered to the barely visible swell of her breasts beneath her cloak. Annastace was more than a little irritated and had as much trouble hiding her irritation as Louis had keeping his eyes on her face.

"You mean until I've confirmed that the amount of wheat harvested here is equal to the amount that arrives at the miller's?" she inquired.

"As I've said before, milady," Louis returned, frustration easing its way into his tone, "we do not know why you have accused us of – "

188

"Actually, Louis," Annastace cut him off, "it had not occurred to me to withhold payment. Perhaps the assumption that I would is the product of a guilty conscience. Now that you've mentioned it, it actually sounds like a good idea."

Louis dropped all pretense of acquiescence. He stood up straight, attempting to affect a subtly defiant posture. When he spoke, he was careful to choose respectful words and a deferential tone. His body language, however, came dangerously close to threatening.

"I don't recommend that," he advised. "The men might misinterpret such a decision. We have families to feed."

The heat of anger flared in Annastace's chest. She wrapped her hand tightly around the long dagger concealed under her cloak even as she flashed her most gracious smile.

"Why Louis," she said innocently, "is that a threat?"

Shrill children's screams caused all three of them to turn. The screams came from August and Arielle. They were not screams of fear, but of startled excitement. The twins hovered several feet in the air, three yards apart, their arms and legs pumping madly as if they were running in different directions.

Little Shandie stood between them, her arms raised. Her sweet little laugh was barely audible under the twins' playful cries. "I got you!" she giggled as she started moving her fingers this way and that.

"Tickle, tickle, tickle!"

The twins' excited cries turned into raucous laughter as the three-year-old girl tickled them without touching them.

Catherine and Annastace laughed. Louis however, looked at the spectacle with genuine fear and then looked at Catherine. He suddenly remembered that the woman sitting next to his employer was Catherine Lorr, wife of the Head Mage and long time friend to Annastace Sureblade.

By the time the two women turned their attention back to him, his nervousness and acquiescence were genuine.

"I'm sorry I gave you the wrong impression," he said quickly. "I in no way meant to threaten. It's just that – "

"Your men will receive their payment at day's end as always," Annastace assured with her dazzling smile. And I am certain that there will be no shortfall this year."

"Of course not, milady," Louis said with deep bow before hurrying back to the field.

As Louis scampered away, four of the King's soldiers rode in from the east, one of them leading a saddled filly with no rider. Annastace and Catherine watched them curiously until they were close enough to speak.

"Madame Lorr," one of the soldiers called. "The Head Mage requests your presence at the castle. He needs your expertise as a healer in his quest to find a cure for those infected with the plague."

Catherine looked at her friend, concern in her eyes.

"Don't worry," said Annastace. "I'll be fine."

"Indeed she will," assured another soldier. "Two of us have been ordered to stay here with Mrs. Sureblade while the other two escort you to the castle."

Annastace cocked her head. "Indeed?" she asked suspiciously, turning to her friend. "And why would Master Lorr give such an order?"

The right corner of Catherine's thin lips lifted in a sly smile. "Let's just say that your workers' discontent, while unwarranted, is not exactly the latest news."

Annastace turned a thoughtful gaze to Catherine. "Maybe I can hire your little Shandie instead of men-at-arms. Considering the way she spooked Louis, she seems to be all the encouragement my workers need."

"She causes enough mischief when she's playing. I don't think anyone wants to see what she does when she's serious. Do you want your employees to respect you or flee from your employ in terror?"

The women laughed.

5.5

Ethan hurried through the maze of corridors, easily finding his way back to his quarters. He did not need a guide as the others did, with the exception of Quick, of course. The changeling not only had the olfactory senses of a hound, he also possessed the keen sense of direction of a bird. In addition to all of that Quick had once lived in these tunnels.

Ethan was not blessed with such advantages. What he did have was an almost flawless memory when it came to direction. No matter how winding the path he always remembered his way back to his starting point. He instinctively internalized the smallest, most insignificant-seeming landmarks that others missed altogether. The guide assigned to accompany Ethan found himself jogging to keep up with the long legged human.

The young Sureblade quickly gathered his most prized possessions: the weapons passed down to him from his father. The broadsword was already resting in its sheath, which hung from the weapons belt that Ethan strapped securely around his waist. The loosely strung long bow was slung diagonally across his back. He slipped the looped lasso over his left arm all the way up to his shoulder. And then he retrieved the javelin from where it rested, propped point side up in the corner of his chambers.

Once the dwarves made it clear that the team had become welcomed guests he was comfortable leaving his weapons in his quarters as he moved around the tunnels and caves. But now that he was collecting all of his gear, his dwarven guide standing in the portal looked at Ethan suspiciously.

"You seem to be bearing for war, human," the dwarf observed.

"No," Ethan said as he followed the dwarf out of his quarters. "I'm..."

Ethan paused, realizing that he did not really know why he was bringing all of his weapons with him. He knew nothing of magic, so he had no idea why he was instructed to bring his gear and he was not overly concerned about why.

All he knew was that this offworlder Child of the Old Ones, a direct descendant of the divine blacksmith called the Gatekeeper and His warrior son Raxe, had decided to forge a weapon for him. That was enough.

Nervous excitement quickened his pace and he had to slow himself down to avoid leaving his guide behind. He remembered the general vicinity of the smithy because they had passed very near to it on their way to the stadium to watch Raxe's "test," but he did not know the exact location. Besides, they may have been captives no longer, but that did not mean he had the run of the underground nation.

The four-minute near jog felt like an hour to the anxious youngster. But when the cool air began to grow warmer and the sound of clanking metal echoed through the corridors, Ethan knew they were nearing the smithy. A few moments later he could see an orange glow spilling out into the corridor from around a corner.

Ethan saw the entrance to the smithy when they rounded the corner. Two large, heavy iron doors hung from broad hinges bolted to the rock walls with large steel rivets. Heat washed over them when those doors opened to admit them.

Ethan looked up at the extra ventilation holes carved into the high ceiling. The walls were much darker from the high amounts of soot in the air from the smithy. Tiny beads of sweat started popping up on Ethan's forehead when they walked through the wide threshold. When the guide led him through the main hall Ethan noticed that, with the exception of the stadium, the ceilings were three times as high inside of the smithy than anywhere else in the sprawling labyrinth.

There were dwarves everywhere. They all wore heavy leather aprons over sleeveless tunics and thick woolen breeches. Big muscular arms slicked over with sweat and soot pounded glowing steel with great hammers while others held red hot metal atop black anvils with large iron tongs. Some dwarves ferried wheelbarrows full of smith's tools or finished weapons and armor while others worked bellows at great furnaces carved into the rough rock walls.

DEMON OF LORR

The room was a flurry of activity and noise. Hissing steam, roaring flames, and the heavy clang of metal on metal joined in with the deep, booming voices of dwarven smiths yelling orders to apprentices and subordinates.

Ventilation channels riddled the high ceiling in such great numbers that it resembled a giant stone honeycomb. Columns of black smoke from the various forges and white steam from water used to cool off orange hot metal were sucked through the ventilation holes in twenty-second intervals. Ethan wondered why the smoke and steam could not be seen from the outside above the mountains. He did not spare much time for the thought, though, because he and his guide reached a wide iron door on the far side of the main hall and Raxe was waiting on the other side of the door. The offworlder sat on the floor in the middle of the small room. His enchanted silver helmet, gauntlets, and cuirass had been removed, revealing Raxe's lean and chiseled chest, shoulders, and arms. Beads of sweat all over his bare skin glistened in the firelight. He faced Ethan on the other side of a cauldron of molten metal that sat within a larger rectangular pit with dense, stone, soot-covered walls that emerged a foot and a half above the ground.

The bottom half of the cauldron was hidden within the red-hot coals that filled the pit and kept the molten metal within the cauldron at a slow simmer. Ethan came closer to inspect the cauldron, expecting to see hot molten iron. What he saw instead was something that looked like thick, liquid silver that glowed with a soft near-white radiance.

"This is called the Divine Forge," Raxe explained. "I know this because Shanderah – the original, not Rionn Lorr's daughter – dumped a bunch of information in my head three years ago. I recall it in fits and starts. This process came to me right after I realized I had to do this for you."

Raxe knew he did not have to explain all of this to Ethan but he felt compelled to. He was making this weapon for Ethan, so he decided the kid should listen.

"The Titan's Ore has already been added," Raxe revealed, his brown eyes alternately reflecting the silver glow emanating from the cauldron and the orange glow from the heated coals. "That's why the liquid metal is pale silver. Now we can begin."

"What do we do first?" Ethan asked.

"First, you have to be sure that you want this."

"Of course," Ethan assured.

"I know that seems like a no-brainer," Raxe began. He stopped when he saw Ethan puzzling at the unfamiliar phrase. "That means the choice seems obvious," he clarified. "Don't make this decision lightly. This is serious business."

"And *I* am serious," Ethan promised. "I am very serious about doing whatever I can to protect the Kingdom of Lorr."

Raxe looked at him for a long time. "So you agree to accept the weapon I'll make for you?"

The offworlder's gravelly voice brought to Ethan's mind the distant rumble of thunder on the horizon preceding a terrible storm. He thought the metaphor might be an omen. If it was, he was determined to weather the coming tempest.

"Yes," Ethan replied. "What do we do next?"

"The magic requires sacrifice," Raxe said solemnly.

Ethan wondered what "sacrifice" would be required of him. He watched with cautious fascination as Raxe placed his left forearm above the cauldron of molten metal. Sweat immediately dripped from his pores and quickly vaporized in the steam rising from the cauldron.

Ethan stood several yards away from the molten Titan's Ore and he could still feel waves of heat washing against his skin. He did not want to know what the offworlder was feeling.

The pain was almost too much for Raxe to bear. He had to resist his initial reflex to snatch his hand away from the intense heat. Instead, he adjusted his breathing, focused his chi, and went into a meditative state. The pain instantly numbed but he knew this would still have to be quick, before his skin started to blister. He brought Demonsbane around with his right hand and pressed one of the axe blades against his wrist.

With a short, quick stroke, the blade easily sliced deep enough to draw blood.

194

DEMON OF LORR

This was the dangerous part. The knowledge imparted to Raxe from Shanderah's mind-merge provided the steps for the Divine Forge, but it did not include the amount of blood that would be needed. He alternately flexed and relaxed his fist to keep the blood dripping but the intense heat was quickening the coagulation process. Raxe was afraid the bleeding would stop before the proper amount of blood was added to the molten ore, and he was not keen on the idea of having to cut himself again.

The bleeding soon slowed to a stop. Raxe pulled his arm away and wondered whether or not he would have to repeat the ordeal. Just then the white glow of the liquefied ore turned a deep crimson and boiled to twice its original intensity. Red steam shot up from the cauldron. Before Raxe knew it he had inhaled a lungful of the acrid vapor.

The heat of the steam scorched his throat and lungs, causing him to rise quickly to his feet and launch into a violent coughing fit. He doubled over as he coughed and stumbled backwards. Ethan jumped up to catch him before he fell and lowered Raxe carefully to the soot-covered floor.

Raxe's coughing finally eased a bit, but the room was spinning. Ethan could see the dazed look in Raxe's eyes and was afraid the offworlder had been poisoned. The teen had no idea what to do.

"I must find a healer," Ethan decided. Before he could rise, however, Raxe reached up and grabbed Ethan's shoulder with a grip like iron.

"The magic requires sacrifice..." Raxe repeated, his coarse rasp of a voice made even rougher by the bitter steam he had just inhaled. His eyes were pink and watery from the blast of crimson steam yet Ethan could feel the strength of the man radiating from his red gaze.

This was a Child of the Old Ones, Ehtan remembered.

The significance of the moment fell heavily upon Ethan and brought with it a wave of fear that dwarfed the considerable heat of the forge.

"Blood?" Ethan asked reluctantly. "My...blood?"

Raxe shook his head "no." His eyes were clearing and he was finally able to sit up on his own. It took him a moment to make sense of the words and images that flooded his mind the instant after the tainted steam flooded his lungs. The microscopic particles from his blood combined with the enchanted ore that rode the heated air into his respiratory system had a hallucinogenic affect. Raxe knew, however, that his flash of vision was not a figment of his own imagination.

The magic had communicated with him. The images showed him exactly what needed to be done, and what he saw filled him with dread.

"It doesn't require your blood unless you want to bind the weapon's magic only to you and your direct descendants," Raxe explained. "Otherwise, the magic will only work for you or for someone to whom you willingly transfer the weapon. Which do you prefer?"

He and Ethan sat facing each other on the hard floor. Ethan considered his choices, and then came to a decision. "I'll not bind the magic – whatever form it takes – to only my offspring. I want children, but who's to say I will ever have them? And if I do, who's to say that they'll choose a righteous path and be deserving of such a legacy?"

"True," Raxe said. "Mar-dah was a descendant of the Protectors but chose the path of the Leaders."

Ethan nodded. "I would rather choose an heir myself." He said. "Better that than to limit the choice to someone who may or may not be worthy."

Raxe nodded. At first Ethan felt relief at not having to draw his own blood, but the grave set of Raxe's countenance worried him. The offworlder had the look of a man about to make a request that he thought would never be granted.

"What now?" Ethan questioned after a moment's pause.

"We're forging a weapon for you," Raxe began. "It's meant to be the perfect weapon, the perfect weapon *for you*. It'll make any other weapon unnecessary. It'll be every weapon you could need, the *only* weapon you'll ever need."

Ethan's eyes narrowed. He had a sickening feeling that he knew where this was going.

Raxe continued. "The price of magic ain't an easy one to pay. I should know. It's especially hard if you have sentimentalities or a conscience."

"You speak of sentimentalities, the need for no other weapon but this. You can't mean that you want me to sacrifice *my father's* weapons*?*"

"I don't want you to," Raxe said sincerely. "The magic requires it."

"You said yourself three years ago that he wanted me to have his lasso, his sword, his javelin, his crossbow," Ethan argued. "How can you ask me to give them up now? What would you do with them?"

Raxe sighed. "We gotta add them to the Titan's Ore. We gotta melt and burn them all down and reshape them into one weapon. So actually, you wouldn't be losing them. You'd be incorporating them into a greater whole. I know it's not an easy thing to do, but that's how the magic of the Old Ones works. It always seems to demand more than most would be willing to pay."

"That is a price *I* am not willing to pay," Ethan agreed.

"And you shouldn't be," Raxe agreed in a genuinely sympathetic tone. "But that's what's required. That's probably *why* it's required. If you choose not to pay, then we end this now. I've bled for nothing. I've used up my Titan's Ore with nothing to show for it."

"I did not ask for any of this," Ethan said defensively. "It was your idea to create a weapon for me. You did not say there would be a cost."

"I didn't know," Raxe admitted. "When I realized that I had to make a weapon for you, I thought I'd be the only one that would have to make a sacrifice. I didn't know what the sacrifice would be but I was willing to pay it. Now that I do know..." he trailed off, having to pause for a moment.

He shook his head as if trying to forcefully shed an unwanted recollection. And then he said, with what sounded to Ethan like relief:

"Let me put it like this, kid... It won't break my heart if you choose not to do this. It just means I misinterpreted my vision. But believe me, I won't be upset with you."

Ethan hid the surprise he felt from Raxe's words. The young Sureblade expected some rebuke, even to be chastised. Despite his relief at not having to give up his father's weapons he still expected Raxe to make him feel more guilt for his selfishness.

His father would have given him a short lecture that would both reprimand him for his childishness and at the same time inspire him to do what he knew to be right. That was why the Child of the Old One's quick concession took Ethan aback. Ethan did not believe Raxe had misinterpreted his vision. His father and hero, the legendary Meldrick Sureblade, taught Ethan and his two younger siblings to never doubt a righteous Child of the Old Ones.

The young Sureblade regarded Raxe suspiciously. Was he being tested? It was the only valid explanation for why Raxe was so certain moments earlier yet so willing to concede now. Raxe met his gaze without any expression that Ethan could discern.

Ethan looked down at his sweaty palms and was glad that the profuse sweating from the oppressive heat of the forge masked the nervous moisture. But he knew it was there, just like the tightening of his gut and the accelerated pace of his heartbeat that always overcame him when he realized he was about to do something frighteningly significant.

Yes, he realized he *was* being tested. His father was probably watching from Heaven, hoping his son would make the right choice. He would not let his father down.

"We both know you did not misinterpret your vision," Ethan declared with an almost accusatory tone. "My father will always be in my heart, no matter what happens to these weapons.

"You may have them."

Ethan thought he saw Raxe's shoulders slump. For a fleeting moment the offworlder assumed a deflated posture but a second later he looked as determined as ever.

"Pass me your broadsword."

Ethan did so. And then he watched Raxe lower the beautiful sword into the cauldron. A captivating red glow illuminated the wide blade where it met the molten metal. Ethan felt his heart melt just as sure as the sword melted within the simmering Titan's Ore.

After the hilt and then the pommel were devoured, the other weapons followed. Despite Ethan's brave words about his father being in his heart regardless of his weapons, his heart sank further and further with the destruction of each one, though the loss of the other weapons were not as painful as the broadsword.

Ethan had watched his father carry each of those weapons with pride and dignity. He had been told tales of how his father used those weapons with legendary skill in defense of the Kingdom of Lorr. His father had even used those weapons to save Ethan and his sibling's lives when they were attacked by a fearsome wallowgrump three years earlier.

The teen quickly wiped away the lone tear that escaped his eye. Even through the heartbreaking ordeal of losing his father during the Cursed Opening, the fact that his father had entrusted those weapons to him had been the most significant occurrence of his life. The weapons had been left to him on the condition that he successfully completed his training at the Royal Military Academy. Ethan had not only successfully completed his training, he excelled. He was the youngest entrant ever admitted as well as the youngest to graduate. His drive to earn his father's weapons elevated him to the best swordsman to graduate the Academy since his father.

For these reasons, Ethan trembled with sadness as the hiss of the molten ore reverberated cruelly in the orange light of the vented cave. The hiss sent a new jolt through him as it consumed the blade, and then the crossbow, and then the lasso, and finally, the javelin.

Ethan did a valiant job of hiding his emotions. Raxe, though, could see in the other's blue eyes the pain that the young Sureblade was feeling. Despite the hardening features and the light growth of blonde hair on the teen's jaw and upper lip, Raxe saw the same heartbroken young boy that had to suffer through the short private memorial to his fallen father in the royal courtyard the day following the end of the Cursed Opening.

And finally, the ravenous hiss of the melted and incinerated weapons died down to the quieter hiss and bubbling of the molten Titan's Ore. Ethan kept his distance from the heated cauldron as he stood and stared at the simmering liquefied metal. It was almost as if he was losing his father all over again.

"Is it over?" Ethan asked, his voice cracking in a near whisper. Beads of sweat fell insistently down his face from the heat within the forge, and Raxe thought he might have spied another tear camouflaging itself within the moisture.

"For you, yes," Raxe answered. "Not for me. The weapon still has to be forged, and I have my own sacrifice to make."

Ethan tilted his head in confusion. "But you just gave so much blood. Was that not your sacrifice?"

"The magic is in the blood," Raxe explained. "My blood was necessary to start the process. It wasn't the sacrifice that I have to make."

"Then...what?" Ethan asked with more than a hint of uncertainty.

Raxe was silent for a time, long enough for four deep breaths. After the fourth exhalation, he looked up at Ethan with a blank face.

"Understand," Raxe began with a dark tone that defied his blank expression. His sandpaper voice grew rougher still, giving Ethan a chill. "I don't really need you here for this part, but you're staying. I'm not showing you this to guilt you into using the weapon we're making. I'm showing you this to make damn sure you understand the significance of this weapon. All magic has a price, and the price is too high for it to ever be used frivolously."

"Raxe," Ethan assured, "I promise you that –"

"I'd prefer you never have to use it," Raxe cut him off. "I want you to dread using it as much as I dread making it, so that when you absolutely have to use it, you will use it responsibly and efficiently. Look at the sacrifice I make and remember how serious this shit is."

Ethan gazed intently after Raxe went silent. The offworlder eyes slid back to the cauldron. He sat cross-legged on the close-packed earth and rocked back in his seated position. Staring blankly into the molten ore, he held his left hand above the molten ore, fingers pointing rigidly forward and his palm facing down.

He ignored the heat as he balled his right hand into a tight fist, thumb side up, and rotated his right forearm up slowly until his fist was level with his left hand. He took in a deep, quick breath. After holding it for a long second, he exhaled with a sharp cry...

And then jabbed his right fist into the molten Titan's Ore.

In the instant it took for what was happening to register with Ethan and widen his eyes, Raxe had yanked his hand out of the Titan's Ore.

Raxe's face was expressionless, with the exception of his eyes, which rolled up in his head from the agony. Tears streamed down his face, leaving clean streaks among the soot-stained sweat that coated his brown skin.

The scorching molten ore began to dry and tighten even as the excess dripped from his fist back into the cauldron. Ethan thought he saw bits of blackened flesh attached to some of the glowing molten droplets.

Raxe strained to open his hand against the searing pain of the hardening, tightening ore and somehow managed to keep his face calm. The energy it would take to frown or moan was diverted to the task of opening his hand. Raxe knew the appendage would be completely useless if it was petrified and completely closed. Sheer strength of will enabled him to partially open his hand before the ore hardened.

The result was something that resembled a bird's claw.

All five fingers were covered with the Titan's Ore. The flesh had been completely burned away on every finger except the thumb, leaving four silvery skeletal digits frozen in a permanent partial clutch. The knuckles were exaggerated by the metal coating to make them appear bulbous in comparison with the rest of the bony fingers.

Only the top half of the thumb was coated. The back of his hand was totally coated, as well, from his knuckles to just above his wrist, stopping at the bottom joint of his thumb and leaving him partial movement in that digit only. The inside of his palm was striped with the hardened metal where the liquid ran across it in several thin diagonal rivulets to drip off of his hand.

Ethan gawked, dumbstruck by what he was seeing. Raxe's face remained amazingly calm even though his right hand throbbed with excruciating agony, as evidenced by the involuntary tears that continued to stream down his cheeks, tears way to big to be mistaken for sweat. Raxe took another deep breath and turned his gaze to the young Sureblade.

"Ouch," he rasped.

"Why in the name of the Seven – " Ethan began to swear.

"*This* is what I had to give up," Raxe interrupted, his voice low and halting, like stone scraping fitfully against stone. He paused to take another deep and controlled breath before continuing. "Like I said, the blood was the catalyst, not the sacrifice. I had to surrender the use of something." He looked down at his distorted hand, "...something I *needed*."

"But that is too much to give," Ethan protested. His own sacrifice suddenly seemed trivial compared to what the offworlder just surrendered for him. Guilt started to get the better of him. "How did you come to such a decision?"

"I've always been afraid for the people I lead into missions," Raxe explained. "That's why I prefer to work alone. I've been unusually afraid for you. I had the same concerns you had. They were playing out in my dreams."

"Dreams?" Ethan asked.

"Well, nightmares, really," Raxe said. "They started on the day I found out Rionn had decided to send you with us. I've been afraid you'd get killed fighting against enemies that had some kind of advantage, either magical or physical, the way your father did.

"At first I thought it was just my subconscious telling me you shouldn't be with us. I thought maybe I was feeling guilty about not being able to save your father. I didn't want the same thing to happen with you.

"That kind of worry could distract me at the worst possible time. Last night I decided to send you back, but then I remembered how adamant Rionn Lorr was about you coming with us. He fears what would happen if you leave the mission."

"What would happen?" Ethan asked with nervous curiosity.

"We'd lose."

"Really?" Ethan asked. A bit of pride began to swell in his chest. "We will lose without me?"

"We may lose *with* you," Raxe rumbled. "So don't get too full of yourself. He didn't say it in those exact words, but he knew we needed you. And after all I've been through since I first came to this world, I don't believe in coincidence any more.

"Rionn Lorr picking you for this mission was the beginning. There's also the promise I made to your mother that I would get you back to her safely. And then there was my unusual concern about your safety. That all happened for a reason. I figured I had better think of a way to protect you without sending you home before this is over."

"So you gave me magic," Ethan concluded. "And you gave up your hand."

"I didn't know I had to give up the hand until that vapor almost strangled me just now," Raxe admitted. "By then, I was committed. Had I known before then, I probably would've just sent your ass back to the palace."

The weight of the guilt Ethan felt from Raxe's great sacrifice grew even heavier with the enormity of what he was hearing. And then a terrible thought occurred to him.

"If you did not have a vision telling you specifically to make a weapon for me, how do you know this was the solution?"

"I don't," Raxe admitted.

"But what if you are mistaken?"

"I guess whether or not we find that out is up to you."

Ethan felt a rush of anxiety wash through him. As flattered as he was to have a Child of the Old Ones craft a weapon for him, the reason for it was chilling. A Child had just told him that without him, the demon would surely win, which meant his beloved kingdom – and likely the rest of the world – would fall. It seemed unfair that such a responsibility would be placed upon him without him having more time to mull over his options.

But then he had to admit that he had no one to blame but himself. He was so excited about the prospect of getting the weapon Raxe promised him that he failed to consider the true cost of what he was accepting.

Raxe saw all of the conflicting emotions flash across Ethan's face and realized the affect his words must have had on the teen.

"Understand that if I'm wrong about this weapon it won't be your fault," the offworlder assured. "It will be my fault for misreading the situation. All I ask is that you do your best and use it wisely."

"I will," Ethan promised.

"I believe you," Raxe said. A wince finally found its way to his countenance as a new surge of pain shot through his hand. "We're done with your part in this." He dismissed his pained expression with another deep breath. "Go get some air and try to get some rest. I'll send for you when the weapon is finished."

Ethan wanted to stay. He realized, though, that if the offworlder wanted him to stay he would have instructed him to do so. This was a polite dismissal, and probably so Raxe could stop trying to hide how much pain he was really feeling. Ethan nodded and took a few steps toward the exit and then stopped to look back at the offworlder.

"If I may ask," Ethan began, "What kind of weapon will you craft?"

"I don't know yet," Raxe admitted. "Something will come to me."

Ethan turned and left. He walked thoughtfully through the doors of smaller forging room, the massive main hall, and then the wide iron double doors to the corridor outside the smithy.

After the loud toll of the closing double doors, Ethan heard a bellowing roar of pain over the din of the smithy's normal sounds. He took a deep breath and paused to ask his father and the Lord Ascendant to give him the strength to live up to the offworlder's sacrifice.

* * *

Raxe seemed to stare at the iron door for a time after he released his agonized cry. But it was not the door he was seeing. He was seeing his grandfather. He looked down at Questblade where it lay less than a foot away from him and wondered what his great grandfather had given up to forge it.

He thought about the Shield of Innocents that was hopefully keeping his grandfather and Lisa safe. He now *knew* what Dan had given up to create it. A pang of guilt stabbed at him and a sad smile spread slowly across his lips.

"Now I understand your sacrifice, gramps."

5.6

Joel sat up, startled, and tried to determine where he was. The air was chilly but the warm sunlight made it comfortable. The smell of fresh grass almost overwhelmed him after so much time smelling nothing but the stink of mold, mildew, body odor and human waste. He still wore the tattered breeches he had worn during his captivity and wore nothing above them save the countless scars and bruises from his brutal treatment in Tauran's dungeon.

His shadow stretched out in front of him and Joel immediately realized that he only saw *one* shadow. Mindful of the aches that still plagued him from head to toe, he turned his head slowly and craned his neck to look up at the sky.

Hope filled him when he saw only one sun shining in the clear blue sky. Tears of joy rushed down his face as he struggled to his feet and turned in a slow circle to take in his surroundings. Tall, deep green grass carpeted the landscape in every direction for as far as the eye could see. He had no idea how he had escaped his chains or how he had ended up in the middle of a grassy field. All he knew was that he was free, and that he was *home.*

Now he needed to know how to find Lisa. After a second look around Joel got a sense of the familiar. The soft roll of the land invoked a vague recollection from years past. He had been in this field before. He had come across the WorldGate into a pasture just outside of Tuskegee, AL. Lisa once asked him to go with her on a farm call to this very field while she was completing her internship in large animal medicine. It was a mild cool winter day in the Deep South instead of a bitterly cold Chicago winter, which would have been rather inconvenient in the rags he was wearing. And it was pure luck that the pasture had not been recently occupied, or he could have easily woken up in a pile of cow dung.

One more turn was taken to get his bearings. If memory served him, a barn was just over a small rise to the west and the road just on the other side of a hill to the east. When he turned east, he saw the hill.

Someone…no, some*thing* was standing at the base of the hill that was definitely not there before. The stench of musk and sulfur and fear chased away the sweet scents of nature. To Joel's horror, the figure was far more familiar than the pasture, and it sent a cold dagger of fear into his gut.

It was nighttime when Joel had last seen this creature. As fearful as it was to behold in darkness, the thing was even worse with the sunlight to reveal it in all of its terrible detail.

It resembled a man, but its staggering size was definitely not human. It was eight feet tall with thighs like tree trunks straining against the taught fabric of woolen breeches. Calf muscles the size of basketballs burst from the torn hem of the breeches and from them stretched broad shins and bare feet that dug into the earth like the roots of an oak.

Scythes of yellowed bone replaced hands at the end of arms that hung almost apelike. Its immense shoulders were misshapen with muscle. From deltoid to deltoid was five feet of bulging sinew. The shoulders rose like mountains to a wide neck roped with tendons. But the hairless head that sat upon the neck was of normal size, which made it look freakishly small compared to the rest of its body.

Its skin was a dull, ashen shade of brown. The brow was so heavy that the eyes were cast in shadow even in the sunlight, but the red glow shimmering in those shadows was all too familiar. The face was familiar, too. It was a distorted version of his face.

It was *the evil*.

Another tear, one of frustration and rage, forced its way down Joel's face. "Another nightmare," he sighed. "I'm still in that damned dungeon."

The creature's answer was a snarl and a charge. Joel was fully aware that he was having a nightmare but he knew how painful a nightmare it could be. The evil meant to kill him, violently, and Joel had no idea whether or not dying in this dream would cause him to die in the real world, so he turned and ran.

The evil took three bounding steps and leapt into the sky.

Joel broke sharply to the right, taking himself out of the evil's path. After only a few fear-fueled steps, the evil hit the ground right in front of him. It landed with a force that made the earth heave and sent Joel tumbling into the grass. As Joel tried to rise, its huge shadow engulfed him. The evil slammed into his back, driving him into the ground and crushing the air from his lungs. He heard the sickening crunch of his ribs breaking and felt excruciating pain that could only be a precursor to death.

But Joel did not die. He screamed and scrambled and worked his way painfully around until he was lying on his back beneath the evil. With the flat side of its left scythe-hand, the creature pinned Joel's wrists to the ground over his head while holding the point of the right scythe over Joel's chest, poised to strike.

Their last confrontation ended in an almost identical position. Joel ended the confrontation by finding the strength to gain the upper position and morphing his own hand into a bone-scythe to drive its deadly point into the throat of the evil. He believed he could do it again. He could feel the strength to do it building within him.

But he refused to, because the last time he did, he came a breath away from murdering his wife. If he had not awoken from that dream when he did, he would have driven fingers deformed into deadly talons into Lisa's throat. Joel feared he was about to do the same to Dayna where she hung suspended from chains bolted into the wall across the cell from him.

Instead of fighting back, Joel tried to wake himself. He tried his very best but he could not manage it. Yet the evil did not strike. It seemed it would at any moment but the bone scythe did not descend. The reason was slowly starting to dawn on Joel.

"You *want* me to kill you so I can kill Dayna," Joel accused. "You're trying to turn me into a willful killer."

The evil's blood-red eyes gleamed sharper. It bared a mouth full of twisted shark's teeth and brought the deadly tip of the scythe blade to Joel's throat. It cut painfully into Joel's skin, sending rivulets of blood running down his throat.

"I won't do it," Joel said. "You can't turn me into a killer."

"Heh," the evil chuckled in a human voice that did not go with its face at all. "You're already a killer. And do not for a moment think that your god can save you. I've heard you praying, asking for forgiveness for the lives you've stolen. Asking to be released from your captivity. Look what all of your prayers have gotten you."

"I couldn't stop the killing then," Joel argued. "But I can now. You won't turn me into a *willful* killer." Understanding suddenly dawned on him. "And *you* won't kill me, will you?"

"Perhaps," the evil snarled. "Though you'll wish you were dead when I'm done with you."

It lifted the scythe hand from Joel's throat and drove it into his chest, but instead of puncturing him, it *burned* him, sending the smell of his own scorched flesh wafting into his nostrils and shocking him with an exquisite agony that dwarfed any pain he had ever felt.

Joel squeezed his eyes shut and screamed. When he opened his eyes he saw Leesil, one of his many tormentors, standing before him pulling a glowing orange-tipped brand away with one hand and holding a blood stained dagger in the other. A shorter man stood next to him stirring a small iron brazier full of red-hot coals.

"No," Joel pled, nearly breathless from the pain. "Please…"

Leesil, with his neatly braided ponytail and overdressed as usual in a gleaming leather vest over a soft cotton blouse and tailored silken breaches tucked into well-shined knee-high riding boots, looked ridiculously out of place in the filthy dungeon. He thrust the poker back into the coals as he smiled and looked over his shoulder to where Dayna hung from the opposite wall.

"He screams like a woman, does he not?" Leesil asked.

Dayna's glare was ice. "So will you when it's you hanging from those chains."

Leeslil chortled. "If this Child of the Old Ones was able to do that, he would have done it by now."

He pulled the brand from the coals and held it up so Joel could see the glowing shape of a wide, broken sword, a miniature version of the sword Tauran carried.

"Cute, is it not?" Leesil taunted as he held the brand in front of Joel's eyes. "The baron so loves his Dragon-fang. Just be thankful he didn't ask me to use his horse brand."

"Why are you doing this?" Joel implored. "No one's asked questions, made any demands. What do you want?"

"Her," Leesil answered, nodding to Dayna. "Tauran says if I do this, he will finally share his coveted brown plaything. Why he wants me to do it is none of my concern. No more talking, offworlder. It's time to scream."

And scream Joel did as Leesil branded him again and again. Joel's voice eventually abandoned him and he could only gasp, choke and cry. His prayers for unconsciousness went unanswered. The few times he felt himself slipping into joyous oblivion, the touch of the brand would shock him right back into excruciating coherence.

But even amid all the pain, one observation did not escape him. He had controlled the evil. That one prayer had been answered, at least. He refused to kill even when his power tried to force him to. It was an unfortunate irony that he finally accomplished that particular goal when it was Leesil standing before him. Giving in to the evil then would have saved him this agony and likely would have freed him.

The memory came back to him of a lesson he was taught while growing up in Catholic school and again while attending Baptist church as an adult: the Lord never gives us a burden greater than we can bear. Joel held tight to this lesson even while a mocking whisper of doubt tried to convince him otherwise. With each burning touch of the broken-sword brand, the whisper grew ever more convincing.

PART II

QUESTS AND ESCAPES

Chapter 6: Blood and Misdirection

6.1

Synn's screams of shock and agony, as short-lived as they were, were music to the demon's ears. She screamed even louder at the beginning, when her killer's eyes started to glow fiery red, and when she saw the reptilian snout suddenly jut from the otherwise handsome human face. The scream only lasted for a moment, though, because the demon quickly silenced her by snapping its terrible maw around her neck, breaking it and crushing her windpipe and severing her jugular veins and carotid arteries, all in one savage bite.

In the middle of the southeastern Texas woods, miles away from civilization, her screams likely would not be heard, but the demon nonetheless sank its rows of fangs deeply into her neck to silence her quickly. It knew that for now, at least, secrecy was its greatest ally, and it would not risk a witness within earshot. Until its greatest threats were eliminated, its true nature had to remain hidden.

The Dierglyorr had indeed missed the screams of its prey while it was imprisoned within the sixth level of hell, but it missed the blood more than anything. The sex was enjoyable as well, but the blood was the real treat.

Especially human blood.

Animals were more of a challenge to hunt than humans. Animals' superior senses, their heightened sensitivity to the supernatural, and their instinctive wariness made them much more difficult to deceive. Of course, all of these things only made the seduction and hunt that much more pleasurable. In addition to the greater challenge they represented, the blood of wild animals was sweeter than human blood. Their diets, at least the diets of the non-carrion eating species, made their fluids more pure than the chemical-laden blood of humans and their domesticated pets. Even the blood of scavengers and carrion eaters, while not as sweet, possessed a bitter and foul tang that lent it a savory quality that was lacking in human blood.

DEMON OF LORR

Men and women were easier to deceive and seduce with simple morphing and spells of rapture. And in this world of technology, virtually bereft of magic compared to many of the dimensions beyond the WorldGate, humans' general lack of true morality and their refusal to believe in the supernatural made them more susceptible to the demon's formidable powers of persuasion. As a result, humans provided almost no challenge in the seduction or the hunt.

What they did provide, though, were exquisite emotions. They were intoxicating. Human moans of lust and pleasure, followed closely by their screams of terror and agony when the demon morphed its member to its inhumanly large and barbed true form while inside its victims, were pleasures that he missed immensely during its two thousand year confinement. Humans' intense emotions added a delightful and addictive flavor to their flesh, blood, and bones that was unmatched by any other species in creation.

The only beings that came close to matching humans in both euphoria and suffering were dragons. They were also much more attuned to the supernatural than any other species and thus even more challenging to hunt. Yes, dragons were the best of both worlds, but the problem with dragons was the risk they posed. The demon knew it could best any dragon – even the mighty Worldhopper, with sufficient preparation. However, the risk of significant injury from a confrontation with those beasts was too great, and with Worldhopper, critical injury was all but assured.

The Dierglyorr had no true fear of injury. It was a fast healer, and in any event, it found immense pleasure in pain. But the Dierglyorr had much to accomplish and could not spare even the brief time it would take to recover from the damage a dragon could inflict upon it while being ravaged and savaged.

Oh, but there would be time enough for dragon hunting. Once all of the Children of the Old Ones were disposed of and the humanoid races were properly subjugated, the Dierglyorr would turn its attention to the dragons...and it would start with their king, Worldhopper.

Other than primary purpose of helping to subjugate the races, the destruction of dragons and Children of the Old ones were, after all, the reasons the Leader gods created the fierce upper level demons.

The human the demon feasted upon this night, or at least what remained of her, was the stripper and prostitute who fittingly called herself "Synn." Synn was even less of a challenge than the average human. The only real challenge had been to seduce her sufficiently to acquire her services for free without using its considerable persuasive magic. The Dierglyorr had plenty of cash in its possession, to be sure, but it had to provide what little sport for itself that it could.

On the other hand, it thought, while it tore into her belly with its pointed teeth and with fingers that had elongated and sharpened into claws, she was more flavorful than the average human because of the taint of the Child of the Ones she bore.

The Dierglyorr could taste the residue of Ryan's sweat on Synn's body. It could detect the last vestiges of the Child's scent upon her breasts as it ripped them from her torso. The woman had bathed often and had been with several other men in the weeks since she had lain with Ryan, but the Child's divine taint was not so easily purged, at least not from the magnificent senses of the Dierglyorr.

Synn's companion, Honey, would not have been as tasty a treat as this one, but she would have been a nice appetizer or desert. Unfortunately, she had a strong enough will to resist the Dierglyorr's miniscule efforts at seduction back at the cabaret in South Houston. It could have easily had her join them if it thought she was worth the slightest extra effort, but the scent of the Child Ryan Franklin on Synn arrested the demon's attention so completely that it had to have her as quickly as possible. It could always return for Honey if it were so inclined, though it doubted it would be.

Yes, Synn would do for now. This small taste of the Child Ryan Franklin went a long way towards re-igniting the demon's passion for its current task.

DEMON OF LORR

It had often found itself terribly bored in this modern time, so different from the one it remembered. There were so many more Children of the Old Ones to kill back then. There were so many more magical creatures to bend to its will.

So many more playthings with which to play.

Heaven's War had wiped out most of them. In fact, a great many of them were destroyed when the Dierglyorr led the Leader Children against the Gatekeeper and Raxe at the Battle of the Bountiful Forest. Even the mighty Dierglyorr lost its earthly life at that battle, but it was victorious all the same. The Dierglyorr and its army successfully killed the last two Old Ones and all but a few of Their Children. The loss of its own earthly life was inconsequential. It knew it would be confined to hell, and because the Old Ones were foolish enough to allow for the creation of the Hell Key, the Dierglyorr knew it was only a matter of time before one or more of Their imbecilic Children used that Key to free it.

For a time, the Dierglyorr had its doubts. Over two thousand years had passed since Heaven's War, and much of the old histories had gone the way of legend: forgotten or dismissed as imaginative faerie tales. The histories concerning the Keys were no exception.

And then Mar-dah, an overly ambitious wizard and Child of the Old Ones, decided to find out if the Hell Key and WorldGate Key were real. If so, he knew those powerful talismans would aid him in his quest for dominion over all of the Known Lands and beyond.

Mar-dah was a fool to think he could control the magic of the Hell Key. He did a fairly decent job of opening the gates of the hells that contained demons he could control, but what he did not understand, or did not care about, was that each use served to temporarily weaken *all* of the gates. The powerful and ever diligent Dierglyorr felt the weakening of the gates – as slight and fleeting as they were – and hurried to put itself into a position to slip free if and when the opportunity presented itself.

And alas, that opportunity came when the foolish Head Mage drew upon Nature's magic at the Tyne River in an effort to thwart the loosed lower-level demons.

Rionn Lorr knew full well the risk of such an action, but in his inanely altruistic desire to save his people, he took the risk. His drawing of magic from Nature to replenish his spent energies compounded Mar-dah's weakening of the Hell Gates for less than a microsecond; all the time needed for the alert and powerful Dierglyorr. That briefest of moments was enough for it to slip through the Hell Gates and begin its own schemes of dominion and destruction.

Those schemes were now in full flower. The demon had pawns, some willing and some unaware, on both sides of the WorldGate. One of its willing pawns had very recently quit its service but that was of little consequence. That one had already fulfilled the demon's purpose and was as inconsequential as the woman the demon was currently devouring.

The demon was mildly surprised that Dan and Lisa had lasted this long, but it was only a matter of time before they were run down. The Dierglyorr briefly considered going after them itself, but the fact that the eldest living Child of the Old Ones had eluded his pawns thus far was evidence that he was cagier than the demon assumed he would be.

He was still a Child, after all. He was a Child whose true magic was ignited by the presence of demons and demon magic. He grew more powerful in proportion to the power and number of demons he confronted. With nearly two hundred years to formulate contingency plans, the old man might still be a significant threat with or without the enchanted battleaxe.

And besides, the age of the oldster would make him dry and bland to the demon's palate.

Ryan, on the other hand – the Dierglyorr refused to call him "Raxe," for the true Raxe was an Old One, and this mere human was undeserving of the name – was more ideal game. He was powerful enough to provide an entertaining challenge but not experienced enough to pose a serious threat. If the

Dierglyorr was careful and patient, and it would be, it would eventually find a way to separate Ryan from Demonsbane and feast upon the Child.

What did concern the demon were the unexpected appearances of the elf and the half-blood faerie Child. Ryan should have been forced to fight off a surprise attack from two *Ken d'Zanir*, an attack he would not have survived. And then, with four of *Ken* warriors against the Sureblade whelp, along with the Head Mage and the changeling runt without their magic, the confrontation would have been decided in mere moments.

That would have been the best way to deal with the wizard. Rionn Lorr, like Dan, was too dangerous to face directly. To human eyes the wizard looked to be in his late thirties or early forties, but he was actually closer to sixty years old. His considerable natural power as a wizard Child of the Old Ones and his years of training made him very formidable. The Dierglyorr had no doubt that it would prevail against all of its foes, including Rionn Lorr, but why risk injury when the Child's magic could be stifled to make him as vulnerable as any other mortal.

The elf's presence ruined that first opportunity to slay the wizard. Rell Kallen saved Ryan and helped fight off the *Ken*. But there would be other opportunities. Now that it knew the elf was accompanying them, the demon would make the appropriate arrangements.

The demon was not surprised or overly concerned by the interference of the water faerie. The Mistress of the Sea of Spirits would be dealt with very soon. Hers and Ryan's daughter, however, was a different matter. Azhju'lestra's unprecedented mix of bloodlines made her an unforeseen wildcard that could not be tolerated.

The Dierglyorr had to admit that the water faerie did an effective job of keeping her hybrid Child a secret, but she was a secret no more. Now the water faerie and her Daughter, along with the Ranger Elf, would all be handled the same way the Dierglyorr handled all of its irritants.

Now finished with its treat, the Dierglyorr stood straight and tall. Its red-furnace eyes burned through the darkness as it looked down at what was left of Synn's blood and gore-spattered corpse. A forked tongue licked away the blood from its muzzle and it smiled a demon's smile.

With the sound of ripping flesh and cracking bones, a pair of leathery dragon's wings, each longer than the demon was tall, emerged from its back. With a powerful leap and an even more powerful thrust of its wings, it soared into the night, leaving the broken and shredded remains of its feast to nocturnal scavengers.

Playtime was over. The time was nigh for the Dierglyorr to take more direct action in its campaign. It was time to wipe away its irritants in a smear of blood.

6.2

Visions of violent deaths haunted Lisa's dreams. She relived all of the killings she had witnessed over the past few days. Only a few hours earlier, Lisa sat less than two feet away as Dan blasted that helicopter pilot out of his own airborne chopper. A few days earlier she watched Dan rip out a man's throat with one bare hand. She would never foget how the wet gargling noises made by the dying would-be thief followed her as she sprinted out of the cheap hotel room. Just moments after that she saw Dan decapitate another man with one perfect shot from his intricately modified shotgun. Each shocking death sent a fresh jolt of terror through her as if she witnessed it for the first time.

She knew she was dreaming and tried several times to rouse herself without success. After what seemed like an eternity, her dreams took her back to the very first time she witnessed a killing.

She and Joel were riding north along a snow-laden southern Illinois highway. The air was colder than she remembered, colder than it should have been in the heated interior of their pickup truck. She had been resting peacefully when a hard thump and crash jolted her awake. The ensuing madness of Joel confronting the driver and passenger of the other vehicle ended with the driver pointing a gun right at Joel's face. They exchanged words that she could not hear, and then time seemed to slow.

Lisa watched breathlessly as her husband, a peaceful man who had always been adept at avoiding physical conflict, who had never even fired a gun, took the driver's weapon with deft movements and ruthless precision. The resulting shots reverberated like thunder in Lisa's mind and finally thrust her from her slumber.

The fading echo of the gunshots, along with the image of one of the dead men with a clean shot to center of his forehead and the other with a perfect shot to the temple, each lying in a spreading pool of blood, lingered in her mind after she woke up.

She was seized with momentary panic. Her sleep-hazed mind tried to figure out where she was. Wherever she was, it was cold and very dark. She looked around frantically, blinking as hard as she could to help her eyes adjust to the darkness. The scent of sawdust and motor oil filled her nostrils and reminded her that she and Dan were in Nathaniel Rogers's work shop and tool shed.

She tried to move her left hand but was unable. Something hard was cutting into her wrist and held it fast. With her right hand she reached over to feel the object. The inspection confirmed that her wrist was still bound by a plastic cuff. Only this time it bound her to a metal table leg. The feel of the table leg jogged her memory of being marched at gunpoint into the shed. By then, the adrenaline of the day had long since faded and was replaced by utter exhaustion. Both she and Dan were too tired and too weak to resist as Nathaniel secured them within the shed.

Dan's voice floated through the darkness from several yards away: "That you moving around over there, girl?"

"Who else would it be?" Lisa asked wryly.

Dan chuckled. "Rats have been scuttling around all night. I think a possum or something scooted through here, too."

Lisa yelped in panic and tried to stand. And then she yelped in pain as she almost snatched her left arm out of the socket and the plastic cuff dug painfully into her wrist.

Dan laughed. "I'm glad my eyes have adjusted to the low light! I would've hated to miss that!"

"That's not funny, god da– "

"Whoa!" Dan cut her off. "Don't forget to respect your elders, young lady. Besides, you're a vet. Little animals shouldn't scare you."

"I don't work on rats and possums, you old bas–"

"When did you develop such a potty mouth, girl?"

"Around the time people started shooting at me."

"We ain't got time for you to cuss me out," Dan cut her off again. He reached up with his free left hand and tapped a long wrinkled finger to his right ear.

Lisa was startled when she heard his voice again because this time it was a loud whisper, literally inside of her ear, and it was laced with static.

"You remember our plan?" he asked.

"Oh," Lisa whispered, pushing her frustration aside and focusing on their predicament. She tapped her right earring. "I forgot about the camouflaged earpieces."

"Good idea, huh?" Dan returned. "I'm pretty sure Nate Junior has some listening devices in here. But he shouldn't be able to pick us up when we whisper this low. So do you remember the plan?"

"Plan?" Lisa asked. She did not have any idea what Dan was talking about. And then she remembered his voice whispering to her softly during the night, apparently through the earpiece. "I thought I was dreaming that."

"You *were* pretty out of it," Dan noted.

"Well *you* slept all the way here," Lisa accused.

"Just answer the question, girl," Dan demanded.

Before Lisa could respond, the door to the shed opened and filled the room with dim, pre-dawn light. Nathaniel's tall silhouette filled the doorway. He was holding something in both hands but Lisa could not tell what it was.

"Rise and shine, people," he ordered with the cadence of a drill sergeant. "I brought some juice and toast. I'd hate to turn you two in with empty stomachs."

"That's sweet of you, kid," Dan said sarcastically.

"Mr. Rogers," Lisa began, wondering if she would chuckle at his name if the circumstances had been different. "I have to use the ladies' room."

"Number one or number two?" Nathaniel asked.

Lisa frowned. "Does it matter?" she asked.

"Sure," Nathaniel answered. "It'll help me decide whether or not watch. No ladies' rooms out here. You'll have to go right there."

Lisa sneered. "I guess I'll have to surprise you," she snarled through clenched teeth.

"I have to go, too," Dan said. "The least you could do is let us go somewhere more private."

Nathanial shot Dan an incredulous look as he set the tray of food on the floor of the shed. He gave it a slight shove with the toe of his shoe, sliding the tray between Dan and Lisa and close enough for both of them to reach.

"You're joking, right? You're lucky I brought you something to eat. I *might* consider letting her go around back. But I'm not taking my eyes off of you."

"What?" Dan teased. "You're afraid I'll get loose and sneak out of here, aren't you?"

"You'll let me go around back?" Lisa asked hopefully, seizing on Nathaniel's earlier comment.

Nathaniel stared at her lustily for a long moment before answering. "I've changed my mind, sweetie," he said with a lewd smile. "I think I'll watch. But I promise I'll go get you some tissue paper afterward."

Lisa's angry glare cut through Nathaniel like a dagger of ice. "Bastard," she whispered. With a frustrated grunt, she managed to shimmy one arm out of the waist-long winter coat she wore and let it slide down her cuffed left arm.

Thank God I'm wearing a long blouse, she thought to herself as she worked her way over to the left and painfully slid her left wrist up along the bolted-down leg of the worktable. She managed to grip it tight enough to balance herself and slide her legs beneath her and then, one leg at a time she rose from a seated position on the floor to a crude squat over it.

True to his word, Nathaniel watched the entire thing. His eyes were riveted even though he was a bit disappointed at the skillful way the shapely young woman managed to work her jeans and panties down below her knees without showing anything above her upper thighs. Her long blouse concealed everything else from that angle, so Nathaniel decided to step around to the other side of the table to have a look.

When he moved, he noticed something troubling out of the corner of his eye. He turned and saw that Dan was gone. Only the plastic cuff remained, still looped around the floor-bolted leg of the lathing table.

Nathaniel's gun was drawn in an instant. He wheeled around in a complete circle but Dan was nowhere to be seen. In confusion and near panic, he turned to Lisa.

"Where the hell did the old man go?" He demanded.

Lisa looked as confused as Nathaniel. "I see an old man right in front of me holding a gun," she griped, "A perverted old man, at that."

"Dan!" Nathaniel snapped, wheeling around once more. "Come out where I can see you or I shoot the girl!"

The only response Nathaniel received was a sharp pain to his right wrist that forced him to drop his gun. That pain was followed by another sharp pain to the back of his head. The room spun around uncontrollably in his vision. He staggered around to see Dan's wrinkled, smiling brown face and a length of two-by-four in his hands just before Nathaniel fell unconscious to the dusty floor.

"Is he dead?" Lisa asked, already hustling to pull up her clothes.

"No," Dan answered. He made an effort – and it took a Herculean effort – not to look at her as he knelt down carefully to check Nathaniel's pulse. "He'll be OK. Those Rogers men have big, hard heads." Dan's concerned look darkened to something else. "If his dad and I hadn't been friends, though, he'd be a dead man."

"Why would you have killed him?" Lisa demanded. "It's not enough to knock him out?"

"Not when he can come after us," Dan explained patiently. "Not when he can give information to the people hunting us. Leaving him alive is a sentimental move that could put us in danger. But I won't betray big Nate like that."

"Little Nate doesn't know how lucky he is," Lisa mumbled, fumbling with her jacket.

Dan struggled to his feet and shuffled over to her. On the way, he lifted a box cutter from the worktable. He cut Lisa free and tried to help her up and almost tumbled over in the process. Lisa had to push herself quickly to her feet in order to steady him.

"You're still weak," Lisa noted needlessly.

"I know," Dan said with no trace of his earlier irritability. "And I'm slow. I thought it'd take forever to get close enough to Nate to hit him."

"How'd you do that?" she asked. "How'd you get out of the cuff? And how did he not see you creeping up with that two-by-four? It took all my will power not to stare at you."

Dan smiled a weak, but sly smile. "You make a damn good distraction. I also used the power of suggestion. He didn't see me because he *thought* I was gone. I planted the suggestion when I mentioned him being afraid of me escaping. A little boost of magic made him think I did. As for the cuff, I used a spell to heat up the plastic tie enough to expand and slip out of it. I got a little burn on my wrist but it'll be fine."

"Magic," Lisa breathed. The look of wonderment on her face quickly morphed to worry. "What's the deal with you? You finally got some sleep but you're still so weak."

Dan sighed reluctantly. "I'll tell you later. We've got things to do right now. Help me over to Nate so we can show him how those damn cuffs feel."

"Talk while we work," Lisa persisted. "I'm prepared to pester you like a four year old until you tell me."

Dan grunted, having no doubt that she would do exactly what she threatened. "Short version: During World War Two, I created the enchanted shield. In exchange for the energy needed to power the enchantment..." Dan trailed off for a few breaths before continuing.

"I had to give up the use of my legs," he went on. "It didn't happen all at once, but by the time the war ended the muscles had started to wither and the bones grew brittle. I could walk for a few more years but it kept getting worse. My daughter, Ryan's mother, kept trying to talk me into going to a doctor. I knew there was no point."

"But you did eventually go, right?" Lisa asked. Her medical curiosity was piqued.

Dan nodded yes. "Cynthia insisted on ruling out the possibility that it was curable. She was persistent like you. I finally went just to make her happy. Of course the doctors didn't have a clue. I decided to go with the wheel chair to conserve my legs for as long as possible before they completely deteriorated."

Lisa was fascinated. "How were you able to walk for all of this time?"

"One of the many enchantments Shanderah taught me decades ago. I've been reciting a chant for years, every day and every night, right before my prayers. It stores magical energies over an indefinite amount of time for later use. I'd been in a chair for a few years before she taught it to me so I was afraid it wouldn't do any good. I tested it every now and then over the years to make sure it worked. It did.

"I used that stored magic to power my legs for this mission. But using it, along with the other magic I've had to use, is making it dissipate faster than I hoped."

Lisa thought about the implications of that. She was not strong enough to be his physical crutch. She could not imagine having to wheel him around in a chair. What if they have to run? What if they have to fight? Her free left arm went to her forehead and she started rubbing worriedly.

"You're scared you'll have to carry me?" Dan teased.

Lisa shook her head vigorously. "This is nothing to joke about, Dan. I don't see how we can do this if you can't walk. I'm sorry, I just…"

Dan's playful smirk vanished. His jaw set firmly. He took her wrist gently and pulled her nervous hand away from her forehead and he looked into Lisa's brown eyes.

"Do you trust me?" he asked without a hint of mirth.

Lisa thought about the many times he had saved her life. Their very first meeting, in fact, consisted of him saving her. His advice and directions, as strange as they were, had kept them alive much longer than she had any right to expect.

"Yes, Dan," she answered. "I trust you."

"Good," Dan said, exhaling heavily, "because you're going to *hate* this plan."

6.3

Hunter used one hand to shield the side of his face from the light of the rising sun and used the other to steer the sedan down Interstate 65 at eighty-five miles per hour. He had a white-knuckled grip on the steering wheel and tried his best not to look in his rear view mirror. To his right sat Shepherd, as stiff as a statue, his eyes wide and his teeth clinched.

Behind them, filling half of the width of the car with its ever-expanding bulk was the terrifying dog-creature that Shepherd's boss told him was called a retriever. Back when they merged onto I-24 from I-57, Chi-Chi started to grow. Every time one of the agents looked back at it, it was bigger than it was the previous time.

So they stopped looking.

By the time they passed through Vienna, IL, roughly thirty miles north of Paducah, the creature had grown too large to fit into the deep back seat while facing forward. So its forepaws rested on the floor just behind the front seats. Its shoulders were almost as high as the agents' shoulders. The Chihuahua-like head had grown almost wide enough to span the entire space between the front seats. The sound of its panting filled the car and threw moist heat into the front of the car. Its eyes shone intensely enough to cast an eerie pale purple glow.

"This damn monster-dog is going to make me shit myself," Hunter complained in a whisper.

"We've *gotta* be close," Shepherd said. "Be glad. The sooner we catch them the sooner we'll be done with Chi-Chi."

Hunter replied by pressing the gas pedal even harder, bringing their speed to ninety-five miles per hour. They flew down I-24 for another few minutes and then Shepherd's cell phone chirped. It was a different tone than the one Hunter recognized. He looked out of the corner of his eye as Shepherd retrieved his cell phone.

Instead of answering it, he clicked a button on the small display and stared down at it for a moment.

"Is that a text?" Hunter asked.

"Yeah," Shepherd answered with a relieved smile. "Someone caught our rabbits for us. They're being held in a barn in Paducah. We'll have 'em in just a few minutes."

"Are any other agents are en route?" Hunter asked.

"Probably," Shepherd said. "And not just our guys. We intercepted a call to the FBI."

Hunter drove even faster. "We have to get there first."

As they approached the exit to State Highway 45, Chi-Chi growled from deep in its chest and abruptly turned to the right. It brought its muscular forelegs back onto the seat and swiveled its head to the right. It had to dip its torso low to stand on the seat and still its wide shoulders pressed against the roof of the car. Its smaller, lower hindquarters were several inches below the roof of the car, but the creature had grown so long that its backside pushed against the rear driver side door.

"What now?" Hunter asked. The nervousness in his voice was still audible just below the tone of irritation.

Shepherd gave him a pointed look. "What the hell do you think?"

"I'm not changing direction," Hunter said stubbornly. "You just got the text. They're in Paducah."

"Man," Shepherd warned, "if I were you I'd head west on forty-five. That's the direction Chi-Chi is indicating."

Hunter shook his head. "We're at least checking out Paducah, first."

"I'm sure our other team will beat the feds to Paducah, Hunter. Don't be a dumbass."

"A quick look at the barn and then we head west," Hunter persisted.

Shepherd did not answer. Instead, he cast a fearful glance over his shoulder and slid to his right as far as he could against the door. Hunter noticed the motion. Any curiosity he had about the strange movement was thrust quickly away when he saw the purple light shifting within the car.

Not only could he feel the hot breath of the animal in the back seat, he could also feel the near-searing heat from the purple light shining directly on him. He risked a glance at his rear view mirror and in the reflection of the weird light he saw the wide brow of the creature turned toward him. He felt more than heard the bass rumble of Chi-Chi's hungry growl. A chill went through him as if he had cracked a window to let in the cold winter air.

Hunter decelerated quickly and turned onto the Hwy 45 West exit.

6.4

Two men wearing long dark parkas that were just a little bit warm even for wintertime in northern Kentucky crept up to the open barn-like door of the shed. As they came nearer, they each pulled HK G36 assault rifles from their coats. One of the men stepped silently around the back of the barn and the other waited patiently until his companion reappeared around the far corner of the small structure.

With practiced synchronicity, one peeked in the door and pulled back quickly and then the other swung into the doorway with his machine gun leveled. The other stepped from the other side an instant later.

Morning sunlight filled the shed and showed them that there was only one person inside. That person was a middle-aged man cuffed to a floor-bolted table leg. He was sitting on the ground looking annoyed and slightly embarrassed.

"Are you Nathaniel Rogers?" asked one of the gunmen.

"Yes," said the handcuffed man. "You're the FBI?"

"Sure," the other agent answered.

Nathaniel eyed them for a moment. "Can I see some ID?"

The agent who spoke first looked around the shed again. "I take it the old man and the girl aren't here anymore."

"How'd you guess?" Nathaniel asked sarcastically. "They stole my plane a couple of hours ago but I don't know where they went. And I'm still waiting for some ID."

The other agent stared at Nathaniel with indifference. "If you don't have the fugitives you don't need to see ID."

The two men slipped their machine guns back into their parkas and turned to leave.

"Wait!" Nathaniel called. "Are you gonna help me outta this?"

His only answer was the sound of the men's fading footsteps crunching on the cold ground outside.

"Damn it," Nathaniel swore. Margaret picked one hell of a time to visit relatives. He hoped he could yell loud enough for his neighbors to hear.

Chapter 7: The Light of Day

7.1

Baron Tauran looked down on Louis from the plush throne atop the dais in his throne room. He wore a crimson doublet embroidered with gold thread with ruffled cuffs and collar, dark purple trousers and black soft leather riding boots. His unruly, dark brown, shoulder length hair was out of place with his garb, but he at least tied it back with a thin leather thong. The broken greatsword Dragon-fang rested on the right armrest of the throne.

It was a most comfortable seat, and Tauran knew it suited him. T'Cheln stood behind him and to his left his sword-breaker dagger hanging from one hip and short sword from the other and his muscular arms crossed. Sitting in the large chair, with the towering *Ken d'Zanir* warrior behind him, Tauran almost felt like royalty.

But it was only a baron's throne, in a baron's throne room, in a baron's castle. It was also a start. Tauran had land and gold and precious gems. Most importantly, though, he had plans. And he had powerful allies that would help bring those plans to fruition. But at the moment he had an annoyance with which to deal.

"You disappoint me, Louis," Tauran admonished. "I granted you a most generous loan three years ago. All I asked in return was a bit of grain at harvest time, and here you come to me with nothing."

The tall, lanky, dusky blonde-bearded man stood several yards away from the foot of the stairs leading to the dais where the baron's throne rested. His worn dun tunic, woolen breeches and scuffed leather riding boots were in stark contrast to the baron's refined garb. Louis wrung his calloused hands with a combination of nervousness and poorly hidden irritation.

"But Tauran, I – "

"*Baron*," Tauran interrupted. "You will address me as *Baron* Tauran, Louis. Our cordial relationship ended when you chose not to join me in the Legion Midnight."

"I was a newly married man, baron, with a son in my wife's belly."

"Which is why I gave you the loan," Tauran said. "I took our past friendship into consideration and took some pity on you for your circumstances."

"That last bit was a lie, Baron Tauran, and we both know it," Louis snarled, his irritation starting to overshadow his nerves and good sense. "You gave me the loan because I had a pregnant wife, yes, but pity had nothing to do with it. You knew I was desperate for money and that working the fields would never earn me enough to take care of my wife and me and our child. You wanted me indebted to you."

"I did not grant this audience to split hairs, Louis. I granted you this audience so you could pay me, and you don't have my payment."

"You know I'm good for what I owe. I repaid you according to our agreement and then some both last year and the year before, didn't I?"

"We're talking about *this* year," Tauran reminded.

"The Sureblade bitch stayed with us from the field to the miller's," Louis explained. "She watched us like a hungry eagle watches a field mouse. I never had the opportunity to remove your share of the grain."

"You should have made an opportunity, Louis. She's only one woman. Women are bad with numbers and easily distracted."

"Not this woman," Louis disagreed. "She was well aware of the last two shortfalls and was determined not to allow another. She threatened to withhold the workers' wages if there was another shortfall, and would not pay us until the correct yield was confirmed by the miller."

Tauran shook his head. "Not acceptable, Louis. Our agreement was an eigth of her yield for five consecutive seasons in return for my loan, not two consecutive seasons and an excuse."

"Yes, baron, that is true. However, Annastace let her dissatisfaction be clearly known after last year's shortfall, so I made sure to prepare for this possibility. I've saved enough money to pay you the equivalent value of your share of this season's yield."

"I don't want your coin," Tauran said, his expression darkening. "I want the grain."

"Money is just as good. Why don't you want the coin?"

"Because THAT WAS NOT OUR AGREEMENT!" The baron erupted to his feet, snatched the broken greatsword from the arm of his throne and pointed it in Louis's direction. Louis took several hurried steps backward even though Tauran was nearly ten yards away.

"I want HER grain, not YOUR bloody coin! I don't give half a damn about your money. I want HER to experience a shortfall and the financial ramifications that go with it. I want HER to suffer, her and her whole buggering family. DO YOU UNDERSTAND THAT, LOUIS?"

"Yes, Baron Tauran." Louis's irritation was gone, his nervousness turned to cold fear. "I understand completely."

Tauran placed Dragon-fang back on the arm of his throne. He sat down again and assumed a relaxed posture. "Good. Then how do you intend to pay me?"

"By making Annastace suffer, Baron Tauran." Louis's fear eased and a sly grin spread across his bearded face. "Does the suffering have to be only financial?"

Tauran raised an eyebrow. "Her suffering has to be at least partially financial. The harvest is done so that's not an option. She may have livestock, though. She may have tenants on her properties paying rent to her. Whatever you do has to have the equivalent monetary value of the grain shortfall. But by all means, if you can find an additional means of tormenting the bitch, be as imaginative as you like. Or you could just kill her and her brats. That might be quicker. But if you do, be sure to make her suffer first."

Louis asked: "How soon? And how do you want me to notify you of said payment?"

"I'll know when you've made the payment," Tauran assured. "As for how soon, I am not an unreasonable man. You'll have until I come for you. Exactly how long that is, I cannot say. I have business to attend here in Darshay first. I'll be sure to take into account the time it takes to travel from here to Fort Bastion."

"Yes, baron," Louis said with a respectful bow. "I am anxious to make payment. And I swear to pay with interest for not having the proper payment at this time."

"See to it that you do," Tauran advised. "If you do not, the man behind me, this *Ken d'Zanir*, will come for you. Are you familiar with the *Ken*?"

Louis's smile faded. "Yes, baron. The *Ken* are the elite warriors and assassins from the S'Zan Rho nation."

Tauran nodded. "Are you aware that they will, if their ordered, cut out and eat the tongues of oath breakers?"

"No, baron, I was not aware of that."

"Well, now you are. And I assure you that I will instruct T'Cheln to do just that should you fail me."

"Understood, Baron Tauran." Louis started wringing his hands again.

"Good," Tauran said. "Take your leave, now. I've wasted enough time with you."

Louis turned and made his way to the door of the throne room. Leesil leaned against the wall near the door with his arms folded. His pose was similar to the one assumed by T'Cheln, but where the *Ken*'s posture was relaxed but wary, Leesil's was arrogant and careless. His hair was tied back much neater than Tauran's and held fast with a black silken thong. As usual, he wore fitted leather vest and white cotton blouse with flared sleeves and baggy, soft woolen breeches tucked into knee high riding boots of polished black leather.

Leesil's eyes followed Louis until he walked out. He gave the peasant a mocking bow as he passed. When the door closed behind Louis, Leesil strode toward the dais.

T'Cheln's eyes shifted to focus on his retainer and he spoke in his usual even, bass monotone. "The S'Zan Rho and

Ken d'Zanir are not cannibals, baron. I do not appreciate you disparaging my people."

"I meant no offense," Tauran chuckled, though he made it a point not to meet the *Ken*'s unsettling gaze. "I just thought I'd give the man a little extra incentive."

"Nevertheless," T'Cheln returned. "In any event, we've wasted enough time here. It is time for our next sparring lesson, is it not?"

Tauran rotated his left arm and winced. "Our last lesson has bruised my shoulder as purple as this frilly doublet. I'm starting to think you're using our sparring lessons to take out your frustrations on me. Is that what you're doing?"

"I've been retained to train you and guard you. Neither has been easy. But I am not easily frustrated."

Leesil grinned as he reached the dais. "I notice our tall friend didn't quite answer your question."

T'Cheln said nothing. He only shifted his eyes to Leesil, whose grin immediately faltered. Leesil turned his attention back to Tauran.

"Do you think it wise, *Baron* Dirk Tauran, to use your riches on such folly as the torment of an innocent and beautiful and buxom widow?"

"They are my riches. I can do with them what I please. That includes docking your pay for your flippant mouth."

Leesil waved his had dismissively. "I'd just make it up at the dice table. These Eastedge bumpkins are so easily fleeced that it's almost ceased to be entertaining."

"Why are you concerned about my money?"

"Because, as you just stated, you pay me. As baron you're an official of the Kingdom of Darshay. What you're doing to the Sureblade woman, the widow of a military hero of another sovereign kingdom, is tantamount to a declaration of war. Your benefactor may not want you to call that kind of attention to yourself for this petty vengeance you're trying to achieve. I'd hate for you to jeopardize *my* livelihood by upsetting your benefactor and getting yourself killed."

"*Petty* vengeance, you say?" Tauran rested his hand on Dragon-fang's grip and continued.

"It was the righteous Meldrick Sureblade who reported my assault of that girl and got me tossed out of the Lorrian military. I'm a fighter Leesil, and a bloody good one. I couldn't even join a local militia after that."

"Meldrick Sureblade is three years dead, Tauran."

"And he's survived by a wife and three children," Tauran argued, tightening his grip around the broken greatsword. "Had I stayed in the military and not had to struggle with peasant labor, I would've been able to afford a family of my own. Sureblade was the cause of all that. The Finder slew him and robbed me of direct vengeance. I'll take my retribution from the family he left behind."

Leesil saw the dark look in the baron's eyes and knew it was time to stand down. Tauran granted Leesil much more latitude than anyone other than T'Cheln. T'Cheln was granted latitude simply because Tauran feared him. Leesil was favored because they were friends since before they were teens. But Leesil knew how fragile Tauran's friendship – and how explosive his temper – could be.

Louis had been his friend before even Leesil, but when Louis chose his family over the Legion Midnight, Tauran felt betrayed and that was the end of that friendship. The same could have easily happened to Leesil because he would never have joined the Legion Midnight. Luckily, during the Cursed Opening, Leesil was part of an extended guard for the wife of a wealthy Lorrian estate lord while she travelled across the Sai-Il continent on a pleasure trip.

"I understand, baron," Leesil relented. "Forgive me my indifference. Perhaps, instead of playing the practice straw man for T'Cheln's frustrations, you can relieve some of your own tension with some sport down in the dungeons. I do believe there are a few nobles' daughters you have yet to sample. And of course, there is always that radiant cellmate of the offworlder."

Tauran's countenance brightened at the suggestion.

"Good idea, old friend," the baron growled lustily. "I knew there was reason I kept you around."

7.2

Twelve armed dwarves led Ethan Sureblade, Quick the Changeling, Ranger Elf Rell Kallen, and the six sky sleigh crewmembers through the maze of torchlit passages beneath Hell's Mountains. They were told that Raxe would meet them on the surface. The moods of the sky sleigh survivors and their dwarven escort were markedly different than they were upon the start of their visit.

The dwarves' gimlet eyes were as wary as ever yet they spoke among themselves conversationally, which was in stark contrast to the threatening silence with which they greeted their captives. The elf remained as aloof as ever while the sky sleigh crew spoke to each other continuously. Quick mingled with both the humans and the dwarven guard, floating between the groups as they traversed the winding tunnels.

Ethan was almost giddy in anticipation of accepting his new weapon and finally getting back to their mission. The only thing dampening his excitement was the loss of Arrowhead and the rest of the Keeper's Hounds. With more than a little effort, he was able to force his mind away from the pain and put it back on the situation at hand.

He had not seen Raxe since the previous night when he relinquished his father's beloved gear. He had spent half the night wondering what kind of weapon Raxe would make for him. A sword of some kind seemed the logical choice. Ethan could not remember if he had ever told the offworlder that the broadsword was his favorite weapon, but Raxe had to notice that the pain Ethan felt when giving up his father's blade was greater than with the other weapons.

And what exactly would the enchanted weapon do? Raxe said he would give Ethan magic and special martial skills. How would it work? Ethan had once heard Raxe mention that when the offworlder's divine magic was new to him, it physically controlled him the way a puppeteer controls a marionette. Ethan wondered if this magic would do the same to him.

DEMON OF LORR

The young Sureblade also vividly remembered Raxe talking about the price of magic. Had Ethan already paid his due when he gave up the weapon? Or would the magic exact a price every time it was used?

The teen soldier's mind whirled with unanswered questions when the small group reached the narrow tunnel that Ethan immediately recognized as the corridor just inside the well-camouflaged entrance through which they had entered the underground nation. Several loud clanks sounded somewhere in their vicinity. The sound was slightly muffled, but they could feel the vibrations through the stone floor.

Those sounds were followed by the sound of gears turning and then the deep, grating sound of heavy stone scraping against stone reverberated in the corridor. A curved jagged line of light appeared before them. The line broadened as sunlight, blindingly bright after days in the dim light and shadows of the underground nation, poured into the cave. The great stone that blocked the entrance to the dwarven world was pulled away to reveal an opening barely five feet high and twice as wide. The ceiling of the tunnel, already just an inch above six feet, sloped sharply and suddenly. Everyone except the dwarven guard had to duck and then crouch in order to walk through the last few yards of the tunnel and through the threshold.

They emerged at the same spot where they entered the world of the dwarves: in a deep gorge on the rocky mountainside. The narrow gully was located at the end of an indistinguishable path riddled with switchbacks that intersected at countless points with false paths that dead-ended at soaring walls of sheer rock.

Only the dwarves knew the subtle natural landmarks that marked the trail. When the thirty-foot high, twenty-foot wide stone that concealed the five by ten foot threshold to the dwarven nation was put back into place, this gully seemed to be just another dead end.

Ethan surmised it was at or near noon. The surrounding earthen walls were so high that the suns had to be at their highest point for its light to shine directly into the narrow cut.

Otherwise, the floor of the ravine would be lost in shadow.

When his eyes adjusted to the midday suns' light, Ethan saw Raxe standing next to Bartok. Azhju'lestra stood at Raxe's right elbow as always. Several armed dwarves stood with them.

The offworlder and dwarf had been talking until the great stone was moved. Their conversation ceased and they watched the company approach. Raxe's gleaming silver armor was almost blinding where it reflected the bright suns' light. He wore Demonsbane in its axe frog at his left hip. Questblade hung sheathed at his right hip. His open helm was tucked under his right arm. But Ethan's eyes were instantly drawn to the instrument in Raxe's left hand.

It was a stick.

To be exact, it was a long staff slightly longer than Raxe was tall, which made it about three inches longer than Ethan was tall. Ethan, while still grateful, was a bit crestfallen. He expected a bladed weapon. Even though he had specifically hoped for a broadsword, he fully expected a sword of some sort. Ethan had received some training in the use of the staff as a fighting weapon in the academy but he would hardly call himself proficient in its use. He was an expert in the use of the javelin, but that was a throwing weapon.

A sharp pang of guilt jabbed him in the stomach when the young warrior's sharp gaze fell upon the offworlder's heavily bandaged right hand. He berated himself inwardly for his selfishness and reminded himself that this was an enchanted weapon that a Child of the Old Ones sacrificed greatly to create specifically for him.

As he neared the offworlder, his appreciation for the staff grew. There was an understated elegance to the weapon. The long, solid shaft of silver metal was the width of three fingers in diameter and perfect in its simplicity. The gleaming surface was smooth and flawless. A faint, sky-blue shimmer ran down the length of the weapon at its exact center. The warm glow was about half a finger's width and barely visible even to Ethan with his famed keen eyesight.

Ethan stepped before Raxe and gave a reverent bow.

"It is a beautiful stave," Ethan declared sincerely.

"But not quite what you expected?" Raxe asked.

Ethan feigned confusion. "Why would you think that?"

"You have a great poker face, kid," Raxe began. "But I've been trained to read people's eyes and body language."

The offworlder noticed the puzzled expressions of the people around him. He realized that they all probably thought Raxe insulted the youngster by saying he had a face like a fireplace or forging tool.

He chuckled briefly and then explained. "Poker is a card game in my world, a game of chance, a form of gambling."

"Ah," Bartok said. "Tis like Jester's Gambit, I'll bet; a game of chance played with a deck of sixty cards, each marked with a different symbol. Jester's Gambit is played among humans, dwarves, and elves alike."

Ethan's confused expression turned into one of shame. His cheeks flushed as he spoke. "Please do not think your gift is unappreciated, Raxe. It's just that I've minimal training in the use of the fighting staff."

"It's called a long staff, or a *gun* in the language of the country where my fighting style originated."

"A...*goo-en*?" Ethan asked.

"Yes, that's how you pronounce it," Raxe confirmed. "It's a little different than a standard fighting staff. A *gun* is slightly wider at the base than the tip. I know it doesn't seem as practical as a sword."

"Aye," Bartok interjected. "King Grimhammer and I be thinking th'same. A skinny stick? Ye'll be in a sore spot with that toothpick against a battle hammer or war axe!"

Raxe ignored the dwarf and continued. "I know the broadsword is your weapon of choice. But the *gun* has a much greater range than even the great sword, and when used correctly it can be just a deadly. And keep in mind this staff is made of Titan's Ore. That makes it unbreakable. It's literally indestructible. Your inexperience with it isn't relevant. The magic within it will see to that."

"How does the magic work?" Ethan asked.

Raxe was silent for a long while. A guilty smile lifted one

corner of his mouth and he shrugged.

"I don't really know, kid."

Bartok guffawed. "How can ye not know, offworlder? T'was ye who made the thing!"

Ethan remained respectfully silent, but Raxe could see the same question in the teen's eyes.

"I know what the magic does, what it will do to you," Raxe began. "I just can't tell you how to invoke it. Understand, Ethan, I have very little experience with magic. Mine works instinctively. I can't invoke it with words or gestures or will it into being. It works automatically. That's my only personal frame of reference with the use of magic. As a result, I can promise you the magic of the long staff will work when you need it to work. When it does, you will fight with my skill, with my knowledge."

Bartok harrumphed. "Think highly of ye'self there, eh, offworlder?"

Raxe turned to him with a sinister grin. "Actually, Bartok, when it comes to fighting: Yes, I do."

"I have seen him use a fighting staff," Quick offered. "It was like nothing I've ever seen."

"You've told me the story," Ethan said. He turned to Raxe. "How you bested the premier swordsman in the kingdom, my father, who wielded a broadsword against you while you fought with a fighting staff in the Rites of Challenge. It is said that you toyed with him and then beat him in a matter of seconds."

"Yes," Raxe confirmed, his expression turned more serious and somber. "When the magic is in use, it will make your body move the way I move, with all of my flexibility and stamina and instincts.

"The problem is I couldn't figure out – and I wasn't sure if I even wanted to figure out – a way to make the magic affect your body to match my thirty years of physical training and conditioning."

"What does that mean?" Ethan questioned suspiciously. "It sounds like you're contradicting yourself."

Raxe nodded his agreement before explaining. "If you're

in a situation that calls the magic forth, you're most likely going to be exhausted when the magic is spent.

"It'll sustain you while you need it, but once it leaves, you'll probably be more exhausted than you've ever been. And you're gonna hurt like hell afterwards."

"The price of magic," Azhju'lestra commented.

Raxe nodded at his daughter and continued. "Your muscles and joints are going to be used, stretched and strained in ways you've never imagined. So starting today, you're gonna have to do a series of exercises. You have to do them every day without fail. If you don't, you risk being injured if you have to use the *gun's* magic."

The Ranger Elf stepped forward impatiently. "We have no time for this," he snapped. His upswept, greenish-brown eyes blazed in anger.

"It's a half-day's walk to the base of this mountain," Raxe countered. "Quick and Ethan can follow us that far and then get back on Joel's trail. I can show him what he needs to know on the way."

"Waste your energy if you wish, offworlder," Rell Kallen said dismissively. "It's not as if you humans have very much energy to begin with."

Raxe held the *gun* out to Ethan. Without hesitation, the young Sureblade reached out and wrapped his right hand around the midpoint of the weapon. A warm thrill spread through him when his bare skin contacted the metal surface. The sensation disappeared so quickly that Ethan wondered if he had only imagined it. He slid it into the strap that had once supported his father's javelin.

The group set off after their dwarven guide along the hidden path. As promised, Raxe demonstrated a number of flexibility exercises as they traveled. He explained to Ethan in detail the order and frequency and significance of each. He also explained the method and importance of proper breathing techniques. Ethan absorbed it all like a sponge. He even attempted the exercises as Raxe had demonstrated, often causing himself unexpected pain.

Raxe had Ethan repeat his instructions. The youngster did

just that, on the first try and without error. The offworlder was impressed.

"You're a natural," he said. Was that good or scary?

"Thank you, Raxe," Ethan beamed. He tried to downplay his excitement, but as before, his eyes betrayed him to the offworlder.

"Don't get too excited," Raxe warned. "Hope you never have to use the *gun*'s magic. If you do, you'd better hope you get at least a few weeks of training under your belt first."

"We won't need a few weeks," Ethan said confidently. "With Quick and I tracking Joel, we should have him within a few days. Don't you agree, Quick?"

"Without question," the changeling agreed with a hearty nod. "We'll start by following the path the scythe wings took when they departed with Joel." His confidence waned slightly as he continued. "But we only know their general direction. Not even I can track a scent through the sky after several days. There is no scent left to track."

Ethan nodded. "Yes, friend, there is. Only the scent is not in the air. We know their general direction, and we know they have recently fed."

"Of course!" Quick realized. "Their western path started to veer to the north as they flew beyond my range of vision. We can retrace their path that far and then track them by their droppings."

With that, Quick raised his hands in front of him, palms out, and fell forward. By the time his hands hit the ground they were transformed into large cat's paws. His hind legs and torso had also transformed into those of a straw-colored great cat. His head and neck were those of a giant eagle and great eagle's wings folded tightly against his back and flanks.

"Whoa," Raxe said, never failing to be amazed by the changeling's transformations.

The gryphon standing before him was much larger than the gryphon form Quick took during Raxe's first visit to the Kingdom of Lorr. The offworlder surmised that as the changeling grew older and grew physically, so did the other forms he took.

DEMON OF LORR

Out of reflex, Ethan reached for the shoulder that usually had his lasso coiled around it. He intended to fashion a makeshift harness for the gryphon to carry their packs.

He paused and sighed when he remembered that his lasso was gone. Or, to be more accurate, it was fused into the enchanted staff. One of the dwarves waiting with Bartok and Raxe stepped forward and offered a saddle. Within minutes, the young Sureblade was riding upon the changeling gryphon as they soared away into the northwestern skies.

Raxe watched them go and thought again of the promise he had made to Ethan's mother. He hoped he had done enough to keep it. A twinge of irritation gnawed at him. Once again he was reminded of how opposed he was to Rionn Lorr's decision to include Ethan on this quest.

At the thought of the Head Mage, Raxe rummaged around in his pack and retrieved his small box of reflection sand, shook it, and opened it. He picked up the stylus and drew the symbol to initiate the magic. It was easier to do, and quicker, because he had done it before. After waiting the requisite few seconds he wiped away the symbol with a finger. He picked up the stylus with his thumb and forefinger and began to write:

You busy, cuz?

A response came immediately. *Always.*

And then the Head Mage added: *Cuz*

Raxe chuckled, drawing a curious glance from Bartok.

We had to take a slight detour, Raxe wrote. *But we are back on task. I need to make arrangements to send the sleigh crew home from Southborough. Can you help?*

Of course, Rionn answered. *I'll send word ahead.*

The elf, my daughter and I will continue on to the Demon's Spine. Ethan and Quick are searching for Joel.

Good, the Head Mage returned. *Those two will find him, even if no one else can.*

How are things going on your end? Raxe wrote.

Slowly, Rionn returned. *No real progress on the cure, but I did find something. In the story of Daniatiae Lorr you asked about the relevance of using her name in some places or*

"Lady" in others.

Research revealed the ancient texts often referred to the Kingdom of Lorr as the Lady or the Great Lady in reverence to Daniatiae Lorr.

Raxe wrote: *Interesting. I'll think on it and let you know if I come up with something.*

As will I, the Head Mage replied. *God's speed to you.*

"Offworlder?" Rell Kallen's sharp voice snapped Raxe's attention back to the small party at the foot of the mountain. "Are we trekking or are you playing in the sand?"

Ignoring the Ranger Elf, Raxe wrote *And to you.* He closed the box and put it back into his pack.

"Southborough be several days walk south of 'ere," Bartok said. "Skirt the base of this mountain until ye see the Forsaken Desert in the southwest. Keep south, keep the desert in view and ye can't miss the town. From there, ye can make yer way to the town of Shaddiston."

"What's in Shaddiston?" Raxe asked.

"If yer purse not be too light," Bartok answered, "perhaps someone t' guide ye or tell ye the path t' Hargathall's Cleft. When ye get t' the mountains overlooking the Cleft, use the elevation t' find the northernmost point of the canyon. Make yer way t' that point before the suns be at their zenith. When they are, from there ye can look due south across the Cleft and see a low pass. Make yer way through that pass and Mardah's mountain will be staring ye in the face. Be mindful of its wards, though. We've spied it from a distance but we've more sense than t' get too close t' the hidden keep of a wizard Child of the Old Ones, even a dead one."

Raxe tilted his head suspiciously. "How do you know where his Mountain is?"

"We may live in hiding," Bartok said with a sly smile. "But our people have been here fer thousands of years. Very little about this region remains hidden t' us."

Raxe nodded. "Good enough. Thank you, Bartok. And give my thanks to the king."

Bartok raised a bushy eyebrow as he looked up at the offworlder. "Show yer thanks by completing yer quest. The fate of both our worlds depends on it. And pray t' yer namesake and the Lord Ascendant that ye haven't wasted the Titan's Ore on that boy."

Raxe almost wished he were a praying man.

7.3

A loud metallic clang, as well as a jolt that vibrated through the heavy chain attached to Joel's manacles, shocked him out of a deep but fitful slumber. He could remember a time during his imprisonment when that sound brought him relief. The sound was indicative of the mechanism on his chains being released...not completely released, but enough to allow him to lower his arms. That meant that food – or what passed for food in this dungeon – was on the way.

And Joel was hungry. He was always hungry. They fed him just enough to keep him alive and never enough to sate him. But still, it was better than starving. During the first few days of his he even looked forward to mealtime.

But this time, his awakening brought him no relief. It only brought him pain. He no longer anticipated the arrival of food with tempered eagerness. The food was either tasteless or foul. And even though the meals meant a temporary respite from near starvation, it was also a reminder of how long he had been held captive.

Through his constant haze of pain, fear, and hunger, he managed to figure out that Dayna kept track of the days by counting meals. They were fed twice a day. Usually. Each meal was a paltry amount of a gray, sticky and bland mush that he could only assume was some sort of hastily prepared grain meal served with a lump of stale bread. Sometimes the bread was so hard he could barely chew it. Other times it was so soggy he could barely distinguish it from the mush.

In the last few days, though, they began to visit him for an entirely different reason. He was beaten daily. Anywhere between four and six men would pound him savagely. There was no set pattern to their visits. They would come at different times during the day. Sometimes it was just before a meal and sometimes it was in the middle of the day or night. As often as not they reeked of liquor.

The burning was the worst. They had returned more than once with the brand and the hot coals. The burn blisters scattered across his torso, arms and neck stung almost as badly as they did when they were made. The itching made them that much worse. Purple bruises and ragged cuts as well as otherwise untouched patches of skin were accentuated with the broken greatsword brand.

It got to the point where dread overcame Joel every time he heard and felt the chains loosen. There was a different group of men each time with one exception. The leader was always the same person.

Leesil, the tall, lean man with sun-browned skin and long brown hair that was always tied back with a thong or red bandana and twisted in the back into a smart ponytail. The doublets he wore and the flared calf-length leggings, the hem of which met with the top of one his many pairs of leather boots, set him noticeably apart from the less sophisticated and more practically dressed men in tunics, breeches and hiking or riding boots.

He usually coordinated the beatings but he let no one else use the brand. He preferred to do that task himself. In between the assaults with the brand or barking commands and yelling warnings that stopped the others from inflicting any potentially fatal damage during the beatings, he cast wolfish leers at Dayna. Joel knew Leesil would not hesitate to ravage her if Tauran had not been so possessive of her.

But there was something off-putting and strangely out of place about the way Leesil looked at Dayna. Beneath the obvious lust was something else, something that resembled a hint of malice in his dark gaze. Had Joel's mind not been so clouded from his physical and psychological abuse, he was sure he would've been able to identify it.

As it was, Joel found it difficult to think about anything beyond his various hurts. Sore muscles, pulsing scorches, countless bruises, raw cuts and stinging scabs kept him in constant pain. The thugs almost always pummeled Joel into unconsciousness. He would usually wake up face down on the smelly, clammy floor with a plate of food or a dirty cup filled with cloudy water next to him. This was what he expected this day when his weary arms fell to his sides.

A savage beating, another session with the dreaded brand,

or barely edible food…this had become his world.

"Food," Dayna said, noticing the shroud of fear that descended over the offworlder's face.

"You sure?" Joel asked weakly.

There was usually a series of loud clangs as other prisoners' bonds were loosened for their meals. The meal times were few and far between, but when they served, they served everyone at the same time; except, of courses, for those who missed meals as part of their torture or punishment. But there were no other sounds at all, and the hall their cell occupied was never completely without sound.

When the sounds of heavy boot falls on the stone floors were not echoing through the corridors, there was the almost constant drone of mumbled conversation among the other prisoners. Joel had long since learned to tune out those sounds. But then there were the impossible to ignore – and all too frequent – moans and screams of poor women prisoners unfortunate enough to catch the eye of a brutish jailer. Even though Joel was thankful that those particular sounds were absent, he wondered at the complete silence.

"I am sure," Dayna assured. "It is the usual time."

"I can't tell anymore," Joel admitted, shaking his head slowly. "I think I'm getting paranoid."

"You have good reason to be," Dayna noted.

"But why aren't your chains giving?" Joel wondered.

When the deep double clank of the disengaging lock on their heavy door rang through the cell, Joel saw that Dayna's chains were still taught and he knew what that meant. He tried to mentally brace himself for yet another pummelling, but this time only one man walked in.

It was a man Joel had never seen before, and he was clearly not one of the usual jailers. He was so tall that the crown of his head nearly touched to top of the high doorframe, which Joel gauged to be close to seven feet. The hood of the stranger's cloak was pulled back to reveal a pale, sharply angled face adorned with an aquiline nose and a thin, neatly trimmed goatee.

The stranger's whiskers, straight eyebrows, and closely

cropped haircut were coal black and stood out in almost obscene contrast to his pallid complexion.

The stranger's long cloak was fastened tightly just below his needle pointed chin. The cloak draped over shoulders as sharp as a coat hanger and tapered severely as it trailed to the floor, covering the stranger's long, slender body and ending where the hem slid along the dirty cell floor. As slight as he was, there was absolutely no hint of physical weakness. He radiated the serpentine power of some giant black viper.

His smooth gait carried him several feet into the cell before the door closed behind him. The cloak was a shade of dark gray that blended so well with the shadows that, once the door closed, Joel could barely make out the outline of the stranger's freakishly tall and narrow body. Without the weak yellow illumination to backlight him, his dark cloak and the dark hair on his head faded completely into the shadows of the cell. Until Joel and Dayna's eyes readjusted to the darkness, it appeared as if a disembodied head was floating through the darkness.

Despite the deathly pale complexion and the narrow build, a frightening aura emanated from the figure. The image was so engrossing that they almost failed to notice that when the door closed, the visitor had made no motion to close it and there was no one there to pull it shut.

When they did realize it, their distress only deepened.

"Wizard," Dayna accused in a harsh whisper.

"Worse," Joel realized.

Joel inhaled deeply through his nose and was repulsed. He detected a smell vaguely reminiscent of the odor he scented upon Ryan, Dan, Rionn Lorr, and many other beings in this weird world. This included the scent that accompanied – but he somehow knew was not a part of – the scythe wings that delivered him to his current predicament. It was unquestionably magic, only this time that all-too-familiar scent was accompanied by the stench of decay and sulphur. The scent obliterated Joel's haze of dizziness, shocked him awake and filled with him dread.

"This is a demon," Joel said. "The Dierglyorr."

Dayna's eyes widened with fear. Before she could utter a word, the visitor turned to her with his crimson, razor-thin lips spread in a grin that turned Dayna's blood to ice. A pale hand materialized from the hem of the cloak's sleeve somewhere far below the gaunt face and a long clawed finger rose to point at her.

"Sleep," the demon bade with a voice like cracking ice.

Dayna's eyes closed and her chin dipped to her chest.

When the stranger turned his gaze back to Joel, the eyes glowed with a deep red hue that cast a blood-tinted pall over the white face. The curving red slit that was the stranger's smile opened to reveal too-big teeth illuminated by the eyes' crimson glow.

"Do my eyes look familiar?" it asked. "I think they must. I think you have seen these eyes in *your* face."

Joel gasped and shook his head. It was less a denial and more a gesture of disbelief, and both of them knew it.

"Yes," the demon countered. "We are more of a kind than you know. We are both slayers, made killers by the Old Ones. I was made by the Leaders, you, by the Protectors, the both of us made for the same grim purpose: to annihilate."

Joel said nothing. He was afraid his voice would not work. If it did, he was even more afraid of what he might say.

"But you already knew what I was," the stranger continued. "You saw through my disguise immediately."

The voice, deep and strong and clear as it resonated in Joel's ears, seemed eerily out of place with the insubstantial, wraithlike appearance. The voice was not particularly threatening. It was calm, in fact. The voice was cloying and almost comforting, though not comforting enough to make Joel respond.

The offworlder willed his body not to tremble and met the hellish glare defiantly. The demon's smile widened.

"Or should I say you *smelled* through my disguise?" it continued with a knowing grin.

Joel tried to hide his surprise but he was not able keep his eyebrow from twitching ever so slightly.

"Yes, *Joel*," the Dierglyorr continued. "You know my

true name as I know yours. But I know so much more about you. No one else is aware, but I know you can smell magic. You keep that tidbit of information a secret from the others, as well you should. You see, Joel? I know your secrets. I know things about you that you do not even know yet."

"What do you want with me?" Joel finally asked. "You try to kill everyone around me but only capture me. Why?"

"You know why," the demon crooned. "You are of much more value to me alive."

Joel's eyes narrowed. A sly smile found its way to his face in spite of the burning pain wracking his body and the cold fear seeping through him.

"You're lying," Joel accused. "You haven't killed me because you *can't*. It's like you said, we were both made to annihilate. The difference is my power can annihilate *you*, and you know it."

The demon's dulcet tones became like acid on Joel's eardrums and brought bile to the back of his throat. The Dierglyorr leaned closer and snarled,

"Do not be smug. Your power means nothing to me. See now how easily you and your power are controlled."

The Dierglyorr drifted ever closer, his prominent nose hovering only inches away from Joel's.

"And there are far worse fates than death, Gatekeeper spawn. For instance, I can let you rot right here in this cell. I can bring your wife and the whelp swelling within her across the WorldGate and make you watch *their* slow and painful deaths."

Joel roared and lunged at the demon. Anger and fear pumped enough adrenaline to allow him to haul the heavy chains up with surprising quickness. The Dierglyorr easily sidestepped and let the offworlder sail past. The adrenaline rush was quickly spent and the destructive power within Joel that he hoped would surface was not forthcoming. The broad lengths of chain pulled Joel clumsily to the floor.

"Leave Lisa out of this!" Joel cried in frustration and worry. "She has nothing to do with any of this."

"Oh, but she has *everything* to do with this, Joel, for she is a means of controlling you."

Joel struggled to his feet. He looked up and was startled to see the Dierglyorr towering over him. He shuffled backwards, almost tripping over his chains but managing to stay upright.

"You have to catch her first," Joel said. "I know you don't have her. If you did, you'd have proven it by now."

"I will have her soon," the Dierglyorr promised. "Honestly, Joel, do you think she and the old man can avoid me for long? Do you think that because he faked his handicap all those years that he can outrun experienced organization operatives as well as my magic? He would not stand a chance on his own and your wife only slows him down. Do not be foolish. Do not leave her fate up to a stooped old trickster that has lived too far past his prime."

"What do you want with me?" Joel asked again in a defeated tone.

Burning red eyes regarded the Child of the Old Ones for a long moment. Joel tried to look away from the horrifically captivating stare but he could not tear his gaze away. The blazing blood-tinted orbs radiated loathing, revulsion and hunger. But beneath all of that, there was something decidedly worse.

The demon was sizing Joel up, he realized. The thought of this hellish beast evaluating him for some fell purpose made Joel's stomach twist and burn with fear. When the demon finally grunted, the sudden sound made Joel shudder.

"In a perfect world I would have you kill the other Children of the Old Ones," the Dierglyorr admitted. "Whether you realize it or not, you have the power to do so. You have absolutely no idea how powerful you really are. I could teach you, you know. Would you like to learn?"

Joel expressed his refusal with cold silence and a murderous glare.

"Of course not," the demon said dismissively. "Had I more time I would...persuade you. And I still may, after my current plans come to fruition.

"In the meantime, here is what I propose: Stay out of my

way. Stay away from this fight. In return I will call off Lisa's pursuers and leave the two of you alone."

All Joel wanted was for his wife to be safe. He wanted to make the agreement but there was a faint yet persistent droning in the deep recesses of his mind warning him against making a deal with the devil.

It's not as if it's asking for my soul, he argued with himself.

"I am not Satan," the Dierglyorr assured as if he had been reading Joel's mind. "The dark lord has many others matters occupying his time. Rest assured that I am not quite the deceiver that he is."

Joel's fear spiked at the thought of the demon hearing his thoughts. He quickly assured himself that under the circumstances, the whole "deal with the devil" analogy was a very easy one to make.

"As much as I'd like to make this deal," Joel said, "How can I believe you? You already know I can smell magic, so you probably know that I smell deception, too. And every word out of your mouth is a lie."

The Dierglyorr's mirthless grin suddenly disappeared. The blank visage slowly descended until its slit of a mouth was nearly touching Joel's right ear. Joel watched the seemingly disembodied face come closer. He tried to lean away but dread froze him in place.

The glow from the demon's eyes was uncomfortably hot on the side of Joel's face while its putrid breath was as cold as ice. Its voice shrank to little more than a whisper yet dripped with malice and dug into Joel's nerves like fingernails on a chalkboard.

"If you say no, you will have chosen a world of misery for yourself and the unfortunate few who care about you, godspawn. Decide. Now."

Joel did not know which would be more foolish: making a deal with a demon or refusing to make a deal when there was so much as stake. He tried to keep his expression blank as he considered his lose-lose options.

He could feel the knit of his eyebrows and the down-turned corners of his thick, dry and cracked lips. His head throbbed painfully and his mouth went dry. There was a debilitating tightness in his chest that had nothing to do with his asthma.

"Promise to leave Lisa alone," Joel demanded. "Promise that she and the baby will be safe if I stay out of this. Say the words, demon."

"I vow, Joel, not to pursue or harm Lisa or your child. All you need do is refuse to assist the other Children. Speak my name when you agree, for that is the only true way to make the agreement binding."

There was no deception in the Dierglyorr's words this time, yet Joel's subconscious screamed vehemently at him to reject the offer. *The demon may have be telling the truth now, Joel, but what's to stop it from breaking the vow later?*

Joel ignored the desperate inner cries. His only concern was the wellbeing of his wife and unborn child. This was the only way he knew of to secure their safety. Not even his own safety mattered anymore.

"We have an agreement…Dierglyorr."

The demon smiled again. "Good. In a moment you will see just the smallest sample of what fate lies in store for that sow who has been cursed to bear your useless seed should you choose to renege on your promise."

"What does that mean?" Joel asked.

He looked away, startled by the loud echoing clangs of the other prisoners' chains being loosened all down the corridors. When he turned back the Dierglyorr was gone. A fleeting but foul breeze rushed inward to fill the space the demon had just occupied.

7.4

The loud noises roused Dayna from her enchanted slumber. She woke with a start and looked around fearfully for any sign of the demon. Her thick, unkempt hair bounced wildly as her head swung from right to left and back.

"Where has he gone?" she asked warily. "Was he really a demon?"

"Yeah," Joel mumbled. "I wish it went back to hell, but no such luck."

Dayna's piercing, suspicious gaze returned and she turned its full intensity onto the offworlder.

"What did it want with you?"

"Something it can't have."

Dayna could tell that no straight answers were forthcoming so she turned her attention to more immediate concerns. She pulled at her manacles but they did not give.

"It sounds like everyone's chains have been loosened but mine," she noted darkly. Joel did not miss the grave look in her eyes or the disgusted frown on her scarred but otherwise pretty face.

"What does that mean?" he asked.

And then he considered the demon's last words to him. He suddenly found himself extremely worried about his cellmate.

The heavy door unlocked and swung inward with enough force to slam it into the interior wall. To Joel's dismay, the silhouette of a tall, bulky man filled the doorway. Just behind the bull of a man stood an even taller man that, from the tightly bound scarf on his head, made Joel immediately remember his attempted kidnapping back at Lakeside. The taller man was a *Ken d' Zanir* warrior.

Leesil and four guards, two of whom carried torches to brighten the dimly lit hall, flanked the newcomer. The added light revealed long, unruly, reddish-brown hair and whiskers and a porcine smirk.

"Tauran," Joel breathed.

"False baron," Dayna spat.

"How do my visitors fare this fine evening?" Tauran taunted as he and all of the men accompanying him save T'Cheln filed into the cell. The *Ken* stood outside the doorway with a disinterested look in his deep-set eyes. Tauran spared a dismissive glance in Joel's direction and let his leer settle heavily upon Dayna. "I have missed you sorely, my chocolate treat."

"Your minions have not," Dayna snarled.

This stopped Tauran in his tracks. His men followed suit and they all looked at each other in confusion.

Tauran's beady eyes narrowed. "Are you saying that someone besides me has sampled you?"

"I'm saying that someone besides you has raped me."

"*Who?*" the big man roared. "Tell me now!"

Dayna nodded to indicate the man standing just behind Tauran and to his right. He was almost as tall as Tauran and only slightly less broad. He looked quick and strong, and he suddenly looked terrified.

"That one."

"Jessup?" Tauran accused.

"No, Baron!" Jessup barked. "The bitch lies!"

"How else would I know about the way his tool bends downward?" Dayna countered.

Tauran started shaking with barely controlled rage.

"Lies, Baron!" Jessup repeated. "You must believe me!"

Dayna went on. "He's bragged about how much more stamina he has than you. He's begged me to confirm it."

Jessup's eyes continued to bulge. "No, Baron! You cannot believe –"

Jessup's shouts were quickly drowned out by Tauran's bellow as he snatched the massive broken greatsword Dragon-fang from its sheath and swung it wildly at his subordinate. Jessup jumped away, causing the deadly edge to miss his face by less than an inch. He pulled his broadsword from its sheath and dropped into a defensive stance.

Leesil and the other guards backed away. Wolfish smiles spread across their faces in anticipation of the baron's wrath.

"I implore you, Tauran! Do not listen to her lies!"

"She is too detailed to be lying, Jessup," Tauran snapped. "You know the penalty for touching what is mine!"

With that, Tauran launched a brutal assault. Jessup, to his credit, was no pushover. He blocked and parried with impressive quickness and skill. He looked to be as strong as the bullish Tauran and perhaps even a bit quicker. But the special martial arts training Tauran had received from T'Cheln, along with the inherent properties of Dragon-fang, soon proved to be too much.

Tauran swung a heavy but controlled blow at Jessup's midsection, which the subordinate easily blocked. But Dragon-fang's diamond hard razor edge bit deeply into the other broadsword. The moment the two weapons were hooked, Tauran gave a mighty tug, pulling Jessup forward and off balance. As Jessup stumbled toward him, Tauran snapped a quick, vicious kick to Jessup's privates that sent him crumpling to the floor.

"You'll not be using that 'curved tool' again, you ungrateful bastard," Tauran growled.

Jessup tried again to voice his denial but his breath was taken from him by the kick to the groin. He was gagging in pain and tears blinded his eyes so that he never saw the killing blow as Tauran crouched low to punch Dragon-fang straight through his chest and pull it free again.

The murderous Baron stood tall, rolled his big shoulders and turned to face each of his men in turn.

"This is what happens when you defy me," he declared. "I have captured this offworlder chained before us, this Child of the Old Ones. Cutting any of you down would be child's play by comparison. Remember this, and remember it well."

All of the men save T'Cheln nodded their understanding. Leesil nodded out of respect but not with the fearful deference displayed by the others. He had known Tauran longer than anyone else in Eastedge. They were petty thieves together in their youth and mercenaries for most of their adult lives. He knew Tauran well enough to recognize when the blustering intimidator was putting on a show. But he also knew better than to disrespect him in front of his underlings.

Tauran returned his lewd glare to his female prisoner. "Did that impress you, my sweet?"

Dayna ignored him and looked at the door.

"You'll not ignore me much longer," Tauran promised. "I've worked up quite an appetite." He sheathed Dragonfang, removed his weapons belt and handed it to one of the guards. "I fear, though, that my little exercise has left me a tad winded. To make sure you get the attention you deserve, I will allow Leesil here to sample you once I am done."

"No!" Joel barked. "Leave her the hell alone!"

"Silence him," Tauran said with a dismissive wave. "But take care not to cause any fatal damage. We need him alive."

The men swarmed Joel. He dropped to the floor and tried to fold himself into a fetal position. The men pulled his arms and legs taut. Two held him while the other two punched and kicked. Through the sounds of his own beating, Joel began to hear bass, animalistic grunts and lewd chuckling from across the cell.

The sounds were punctuated by intermittent female whimpers. Joel could tell that Dayna was trying not to give them the satisfaction of any sounds of suffering. It was impossible, however, for her to remain completely silent under such a horrendous assault. Joel closed his eyes to avoid seeing the blows or catching a glimpse of Dayna's violation.

There was nothing he could do, though, about the terrible sounds. As Tauran's and later Leesil's sounds of dark pleasure grew louder, Joel's beating grew more intense. His attackers fed off of the assault, letting their jealousy of their omission from Dayna's attack fuel their anger.

Tears streamed down Joel's face. They were not tears of pain from kicks and punches. They were tears of sorrow for Dayna. He was powerless to do anything to help her. That helplessness added anger to his sorrow. The mental and physical anguish pressed down upon him until the weight was too much to bear. When his world finally went dark, a small part of him hoped he would never see light again.

7.5

Joel woke up face down on the clammy floor yet again. He awoke with a cry from the pain of his burns pressing against the floor. A tray of foul-smelling mush rested beside him as always. It took him a moment to get his bearings and gather himself to a seated position. He looked up and saw Dayna finishing off her unsatisfying meal while silently eyeing him.

"I'm sorry," Joel said.

"For what?" Dayna asked in a small voice. "You did nothing."

"That's why I'm sorry," Joel returned. "I should have done something."

"What could you have done?" Dayna questioned with grim humor. "It's obvious that everyone knows how to control your power but you."

The truth of that statement stung Joel and left him speechless for a moment. All he could do was lower his head and begin to force down his mush with dirty fingers.

Dayna sighed. "It was not my intention to insult you, offworlder. The truth, however, is often painful."

"How many men has he killed for touching you?" Joel asked. "That doesn't seem like a good way for him to keep up the morale of his men."

"Jessup was the first," Dayna said, managing a sly smile. She added in a confidential tone: "And Jessup never touched me. Today was the first time anyone other than Tauran attacked me. And that was only because Leesil is his longest acquaintance and what passes for a friend among those heathen jackals."

"What?" Joel gasped. "You lied?"

Dayna shrugged. "Not completely. He exposed himself to me more than once. The sight of me excited him, apparently, and the fool wanted me to see how much. That was how I knew how he looked down there. He often bragged about having more size and stamina than the false baron. But he was never stupid enough to actually touch me in that way."

"So you got him killed for nothing? That's some cold shit, Dayna."

"Cold indeed," she concurred. "Although it was not 'for nothing' as you say. All of these motherless animals deserve the same fate. They have all stolen and raped and murdered. Jessup may not have savaged me but he has victimized other women in these cells. He bragged about it to me, about how he sometimes pretended they were me, how they enjoyed it, how their cries and screams were from pleasure.

"None of them are innocent," she concluded. "I see no problem in winnowing their numbers if the opportunity presents itself. Would you disagree?"

Joel shook his aching head slowly. "I guess I can't argue with you on that one."

"Besides," she went on. "I thought Jessup might have had a decent chance of besting Tauran. My only regret is that he was not able."

Joel found himself respecting Dayna's tenacity. Her ability to find any measure of revenge and satisfaction in this hell was more than admirable. He grinned in spite of himself. The grin, however, was very short-lived.

Dayna was beautiful, proud, and strong. She did not deserve the fate she was suffering. No woman did. Yet she managed to find a small victory in the midst of such horror. Dayna's strength and tenacity only emphasized Joel's weakness and despair.

He was tired of feeling helpless, of *being* helpless. His vow to the Dierglyorr would be kept, but in that moment, he made another vow to himself.

"I won't let them do that to you again, Dayna."

Dayna smirked incredulously. She almost laughed. "And how in the seven hells would you stop them?"

Joel again shook his head slowly. That was a good question. His power only manifested for him, and it only manifested when his life was in danger. There was the one exception: It flared for Lisa on that highway in southern Illinois when the organization agent, posing as a common thug, threatened to rape and kill her.

But Joel loved Lisa.

The moment the threat was made Joel decided that he was going to sacrifice his own life to protect his wife. He knew he could not manufacture that feeling for a woman he barely knew.

As he downed another bitter swallow he leveled a cold, serious stare at his cellmate. "I don't know how I'll stop them," he admitted. "But I promise you, as long as I'm breathing, no one will do that to you again in my presence."

"Eat, foolish one. You're delirious with hunger."

Dayna's gaze lingered on Joel for a moment longer. "If you want to do something for me that is *actually* possible, tell me what the demon wants from you."

Joel's instincts were to be evasive. And then he asked himself: What was the point of keeping it a secret? As uncomfortable as the subject was, any topic was better than the one they were discussing.

"I didn't really know until it told me today," Joel admitted. "And now I wish it had never told me. It wants to use me to kill the other Children of the Old Ones, to save it the trouble, so it won't have any opposition."

A shroud of worry and doubt darkened Dayna's stare. "Rionn Lorr is the most powerful wizard in the Known Lands. The Offworlder Raxe is a dragon rider and demon slayer of near godlike strength. Surely the demon is not insane enough to believe that *you* can defeat them."

"Sounds crazy to me, too," Joel said, taking no offense at her words. "But that's what it told me. It also said that it would take too long to teach me how, so instead, it made me promise not to stand in its way."

"That's a strange promise to make, considering you don't expect to ever leave this cell."

"Exactly," Joel noted. "What do I have to lose? If the demon doesn't keep its side of the bargain, what's the difference? If it does, my wife will be safe."

A knowing look flashed across Dayna's expression. "It threatened to have what's happening to me here happen to your woman."

Joel nodded.

Dayna continued. "Yes…that gives me some insight into my own predicament."

"And what would that be?" Joel asked. "You still haven't told me why *you're* here."

"Our situations are more closely related than I realized. And that frightens me to no end. I thought we were mere victims of a power-hungry despot. Now I know that is only a small part of it. It is no coincidence that we are both here in this cell. I wonder if that fool Tauran even realizes this."

Joel cocked an eyebrow. "Why do I get the feeling that 'we' doesn't include me?"

He was being completely honest with her, now, so her half-answers to his questions were starting to frustrate him. He wanted to press for details. After what she had just been through, though, he could not bring himself to badger her.

"I have my suspicions, although I dare not say," Dayna replied. "Not now." She looked at door as if she believed someone was listening from the other side. "Pain and exhaustion have made me careless. I fear I may have already said too much.

"But I *can* say this, offworlder: What's done is done. It is time to think about what you will do from here. You are clearly a threat to the demon or a powerful tool for it to utilize. It made that deal with you because it knows you have the potential to free yourself. You must figure out how to tap into that potential and use it to your advantage. If not, you will not be able to do anything to protect yourself, me, or your wife."

Joel thought again about the Dierglyorr's parting words:

In a moment you will see just the smallest sample of what fate lies in store for that sow who has been cursed to bear your useless seed should you choose to renege on your promise.

Dread stabbed at him like a blade of ice through the heart. *No,* he swore to himself. *It won't happen to Dayna again, and it* damn *sure* won't *happen to Lisa.*

Chapter 8: Search and Research

8.1

The creatures resembled light gray and dull brown mottled puddles of water with countless short, spindly legs sprouting from all around their circumference. They clung to the darker gray shriveled skin cell, pulsing every few seconds. The creatures that Raxe referred to as "bugs" were roughly an eighth of the size of the cell to which they attached, so several of the bugs resided on each cell that Rionn and his group of healers and alchemists viewed through their magnification scopes.

Rionn Lorr focused his will on the creatures, lifted his pinky finger and held its tip just out of view of the scope. He used his visual connection with the specimen through the scope to channel his will. With great concentration, he sent tiny slivers of energy in the form of miniscule – yet proportionally intense – puffs of air at the bugs.

His jaw dropped when he saw the bugs tumble wildly away from the cell. The bugs that remained within view flailed their tiny legs for several seconds before pausing and then suddenly moving back toward the skin cell. Rionn sent another pulse of concentrated air, but this time with enough force to crush the microscopic organisms into disintegration. The wizard watched in fascination as the skin slowly, but steadily, began to change color from gray to clear and translucent and then to black, crumbling into particles too small to see even though the scope. Rionn Lorr stood up straight and grimaced. He grew excited and crestfallen all in the same instant.

Catherine, standing by her husband, saw the changes of expression. "What did you see, Rionn?" she asked.

"This cell," Rionn explained, "is from the flesh of Captain Johnican's severed head and has been long dead. The bugs apparently kept it, not alive, but animated. Once they were removed the cell disintegrated."

"I only wish I could get a sample from a victim I knew to be alive at the time of infection, one that had not suffered a fatal wound after turning. I want to see if the cell would return to normal once the parasitic bugs are destroyed."

"I wish I could be of more assistance," Catherine said apologetically.

"Your presence is enough, my love," assured Rionn. "And I want you near in case your knowledge is needed. If we can get a better idea of what these creatures are, perhaps you can use your expertise in medicines to counter them."

Catherine glanced down at the scope and sighed. "Perhaps. Though this seems more in the realm of conjuring and alchemy than healing."

He nodded gravely. "Yes. I could destroy the bugs at the cell level, but only with the magnifying scope to focus on individual organisms. There is no way I could do this to the millions upon millions of cells that it must take to form even one human body."

"Perhaps," Catherine said thoughtfully, "a compound can be produced that has the same effect on infected cells as your magic."

Rionn perked up a bit and looked at his wife. "Of course. I will inform the alchemists of my discovery. If I can make sufficient headway, would you work with them to develop such a compound?"

"You know I will, my love. How long do you think that would take?"

Rionn shrugged just as the sound of rushing footfalls floated through the threshold of the open laboratory door. As a matter of habit, he sent his perception on a tendril of magic that carried it through the doorway and down the hall. He exhaled heavily.

The Head Mage was already thoroughly frustrated from countless failed attempts to find a cure for the demon's plague. The last thing he wanted or needed was the confrontation he knew was forthcoming. He also knew there was no way to avoid it. So when the messenger rushed into the palace alchemy laboratory, Rionn was waiting for him at the open wooden door.

"Master Lorr," the chubby young man said with a reverent bow, "King William has requested your presence in the Command Room."

"Yes," Rionn Lorr replied politely. He turned to Catherine. "Can you stay and oversee things here, my dear?"

"Of course," answered Catherine.

The Head Mage turned to the messenger. "Lead the way, young man."

Rionn smoothed his long unkempt locks and took one last look at the lab. The Head Mage was amazed by the microscopes fashioned by the hastily assembled team of craftsmen and alchemists, as well as a few conjurers who showed a talent for manipulating solid matter. Spectacles, magnifying glasses, spyglasses, and celestial telescopes were already widely used in the Known Lands, but this new application of lenses excited the team. They attacked the task with urgent enthusiasm.

From Raxe's rudimentary and laymen's explanation of the mechanics of a microscope, the team made breathtaking strides in a very short period of time. Already they could see the miniscule creatures that attached themselves to their human hosts, to what Raxe referred to as cells. And while seeing them was intriguing and promised many possibilities, it had done them little good to this point because they had not yet found a way to destroy the invading life forms without destroying the cells to which they were attached.

"Forgive me, Master Lorr," the messenger began nervously, looking at the floor. "But the king was adamant that we hurry."

"Yes, of course," Rionn said distractedly before closing the door and following the messenger.

The laboratory was housed in the Academe Complex situated in the northeast area of the palace grounds. The building was not connected to the castle proper, so Rionn and the young messenger had to pass through several corridors to reach the southern exit.

The messenger mounted a small mottled gelding while the Head Mage made his way to Ebony and swung up onto her saddle. A short ride across the palace grounds brought them to the northeastern gates of the castle's primary keep, where a pair of guards greeted him with quick bows.

The messenger rode away as Rionn Lorr dismounted. The guards escorted the wizard through a maze of corridors until they reached a narrow staircase well away from the most frequently used areas of the keep. This was one of the many remote stairwells scattered around the castle that offered not only privacy for select visitors but speed as well. These passages provided a more direct route to important areas than the wide, ornate stairways used for the more common visitors and the dim, winding ones used by the custodial and maintenance staffs.

They went up several flights of stairs until they arrived at the stout wooden door to the king's private conference chamber. Rionn was relieved that this meeting was not in the larger, more formal royal conference chamber. That room evoked bad memories for the Head Mage. He had almost died in there at the hands of Mar-dah. So had his wife, King William and Queen Mary, and the king's advisors, as well.

Two more guards stood on either side of the door. The one to Rionn's right opened the door and bowed in greeting while the other nodded and waved him into the room. King William was having an intense conversation with Tyus, high admiral of the Royal Navy, Artemis, high commander of the Home Guard and Ramos, the general of the Royal Infantry.

There was a fifth man at the table, a man with whom Rionn was very familiar although he was surprised to see him here. The fifth man was Prince Graham Broadbow, King William's first born and heir to the throne of the Kingdom of Lorr. The Head Mage sighed inwardly in amazement at the swift passage of time, even to a Child of the Old Ones with their longer-than-human lifespans. It seemed like only days ago that this broad-shouldered young man was a chubby little scamp running roughshod through the palace bossing his younger siblings around.

Rionn wondered if the maturation of his three-year-old daughter Shanderah would seem to move this fast.

The prince spared a glance and nod at the Head Mage while he listened intently to Tyus, who was in the middle of a sentence as Rionn entered the room, his smooth tenor voice low but intense. The king was not sitting at his customary place at the head of the square oaken conference table. Instead, he was sitting on the long side of the table two seats away from Artemis and next to his son. This was not a formal conference, which made it that much more significant. At this very table, the five older men, along with Minister Geoffrey, who was still out east facing the plague victims, had made decisions that affected the Kingdom of Lorr and had ripple effects across all of the Known Lands.

At this table they were not the king and his advisors. They were old friends talking as equals. These men had known each other for decades. They had grown from adolescents into men together. They had fought wars together. As such, they did not stand on ceremony when it was just the five of them together.

Each man had a tankard of wine or ale at his side. Ramos and King William smoked strong-smelling pipes. They used rough language that they would never use at a formal conference. And even though the prince seemed out of place from Rionn's perspective, the young man looked completely at ease among the grizzled old warriors, as if he had been a part of the group all the time.

The other four men nodded in greeting and the king motioned for Rionn to sit. He took a seat next to Tyus as the veteran navy man continued to speak.

"...Yes," Tyus was saying. "We found the bleeding transport barge. It was more than large enough to hold a company of *Ken d'Zanir* along with their giant lizard war mounts. The barge had been abandoned when it was found but there was ample evidence that it had been used to carry heavy wheeled equipment as well as men."

"Ballistae," Ramos snarled. "That's how the bastards transported them. Had they towed the weapons across land the entire way, our battalion would've spotted the tracks and been much better prepared."

"Of course," Artemis added. "The *Ken* used Lake Onyx and the Tyne River's western stem to move half their company and ballistae behind our battalion to outflank them without being detected."

Artemis leaned forward angrily. "That maneuver would have required foreknowledge of our strategy. While they would have expected us to pursue them, the timing was such that they had to have precise intelligence of our movements."

King William clenched his large fist tight enough to send the sound of his cracking knuckles echoing off of the walls. "We *have* to find this spying sack of dung."

"I must add that the *Ken* are not known for being water-faring folk," Prince Graham offered. "They tend not to go anywhere that their land dragons cannot carry them."

Ramos grunted. "Neither are they known for employing war machines. Catapults, ballistae…those things contradict everything the *Ken* believe in. They hunt food with bows and arrows but they fight man-to-man, close quarters. It's not beyond them to use stealth or their land dragons, but they always get in close for their kills."

"And they've found a way to neutralize magic," Rionn Lorr added. "I have surmised that they're using some sort of talisman. Call it anti-magic, if you will. But the *Ken* detest and reject magic in any form. Even though this talisman extinguishes magical energy, it is still in truth just another form of magic. It seems unlikely that they would obtain such a tool on their own."

The king sat back in his chair and drummed his thick fingers on the table. "You are all saying that the *Ken* are receiving aid. Since we've long suspected that they are in the demon's employ, even if they don't realize it, the insinuation is that they are receiving aid from some other entity than just the Dierglyorr."

"It is a safe guess that the demon is not dealing with the *Ken* directly," Rionn offered. "But it must be orchestrating their new methods."

The king turned to Tyus. "Were there any markings on the barge?"

"No," Tyus returned. "And you can be damn sure that there was an exhaustive search. We discovered nothing to indicate the barge's port of origin or where it was built. Its design was a basic one common to every kingdom in the Known Lands that sail those types of vessels."

The king was silent for a moment as he considered everything that had been said. He turned to his son.

"Graham, you spent four years in the Carthan Kingdom. Perhaps you heard or saw something, anything, that would indicate their potential involvement?"

Prince Graham shrugged. "I was well-known while I attended the Royal Carthan University, much like Prince Vergoth was well-known while he attended our military academy. Students and teachers were careful with their words in my presence." He thought for a moment and continued. "However, I entered a tavern or two during my stay. Knights and noblemen and their mistresses, while filled with spirits of various types, were sometimes slow to recognize me and therefore slightly looser with their tongues."

King William gave his son a stern look. "And what, Prince Graham, did these men and women say in these taverns you frequented when you were supposed to be studying?"

"I didn't say I *frequented* these establishments, my king," the prince answered with a sly smile. "I cannot say that I learned much of anything that would assist us. I heard the usual griping. They envy us and fear the Children of the Ones. Many wish their king would do something to 'even the balance,' as they put it. They say there is even some unrest in the southern borderlands of our very own kingdom. But I've never heard anything specific."

The king blinked. "Unrest in the southern borderlands, you say?"

Tyus scoffed. "There is always unrest in the borderlands, especially the southern ones. They feel neglected because they're so far away from the capitol city."

"Perhaps," the prince allowed. "But there is a difference between general unrest and *organized* unrest."

This got Artemis's attention. "My spies have mentioned nothing of organized unrest. Church-based emissaries from Cartha have been traveling the southern territories for years preaching stuff and nonsense against the Children of the Old Ones, but no one takes them seriously."

"True," Prince Graham agreed. "That was indeed the case for years. They used to be chased away by raucous crowds hurling ridicule and rotten vegetables. Now, according to the rumors, the southern Lorrians no longer chase them away."

"I don't know that that rises to the level of *organized* unrest," Tyus noted.

"Perhaps not," the prince allowed. "But perhaps it's the foundation. If they start to listen, they may start to agree. If they start to agree, the soil becomes fertile for those who would sow the seeds of an uprising."

"Interesting," Ramos observed. "What would you have us do about this potential for the sowing of seeds?"

The prince did not miss the Minister of War's incredulous, almost teasing underlying tone. He turned an angry glare to Ramos. "Simple, Minister. I would remove the threat from my beloved kingdom. I would have the outsiders silenced, those who dared to listen to such seditious rhetoric detained and reeducated, and future emissaries banned."

All of the older men were taken aback by the prince's harsh words. But it was the king's son who had spoken, so the king's main council waited for the king to reply.

"Are you advocating the execution of visiting clergy, son?" William asked. "You would close our borders to peaceful emissaries? And from your tone I don't dare ask what sort of 'reeducation' you would employ."

"I fear you may have spent too much time in Cartha, Prince Graham," Rionn suggested. "That is the kind of intolerance and heavy-handed approach for which King Vergoth is renowned."

The prince's pointed glare turned to the Head Mage. "And I fear you may need to spend some time in Cartha," Graham snapped. "That type of intolerance and heavy-handed approach would have served my kingdom well when you dealt with your fellow Child Mar-dah."

A rueful smile came to Rionn Lorr's lips. "*Your* kingdom, is it?" he challenged.

"Graham," King William rumbled. "Every member of this council has defended this kingdom longer than you've been alive. You *will* respect them as you respect me."

"But father, I was only – "

"Forgetting your place!" William interrupted. "You may be a prince, but as long as I draw breath, every man here has a higher functional station than you. You would do well to remember that."

Prince Graham's face reddened as he bowed his head. "Yes, my liege and father. I apologize for speaking out of turn."

"All right," the king said, coming to a conclusion. "Tyus, continue to conduct interviews at every port and shipyard along the perimeter of Lake Onyx and the length of the Bountiful River. If anyone has seen anything out of the ordinary, we have to know. Ramos, keep the rest of the infantry ready and pray we do not have to deploy them.

"Artemis, have your agents conduct investigations at every port and shipyard along the western stem of the Tyne. I don't have to tell you that they must be as discreet as possible. That is another kingdom, after all. The Kingdom of Darshay may claim to be our ally, but if that is *only* a claim, it's best not to alert them. And do whatever it takes to find that damnable spy. When this crisis has ended," William continued with an annoyed glance at his son, "I want you to look closer at these rumblings in the south."

"As you command," Artemis said.

King William turned to Rionn Lorr. His thick and ruddy eyebrows knitted over intense brown eyes. The bronze skin of his forehead creased in disappointment. The king's advisors also turned concerned gazes to the Head Mage. This was the moment Rionn Lorr had been dreading.

"And what say you," the king demanded, "about the conduct of your Master Mage and old mentor?"

"I in no way condone what he did," Rionn assured.

"I should hope not," the king returned. "What would you suggest we do about it?"

Rionn Lorr sighed. This was going to be a delicate conversation.

"By law," Rionn began, "Delthar was well within his rights. Colonel Stottlemeyer – "

"Is a colonel no longer," King William finished. "Yes, yes. I am well aware that his retirement effectively made him a civillian despite his status as Earl of the Allanville Territories. And since the walkers have not been classified as enemies of the kingdom, and in fact consist of both citizens and enlisted men, Delthar was doing his duty by protecting them. But did the wizard have to *kill* Stottlemeyer?"

"No," Rionn admitted. "And I told him as much. I told him that it would have been a simple matter to incapacitate the poor man. But Delthar has always been one to see the larger picture. He feared Stottlemeyer's actions would embolden others to strike out against the infected. He felt a strong statement had to be made to discourage any other potential vigilantes. He wanted to send the message that such action would not be tolerated by the crown."

"Yes," Ramos grunted. "But some might interpret the message in a different way. The king has not officially declared the walkers enemies of the crown but they are nonetheless viewed as such by a great many people. They are, without question, a danger to all who cross their path. Those already inclined might easily perceive the Master Mage's actions as protecting our enemies."

"And retired or not," Tyus warned, "Stottlemeyer was greatly respected by the Royal Army. Many will take his death personally. Some soldiers may view the incident as evidence of a rift between the military and the Conjurer's Alliance."

"A *rift?*" Rionn asked. "I'd say that is a rather extreme conclusion to draw from this one incident."

"I wonder if that's so," Artemis said. "*We* know the notion is so much nonsense, but there have been whispers…"

Rionn Lorr cocked an eyebrow. "What whispers? The Conjurer's Alliance and the Royal Military have worked in harmony since the Alliance's conception over five hundred years ago. After all of these centuries, why would there suddenly be rumors of a rift?"

"The rumors began shortly after our costly success in the Cursed Opening," Artemis said, his full cheeks reddened just a bit beneath his neatly trimmed beard. Rionn could not tell if it was because he was embarrassed to be relating such outlandish gossip or if he was ashamed for not revealing it sooner.

"Many of the soldiers that fought at the Tyne felt marginalized. Some even felt like they were used as demon fodder for the conjurers. It fostered a general sense of mistrust. Mar-dah's ability to release the demons – as well as yours and the offworlder's ability to destroy the demons – served to strengthen that feeling. People are in awe of your power…and many of them are fearful of it."

"Alas," Tyus said. "Artemis speaks true. The Battle at the Tyne River poisoned the river and left it barren for over a year, as you well know. Many citizens' livelihoods were devastated by the loss of the river, temporary though it was."

Rionn Lorr frowned. "And it was through the efforts of the Conjurer's Alliance that life returned to the river as soon as it did," the wizard reminded. "Those who depend on the river have nearly recovered. Surely they do not blame the Conjurer's Alliance for the river's poisoning. It was Mar-dah who set the demons upon us."

King William shook his head slowly. "You miss our point. Many of our citizens have never knowingly been directly affected – or threatened – by magic in their lifetimes. Even during the incident with the Wizard Drake, when he nearly sparked a second Dragon War, most of the battles were fought in relative obscurity.

"But in the Cursed Opening the demons marched from the southern regions of the kingdom to the northern ones, cutting a swath of death and destruction along the way. Even after the Cursed Opening, many innocent citizens were killed by stray demons before the Keeper's Hounds could destroy them. The collateral harm from the Battle at the Tyne bankrupted small companies and private business. Do you understand what we are trying to say?"

Rionn nodded reluctantly. "I'm afraid I do. They fear the destructive potential of magic."

Artemis winced slightly as if pricked by a small pin. "Not exactly, old friend. It is not magic in general they fear. It is *your* magic they fear, your potential destructive power, and that of the other Children of the Old Ones. And since you lead the Conjurer's Alliance, it stands to reason that those who fear you would fear the entire organization. Think about it. If Mar-dah had power enough to release the demons and only you and the offworlder had power enough to stop them, who or what could stop *you* if you ever chose to follow Mar-dah's path?"

Rionn Lorr's frown deepened. "From where would such slander originate?" he demanded. Rionn's voice began to rise in volume. "I have dedicated my life to the protection of this kingdom. Has the drivel of the southern and western kingdoms really started to infect the minds of Lorrian citizens to that extent?"

"Unfortunately, yes." King William said. Out of the corner of his eye he saw his son square his shoulder and grin a smug little grin. He ignored Graham and went on. "The Cursed Opening was exactly the type of scenario that the southlanders and westerners have been screeching about over the years."

"Indeed," Ramos concurred. "So when a veteran as popular and decorated as Colonel Stottlemeyer is killed by a Master Mage, who operates under the command of a Head

Mage who is also a Child of the Old Ones, it only adds kindling to already smoldering doubt and suspicion."

"Which is exactly what the Dierglyorr wants," Rionn Lorr pointed out to them all.

"Which is why Delthar should have exercised better judgment," King William countered.

The Head Mage could only sigh. He knew the king was right.

"I trust nothing like this will happen again," King William said.

"I have ordered the Alliance to refrain from similar action," Rionn assured. "No conjurer in my charge will repeat Delthar's mistake."

King William huffed and leaned back heavily in his chair. His bulk, mostly muscle with the exception of the well-earned paunch around his middle, caused the sturdy wooden chair to groan in protest. His usually stern and often fierce expression softened to an exhausted scowl.

"We must end this crisis as soon as possible," the king exhaled. "It is crushing morale. Our military has not yet returned to full strength after the Cursed Opening. Now we face the grim possibility of having to strike down our own citizens and brothers-at-arms."

That last sentence caused everyone to turn their attention to the Head Mage once more. They all knew that there was only one alternative to destroying the walkers.

"Rionn, how close are you to finding a cure?" King William asked hopefully. "That is precisely what we need to restore morale and focus all of our efforts on the demon... and those damned *S'Zan Rho* cutthroats, if the pursuing regiment fails to stop them."

The Head Mage shrugged slowly. "We have learned more about how the infection behaves but we have made little progress in finding a cure."

Ramos drove a meaty fist into the table with almost as much power as the king. None of the men so much as even flinched. They all felt the same frustration and they all had known Ramos for years. The only surprise was that he had not done it sooner.

"By Hargathall's blade, mage," Ramos swore. "I loathe the prospect of engaging the walkers, but the longer we wait the more of them we will likely have to destroy. How long are we to wait?"

Rionn, not at all offended by the familiar gruff tone, replied, "That question is for the Minister of War and King."

William sneered. "The infected hordes are composed of our own military and innocents from all corners of the kingdom. If I give the order to wipe them out, half of my kingdom will accuse me of slaughtering my own subjects. If I don't give the order, the other half will damn me as a coward. No matter which choice I make, those who mistrust the Children of the Old Ones will twist the facts to make me out to be a pawn of my Head Mage."

"A king must make the hard choices," Ramos said needlessly. "The ultimate safety of his kingdom must be put first, whether his subjects understand his decisions or not."

William gave Ramos an annoyed sidelong glance. "You seem to be so knowledgeable of what is required. Do *you* want my job?"

"Hell no," Ramos said with a grim smile. "I've never wanted your job, Will. You know that."

The prince spoke up. "But you did say that you wanted to end this as soon as possible, father. As terrible a solution as it may be, I cannot imagine a faster end than the wizards' whitefyre."

Tyus disagreed. "Whitefyre may quickly put an end the plague-ridden in the east, but it may very likely ignite dangerous unrest throughout the entire kingdom. It's one thing for the military to put an end to them, but if the wizards do, that would be all the fuel the Children-fearing folk need. Then we will be dealing with the demon *and* the prospect of civil war."

The king was growing visibly frustrated. He again clenched his fists hard enough to send the sound of his cracking knuckles echoing off the walls.

"Enough," he said. "What say you, Rionn?"

"For now," the Head Mage said, "Geoffrey and Delthar are of one mind on this. They support the position of standing down. The infected do not pose an immediate threat."

"That is only supposition," Ramos argued. "We have no idea what the demon's plans are. And I must admit that I am surprised Delthar would take that position. His past would indicate a willingness to eliminate the greater threat."

"Delthar is a hard man, yes," Tyus said. "But he cares for this kingdom and its citizens above all else, most especially the innocents. Not even he would kill women and children unless he was left with no other choice."

Ramos turned a challenging glare to Rionn. "He may be left with no other choice sooner rather than later."

Rionn met Ramos's gaze. "It may very well be that the demon wants us to wipe out the infected for the very purpose of splintering the kingdom. How easy it would be for a rival kingdom, under the demon's manipulation, to sweep in and conquer us while we fight each other."

Prince Graham leaned forward insistently. "And what if the demon has an even more dire consequence in store if we do not wipe them out?"

The Head Mage felt a twinge of irritation that the youngster was even there. He had already spoken out of turn and seemed determined to test his father's patience. It was not that Graham disagreed. Rionn would have been just as irritated if the youngster agreed with him. He just did not think Graham should have been there.

While Rionn knew how important it was for William to prepare his eventual successor, he did not think such dire circumstances made the ideal setting for a lesson in kingship.

He would not say this to the king, though. When it came to his family, William was thrice as stubborn as usual. Rionn answered the question, but when he spoke, he directed his reply to the king and not the prince.

"I'm convinced, William, that a cure is the best solution and I'm confident that one will be found. I cannot, however, predict how long it will take. I only ask for patience."

"And we will have patience," King William declared. "The situation is contained for now. Delthar was as creative in effectively slowing the walkers as he was brash in his decision to slay Stottlemeyer. He has bought us valuable time."

The king paused for a moment and met every man's gaze until his dark brown eyes finally rested on Rionn's.

"But we will have to re-evaluate our strategy once the walkers resume their march."

And with those words, the king set his timetable.

8.2

Ethan's body ached when he finished his exercises. The joints in his back, shoulders, arms, and legs protested painfully. The muscles in those very same areas burned. The only good thing about the discomfort was that it was not as bad as it was after the first day he performed the exercises. If he had found himself in a fight that day he would have been in serious trouble. He could barely walk or even lift his arms for two days.

On the third day his body had recovered enough to resume the exercises, and even though his body hurt too much to exercise the next day, it did not ache as severely as it did after that first day. And now on this, the fifth day of his and Quick's search, the pain was noticeably less intense. In fact, he felt unexpectedly energized even through the residual soreness.

When his labored breathing finally returned to normal, he turned his attention to supper. He wolfed down his evening ration, which consisted of a thick strip of dried beef, a hard, fist-size biscuit, a small chunk of pale yellow cheese, and then washed it down with a few healthy gulps from a water skin. He sat in patch of dry grass at the side of the intersection of two wide roads. The roads, seldom used so far away from the nearest town and so close to the Forsaken Desert, were barely discernable in the dry, hard packed earth of the barren foothills just west of Hell's Mountains.

The vast rocky mountain range to his left, Ethan looked to the southern horizon. From the elevation of the foothills he could just make out the edge of the Forsaken Desert as an even paler swath of land. The air in the distance shimmered from the heat of that cursed region even in the dim light of the setting suns. The cool dry autumn breeze forced Ethan to pull his cloak about him. Across the arid western plains, half of the smaller southern sun had already dipped below the curve of the earth and the lower edge of the largest sun was just kissing the horizon.

Having lived the last few years of his young life in the eastern regions of the Kingdom of Lorr, he was used to seeing the suns devoured by Hell's Mountains at nightfall. Lately, though, he only saw the suns sink below a flat horizon on his trips beyond the Hell's into the Kingdom of Darshay with the Keepers Hounds demon hunters, or when sailing upon the great Lake Onyx. It was a beautiful sight, one that Ethan did not see as often as he would have liked.

This was his favorite time of day. The clear, near-dusk skies were a breathtaking combination of pink and orange. Soon the lower sun would dip below the horizon and the sky would turn into a spectacular rainbow, flowing softly from west to east in bands of orange, gold, silver and finally blue-black on the eastern horizon as the three moons ascended to take their turn in the evening sky. The dazzling beauty made Ethan think that was how heaven must look all the time.

The thought of heaven made him think of his father. Yes, he was sure the legendary Meldrick Sureblade stood somewhere in those heavens, in the company of the Lord Ascendant and the Old Ones, looking down at his son.

"What do you see, father?" he wondered. "Are you proud of what I've become? Have my accomplishments honored you? Have my mistakes made you ashamed?

"It pains me to have relinquished your weapons, father. I pray that I've made the right decision. I've done what I thought you would have me do."

He stopped and turned when he heard the sound of flapping wings. A large eagle circled smoothly as it descended. When it was just at twenty feet above the ground, it curled in on itself and began to shudder. The image of the creature grew, wavering as if it was being viewed beneath stirring water, and then began to drop straight down. Quick unfolded from the shifting image and landed lightly on the soles of booted feet a few yards away from the young Sureblade.

The tall, lanky teen took a moment to adjust his leather jerkin before he spoke.

"I would have returned half a day sooner," Quick said, "But I had to stop to rest."

"I imagine you would have to rest sometime." And then: "Oh, you mean 'rest' in the unique way changelings rest."

"Indeed," Quick affirmed. "Mountain ranges are the ideal settings. There are countless places to hide from predators during my short hibernation in my true form."

"And what *is* your true form, my friend? You've never said. Is it something you wish to keep secret?"

Quick hesitated for a brief moment, as if uncertain whether or not to answer. And then he shrugged. "I honestly do not know. I do know it is very small and unlike any earthbound, airborne, or aquatic animal. I perceive things much differently. My senses become less like sight, sound, touch and smell and more like an acute awareness of the world around me. But I have no idea how I would appear to another being."

"Interesting," Ethan said thoughtfully.

Quick grasped Ethan's shoulder. His ever-present half smile tightened into a stern grimace. "Understand, my friend that I tell you this in the strictest confidence."

"Of course," Ethan said. "I guess that's not something you'd want an enemy to know. On my honor and before the Lord Ascendant, Quick, I will not speak of your secret to anyone."

Quick nodded. "Thank you, Ethan."

The two young friends clasped their right forearms and shook once before disengaging.

"So what have you discovered?" Ethan asked.

"This is the last place the scythe wings stopped before returning to their hidden roost in the heart of the Hell's. I got close enough to their roost, in the form of a wasp, to search for any evidence of Joel. There was none. You know, Ethan, it was an excellent idea to follow their dung trail."

Ethan shrugged. "I only wish I could have thought of a quicker way. They veered many times in search of food. Such a large flock has to feed often. Not even the attack on our sky sleighs sated the giant hawks even though they devoured horses, avicaws, and people.

"Every time we found the remains of their feeding you had to circle miles to find more evidence of their passing. It probably took several hours for them to get here but it's taken us several days."

"It would have taken much longer, otherwise," Quick reminded. "And we've learned some valuable things. For one, we found no traces of fresh human remains along they way. At the very least we would have found bones or blood if they had devoured Joel."

"Yes," Ethan agreed. "We've seen dung and feathers in this area, but no evidence that they killed human prey. That means they only fed on animals before going to roost."

Quick nodded. "At least one human died here, though." He indicated the faded blood spatters. "There are signs here that indicate a body being dragged off by scavengers. It wasn't Joel, though. I don't recognize the scent."

Ethan nodded. "And there are faint traces of boot prints and hoof prints that the soft breezes haven't yet completely concealed. There's drying horse dung, as well. It's all only a few days old, like the nearest traces of the scythe wings. There is no evidence that any others have passed this way in very long time. Quick, I remember you saying you sensed a faint trace of magic among the scythe wings."

"Yes. The scythe wings must have brought Joel here to the person controlling that magic," Quick concluded. "I'm sure he is alive. We have to stay earthbound to follow their spore from here, though I fear we will lose the trail once we get to the nearest town."

"Eastedge," Ethan acknowledged. "That's the closest town. This trail leads north in that direction. On my travels with the Keeper's Hounds…" he paused at the mention of his lost team and the memory of Arrowhead, took a breath, and continued. "I've heard there has been much traffic in that remote town of late, an upheaval of some sort."

"If the trail becomes too obscured, how will we proceed?" Quick asked. "Their scents are fading even now in this low-traffic area after so many days. It will be impossible to track them if the town has been as busy as you say."

Ethan thought for a moment before giving Quick a knowing glance. "There are no wagon wheel tracks here," Ethan noticed. "That means they had to carry the Child of the Old Ones into town on horseback. Surely someone knows something. Even if no one in town knew who he was, someone *had* to notice a man being taken under guard through the city streets. We'll ask around in Eastedge."

"Let us ride, then," Quick declared. A devious sparkle danced in his eyes. "For speed and following a scent on the ground, a land dragon would be the best form to take." The teen suddenly shook his head in the negative. "No. Such a beast would certainly not go unnoticed. We do not yet know who or what has Joel, so it would not be in our best interest to draw attention to ourselves."

"We can follow this trail visually for a time, as well as their scent," Ethan said. "If they lead to Eastedge as we suspect, the fastest and safest way to transport us both there would be as a gryphon, but only royal agents and the wealthiest citizens ride gryphons. A lone Gryphon Ryder out here would stand out.

"A fast horse would be the most practical, and you can take your human form when we reach the town." Ethan turned a suspicious glance on his friend. "But you already knew that. You're just trying to find a reason to take the form of a land dragon."

Quick shrugged. "They're fascinating beasts. I'd never seen a land dragon before. Now that I am familiar with them, I would love to take its form."

"A fast horse will do," Ethan said with a smirk.

Quick decided to take the form of the fastest breed of horse in the Known Lands, called a *Zephïrra Tul Fey* in the old tongue, which meant "divine wind," so it was only just past the twilight hour by the time Ethan and Quick had covered roughly one hundred miles to reach the road that would take them into Eastedge. The intersecting road stretched out to the east and west and was marked with considerably more signs of traffic.

From where it emerged from the crossroads and continued north, the road on which they traveled also displayed evidence of higher traffic. The more populated regions of the Kingdom of Darshay, including the capital, lie to the west.

To the east, down a long, steady decline in the earth, the light forest surrounding them ended abruptly and gave way to the dry, rocky, bowl-like valley where the border town of Eastedge was situated. Further to the north, among forested foothills and overlooking the valley, was the castle belonging to the baron of Eastedge.

Ethan called to Quick to stop. He swiftly dismounted and removed the saddle and makeshift harness that held his and Quick's packs when the changeling horse halted. Quick morphed back into his human form while Ethan surveyed the immediate area. The young Sureblade took note of how it was lightly forested, but the woods grew denser to the northwest and east.

"I could have gone on a few miles further before stopping to rest," Quick assured as he accepted his pack and straight sword. "We should be able to reach Eastedge before midnight."

"I'd prefer to enter the town by light of day," Ethan said. "Eastedge is in a state of transition. All newcomers are likely to be thoroughly appraised by the locals. People tend to take particular notice of visitors who arrive in the dead of night."

"Good point," Quick agreed. "I hear sounds of an inn or a tavern less than a mile west down the road, a rather raucous one, at that. Perhaps we should pay it a visit."

Ethan gave Quick a sidelong glance. "You don't drink. I've taken a mug of mead or ale when I've had the chance, but I doubt they'd believe we were old enough to serve."

Quick chuckled. "Not for drinks, Ethan. Maybe men and women with a few drinks in them will have less suspicion and looser tongues."

DEMON OF LORR

"And if they're raucous, perhaps they'd be less tolerant of outsiders and looser with their swords," Ethan countered.

"There is that," Quick agreed.

Ethan kneeled down to inspect the various tracks on the dusty road under the pale silver moons' light. As he suspected, countless tracks of man, beast, and wheeled transports converged and made it almost impossible to distinguish the tracks they had been following. The young tracker thought their targets had veered east but he could not be sure. He was about to stand up when he noticed a set of recent tracks that arrested his attention.

The outline of a pair of small, slender feet wearing soft-soled tracker's shoes painfully reminded him of Arrowhead – or Nicolette, as she asked him to call her that night weeks earlier. Ethan immediately thought back to that special night.

They had almost kissed for the first time after Ethan finally confessed his feelings her and she for him. The image of her tiny, perfect feet and delicate ankles were still vivid in his memory. He remembered how the moons' light played softly off of her long, jet-black hair and accentuated every perfect curve of her beautiful face.

Even though that night ended terribly – like almost everything else that was good in his life – when another of the Keeper's Hounds attacked while transforming into one of the horrid walking dead, Ethan remembered the near-kiss fondly. He had hoped she would be a part of his life from that moment on. That turned out to be a boy's foolish dream that was not to be. She and the rest of the Keeper's Hounds were aboard the sky sleigh *Sundance* when it was brought down by the savage scythe wings.

Guilt soon accompanied the heartbreak of her loss. Ethan was supposed to have been on that sky sleigh. He knew he was blessed to have survived but he could not help feeling that it was unfair for all of the other Hounds to have perished while he lived.

He tried to look away from the footprints, to banish the images that were causing him such pain. Try as he might, though, he could not tear his eyes away.

"What troubles you?" Quick asked, seeing the pained look on his friend's face.

"Nothing, Quick. I'm all – " Ethan stopped short when he noticed something else. Not only did the size and shape of the prints remind him of Nicolette, the angle of the impressions and length of stride were similar.

Ethan did not normally read human tracks so closely. He usually hunted animals and demons. The only time he tracked people was when he tracked his siblings back at his home at Fort Bastion as they played their hunting games.

Nicolette was different. He had long since committed to memory everything about her, from the sublime to the most seemingly insignificant details.

He shook his head, admonishing himself for wishful thinking, for seeing not what was there but what he wanted to be there. He was torturing himself. Still, though, he could not look away.

"Tell me Quick," Ethan started. "What do you scent in the air?"

The changeling sniffed. "Quite a few things: Human sweat, animals, road dust, plant life…" Quick paused. "And strangely, I smell a faint trace of lilacs. There are no such plants around here, but that scent lingers."

Ethan's eyes widened. "Maybe you were right, Quick. Maybe we *should* pay a visit to that inn or tavern you hear in the distance."

8.3

It was a short walk to the tavern, and a disturbing one as well. A frown had creased Quick's narrow face by the time Ethan was able to hear the noises coming from the tavern, and then Ethan frowned as well. The sounds were not just raucous. They were violent. There was a brawl in progress and a fairly sizable one by the sound of it. Ethan and Quick could hear metal clanging, furniture breaking, and roars of anger and pain.

They reached the one-story ramshackle construction, little more than an oversized shed with gaudy red paint that looked more like a deep purple in the moonglow. A dozen horses were tethered to a hitching post but Ethan judged from the number of fairly recent footprints, including the ones that led them here, that there were *many* more people in the tavern than just the riders of the twelve steeds.

Instead of entering right away, the two teens sidled up to a window with no panes and peeked in. A wild fracas filled the room. A large group of burly, drunken men surrounded and and attacked a much smaller group. Several one-on-one and two-on-one scraps were taking place on the periphery of the main clash. There were too many people obstructing the view to get an accurate count of the seriously outnumbered fighters. One of the targets was at least a head taller than anyone else in the room, but countless raised fists, arms, and weapons hid his face. Whoever they were, though, they were more than holding their own.

Quick turned to Ethan. "Maybe we should wait," he said with a smirk.

"Do you still smell lilacs?" Ethan asked, never turning his eyes away from the brawl.

Quick sniffed. "Amid the sweat, alcohol, and road dust?" He sniffed again, paused, and said, "Yes. It's faint, but yes."

"I'm going in," Ethan said. He reached over his shoulder and pulled the gleaming silver staff from his back and stalked toward the open front double-doors of the establishment.

"Ethan!" Quick called. "Maybe we should –"

Ethan was not listening. He was already entering the tavern. Quick sighed, unsheathed his longsword, and followed his friend into trouble.

Ethan sidestepped to avoid a stray scuffle. He ducked a chair that was swung at his head by one of the bruisers and jabbed his staff into the man's solar plexus before he could swing the chair again.

As the would-be attacker doubled over in pain and fell to his knees, Ethan turned his attention back to the main confrontation. He saw the head of a massive war hammer swing high above fray and then quickly down. Ethan raised his eyebrows. There was only one person he knew of that could swing a war hammer that big that quickly. The young Sureblade leapt onto the nearest table in order to look over the top of the attackers. When he saw the defenders his knees almost buckled.

In the midst of five strangers, with their backs to the rear wall and fighting valiantly against the mob, were two members of the Keeper's Hounds.

Hammer and Arrowhead.

The mention of lilacs reminded Ethan of Nicolette, the seemingly dainty, almost fragile beauty with flowing black hair, the woman that appeared at his cabin door bathed in the soft moons' shine. But other than the long raven hair, which was now tied back severely into a coiled ponytail, the woman in the midst of this brawl bore little resemblance to Nicolette.

Gone were Nicolette's gentle facial features. They had been replaced by a grim scowl, her teeth bared like a feral wolf. Her warm hazel eyes locked with ice-cold intensity on her opponents. Nicolette's soft curves gave way to diamond-hard toughness. Tendons stood out in her neck. The muscles in her slender arms could be traced beneath her tunic sleeves.

This was unmistakably Arrowhead, the fierce Keeper's Hound with the small crossbow at her hip and a straight sword that she wielded with the mastery and savagery of a fighter far more experienced than one would expect from an eighteen year old. Though arrowhead and Nicollette was the same person, their personas could not be more different.

DEMON OF LORR

Arrowhead, Hammer, and their five companions did an exceptional job of holding the throng at bay. It helped that the attackers were, to a man, almost staggering drunk. Not only were their reflexes slowed by the alcohol in their systems, they were completely disorganized. For the most part they attacked seven at a time, taking turns challenging each of their targets one-to-one.

The small group would not have had a chance if the mob attacked in force. As it was, the five strangers, all very sober and learned swordsmen as evidenced by the precision and quickness of their movements, overcame each of their attackers in relatively short order. Arrowhead and Hammer dispatched their opponents even quicker.

The problem was that other drunken brawlers kept stepping in to take the place of the downed ones. Ethan knew that eventually even Arrowhead and Hammer would tire. Or worse, it would finally occur to the mob to attack as a group.

Once Ethan assured himself that what he was seeing was real, he vaulted from the table and charged into the outer perimeter of the fracas with his staff at the ready. One of the inebriated men waiting for his turn at the one of the seven saw the teen rushing toward the fray. He had no idea if the boy was part of the mob or coming to help the seven targets, and since the boy was a stranger, he assumed the latter. With a slurred battle cry, he ran at Ethan with his hand-and-a-half sword raised high.

Ethan expected – and waited for – the magic of the staff to come forth but he felt nothing. It was at that moment that the significance of what Raxe told him sunk in. There was no way to purposely invoke its magic.

With no time to waste pondering how to use the magic, Ethan had to call upon the training in stave fighting that he received at the Royal Academy. He pushed the silver staff up and forward in a wide two-handed grip to catch the sword as it swung down at him. As the blade rebounded, Ethan snatched the right side of the staff down and around to smash his assailant on the left side of the head. The man went down in a heap. Ethan hurdled him and kept moving forward.

Two more thugs saw their companion fall and converged on Ethan. One wielded a dirk and the other a mattock. Both were short-range weapons, and if either man had attacked alone Ethan would have been able to dispatch them with little effort. Had he been a more accomplished stave wielder, or if he had his broadsword, he would have known the best way to counter and stop them quickly. With them attacking together, the teen was hard-pressed to block the wild but powerful blows. He knew that he would be in serious trouble if another attacker approached him from the rear.

Quick noticed his friend's plight. Unfortunately he was in no position to assist him. He was embroiled in his own fight against three of the drunken brawlers who attacked him simply because they did not recognize him. Two wielded swords and the third a large club. Quick parried and ducked and dodged the sloppy attacks while trying to find openings in their guard.

He saw several openings that he could have easily used if he had wanted to kill them, but Quick was as loathe to take a life as he had always been.

He almost wished the men were sober, at least that way he could have inflicted injuries painful enough to incapacitate them. Quick knew that in their inebriated conditions they would feel little pain and would simply shrug off any such attacks. Of course, there was always the option of transforming into a formidable animal that would terrify everyone in the tavern and send all of them scattering. He decided against that move, though, fearing that revealing his power would unquestionably expose his identity. That news would quickly find its way to Joel's captor or captors sooner than he would like.

Quick allowed the men to push him back further and further until his back was only inches away from a window that actually contained a pane of glass. The club wielder swung a vicious blow that Quick could have easily ducked. Instead, Quick held up his weapon vertically with one hand, braced himself by placing the other hand high on the flat side of the blade, and let the long sword absorb the blow.

The club struck the blade forcefully, bending it and launching the changeling up, back and crashing through the thin glass window.

Ethan had finally dispatched the mattock wielding assailant and was about to do the same to the thug with the dirk when he saw Quick, out of the corner of his eye, go through the window. The sight alarmed him but it did not distract him. His opponent attempted a reckless jab at Ethan's neck. The teen stepped back and to the side and then used the far superior reach of the staff to rap the thug on the fist holding the dirk. He heard the sound of the man's knuckles breaking over the din of the brawl. By the time the dirk clattered to the floor, the young Sureblade had already hit his opponent on the top of the head and knocked him senseless.

The mob had increased their pressure on Arrowhead and the others. Each one of them was fighting off at least two opponents. Ethan took two steps toward their attackers when three men confronted him, each with a broadsword. Their number, along with the reach of their weapons, gave Ethan pause. He looked at his staff, calling for and then hoping for and then finally praying for its magic to come to bear.

Nothing happened.

Fending them off was even more difficult than Ethan expected. With the men wielding the mattock and dirk, all he had to do was put space between him and them and use the reach of the staff to his advantage. Against three men with broadswords, the reach advantage was considerably less. To make matters worse, these men did not seem to be as intoxicated as Ethan's other opponents. All the youngster could do was protect himself, and he was only just barely able to do that. His attackers left him no time or space to go on the offensive.

Hammer was pleasantly surprised when he noticed Ethan entering the tavern. He was so distracted that he actually let one of these fools pass within the perimeter of the massive head of his long-handled war hammer. He quickly corrected the error by yanking the war hammer backward and jabbing the fool in the face with wide end of the handle.

His wide, frighteningly fast sweeps of the great hammer then provided plenty of space between him and the rest of his opponents. The blunt side of the hammerhead resembled a sledgehammer and was almost as big as a grown man's head. The weapon was even more deadly on the opposite side, which was a foot-long, curved spike. At its base, the spike was as broad as its wielder's large, meaty fist. The other end was sharpened to a deadly point. Altogether the weapon weighed more than forty pounds yet the mountain of muscle and sinew that was Hammer handled it as if it was a toy.

The drunken attackers' judgment was clearly impaired. They kept trying to dart within the circumference of the great weapon and almost to a man were sent flying across the room, or driven with fatal power to the floor, or torn open violently. The lucky ones caught vicious elbows and club-like forearms to the head or upper torso.

As pleasantly surprised as Hammer was to see Ethan, he was even more surprised by the weapon the young Hound wielded. He was doing well with it until the three swordsmen jumped him. Hammer took a wide, wild swing to send several men scurrying back, stepped over to an unoccupied table – all of the tables were unoccupied by this time – and took a powerful underhand swipe at it with his war hammer.

The heavy table went skidding across the floor in Ethan's direction. Those nearby dove hastily out of the way to avoid the table. Ethan and his attackers also saw the approaching table. They all jumped in different directions and watched the table barrel into several people who could not get out of the way in time. They went flying.

Arrowhead used her foot to flick the handle of a discarded broadsword up and over to Hammer's waiting hand. Hammer grabbed the broadsword and tossed it toward Ethan as if it were a large dagger. Once again, attackers dove out of the way as the large sword spun through the air end over end. Ethan, however, did not move. They had practiced this maneuver many times.

Ethan dropped the staff and reached up and to his right to pluck the broadsword out of the air with both hands. He had to immediately whip the blade to his left to block a broadsword arcing toward his left shoulder.

He looked over his enemy's shoulder and saw the other two swordsmen returning to the fray. The one with whom he was engaged took another hard swing at him. This time Ethan did not just block the strike. He attacked it with a vicious two-handed hack. His broadsword met the other with enough force to make it rebound and force its owner to take a step back.

Before the man could bring the broadsword back into a defensive position Ethan quickly reversed his swing and brought the tip of his blade across his opponent's stomach. The man dropped his blade and fell to his knees in an attempt to keep his guts inside his belly.

The other two swordsmen reached Ethan, but the teen slid quickly to one side and took on the man to his left, who was jabbing his broadsword straight at Ethan's chest. Ethan stepped further to his left and forward while batting the thrust away. Once again he reversed his swing and deeply sliced the wrist of the swordsman before he could snatch his hand away.

The attacker roared in pain and shuffled away as the third man came around and attacked Ethan from the right. Ethan turned and raised his broadsword to catch the middle of the opposing blade with the long cross guard of his weapon just an inch away from his face.

The teen twisted the handle firmly to trap the other blade between his cross guard and the base of his blade and then stomped his attacker's foot. The man howled in pain. The howl was cut short when Ethan swiftly pivoted and elbowed him in the mouth. As the man tried to scramble away, Ethan clutched the man's wrist to stay his weapon, shifted the handle of his broadsword to disengage it, and then brought his own blade down to cut the other across his torso diagonally. He released the man's wrist and let him crumple to the dirty floor.

Ethan turned to face the next attackers and was shocked to see that there were none. No one approached him. All of the thugs near him were staring slack-jawed in his direction.

They were not staring at him, he soon realized. They were actually staring past him. A few of them were even gasping and pointing. Ethan turned and saw why.

The bulk of a wallowgrump filled the same window through which Quick had fallen. The creature, resembling a giant frog standing upright on reverse-articulated legs, loosed a terrible hiss-growl and vaulted through the window. The wallowgrump was so broad that it tore away some of the wood on either side of the broken window frame.

When the wallowgrump stood to its full height, it was slightly taller than Ethan. Its wide mouth was lined with rows of wickedly sharp teeth. It chased the tavern patrons all through – and out of – the establishment. Some dashed through the open front doors while others jumped through windows, whether they contained glass panes or not.

The animal propelled itself after everyone with its heavily muscled amphibious legs. It reached for some with its short arms that ended with long, dangerous, talon-like claws.

Those who were caught were tossed roughly around the room. The wallowgrump battered men with its thick, long tail. It snapped at some with its wide mouth and razor-edged teeth. It tore small bits of cloth, and sometimes a bit of flesh, from fleeing men's backs, thighs, and buttocks, eliciting almost comical high-pitched screams from its victims.

The young Sureblade squelched his first reaction, which was to run screaming the way the others did. He had been deathly afraid of wallowgrumps ever since his first encounter with one when he was three years younger and a wallowgrump attacked his younger siblings. Both he and his father had shot it in critical areas with an arrow and a crossbow bolt. His father had even pinned it to a tree with his javelin, and still the beast did not die. Meldrick Sureblade had to take the animal's head to finally kill it.

Just as three years ago when the wallowgrump appeared outside the military town of Fort Bastion, this wallowgrump was far away from its natural habitat of the Badlands and the Demon's Spine Mountains, both of which were hundreds of miles away to the south and southeast.

Ethan realized that the beast was not actually attacking anyone. While it snapped its fierce jaws while darting this way and that with remarkable speed in pursuit of the drunken patrons, it never did anything fatal even though it could have at any time it chose. Ethan smiled.

Arrowhead, Hammer, and the men who had been fighting by their side looked on in fearful astonishment with their backs pressed firmly against the rear wall. The wallowgrump seemed to be targeting everyone but them so they thought it prudent to remain where they were. Their fear magnified a few moments later when the wallowgrump finally turned and looked in their direction. The beast suddenly flung itself at them, causing all seven fighters to brandish their weapons.

"No!" Ethan called.

The wallowgrump's webbed feet landed a few yards away, almost exactly between the seven companions and Ethan. It released an evil hiss and bared its teeth at them and then turned to Ethan. It closed a vertical, opaque lid over one of its wet bulbous eyes in a gross wink before turning its back to the eight of them and resuming its pursuit of the few remaining thugs inside the tavern.

"Let's go!" Ethan beckoned to Arrowhead and Hammer as he retrieved his supposedly enchanted fighting staff.

The five strangers turned incredulous glares to the small woman and the hulking man, but the two Keeper's Hounds only beckoned for them to follow and ran off after Ethan. With only the slightest hesitation, the other five followed. The wallowgrump completely ignored them as they sprinted through the open front doors.

The five strangers untethered their horses and mounted up. Arrowhead and Hammer did the same to the two horses that remained at the hitching post. Their owners made the mistake of leaving them unattended so the two Hounds made good use of them. Arrowhead beckoned for Ethan to join her.

He wasted no time in swinging himself onto the saddle behind her. The eight of them tore off into the night, riding west, away from Eastedge.

Chapter 9: Strategies

9.1

The Hounds followed Arrowhead and Hammer's companions a little over two miles down the main road and into the woods. At that point they slowed from a full gallop to a trot and rode north by northwest away from the main road through the forested foothills with the stars and the full moons' light to guide them. Their path was winding yet Ethan took note of every detail, as he always did, knowing he could easily find his way back to the main road if he had to. It was not an easy feat, though, as distracted as he was by the beautiful young woman pressed against him.

Even through the smell of perspiration and stale road dust, the faint scent of lilacs still wafted from her hair, clothes and flesh. She was not wearing a cloak, only a leather vest buttoned fast over a cotton tunic, thick, brown, woolen riding pants and soft-soled tracking boots. Ethan was tempted to remove his cloak and place it around her shoulders but they were pressed together firmly in the saddle. The exchange would be awkward while the horse was moving. And in any case, she was probably not cold. The heat of exertion from the brawl continued to radiate from her and washed over him soothingly.

Ethan noticed how her slender waist fit within his arms perfectly. Without realizing it, he had lowered his head until his nose and mouth were barely a half an inch away from the end of her coiled ponytail. Beads of sweat still dotted the smooth skin on the nape of her neck. He inhaled deeply, breathing in her warmth and her scent. The last time they were this close they almost kissed. The missed chance still tortured him.

"I thought you were dead," Arrowhead whispered, startling Ethan and making him pull away.

He heard relief in her tone. He also noticed a slight tremor in her voice and wondered if it was caused by the movement of the horse beneath them or by her emotions.

"I thought the same about you," Ethan said. "And the rest of the Hounds. It was great to see you and Hammer, even under those circumstances. I'm sorry I wasn't with you on the *Sundance*."

"I'm glad you weren't," Arrowhead returned. "I'm fairly certain that Hammer and I were the only survivors."

They rode on in silence for a time, both thinking about their lost friends and fellow comrades in arms.

"How did you find us?" Arrowhead finally asked, breaking the somber silence.

"We were already coming this way," Ethan told her. "I thought I recognized your footprint...and Quick could smell the lilacs."

Arrowhead glanced over her shoulder. "You remember my *footprints*?"

"And your perfume," Ethan said. He glanced ahead at Hammer and frowned suspiciously. "Why are you wearing it, anyway?"

"I like it, silly," Arrowhead chuckled. "The only time I don't wear it is on a hunt. You only noticed that first time on the ship because the hunt was over. We were sailing home and there was no need for stealth."

"I like it," Ethan admitted.

"Do you?" Arrowhead asked, one corner of her mouth rising.

They stopped talking when Hammer dropped back to ride beside them.

"Eagle Eye!" he called boisterously, using the moniker given to Ethan when he joined the Keeper's Hounds. "You and Quick escaped the scythe wings, too! I take it he was the cause of the wallowgrump sighting. Where is he, anyway? And why in the world were you fighting with a *stick*? Did you lose your sword when the sky sleighs went down?"

"I'm not sure where Quick went," Ethan answered. "And yes, he was the wallowgrump. We'd like to keep his changeling ability and his identity secret for now. It would be to our advantage if no one knows who we are. Do your new companions know that you're Keeper's Hounds?"

"Of course not," Hammer assured.

Ethan nodded. "Good. As for my father's sword, no, I didn't lose it. It's a part of this *stick* strapped to my back."

Hammer looked at the long staff, looked at Ethan, looked back at the staff and then looked at Ethan again.

"What?" the big man asked.

"Raxe melted it down," Ethan explained gloomily. "He added the sword and the rest of my father's weapons to molten Titan's ore in order to cast this fighting staff for me."

"It's enchanted?" Hammer asked. After Ethan nodded in the affirmative, Hammer commented, "That is quite an honor, having a Child of the Old Ones craft a magical weapon for you. But, Eagle Eye, while the stave appears to be a formidable weapon, it didn't look like it had any power back at the tavern."

Hammer's bluntness brought on a flare of frustrated irritation that reddened Ethan's cheeks. He could only hope the darkness of night hid it. If it had not, Hammer would have certainly mentioned it. Ethan knew his friend did not mean to be crude or insulting. Delicacy and tact were simply not a part of the big warrior's personality.

"Raxe assured me it would work when I needed it," Ethan said. "I guess I didn't need it back there."

Hammer scoffed. "Not when we finally got that broadsword to you. If we hadn't, you would've gotten your arse handed to you!"

"Hammer!" Arrowhead snapped. "I don't think Ethan needs you to give him the details."

Hammer smirked. "So he's *Ethan* to you now, eh?" he teased. "All right then, *Nicolette*. I'll leave your boyfriend alone." Hammer chuckled, heeled his horse to a faster trot and pulled away.

"Big lummox!" Arrowhead called to Hammer's back.

"Don't mind him," Ethan said. "If he didn't act like a horse's arse I'd know something was wrong with him."

Arrowhead giggled, the lilting sound quickened Ethan's heartbeat and gave him gooseflesh. He involuntarily held her tighter. To his delight she did not pull away.

In fact, she relaxed and leaned into him. The warmth radiating from her grew warmer. At that point Ethan knew he had to distract himself lest he have a truly embarrassing involuntary reaction.

"So how did the two of you come to be here?" he asked.

"Hammer and I were nearest the escape hatch in the *Sundance*," she explained. "We jumped first. It was the only thing that saved us. We were able to guide our uniwings to the safety of the Hells just before the scythe wings could reach us.

"The rest of the crew, and the Hounds, weren't so fortunate, I'm afraid. We drifted deep into the heart of the mountains, closer to the Darshay side than the Lorr side. We never had time to collect our packs. We had no rations or supplies, only our weapons.

"We decided to find a border town in Darshay where we could re-supply before making our way back home. It was a difficult trek, but we managed to hunt and forage as we made our way to Eastedge. During our very first day here we heard about the unrest. There are a lot of rumors going around about the new baron and the way he came to power. The men we're following look to overthrow him and re-establish the family of the previous baron."

Ethan nodded. "What started the brawl tonight?"

"We were supposed to meet with one of their spies," Arrowhead told him. "But one of the locals, one who pledged his loyalty to the baron, recognized the men accompanying us. He rallied a group of like-minded traitors and confronted us. The fracas soon took on a life of it's own."

Ethan frowned. "Is it wise for you and Hammer to involve yourselves in this? As agents of the Kingdom of Lorr, assisting in the overthrow of a baron in another kingdom could be interpreted as an act of aggression against the crown."

Arrowhead glanced at Ethan over her shoulder. "We've also heard rumblings about the baron holding a Child of the Old Ones captive."

Ethan sat up straighter in the saddle.

"There is more," she went on. "We heard descriptions of the current baron. They say he is a ruddy-haired man as large as Hammer, and that he is accompanied by a strange foreigner who is leaner but taller still."

"No," Ethan breathed.

"Yes," Arrowhead confirmed. "They say that the baron carries a broken great sword that looks more like it is made of ivory than steel."

Ethan smiled a dark smile.

"That's right, Eagle Eye," Hammer said with a grin just as sinister. Ethan was so engrossed in Arrowhead's tale that he did not notice the big man riding near them again. "We can free the offworlder *and* finish what we started back at Tohrfell's Valley." Hammer paused thoughtfully before continuing. "And afterward, I will go east to Ridgeland."

"What's in Ridgeland?" Ethan asked.

"Trouble, my friend. We've heard that an army is on the move. They call it the 'army of the walking dead.' It has to be of the demon's making and it's marching to Ridgeland."

Ethan felt Arrowhead stiffen in the saddle. "Ethan," she said, "we've heard talk of this dread army. Their description is similar to –"

"Magnus and Lance," Ethan realized.

He thought about the Keeper's Hounds that were lost while sailing across Lake Onyx. Both men had changed into creatures that had the look of corpses, but they were inhumanly savage and strong. They were impervious to pain and not even slowed by what should have been mortal injuries. Hammer knocked Magnus overboard with his war hammer before the transformed Keeper's Hound could kill Ethan and Arrowhead. The three of them had watched Lance tear through the ship's hull with his bare bloody hands and throw himself into the great lake.

How in the world were the Kingdom of Lorr's protectors supposed to fight against an army of those things?

*   *   *

They traveled another two miles in thoughtful silence before topping a rise and riding down into a small dell at the base of a grassy hill. The five strangers reigned in their mounts and then turned to face the three Keeper's Hounds as they followed suit.

Arrowhead and Hammer halted their mounts. One of the five strangers, apparently the leader, flicked the reins of his mount to lead it a few feet away from the others. He rode high in his saddle. He was long limbed and thin but broad shouldered. An unadorned doublet stretched snugly across his torso and was buttoned almost to his chin against the chill winter night. Buckskin-trimmed trews tucked into knee-high, hard soled leather riding boots covered his long legs.

He was ruggedly handsome, with thick dark eyebrows, a strong jaw line and thin lips. Medium length dark hair was held in check by a strip of braided leather tied around his head. The moons' light made his pale gray irises almost indistinguishable from the whites of his eyes. He appraised Ethan suspiciously and thrust his dimpled chin in the teen's direction.

"We ride no further until one of you gives us the identity of the boy," he declared.

"He is called Ethan," Hammer returned. "He is a friend of ours, a fellow bounty hunter come to assist in the rebellion. He was with us when our sky sleigh was shot down and we thought him lost to us. I assure you, David Northforest, he is as trustworthy as Nicky and I."

David scoffed. "I will determine that for myself." With another flick of the reins, David brought his horse right beside Arrowhead's stolen mount. He continued to eye Ethan distastefully as he approached. When he reached them he turned to Arrowhead, his gaze softening to something that Ethan did not appreciate in the least.

"He fought well…with the sword, at least," David noted. "Yet he's rather young for a bounty hunter. When he arrived at the tavern he fought with a stave…if you can call that fighting. I have to question the reliability and wisdom of a boy who battles with a weapon so ill-suited to him."

"My weapon was lost when the sky sleigh went down," Ethan lied. It took all of the constraint he had to keep himself from upbraiding the stranger for the *boy* comment. "I had to make due."

"Where is the child that accompanied you?" David questioned, finally addressing Ethan directly. "And what kind of soldier leaves a fallen companion behind? You did not even check to see if he survived."

"Neither one of us are children," Ethan said evenly.

Another horse and rider trotted into the clearing. David and his four men drew their swords. Ethan, Arrowhead and Hammer smiled in recognition.

"You," David said, sheathing his sword while the other four did the same. "How could you have tracked us among all of the traffic on the main road?"

Quick shrugged. "What can I say? Ethan and I are gifted trackers."

"Elbert!" Ethan called to Quick. "I'm relieved that you found us."

"Indeed," David said incredulously. He looked at Arrowhead and Hammer in turn. "Nicky, Derrick, I suppose the two of you can vouch for this one, too?"

"Of course," Arrowhead said. "The addition of these men will greatly improve our chances of success."

"Men?" David grunted derisively. "Hardly. This skinny youngling looks even less formidable than Ethan. At least Ethan has a bit of muscle on his frame. This…Albert couldn't even hold his own against drunken thugs."

Quick chuckled, not at all phased by the other's attempts to rile him. "It's *Elbert*. And looks can be deceiving."

"What is so special about you, then?" David demanded.

Quick cast a swift glance at Ethan and saw the young Sureblade twitch his left eyebrow.

"As I said," Quick began. "I, like Ethan, am a gifted tracker. I'm also a better fighter than I exhibited at the tavern. It's just that I saw the wallowgrump approaching. You can imagine how distracting that was. Luckily for me the ruckus in the tavern was more interesting to the beast than my skin and bones."

"I don't think I like these new additions," David said stubbornly to Arrowhead. "We barely know Derrick and you, pretty one. Why should we take your word for the trustworthiness of these two?"

Ethan stiffened at the unsolicited compliment directed to Arrowhead. He somehow managed to contain the sharp retort at the tip of his tongue. Instead, he asked a question.

"How have Derrick and Nicky earned your trust?"

David tore his eyes away from Arrowhead long enough to fix an annoyed stare on Ethan.

"If you must know, young one," David began. "They happened upon us when we were in a bit of a spot, just as a group of Tauran's cronies cornered one of my men and me just outside of Eastedge. They helped us slay the fools and explained to us that Tauran is an enemy of the Kingdom of Lorr, as well. They volunteered to help us wrest control of Eastedge back from the false baron."

David clenched his trembling fists so tightly that his knuckles turned white. "He used treachery and a small army of bloodthirsty mercenaries to kill my father, the true baron, as well as my uncle, the next in line for the barony. They presently hold my cousin and many others hostage in the hopes that they will tell them how to find my group and me. I am next in line to rule Eastedge, so if he kills my cousin and me, there will be no one left to officially challenge his rule of the barony."

"Then you need as many fighters as you can gather," Ethan remarked. "Elbert and I will be more than happy to throw in with you."

David turned an admiring gaze back to Arrowhead. "If he and Elbert are more formidable than they appear, like you Nicky, then we can indeed use their assistance."

"If anything," Arrowhead returned, ignoring his leer, "they are even more formidable than Derrick and I."

Hammer harrumphed and started to disagree. Ethan stopped him with an exaggerated of clearing his throat.

"We should waste no more time, David." Ethan said. "What would you have us do?"

"For now, we will camp here," David answered. He and his men dismounted. Quick and the Keeper's Hounds did the same.

"In the morning," David continued. "We will ride into Eastedge. There are several groups of soldiers faithful to my family who are hiding in the woods surrounding our castle. We will join them, and when the time is right, we will storm the castle and take it back."

Hammer tapped his chin thoughtfully. "How will you know when the time is right?" he questioned.

"We have our own informants in the castle," David explained. "The usurpers are unruly drunkards like the fools at the tavern. One of our informants will give us a signal the next time the baron has one of his rowdy gatherings. It is then that we will strike, while they're inebriated and distracted."

Quick shook his head. "I would advise against that. In fact, it may be best to find a way to get your people out of there as quickly and quietly as possible."

"What nonsense is this?" David spat. "We have the equivalent of a light company in position, more than two hundred and fifty men, easily outnumbering the baron's forces. We're poised to take our barony back and you make such a suggestion?"

"Ethan and I are not only gifted trackers," Quick said without a hint of bravado. "We are outstanding scouts. The news of the unrest here is well-known in Lorr, so before coming to the tavern, we thought it best to do our own investigation."

Ethan was surprised by the tale his friend was spinning. He trusted Quick with his life, though, so he kept his confusion hidden. Instead of making any reactions that would betray his surprise, he merely nodded in silent agreement when anyone looked to him for confirmation.

"We spotted your people on the perimeter of the castle," Quick went on. "But there were more men out there, close to a full company of over three hundred, forming an even wider perimeter around your force. Their armor bore royal markings. I was able to get close enough to the commander's platoon to hear a bit of their conversations and learned that they were definitely not there in support of your company."

The other four men gathered around closely to hear the story. Quick continued. "They await the arrival of one more royal platoon before they attack and put the revolt down for good."

"Revolt?" one of David's men exclaimed. "This is no revolt! Those mercenaries have stolen Eastedge from *us*!"

Quick shrugged. "The royal soldiers don't seem to see it that way. In any event, I heard one of them say that a squad would be dispatched sometime tomorrow to meet the platoon and escort them to the site so they can bolster their flanking positions. They intend to have everyone in place late tomorrow afternoon and to attack at sunrise the following morning."

"A platoon," David snarled. "Counting Tauran's men coming at us from the castle, they will almost triple our numbers, and they'll have us completely surrounded."

"Overwhelming force," Arrowhead sighed. "They want to put a quick and decisive end to this."

Hammer knitted his eyebrows in confusion. "I don't understand," the big man said. "Why would the crown send men to help a usurper?"

David shook his head in despair. "They don't see him as such. The monarchy doesn't keep a close watch on the outlying counties. They send tax collectors twice a year and field marshals twice a year to inspect the readiness of the local militias in case of war. Otherwise, as long as the outliers don't do anything to bring unwanted attention from the surrounding kingdoms, they leave us to our own affairs."

Another of David's men chimed in. "Neither the king nor anyone in the royal court appoints the lords in the outliers. They aren't concerned with how power changes hands. It is no secret that Tauran took the true baron's estate by force and then bribed and threatened the lords of the other four estates into supporting his claim to the barony.

"In the end the neighboring lords signed the formal writ of transfer verifying him as the new baron, so, as far as the crown is concerned, Tauran is the rightful baron. If he petitions the king for assistance with putting down a so-called revolt that might interfere with tax collection, he'll get it."

David looked angrily to Ethan. "Why did you not tell us about the royal soldiers?" he demanded.

Ethan had his lie ready. He answered without hesitation. "We weren't entirely sure what was happening. Until tonight, we only knew that there was a fight for the barony. We couldn't tell the difference between who had the rightful claim and who did not. Now we know, and we fully support your struggle."

"But I must ask," Hammer chimed in. "How do you intend to get the other estate lords to back your claim if you're successful in removing Tauran? Do you plan to use the same underhanded tactics?"

"Of course not," David said, offended. "Tauran is lining their pockets now but they see that he's running this barony into the ground. When he does, their extra income will dry up as sure as the river that once ran through the valley. While they're too cowardly to oppose him, they'll happily support a more competent baron once he's out of the way."

"You've no fear one of them will try to rise up to claim the barony for themselves?" Ethan asked.

David rolled his eyes with ill humor. "Their estates, including the peasants and farmers that work the land and tend to their livestock, have been passed down from generation to generation. They've never had to put in a real day's labor in their pampered lives. Actually *managing* the entire barony would be too much like work for those spoiled, fat slackers.

"But none of this matters if we don't stop that platoon," David concluded. "We won't stand a chance if they form up with their full company and Tauran's forces."

"You barely stand a chance against the existing opposition," Ethan reminded them. "And I don't think taking back your barony by killing royal soldiers will sit well with the king." A mischievous glint sparked in Ethan's eyes. "But perhaps there's a way to remove the king's men from the equation without having to raise a sword against them."

David turned a suspicious glare on the young Sureblade. "How do I know we can trust you? Perhaps you are hatching a plan to remove *us* from the equation for Tauran."

Arrowhead scoffed in exasperation. "How many times do we have to save your skin before you trust us?"

David was silent for a moment. He cast one more suspicious glance at Ethan and Quick before turning to his surrounding men.

"Come," David commanded. "Let us discuss this."

The five men stepped to the far side of the clearing and spoke in hushed tones.

"So," Ethan began, looking at Quick. "Where did you get the horse?"

Quick shrugged innocently. "One of the drunkards fleeing the tavern was frightened by a low-flying owl. He fell from the saddle but the horse ran on. I thought David and company might be suspicious if I was able to catch up to you all without a horse."

"Low flying owl, eh?" Hammer said with a grin.

They turned their attention to David and his men. Ethan, Arrowhead, and Hammer tried to listen but they could near nothing of their conversation. Quick, on the other hand, could hear every word.

"They are deciding if we are spies for Tauran," Quick whispered. "There is some suspicion among them that we may have been sent to deceive and capture David."

Hammer harrumphed again. "We've been with them for days and saved their hides twice already. Doesn't the fool realize that if we wanted to capture him we could have done so long ago?"

Quick grinned. "One of his men is saying the same thing at this very moment." Quick listened for a few more seconds before he spoke again. "They also realize that with the way you two fight, they would have no chance of stopping you."

Arrowhead turned an accusing glare to Ethan. "Why did you not tell *us* about the king's men surrounding David's?"

"Because I didn't know," Ethan said. "This is the first I've heard of it."

All eyes turned to Quick.

"Oh, yes," the changeling said, as if just remembering. "After clearing out the tavern, I became an owl and did a bit of reconnaissance to make sure you were not being pursued. I happened to overhear a couple of people talking about a surprise the baron had waiting for the rebels in the woods surrounding the castle.

"At that point, I decided to fly over those woods and discovered what I just told David. I made up the ruse because Ethan warned me against revealing my identity. Why that is, though, you'll have to ask Ethan."

All eyes then turned to Ethan.

"It's simple," Ethan said in a matter-of-fact tone. "Remember all that Rionn Lorr told us about the loosed demon, the Dierglyorr? It may have agents anywhere. The fact that Tauran is holding Joel prisoner is evidence that he is working for the demon whether he realizes it or not. Rumors of a changeling would alert them to Quick's presence. It's common knowledge that the only known changeling in existence is named Quick, and that he is an agent of the Kingdom of Lorr. His discovery would endanger him and anyone accompanying him."

"Good point," Arrowhead noted. "Ethan, you said you had an idea about what to do about the royal soldiers."

"I may," Ethan said. And then his tone chilled just a bit. "But I think we should wait to see if your new admirer has any ideas."

Arrowhead rolled her eyes. "Oh, that," she said dismissively. "If we didn't need his assistance in our own mission, I assure you I would've blackened both of his wandering eyes long before now."

Ethan cocked his head. "Are you quite certain?"

Arrowhead sighed. Ethan mistook the reaction as an admission and was about to say as much when Arrowhead stepped quickly over to him and kissed him. She pressed her lips firmly to his and let the kiss linger for what seemed to Ethan like forever. When she finally pulled away he knew it could not possibly last long enough.

She stepped away and stared at him with a serious look in her eyes but with one eyebrow raised and a half smile on her lips. Ethan could not turn away from her gaze and had no desire to. And then he remembered that they were not alone.

His face flushed when he looked around to see everyone staring at them, even David – whose gaze had darkened considerably – and his comrades. When Ethan turned back to Arrowhead she was still staring at him as if he was the only person in the moonlit clearing.

"Any more questions, Ethan?" she asked authoritatively.

"No, m'am," Ethan said with a salute.

"If you are quite finished, *children*," David snapped as he stalked back across the clearing and stopped in front of Ethan. "At first light I will send out our own scouts to confirm the information you have provided. If the situation truly is as you say, we will allow you to assist us."

"Good," Arrowhead exhaled in mock relief. "With the help of these two we will be that much more effective."

"I have one condition," David said, his gaze never leaving Ethan. "No more carrying on like lovesick pups."

Ethan smiled at this. "Of course, not," he said. "No more carrying on is necessary."

9.2

The remains of Colonel Rheingold Strong's battalion were settling down for the night. Cook fires were being doused, scouts and sentries had been deployed, and tents had been raised. Squires hobbled horses at the south end of the camp while the Gryphon Ryders tethered their gryphons on the north end.

Bird cats were carnivorous animals, and while the Ryders' steeds were well trained and not likely to attack the horses, Captain Zedek thought it best not to tempt his gryphons with both the tantalizingly close view and scent of fresh horseflesh all night.

Strong stood outside his tent surveying his battalion, even though it was more like a company now. Sword and shield had suffered the heaviest losses. Only eighty-seven of the original two hundred survived the massacre outside of Port Lorrian.

Seventy-four of the ninety-eight archers remained. Sixty-six of the one hundred soldiers of the lance company survived. The spear took the lightest losses, with twenty-one of their one hundred falling to the *Ken d'Zanir* onslaught.

The Gryphon Ryders were not part of his battalion, but they took significant losses as well. A quarter of Captain Zedek's company of one hundred Ryders were brought down by the *Ken.*

The colonel was waiting for Echelon One mage Gilder Raynard to return with a report on the construction of their portable ballistae and its ammunition when, from his peripheral vision, he spied a pigeon swooping in from the east. The bird was barely more than a speck flitting across one of the three pale moons as it circled above his column of infantrymen.

After a couple of deliberate passes it apparently spotted its target and dropped out of sight.

"Carrier pigeon?" asked Mage Gilder from over Strong's left shoulder.

Strong looked back with a start. He was so distracted by the bird that he did not hear the wizard's approach. "Try to make a little more noise when approaching an armed man in the middle of the night, wizard." The wizard grinned as Strong continued. "A lone bird would not fly into the midst of this much human activity without a significant purpose. It has to be a carrier pigeon."

"And a very well trained carrier pigeon," remarked Mage Gilder. "I've never seen one deliver messages to a mobile destination."

"It's a fairly new training method," Strong explained. "They train the birds to fly to a specific region and look for certain indicators to locate their target. It's ideal for sending messages to ships at sail, sky sleighs in flight, or ground forces on the move. To lessen the possibility of intercepts, the indicators are known only to the sender, the bird, and the recipient. But this troubles me. We have you and your magical means of communication with other mages stationed around the kingdom. We've no need for carrier pigeons."

The wizard stroked his stubbly chin thoughtfully. "It appears someone in your battalion is not satisfied with the Conjurer's Alliance, despite our incomparable speed and dependability compared to messenger birds."

Strong frowned. "Perhaps someone here is sending and receiving messages they don't want you or I to see. In the night sky, a lone bird's arrival would be nigh undetectable. It was only by chance that I saw it. How is it that you saw it, as well?"

"I saw you looking and followed your gaze."

"Nosy wizard," Strong accused.

Gilder nodded. "It's a critical part of the job."

"And did you notice, by chance, the direction from whence the bird approached?"

"No. It was already circling when I spied it."

"The east," Strong said. "Perhaps that is a hint as to what message the bird delivered."

Mage Gilder sighed. "Perhaps it does. As troublesome as *that* might be, I fear it could be worse than we imagine."

Strong raised an eyebrow as he peered in the general vicinity of where the bird disappeared. "How so?"

"Colonel, you are aware that the enemy has employed a spy, or perhaps several, are you not? Which of your men have been trained to handle messenger birds?"

Strong turned back to the wizard. "Lieutenant Colonel Caleb Godson, my second in command," he admitted. "But Caleb *cannot* be a spy. I've known him too long to believe that. He's a knighted warrior of the royal infantry and the most honorable soldier I've ever commanded." *And a longtime friend* he said to himself.

"Well, it looks like we're about to get an opportunity to question him," the wizard said, pointing to the south. "He approaches as we speak."

The Colonel turned again to see Lieutenant Colonel Caleb Godson leading a dozen soldiers toward the commander's tent. His stride was purposeful, as were those of the men trailing him.

A closer look revealed the twelve men were men of rank: the lance and spear company captains and their first lieutenants; the first lieutenant of the archer company, who became the company commander after the attack at Port Lorrian resulted in the death of the captain, along with his second; and the second lieutenant of the sword and shield company, who took command after his captain and first lieutenant fell to the *Ken* and their land dragons in the same battle. He was joined by all five of his platoon sergeants.

As they came closer, the pale moons' light revealed the small slip of paper in Caleb's right hand and the dark look on his face.

Seeing the slip of paper in Lieutenant Colonel's hand gave him a bit of relief. The fact that Caleb was not hiding it reassured Strong that Caleb was not a spy. But the look on his face tempered Strong's relief, for he had a fairly good idea of the contents of the message.

When the Lieutenant Colonel and his followers were within ten yards, Strong asked: "A bit of bad news there, Lieutenant Colonel?"

313

"I'd say so," Caleb answered tersely, casting an accusing stare at the Echelon One mage.

"I suppose the pigeon was sent from Ridgeland, or Allanville, perhaps." The wizard said. It was more of a statement than a question.

Caleb gave a curt nod as he and his retinue came to a halt. "It came from Allanville by way of Ridgeland, in fact. And your accurate supposition reveals that you know the contents of the message." He held out the slip of paper to his commander.

Strong took the proffered slip and held it up to see it by the light of the pole-mounted oil lamp behind him.

> *RETIRED COLONEL ROBINSON STOTTLEMEYER, WHILE PERFORMING HIS RIGHTFUL DUTY OF PROTECTING THE NORTHEASTERN REGIONS, AND THE BLESSED KINGDOM OF LORR AS A WHOLE, BY DESTROYING THE WALKING DEAD ADVANCING ON RIDGELAND, WAS SLAIN BY MASTER MAGE DELTHAR TO PROTECT ENEMIES OF THE KINGDOM.*

The Colonel exhaled slowly as he read the message. When he was done he handed the slip back to Caleb and asked: "Lieutenant Colonel Godson, how long have you been transporting messages without my leave?"

Caleb's gaze shifted from Mage Gilder Raynard to his superior officer, his gaze changing from one of accusation to confusion. "Did you not read the message, sir? It clearly... Wait...you're not surprised. You already knew."

"Of course I did, Lieutenant Colonel. Mage Gilder was told the day it happened. He was informed through the Conjurer's Alliance and then he told me. And you have not answered my question."

Caleb's gaze darkened again. Strong could see the sting of betrayal in his second's eyes. Caleb squared his shoulders defiantly.

"This is the first message I've received, sir. Our colleagues protecting the east thought news of this magnitude should be shared with *all* of the kingdom's protectors.

"They did not trust the conjurers to deliver such a message to the military. But now I see that they have, and you did not see fit to share the news with your second in command."

Mage Gilder spoke before Strong could respond. "As the commander, it is his prerogative to – "

The Colonel stopped the wizard with a raised hand. "To what end, Lieutenant Colonel?" Strong asked. "What would be the point of telling you now? How would that news help us on our current mission?"

"Colonel Stottlemeyer was a famed and respected warrior," Caleb said, nearly aghast at the question. "He was a great commander, legendary for his contributions in the Cursed Opening and the Carthan Defense. To not immediately pass along the news of his passing, and especially the *manner* of his passing, is bloody near criminal."

The wizard looked at Strong with disbelief. "Do you allow such latitude to all of your subordinates, Colonel?"

Strong shot the wizard an irritated glare. "This is my battalion, wizard. You were dispatched to *assist* us, not command us. I would ask that you grant me the respect of silence until you are called upon, or take your leave until your assistance is needed again."

"My apologies, Colonel," Gilder said with a respectful nod. But he did not leave.

Strong returned his attention to his Lieutenant Colonel. "The wizard speaks out of place but he speaks true. I respect your council, as you well know, but you overstep your bounds. We no longer pursue the infected. Our charge is to pursue the *Ken d'Zanir*. I did not inform you of Stottlemeyer's death because what's happening in the east has nothing to do with our mission."

"Stottlemeyer's murder is more – "

"*Enough,*" the Colonel barked. His commanding tone made it clear that they were no longer speaking as friends, but as superior and subordinate officers. "You will stand quiet and listen until I give you permission to speak.

"Stottlemeyer was a *retired* colonel and not acting as an agent of the Lorrian military. He was leading a militia outside of its jurisdiction. The wizard Delthar's response was extreme, and unfortunate, but within his rights. The militia was acting outside of the law the moment they attempted to attack the infected against King William's orders."

"Permission to speak freely, sir," Caleb requested. When Strong nodded, Caleb continued. "There is a growing number of us that wonder if those were really King William's orders…or the Head Mage's."

"This is an issue concerning magic," Strong pointed out. "The order came from the king, but he obviously would have received the Head Mage's counsel."

Caleb gave his superior a dubious look. "And you're quite sure it was *counsel* that Rionn Lorr gave King William?"

"As opposed to what?" Strong demanded. He could see the Echelon One mage stiffen with anger, but Gilder remained silent.

A hush fell over the camp. The soldiers closest to them all watched expectantly. Those too far away to see remained silent and listened with rapt attention to the voices carrying through the cool night air.

"I think you both know the answer to that question," Caleb accused. "It is just as I feared. The Head Mage influences the king. Master Mage Delthar influences Minister Geoffrey. Now it appears this Echelon One mage influences you, commander. Why else would you condone the killing of a warrior such as Colonel Stottlemeyer by a wizard who is supposed to be on our side?"

"Influence?" Strong growled, now seething. It was all he could do to keep from throttling his second in command. "You dare accuse us of allowing ourselves to be manipulated by magic like puppets, then. Is this why you've confronted me with all of my officers? Is this an attempt to relieve me of my command?"

Caleb stood firm under the colonel's withering glare.

"With all due respect, sir, it's not a matter of 'allowing' yourselves to be manipulated. I have no doubt that such a feat could be performed without your knowledge by conjurers of their ability."

Mage Gilder could keep silent no longer. "What you have, Lieutenant Colonel is absolutely no idea of the complexities of magic. The only thing you do have is a perilous mistrust of a power you have no hope of understanding."

"I'll not deny that, wizard," Caleb agreed. "I trust steel, and I trust the men who wield it. A man who chooses magic over metal chooses trickery over honor."

The wizard shook his head with something resembling pity. "To doubt my honor only because I am a conjurer is as foolish as believing a thief, rouge, or rapist is honorable simply because he also happens to be skilled with a blade. You prove your ignorance more thoroughly with every word you utter, Lieutenant Colonel Godson."

"If you did not have your magic to hide behind, wizard," Caleb threatened, "I would shove those words down your throat with the point of my blade."

The Echelon One mage smiled. "I ask you, Lieutenant Colonel, would you continue to doubt my honor if I bested you with a blade...*without* the use of any magic?"

Caleb scoffed. "Small chance of that."

"What say you, Colonel Strong?" Gilder continued. "If your man bests me, he takes command. If I win, he and his followers stand down and stay in their respective places."

"Hell no," the Colonel answered. "If anyone is going to fight for command of *my* battalion, it'll bloody well be me. What say you, Caleb?"

Captain Zedek shouldered his way through the onlookers from the north end of the camp. "What idiocy be this?" the Gryphon Ryder captain demanded. "T'is not enough that we had the *Ken* hand our arses to us on a silver platter? We have

317

to do for ourselves as well? We're s'posed to be fixin t'pay them back in kind when we catch 'em, not kill each other!"

"I trust you completely, sir," Caleb assured, ignoring the boisterous Gryphon Ryder commander. "As do all of your men. It is the conjurers we mistrust."

"How can you say that?" Zedek questioned. "Conjurers have fought 'longside the Kingdom of Lorr's warriors since Heaven's War."

"Perhaps the Old Ones make today's conjurers of different stuff," Caleb suggested. "It's not their dedication we mistrust, it's their judgment and tactical expertise."

Zedek shook his head. "You have it wrong, lieutenant colonel. T'is not the conjurers giving orders to the military."

"We were woefully underprepared for the walking dead, an enemy brought forth by fell magic the Head Mage himself seems powerless to counter, " Caleb argued. "Master Mage Delthar *killed* one of our most decorated soldiers to protect those abominations. We've lost nearly half our battalion and an Echelon Two mage to the *Ken,* yet we still pursue them. And the Head Mage has no answer for their ability to extinguish magic.

"Competent leadership would pull back until answers are found, yet we continue to waste brave lives. King William, Minister Geoffrey, General Ramos, Colonel Strong are more than competent leaders who know better. What else can this debacle be but the conjurers influencing them to continue these senseless courses of action?"

"You forget, Lieutenant, the Head Mage suggested that we return to Fort Bastion," Strong reminded. "It was my idea to continue to follow them, and Zedek agreed."

"And so did Mage Gilder," Caleb pointed out. "And he seems the most enthusiastic about it. I would not be surprised if he is influencing the two of you in order to get revenge for the death of his student."

"Hmmmm..." Zedek said, "So you propose to take command of this battalion and dismiss Mage Gilder. Then what'll you do?"

"Wait for the regiment that is being sent, form with them, and then catch the *Ken* bastards and kill them."

"And what if you lose their trail while you wait?" Zedek challenged. "All it would take is one hard rain, perhaps a strong windstorm. Our charge is to track 'em 'til the regiment catches up with us so that nothing of the sort happens."

"And if they ambush us again?" Caleb asked.

"They won't," Mage Gilder promised. "We have their measure as far as that goes."

Caleb grunted. "I have a hard time taking your word for that."

"Ah yes," Gilder remembered. "Because I'm a conjurer and not a warrior, my strategies cannot be trusted. What if I can best you in a duel, lieutenant colonel? Would you trust my judgment then?"

"I'll say it once more, and not again," Colonel Strong warned, "I'll do the fighting if there's any to be done."

"I don't know, colonel," Zedek offered. "First off, you'd beat Lieutenant Godson like a drum. Hah. What's more, that'd prove not a thing. He and your commanders'd still think you were under Gilder's sway, and if the majority of these men agree with them, as it appears they do, you'd still be relieved of your command. But if Gilder can somehow spank your second without magic, they'd give 'em his due. That the gist of it, Godson?"

Caleb nodded. "I'd say so, captain."

Colonel Strong grunted wordlessly. He had no desire to fight his longtime friend, but under normal circumstances he would never let another man fight his fight regardless of the opponent. These, however, were far from normal circumstances. The mistrust of magic wielders in general – and Children of the Old Ones in particular – made it very likely that the result of Strong dueling Caleb would yield just the result Zedek cautioned it would, no matter the outcome. Strong turned reluctantly to the wizard.

"Is this really what you wish, Mage Gilder?"

Never taking his eyes away from Caleb's, the Echelon One mage shifted his conjurer's staff from his left hand to his right, turned it so that it was parallel to the ground and thrust it to Captain Zedek.

He held his left hand out to Colonel Strong and beckoned for a weapon. "Your straight sword, colonel, if you please."

Colonel Strong unsheathed his blade and handed it to the wizard. "I'll be sorely and thoroughly pissed if you get yourself killed, man."

"It's not my intention to kill Mage Gilder, sir," Caleb promised. "I will only soundly defeat him and send him back to Greenglenn. The first one to drop his sword loses."

The surrounding soldiers formed a circle around the combatants roughly ten yards in diameter. The colonel and the Gryphon Ryder stepped back to join them. The Lieutenant Colonel wrapped his hand around the pommel of his straight sword.

Captain Zedek held up a hand. "One moment, gents," he began. "Tell me something, Caleb, since you're so worried 'bout trickery and such. If the wizard decides to use magic during the duel, how in the hell will you know?"

"Oh, I'll know. Even the Head Mage has to utter words or employ hand gestures or use a staff or wand or some other talisman to work his magic. Isn't that right wizard?"

Mage Gilder nodded reluctantly.

Caleb continued with a satisfied grin. "Not as ignorant to magic as you thought, eh?"

The wizard shrugged as he took a practice swing to test the weight of Colonel Strong's straight sword. "Perhaps not. I'm mildly impressed."

"You're about to be *very* impressed, wizard." Caleb directed his attention to Captain Zedek and went on. "When Gilder fights me, captain, he won't have his staff. His hands will be too busy trying to hold on to his sword for any conjuring gestures, and I assure you he'll be breathing and likely grunting in fear too hard to utter any magic words."

"Get to it, then," Strong ordered.

Lieutenant Colonel Caleb Godson drew his longsword and advanced. He was half a head taller than Mage Gilder. Caleb's arms were longer and his reach was extended even more by his longer sword. He outweighed the shorter man by at least forty pounds.

And it was fairly obvious that the seasoned warrior wanted to end the duel quickly. He came on with a barrage of fast, heavy blows meant to knock Gilder's sword free. The light from the moons and stars and the flickering yellow-orange light of blazing oil lamps shimmered off of the dancing blades. The soldiers watched quietly, so the only sound was the loud toll of steel on steel.

The wizard surprised everyone by holding on to his sword as he deflected blow after powerful blow. His footwork was solid but Caleb gave him no room or time to counterattack or even feint. Each block shook Gilder and drove him back a step or two. Each parry gave him just enough time to sidestep to the left or right before having to defend himself from another thrust or swing.

Before long Caleb was huffing and puffing, yet his attack never slowed. Gilder appeared to be tiring, as well. He labored just to lift his sword but he somehow managed to maintain his defense. When it seemed he could no longer lift his sword against the jarring strikes, he would duck or dodge or backpedal far enough to stay out of range.

Another couple of minutes of this left both men breathing raggedly. Caleb's sword was held lower but the tip of Gilder's sword was literally dragging in the dirt.

"You sure you want to continue, wizard?" Caleb panted. I'd hate to kill you by accident. You can't even lift your sword."

"But I'm still *holding* it, soldier."

"Not for long!" Caleb snarled and attacked anew.

With his left hand holding the sword grip, the soldier swung his sword high and wide. The wizard lifted the sword with two hands and pivoted to his right to put his weight behind the block. He just barely deflected the blow. As he did so, Caleb stepped forward and delivered a stinging right jab to Gilder's jaw.

The Echelon One mage spun with the blow while going down to one knee. But instead of dropping his sword, he used the momentum of his dazed spin to swing the blade viciously at Caleb's right shin.

Caleb had to bring his longsword to his right and stab it into the ground to stop Gilder's blade. Gilder rebounded violently from the block and used the momentum of the rebound to spin quickly in the opposite direction.

He miraculously managed to hold on to the sword with his right hand but he let go with his left, let the impetus of this second spin take him, and lifted his left elbow to drive it into Caleb's crotch.

As the pain froze Caleb and made his eyes bulge, Gilder quickly gathered the grip of his straight sword and swung it like a club. The flat of his blade struck Caleb's blade near the hilt, tore it from the Lieutenant Colonel's hand and flattened it to the ground. Caleb toppled to the ground just beside it, clutching his manhood and gasping for air.

A roar of surprise and mirth exploded into the night. Mage Gilder held the straightsword across his lap, lowered himself to his backside and panted like an exhausted hound.

"Looks like I'm *still* holding it, Lieutenant Colonel."

The soldiers laughed and jeered as they helped both men to their feet. Mage Gilder handed the sword back to Colonel Strong and immediately bent over to rest his hands on his knees and gasp with exhaustion. When Caleb was finally able to stand on his own, he assumed an identical pose and gasped in pain.

"That was a bloody foul move, wizard."

Mage Gilder chuckled breathlessly. "Only slightly fouler than your punch."

Caleb found the strength to almost smile. "Only slightly."

"You do realize that I didn't beat you with strength, speed, skill, or magic, don't you? I beat you with strategy. Most of that duel mirrors our battle against the *Ken* and the infected."

"That it did," Caleb conceded. "They've had the upper hand most of the way, as I did in the duel, but you found a way to win."

"Exactly," Gilder returned. "And with steel, magic, and cunning, both the military and the Conjurer's Alliance will find a way to win this war. Of that you can be sure."

Strong stepped in front of his second in command. "Is it safe to assume my command is safe, Lieutenant Colonel? That there will be no more challenges to my authority?"

Caleb nodded and weakly lifted his right fist to his chest. "It is, sir. You have our word of honor."

The company commanders and sergeants all saluted in kind. Colonel Rheingold Strong returned the salute.

"That's good to hear," Strong said. "Because next time it's *me* you'll be dueling, and I fight much dirtier than this skinny little mage."

"Yes, sir," Caleb acknowledged. Two of his followers helped hold him steady as he limped back to their campsite.

"If the pissing contest is done," Zedek said, "I'll be goin' back t' my Gryphon Ryders." The captain turned and made his way back to the north end of the camp.

Strong looked down at Mage Gilder. "Straighten up, loafer. You still have a report to give. I want to know how the construction of the ballistae and bolts is going."

The colonel led the wizard into the commander's tent. He took a cautious look around the outside of the entrance, closed and secured the tent flap, and then turned to the Echelon One mage. He spoke softly so that his deep voice would not carry beyond the walls of the tent.

"You used magic."

A confused frown darkened Mage Gilder's face. "What?"

"I've fought alongside, well, not shoulder to shoulder, but near more than one of you Echelon mages in my nigh on twenty years in the Royal Army, and I've heard tell that you in particular do more than a bit of sword training."

"That's correct," Gilder confirmed.

"But Caleb is one of the best swordsmen I know, wizard. There's no way you've done enough training to keep him off you that long without some kind of edge."

"Are you sure about that, colonel?"

"Positive. Tell you what else I know about you conjurers. The better ones, like you, can barely move your lips while you mutter spells quiet enough for no one but a dog to hear."

Mage Gilder exhaled heavily and took a seat at a small bench near a conference table constructed of two carved square stones and a slab of oak. Instead of responding, he only stared stone faced at Colonel Strong.

"And the way you handed Zedek your staff and beckoned for my blade, along with your little warm-up with it…those were gestures. You were doing some sly spellcasting before the fight, weren't you?"

The wizard smiled. "*Of course* I was," he admitted. "The man fights like a demon. There's no way in the seven hells I'd've taken him otherwise. I'm impressed, colonel."

"You don't get to be an old battle commander without knowing a little about strategy. I know wizards are tight with secrets, but I have to know, what kind of spell was it?"

Gilder looked at Strong for a long time. Strong was absolutely right about wizards and their secrets. Secrecy was part of a conjurer's nature. It had to be. But it was critically important that he and the colonel trust one another on this campaign. He took another moment to weigh the pros and cons of his choices.

"An adjustment here and there," he answered. "A sphere of lighter air around his head so he would get winded a bit faster than usual, a sphere of heavier air around his torso to slow his movements. They're subtle but usually effective spells, and yet that bloody maniac still nearly bested me."

Colonel Strong shrugged. "As I said, he's one of the best swordsmen I know. And I know a *lot* of swordsmen."

"Tell me something, colonel," Gilder bade. "Do you think my actions lacked honor?"

"Hell no, man," Strong flashed a rare smile. "You fought for *my* command of *my* battalion. Caleb's an excellent soldier and fiercely loyal to his kingdom, but he's still young. He's yet to learn that in the field, honor must often take the rear guard to good, sound strategy. And speaking of strategy, where are you and the men with my ballistae?"

9.3

The two suns were just beginning into creep to the western skies when the forty-eight-man mounted platoon sent by King Joseph of Darshay travelled along a wide road that cut through the forested foothills west of Hell's Mountains. They were in no particular hurry. The platoon leader, Lieutenant Granson Black, led his men at a leisurely pace without much urgency across the Tul Darshay'n River in four columns of twelve riders. The light company already deployed there had arrived so soon only because they had already been stationed at the river at Fort Darshay'n performing joint exercises with the royal navy.

When the king granted the petition to send troops to Eastedge, it was little more than an afterthought, but that was not why Lieutenant Granson was so unenthusiastic about this operation. The king's lack of urgency was because of his nearly nonexistent regard for the backwater border county. To completely ignore or refuse the petition, however, would have sent a bad message to the larger, wealthier, more influential baronies and townships in the Kingdom of Darshay.

The source of Lieutenant Black's lack of urgency was his reluctance to battle citizens of his own kingdom. Unlike the king and most of the nobility, the lieutenant made it a point to stay abreast of what went on in the outlying territories. He knew about Baron Tauran's bloody takeover of Eastedge and was not keen on helping him keep it. But Tauran made sure to submit all of the necessary documentation. He paid his taxes and then some to curry favor with the monarchy. That was all it took for the outlying territories to satisfy the crown until the time came to inspect their martial forces; and the next inspection was months away.

From what he knew of the baron, the lieutenant had serious doubts that Tauran's forces would be up to the kingdom's military standards, but until then he would be recognized as the lawful baron. And the lieutenant would have to follow orders.

Up ahead, a squad of armed men on horseback rode into view around a wide turn in the road. Lieutenant Black immediately recognized the lead rider and was surprised. He continued on until the approaching squad was nose-to-nose with his platoon. The lieutenant put his left fist into his open right palm and pressed both to his heart in salute.

"Captain Gesner," the lieutenant greeted.

"Lieutenant Black," the captain returned the salute.

"I'm surprised to see you with the squad, captain," Black said. "I thought you might send a corporal to lead the escort."

"Yes," Captain Gesner confirmed. "I normally would have, but I was bored nearly to tears waiting around in the woods."

"I'm sorry we didn't arrive sooner," Black said immediately.

Captain Gesner held up a hand to stay his lieutenant's apology. "No explanation needed, lieutenant. You got here sooner than I anticipated. I've been bored from the moment we got here yesterday. And to be honest, I'm not looking forward to this mission."

"Neither am I, sir," Black agreed. "They're only fighting to take back what is rightfully theirs. They've been citizens of Darshay their entire lives. It is the baron who is the outsider."

"The rebels aren't even trained soldiers," the captain added. "They're farmers and miners and such. Most of them are barely out of their teens. They have no idea they're already outflanked. An experienced force would have known we were here."

"Perhaps the size of our force will convince them to concede without resistance," the lieutenant said hopefully.

Gesner shook his head slowly. "This is their home, lieutenant. I doubt they'll give it up without a fight. But I suppose one can always hope."

The platoon and the squad milled about casually as the commanders conferred, but all conversation stopped abruptly when a shrill female scream rang out from the surrounding woods to the west.

A moment later, a beautiful and terrified raven-haired young woman came tearing out of the trees on horseback from the north edge of the road. The soldiers watched in confusion that quickly turned to terror when, as she reached the middle of the road only a dozen yards or so behind the captain's squad, a slavering wallowgrump burst from the cover of the trees in pursuit. It landed at the midpoint of the road a second after its prey and took another powerful leap. By the time the girl disappeared into the woods on the far side of the road, the giant froglike beast was almost nipping at the horse's tail.

"What in the name of the seven hells!" the captain exclaimed while countless other expletives were shouted out by other shocked soldiers. "A wallowgrump has no business this far north!"

"Captain!" Lieutenant Black said, "We must help the girl…" the rest of his sentence was drowned out by the girl's shrill scream of agony and horror. The scream frightened a large flock of squawking birds from the trees before it was abruptly cut short.

Captain Gesner drew his sword. "The girl is beyond help, now, but we can still slay the beast. Bring a dozen men. Wallowgrumps are nigh impossible to –"

Another cry boomed out from the northern edge of the forest. It was a man's roar, this time. They turned to see a hulk of a man sprint from the woods faster than any man his size had any right to move. His wide face was twisted in a mask of horror.

"RUN!!" he yelled. "They're EVERYWHERE!"

Before he could reach the midpoint of the road, another wallowgrump soared down from the trees and landed on the man's back, driving him into the ground. With a terrible hiss-growl, the wallowgrump gathered the massive stranger easily in its short but sinewy arms as if the man weighed next to nothing and then it bounded back into the shadows of the trees. The big man's frantic screams, like those of the raven-haired girl, were also cut short in horrifying fashion.

"Did he say 'everywhere'?" gasped the lieutenant casting wild glances in every direction.

"We heard rumors that a wallowgrump was spotted last night at a tavern," the captain said, his eyes also darting this way and that along the trees lining the northern edge of the road. "I dismissed it, believing it was some other large lizard mistaken as a wallowgrump by ignorant and drunken peasants. No such creature had been seen this far north since the Cursed Opening. Even then there was only one of them."

And then they saw them.

At least two-dozen wallowgrumps crept to the edges of the road, both north and south. Most of them clustered near the front of the platoon's columns and the space between the platoon and the squad. They bobbed on their reverse-articulated legs almost rhythmically. Their long tails, thick at the base and tapering to a point, swayed hypnotically or coiled beneath them, poised to spring them forward. The creatures' impossibly wide maws were lined with stubby but razor-sharp teeth that clacked ominously as they snapped open and closed. Low hisses with an undertone of hungry growls made every man and horse's hackle's rise.

"What are your orders, captain?" Black whispered.

The men and their mounts had grown restless. Weapons were drawn or raised slowly and carefully. Hooves stomped. Men struggled to keep their horses from bolting.

"We run," Gesner said, fighting panic. He spoke quickly but calmly and loud enough for the surrounding men to hear. "You and I will lead the squad and the first four rows of the platoon east. If we flee first, most of the wallowgrumps should chase us. We'll form up with rest of the company awaiting us outside of Eastedge. The rest of the platoon rides back west, all the way to Fort Darshay'n, if necessary. If they have to fight, they should have enough men to hold off the few beasts that will pursue them.

"If we have to, we'll leave the road and ride through the woods. Our horses can weave among the trees faster than the wallowgrumps. They move fastest when they leap. They won't have enough room to move as fast through the trees."

DEMON OF LORR

The lieutenant nodded and then gulped. "And what will we do when we get to Eastedge?"

Captain Gesner looked at his lieutenant as if his subordinate had gone mad. "We get the hell out of this gods-forsaken countryside. Once there we'll have more than enough numbers to fight our way past these creatures and back to the palace. We'll not fight rebels with a host of wallowgrumps at our backs. Let the baron deal with this infestation on his own...or petition the crown for a larger extermination force."

The lieutenant nodded again. "Everyone ready to ride?" he asked carefully. The trailing eight rows of riders turned their mounts slowly while the glares of the wallowgrumps hungrily followed their every move.

After a host of slow, silent nods, the captain grimaced, took a deep breath and barked: "Now!"

The squad and first four rows of the platoon bolted. As expected, the vast majority of the wallowgrumps exploded into motion behind them, roaring and hissing all the way. A moment later the rest of the platoon thundered east, with less than a third of the remaining wallowgrumps snarling and bounding off after them.

Within a few seconds the road was empty with the exception of four wallowgrumps standing in the middle of the road. In the blink of an eye three humans stood in the place of three of the giant amphibians: Arrowhead, Hammer and Ethan. The fourth one underwent a slightly more lengthy transition. Its image wavered, its arms and torso growing thinner and longer and its reverse-articulated legs snapping straight.

The shape of its massive head changed color from green to tan flesh tones and sprouted brown hair. The animal's tail retracted, and then a tunic, breeches and riding boots replaced the thick hide covering its torso, legs and clawed feet. Quick stood next to Hammer looking at the three humans with his narrow face brightened by a wide grin.

"Told you it would work!" Ethan chuckled.

"Like a charm," Hammer agreed. "It was a great plan, Eagle-Eye."

"It wouldn't have worked without Quick's help with the details, and all of the real work." He looked over at his best friend and smiled.

"How long do you think the illusion will fool them?" Arrowhead asked, cautious not to get too excited.

Ethan shrugged. "Long enough, and when they do realize it was a ruse, they'll realize that the rebels have a powerful conjurer in their employ, in which case they'll still be hesitant to stick around."

"Powerful conjurer?" Quick asked, his grin widening. "I like the sound of that!"

Hammer guffawed. "You should, skinny, one. It's true!" He clapped the lanky youngster on the shoulder, almost knocking him off of his feet.

"It wasn't that complex," Quick confided after regaining his footing. "Illusion spells are fairly simple, and they're stronger when the target is preconditioned to believe what he thinks he sees. The rumors of the wallowgrump that attacked the bar patrons last night laid the foundation. When they saw me chasing you, Arrowhead, and attacking Hammer, the physical interaction between a flesh-and-blood wallowgrump and humans solidified the illusion." Quick turned to Hammer. "I hope I wasn't too rough with you, big man."

Hammer dismissed Quick's concern with a wave of the hand. "It was fun. It's been years since anyone or anything picked *me* up. It was worth a few bruises." He gave Quick a playful punch on the shoulder that surely would have dislocated it if Quick had not been leaning away from it. "But I have a question," the big man continued. "As you instructed, I stood at the edge of the tree line and counted to three after Arrowhead's most convincing scream, but how did you get across the road so quickly without being seen?"

"I was one of the birds that scattered from the trees," Quick revealed.

"Clever," Arrow complimented. "And powerful, indeed. To cast so many images moving independently must have been incredibly complicated."

"They weren't really moving independently," Quick admitted. "I had the four of you stand at the roadside and imitate a wallowgrupmp's movements so I could use your physical presence to weave the original illusions around you. Your different sizes lent variety to the images. I duplicated each image, including mine, five times. The movements of each duplicate were identical to ours but I scattered the duplicates randomly and delayed the movements of each so they wouldn't all appear to be moving the exact same way. A sharper eye would have caught it but the soldiers were far too distracted and frightened to notice."

"I don't know much about magic," Ethan admitted. "But from what I know, illusion spells of that magnitude are fairly advanced. Has Master Mage Delthar already promoted you?"

Quick scoffed. "Of course not. The chances of that crotchety windbag promoting me ahead of schedule are about the same as a pack of *real* wallowgrumps migrating this far north. Delthar would soil himself if he knew that I knew the duplicate illusion spell. I spied old Shanderah using it years ago and memorized it. I was never strong enough to invoke it successfully, though."

"When did you discover you *were* strong enough?" Arrowhead asked.

The changeling thought for a moment, counting silently to himself. "About…ten minutes ago."

Hammer laughed again. "I LIKE this kid!" He swung a gigantic arm to clap Quick on the back once again. This time the changeling lived up to his name as he ducked and let the meaty paw whoosh through the empty air above him.

9.4

David Northforest, his four companions from the previous night, and seven others who had joined them earlier in the day perched behind large boulders on a high hill strategically overlooking the forest edge. The tall spires of the baron's castle, David's rightful castle, were just visible above the crown of the trees in the distance.

To the east, the whole of Eastedge proper was visible from their vantage point. David looked down longingly at the sparse fields of grain and small livestock, the modest dwellings of the hardworking farmhands and field hands, and the wheeled merchant carts and small storefronts, and recalled how much more bustling the valley had been before the false baron stole the land from David's father.

Many called the valley a dried out, godforsaken dust bowl. With the gentle slope of its walls and its oblong shape, the valley looked more like a giant earthen platter. Where outsiders and even some natives saw a nearly desiccated wasteland, David saw opportunity. Eastedge was a basin of hidden treasures that was more than willing to share her wealth with those with enough vision, determination and strength to coax it free.

The lords of the four other estates that comprised the barony cared nothing for the town down in valley. They only cared about the money they could squeeze from her. All of them owned properties within Eastedge proper, but none of them ever deigned to step foot even on the slopes of the valley, let alone trek to the valley floor. They were satisfied to send peasants down to labor in the quarries or work their goat farms and millet and potato fields.

They did not love the valley the way David did. He would have her back, and he would be the just and competent lord and baron that his father and grandfather were.

He looked away from the valley when he heard the sound of hoof beats. David and his men watched the royal soldiers gallop from the wide road that led into town and into the surrounding forest where the other royal soldiers surrounded David's hidden forces.

"What's this?" David's second in command asked with anger and alarm. "Nicky and Ethan were supposed to turn them away, not send them charging in for battle!"

"We must alert our men," said another.

"Wait!" David ordered. He looked closely at the royal soldiers.

Most of his companions had no military experience. David, however, had served in the local militia and served a stint in the royal infantry. He spotted the captain easily and he recognized the markings of a lieutenant. All but five of the soldiers entered the forest. The remaining five held back and turned their horses back the way they had come. They did not ride away, but stood alert...and clearly nervous.

"That wasn't the entire platoon," David observed. "That was only the escort squad that we watched leave and an additional small group, likely a detachment from the approaching platoon. And those five are standing guard. Where are the rest of them?"

No one had an answer. They followed their commander's lead and watched and waited patiently. Their patience was rewarded when, less than ten minutes later, the captain and lieutenant rode out of the forest again. This time, though, the two of them led far more than just the squad and the platoon detachment.

All twelve "rebels" watched with wide eyes and open mouths as the royal company filed out of the forest and onto the road. They rode west, *away* from the barony. They traveled slowly and cautiously, as if they expected an attack at any moment.

"Daniatiae's heart," David swore. He had enough military experience to know a strategic retreat when he saw one.

"I don't know how, but the Lorrians did it!"

PART III

DEMON

Chapter 10: By Hargathall's Blade

10.1

Raxe was getting tired of traveling on foot, and he was sure the rest of the party felt the same. Southborough turned out to be a four-day walk. It might have been three if it were just the elf, the offworlder, and half-faerie. The survivors from the sky sleigh crew were a hearty lot, but they were flyers, not hikers.

The Ranger Elf Rell Kallen cast a disgusted glance over his shoulder at the crewmembers. The six of them slogged along nearly twenty yards behind.

"They're slowing us down," the elf complained to Raxe, who trudged along five yards or so behind the impatient elf.

The offworlder's daughter scampered along beside him, her shorter legs needing three quick strides to match one of Raxe's.

"They can follow the dwarf's directions as well as we can," the elf continued. "Let them keep their snail's pace whilst we go on without them. It's bad enough that I have to slow my stride for the two of you."

"You don't *have* to do anything," Raxe countered. "You're free to go on ahead and find Mar-dah's mountain if you can. But wait, I guess you would have to wait for us to actually find the Hell Key. I doubt it'll be just lying out on the ground waiting for you."

"You continue to make light of all this," Rell Kallen growled. "This is no joke. The fate of our worlds is at stake yet you dilly-dally like a child. Let us leave them."

Raxe would not hear of it. "We're trekking through dangerous territory. The mountains were full of predators. Now, we're so close to the Forsaken Desert that we're at risk of attack from sand creatures. Bandits harass travelers near the borderlands and the crew doesn't have weapons. Those men and women risked their lives to get us to the Demon's Spine. I'm gonna make sure they get to Southborough safely and get safe passage back to Port Lorrian. If you don't like it, go on ahead. I'm sure you can find something to do while you're waiting for Azh and me to catch up."

The Ranger Elf gave Raxe a contemptuous glare as sharp as his elven features and walked on, putting more distance between himself and the rest with every stride.

It was dusk when the group reached Southborough. By then they had lost sight of Rell Kallen among the outlying buildings and intersecting streets. Raxe was not concerned. The respite from all of the complaining was refreshing.

And while Raxe would never admit it to a living soul, the irritated glares the elf constantly leveled upon him freaked him the hell out. With his canted eyes, upswept eyebrows, razor-sharp cheekbones, pointed ears and thin-lipped grimace, the angry Ranger Elf was an intimidating sight.

As it turned out, the Head Mage was true to his word. A squad of eight royal mounted soldiers met them at the edge of town. The squad leader led his team up to Raxe's group, stopped, and saluted.

"Master Raxe," the leader greeted, his right fist held firmly to his chest. "I am Sergeant Samuel Nichols. It's good to see you again, sir."

"Again?" Raxe questioned as he returned the salute. "When did we…? Wait, this is Southborough. You were here when fought the Legion Midnight."

"Yes," the sergeant said, surprised that the Child of the Old Ones recognized him. "I'm honored to be remembered by such a legendary warrior."

"I never forget the face of someone I've gone into battle with," Raxe assured.

And I never forget the face of someone I've killed, he thought bitterly. The Battle of Southborough during the Cursed Opening was one of the most memorable skirmishes in which he had participated. For an ex fighter pilot and assassin with dozens of kills to his name, every aspect of that battle held a special significance for him.

It marked the last time Raxe had taken a human life.

"I was only three years in at the time," Samuel shared. "That was the first action I and most of my platoon had ever seen. The skill you and Captain Sureblade displayed is still talked about by the men who survived that day."

"What about Shanderah?" Raxe questioned, strangely irked at the fact that the exploits of a fellow Child of the Old Ones would be omitted.

"Well," Samuel began, somewhat uneasily, "We don't discuss her as much. Hers is a skill we can't hope to emulate. And to be honest, sir, her display of ability was, well, somewhat…unsettling."

When Raxe thought about the old sorceress in combat he had to smile. The way she used her magic to toss devastating bolts of lightening at her enemies with such apparent ease, he could understand if even her allies found her at bit frightening.

"I can't argue with that, sergeant," Raxe allowed.

"I thank the Lord Ascendant we don't have a battle to fight this day," Samuel declared. "My squad is here to escort the sky sleigh crew to the airfield on the western outskirts of Southborough."

Morgana, one of the crewmembers from the ill-fated sky sleigh, heard Samuel as she approached with the rest of the crew. She stepped forward.

"If I may ask, sergeant, is there a reason an entire squad is needed? Is there some danger?"

Sergeant Samuel gave the young woman a look that was haughty and incredulous, surprised and slightly offended that a civilian would dare question him.

"You may work for the crown, girl, but not in a military capacity. It is not your place to question a sergeant in the Royal Army."

"She has a point, though" Raxe added firmly. "I'm kind of curious about that, too."

Samuel nodded deferentially. "I was about to explain before the interruption, Master Raxe," he said, glaring at Morgana, who responded with a smug grin.

"Of late, there have been demonstrations here in Southborough and in Shaddiston. We were already stationed here so the crown instructed us to assist with containing the unrest. Rabble-rousers from Cartha have been stirring passions among some of the citizenry, encouraging them to protest against King William and the Head Mage. A few of the demonstrations grew beyond the local constabulary's ability to contain.

"Unfortunately, outsiders don't go unnoticed here, Master Raxe. The elf and the…unique girl accompanying you make your group conspicuous enough. And even if they've never seen you in person, many people would recognize you from your singular armor and battleaxe. They'd know you are acting as agents of the crown. I've no doubt that news of your arrival has already been spread. The King wants neither the crew endangered nor your progress impeded by trivial protests."

Raxe was tempted to tell the sergeant to leave off the "Master" and just call him Raxe. He was put off, however, by the man's superior air and decided the good sergeant needed a dose of humility, sincere or otherwise.

"Sounds good to me, sergeant," Raxe said. "I have one request. We've been walking for days and we're pretty worn down from our journey. How 'bout you let us ride those horses? There are eight of you guys and there just happens to be eight of us. Seems like it was meant to be, doesn't it?"

The sergeant hesitated for the briefest moment before forcing a smile and nodding. "Of course, Master Raxe. How can I refuse a request from a Child of the Old Ones?"

Samuel and his men dismounted. Raxe insisted that the sergeant help Morgana upon Samuel's horse while Raxe helped his daughter mount the steed of the second in command. He then found another horse for himself.

"Master Raxe," the sergeant called over his shoulder as he led his horse by the reins. "As you say, there are eight of you. We were told there'd be nine. Has misfortune befallen the Ranger Elf? I was looking forward to meeting him."

"You haven't missed anything," Raxe assured. "He went on ahead of us. Patience isn't one of his virtues. But don't worry about him. Wherever he is, he'll keep to himself and stay out of sight. His social skills suck."

Samuel frowned. "'Suck' you say?"

"That means bad," Azhju'lestra explained with a grin.

Raxe smiled.

"Ah," Samuel said.

* * *

After accompanying the sky sleigh crew to the airfield and seeing them safely away, the sergeant offered to assist Raxe and Azh with replenishing their supplies for the trek to Shaddiston. Raxe quickly accepted. Two of the squad members volunteered to remain at the airfield so that the two Children of the Old Ones could ride along with the mounted squad to save time.

Azh rode to Raxe's right while Raxe rode to the right of Sergeant Samuel. The soldier eased his mount closer to Raxe.

"If I may, Master Raxe," the sergeant began, "Since your last visit to Southborough, I've wondered about your fighting style. Do many people fight the way you do?"

Raxe shrugged. "A lot of people study martial arts in my world. There are many different styles. Some study some of the same ones I study, some study similar styles, and some are quite different."

"How long does it take to learn to fight like you?" Samuel asked.

"Well," Raxe said thoughtfully, "I began my studies when I learned to walk, so, at about six months old. So I'd say a little over thirty years."

Sergeant Samuel chuckled for a moment, and then he realized that the offworlder was serious. "They say the same about the *Ken d'Zanir*. They have a warrior culture. Is that how it is in your world?"

"My world is not *that* different from this one in that there are a lot of different cultures," Raxe explained. "There are some cultures that incorporate martial arts much more than others. I didn't grow up in that kind of culture, but my grandfather spent decades in one. He taught my mother and both he and my mother taught me."

As the sergeant considered his next question, he pulled a

wineskin from his hip, flipped the cap on it, and squeezed a long stream of purple liquid into his mouth.

Raxe noticed that the man did not put his mouth on the stem and the sweet smell of the drink made his mouth water. Sergeant Samuel was about to close the wineskin when he saw Raxe's interested look. He smiled and held it out.

"You look thirsty, sir. Would like a belt?"

"Is it that obvious?" Raxe grinned.

"I'd be honored to share with a Child of the Old Ones."

Raxe took the proffered wineskin gratefully, popped the cap and imitated the sergeant, squeezing a stream of wine into his mouth. No stranger to the strong liquor in the Kingdom of Lorr, he made it a point not to drink as much as Samuel had. Nevertheless, he had to fight to keep from coughing. Samuel called it wine, and it was indeed sweet, but it seared his throat like strong whiskey and gave him an immediate – though not unpleasant – head rush.

"Good," Raxe said, his sandpaper voice made even rougher from his burning throat and chest. He quickly handed the wineskin back.

"The best," Samuel bragged. He looked around warily. "I wonder about the Ranger Elf. Are you sure he's not nearby?"

"Positive," Raxe burped. "He's probably at the southern border of town by now, sulking and wondering what the hell is taking us so long."

"Good," Sergeant Samuel said with a nod.

Raxe raised an eyebrow. The sergeant did not seem to be nodding at him, but past him. He turned in time to see two men riding up behind his daughter. One threw a hood over her head while the other coiled a rope around her narrow shoulders. Raxe tried to reach for Demonsbane but he was suddenly too exhausted to move. His blood felt like it was turning into fire in his veins.

Azh swooned a second after the hood fell over her head. A cloud of white powder puffed out from under the hood as the soldier tightened it about her face.

Raxe's vision started to waver. He turned back to Sergeant Samuel, who wore a menacing smile.

"The offworlder's done," the sergeant observed. "Let's get him and the girl to the red mage and collect our bounty."

"You son of a bitch..." Raxe swore as his throat began to constrict painfully, his gravelly voice turning the words into a bass, feral growl.

"Oh, did I not offer you the counteragent to the poison you just drank?" the sergeant taunted. "I took a nice big swig of it back at the airfield. How forgetful of me!"

Raxe mumbled a few unintelligible words and managed to flutter his hands before he went completely still and silent. He slumped in the saddle and then tumbled from his horse. Samuel's eyes followed the offworlder as he fell, but then they widened when the Child of the Old Ones disappeared mere inches above the ground. There was a small pop as air rushed in to fill the space his falling body had just occupied.

"What in the seven hells?" Samuel wondered aloud.

His second in command rode to his side. "He's not supposed to have that kind of magic, is he, sergeant?"

"He's a Child of the Old Ones," Samuel said. "There's no telling what they can and can't do. Doesn't matter where he went, though. The poison will have killed him by the time he gets there, or a scant moment after."

10.2

Shaddor Rinn's black, beady eyes peered at the approaching squad through the arrow slit cut into the slate wall on the second floor. The little man peaking through the slit relaxed his grip on the crossbow he held in his right hand once he recognized his visitors.

He relaxed his grip, but did not put the crossbow down.

As the squad came closer, he finally saw what he was looking for. The sight of the unconscious hooded girl draped across the sergeant's saddle made the little man smile an evil little smile that boasted dark purple gums and a sparse scattering of yellow and brown teeth.

The smile faltered, though, when he noticed that hers was the only passive body being brought to his home. His small hand tightened around his crossbow once more.

Were they imposters? Or did they merely plan to cheat him? Other's had certainly tried to their peril. Everyone underestimated him because of his size.

As a child he was bullied because he was smaller than everyone else. However, when he realized his interest in magic as a teen, the bullying quickly came to a halt. Back then he was not a powerful mage by any stretch of the imagination.

He was a warlock, so he had a heightened sensitivity to magic but no inner power to call upon. But even a minor spell caster – such as he was at that time – could inflict serious pain upon those without the capacity to use magic.

When he realized his full potential as a disciple of the Wizard Drake, any would-be tormentor was repaid with far more than just pain. The dozens of bodies buried all around his property attested to that.

He brought up his crossbow and fitted it through the arrow slit as the squad came ever closer. Though he doubted he would have to use it. The fools were about to stumble right over his warded boundary line. If they were impostors, in a moment he would have eight more bodies to bury: the girl and the seven soldiers.

DEMON OF LORR

He had never pulled in a cache of this many subjects at one time. The effort it would take to bury their exsanguinated bodies would be well worth the resulting exhaustion.

A red mage required quite a bit of blood to fuel his power properly.

To his slight dismay, Sergeant Samuel brought the squad to a halt just a few feet away from sure death. The observant soldier could see the line of slightly discolored grass that marked the boundary to the property even in the fading daylight. Perhaps the crossbow *would* have to be employed.

*   *   *

"We will come no further, mage!" Sergeant Samuel Nichols called to the oddly shaped two-story dwelling. "Not until you grant us safe passage!"

The plain gray building looked like nothing so much as a giant, capped stone bucket with windows, doors, and arrow slits cut randomly into its walls. It sat on an acre just southeast of Southborough, in the middle of a half-mile of flat land among the softly rolling foothills surrounded by Hell's Mountains to the north, the Forsaken Desert to the west, the Demon's Spine Mountains to the south, and the Badlands to east.

The structure's utter starkness lent it an ominous air, like a thing cold and lifeless. While it looked to be only two stories tall, it was a poorly kept secret that there was an underground level. And even though the sergeant could not see it, he knew one of those arrow slits was fitted with a loaded crossbow aimed squarely at his squad. The red mage's reputation most certainly preceded him.

Shaddor Rinn had warned against approaching too close to his home without the mage's leave, but he never said how close was "too" close. The sergeant knew that powerful conjurers – especially those of high station or paranoid lunatics like Shaddor Rinn – most often protected their domiciles with dangerous enchantments, so when he saw the vague line of slightly duller grass he decided not to take any unnecessary risks with his life or the lives of his men.

"So you *can* follow instructions!" Shaddor Rinn shouted

back. "I thought perhaps you could not, seeing as how you only bring me the little one. You were instructed to bring the offworlder, as well."

"Raxe was given the poison as directed," Sergeant Samuel yelled. "And it worked. He fell from his horse but managed to teleport as he fell. No doubt he is somewhere dead or dying at this very moment."

"Teleport? I have it on good authority that he does not have that kind of ability. His magic does not lend itself to conjuring. What trickery are you trying to pull, Sergeant?"

"Damn it Rinn!" Samuel barked. "Either grant us safe passage onto your land so we can talk like civilized men or we will go and find another buyer for the girl. Perhaps no one will pay as much as you are offering but an exotic little thing like this will certainly fetch a handsome price. I'd actually *prefer* to sell her as a slave or hostage than as a specimen for your foul machinations."

Shaddor Rinn stared for a moment and then growled. If Samuel spoke true, the red mage could not risk losing such a prize as Azhju'lestra, even if her father did not accompany her. Should this be some sort of duplicity, though, he and his traitorous soldiers would pay dearly.

The diminutive wizard stepped back to inspect the crude drawing on the wall to right of the arrow slit. He set his crossbow down on a table a few feet away and turned back to peer through the arrow slit once more.

Once he was sure of his guests' position, he turned his attention back to the drawing, which was difficult to see in the gloomy room. The north-facing arrow slit let in only a small amount of natural light, and that light was fading as the suns drifted lazily toward the western horizon. The candles burning around the room added barely enough to illumination to see. Fortunately the red mage did not need to see the drawing clearly. He drew it years ago and had used it countless times. It had long ago been committed to memory.

Rendered in reddish-brown lines that emitted the faint scent of copper, the drawing consisted of concentric circles, the outer one about twice the size of the inner one.

DEMON OF LORR

The inner circle represented Shaddor Rinn's home. The larger one represented the circumference of his boundary ward. The space between the circles was filled with a seemingly haphazard pattern of two symbols rendered multiple times.

One of the symbols was that of a heart being cloven by a broadsword. It was the symbol of the Old One Hargathall, also called the blood god within certain clandestine factions.

The other symbol was a six-pointed star composed of intersecting equilateral triangles set within a circle. The triangles that made up the six tips of the star had smaller images within: a symbol to represent earth, wind, fire, water, air, and spirit. Novices assumed air and wind were the same entities. Those who studied blood conjuring passed down by the ancient high priests of Hargathall, the original red mages, knew the significant difference between the two.

Air was obviously important because it was needed for life and fire alike, but it was static and relatively harmless. Wind was altogether different. It was the dark twin to air. Wind was energy, a force of potential devastation. It turns water into waves. It extinguishes a flame or transforms it into an inferno. Wind could turn inert sand into a deadly sandstorm or kill by ripping the breath from a living creature's lungs.

Lines were drawn to connect all of the symbols of Hargathall, with care not to intersect the circle-star symbols.

Shaddor Rinn intoned a brief incantation, licked his right index finger, and used the wet fingertip to rub a small gap into the top of the large outer circle. He licked the finger clean and used his left hand to draw a flask from a pocket in his robe. He pulled the cap from his flask with his teeth, pressed his moist index finger over the rim of the flask, quickly tilted it upside down and righted it again just as quickly. When he pulled his finger away to put the cap back on the flask, he took care to not let any of the thick crimson fluid coating his fingertip to drip free. He poised his blood-soaked finger near the drawing and called to the sergeant through the arrow slit.

"You may pass, sergeant. *Only* you and the rider carrying the girl may pass. No one else!"

"As you wish," the sergeant returned.

Shaddor Rinn watched his barrier spell drawn on the wall. He peered closely at it as the men rode onto his property. Just as they crossed the barrier he saw a small spot on the bottom of the outer circle – almost exactly opposite the point he had opened with his finger – turn moist. That spot represented the rear of his home, the back of his property. A small droplet broke away from the wet spot and ran. It did not toward the floor, though. It defied gravity and ran up into the space between circles, where it merged with one of the existing symbols.

The red mage's thick lips curved into a malevolent smile.

"Fools," he murmured.

Shaddor Rinn used his bloody fingertip to close the circle the moment Sergeant Samuel and his underling crossed the barrier. He immediately stepped to his left, to one of the curved walls, in which was built a set of floor-to-ceiling shelves nearly fifteen feet long. There were six shelves, each roughly two feet high and deep. The top three shelves contained cans and vials and jars and beakers and tubes of alchemist chemicals. The second and third shelves from the bottom contained books and pamphlets and scrolls. The bottom shelf held weapons. Knives, dirks, straightswords, rapiers (but not broadswords and greatswords, for they were far too big and heavy for the diminutive conjurer to wield), slings, cudgels, unstrung bows, crossbows, arrows, and crossbow bolts, were all stacked in no particular order along the bottom shelf.

Shaddor Rinn took out his flask again and poured a bit of blood into his palm. He rubbed his hands together, chanting as he did so. The language was that of the wizard's tongue, unfamiliar to all save the most learned conjurers, but those who knew it, had they been there to listen, would have heard these words:

> *In the sacred name of the Old One*
> *Hargathall, and by Earthsplitter, His blessed*

*greatsword, and on the honor of the Red
Priests of His holy order, I beseech thee, use
this blood sacrifice to let my missiles fly true,
and bend their targets to the will of your
humble servant.*

After scooping up a handful of crossbow bolts and
slipping them into a hidden pocket in his robe, he turned and
scampered around the table behind him. He snatched up his
crossbow as he passed, careful not to upend any of the jars
filled with the blood of various small mammals. The wake of
his passing caused the candlelight to flutter and the shadows
to dance, seeming to animate the countless spells, spell
forms, symbols and diagrams rendered in dried blood all over
the walls, floor and ceiling.

He hurried down the narrow spiral stairway that ran down
the center of the structure like a twisted spine. At the front
door he had just enough time to set the crossbow on the floor,
pull the flask from his robe, pour another small puddle of
blood into the palm of his right hand, and replace the flask in
his pocket. He rubbed the blood on both hands again,
snatched up the crossbow, and wiped some of the blood on
the loaded bolt. That done, he snatched open the front door.

Sergeant Samuel stopped his horse several yards away
from the entrance. He looked at the crossbow hanging
unabashedly down near the red mage's shin.

"What's this, then, Shaddor?" he demanded. "I thought
this was to be a civilized exchange."

"As did I," Shaddor returned, his cold black eyes boring
into the sergeant. "But you've only brought me half of what
was agreed upon."

"It is as I told you. The Child of the Old Ones teleported
as he fell from his horse."

"Then why do I get the strong sense that you are trying to
betray me?" Shaddor demanded. "You've betrayed your king
with treachery against the Children of the Old Ones. Why
should I trust you?"

"I did *not* betray my king," the sergeant snarled.

Shaddor scoffed. "That's not how it seems from here."

"I am protecting my king and kingdom against the treachery of these Children of the Old Ones. He's allowed himself to be a pawn in their game of domination of the mortal races, as have many in our military.

"They say they want to protect us. They really wish to control us. There are whispers that the offworlder was on a quest to recover the Hell Key from Mar-dah's hidden lair. To what possible end, I ask? They crave the power to unleash the demons again if they so desire. I'll not allow it."

"Passionate about this, are we?" Shaddor taunted.

The sergeant sneered at the mocking tone. "Yes, passionate enough to throw my lot in with the likes of *you.* "

The red mage studied the sergeant for an uncomfortable moment and then turned his black gaze to the hooded girl sprawled over the sergeant's saddle.

"Is she alive?"

"As promised," the sergeant assured. "Why do you want the daughter alive but the offworlder dead? Not that I mind, but I'm curious. Afraid he'd cause too much trouble?"

"What does it matter? He is not here. Bring the girl." Shaddor had grown weary of the pointless banter and was certain the sergeant was stalling. "There is a bench here in the foyer. The two purses on the bench contain your payment. Place the girl on the bench and take *one* of the purses when you leave."

"Understood," Sergeant Samuel said with a nod. "I'd not expect full payment for half the job. We will look for the offworlder's body. Perhaps you will give us the other purse when we bring his corpse to you."

"Don't bother. By the time you find him his blood will be cold and clotted and useless to me. If I work with a corpse, it must be freshly dead."

The sergeant suppressed a disgusted shiver and beckoned his soldier to bring the girl. The soldier dismounted, rushed to pull Azhju'lestra from his superior officer's saddle and carried her toward the front door.

"Wait," Shaddor commanded. When the soldier stopped, the red mage continued. "Remove the hood and open her eyes. I want to be sure you did not snatch some peasant girl with the intention of deceiving me."

When the soldier removed the hood Shaddor was struck dumb by the little girl's beauty. Her skin was a light shade of bronze that shone even in the dying light. Her long hair was a mesmerizing combination of aquatic hues. Deep blues flowed into ocean greens and soft strands the color of sea foam reminiscent of whitecaps cresting strong waves.

The little girl had an oval face and small round chin, full lips, and thick eyebrows with a soft arch. Her long curving eyelashes twined around the soldiers fingers as he held her eyes open for the red mage's inspection. Her wide oval eyes were such a light shade of brown they were only just slightly darker than desert sand. Streaks of darker brown and paler shades of brown shot through irises that reflected the deep red of the setting suns like twin prisms.

"She is truly daughter to the Mistress of the Sea of Spirits," Shaddor breathed. His black eyes glinted hungrily as he ran his bloody right thumb across the other four fingers of his right hand, savoring the slick wetness in anticipation of having the Child's hot blood smeared on them soon.

He stepped to the side of the doorway but remained at an angle that kept both men in his line of sight. "Place her where I commanded, take your payment, and be gone."

The soldier glanced at his commander with an unspoken question is his eyes. Sergeant Samuel frowned and nodded.

"Do it. The sooner we're away from here, the better."

Shaddor Rinn managed to tear his gaze away from the girl long enough to study the squad leader. Sergeant Samuel watched as Hoff did as instructed, but his eyes momentarily flicked over to the right.

"Looking for something, sergeant?" Shaddor asked.

Sergeant Samuel ignored him. Hoff eased passed Shaddor Rinn, stepped to his commander, and handed off the purse.

"I'll take you at your word that it is all here," the sergeant said. "But if it is not, we shall return."

Shaddor Rinn favored him with a smile as black as his eyes. "You never answered my question, traitor. Were you looking for something just now? Or was it some*one*? Perhaps you were looking for the man who tried to sneak onto my property from the rear of my home."

A choking cough sounded from around the curved wall of the house. A man followed the sound, crawling on his hands and knees. His skin was pale white and riddled with blue veins. He was gagging as he hawked up gouts of blood from his mouth and nose. A stream of thick red tears poured from his eyes and thin lines of bloody wax dribbled from his ears.

Sergeant Samuel was frozen for the barest instant with disgust and alarm and then he drew his broadsword, roaring for his underling to do the same. In that instant, however, Shaddor Rinn barked an unrecognizable word that froze the young shoulder in place. His hand was on the grip of his sword, but it stopped moving.

The sergeant spurred his horse to charge the wizard but the horse had gone as still as the young soldier. The horse made a deep-throated choking noise as the soldier began to gag. In the next moment both crumpled to the ground, lifeblood evacuating from their orifices as it had from the soldier who stole onto Shaddor Rinn's land uninvited.

Sergeant Samuel noticed that he was not suffering the same fate and he thought he knew why. As his horse faltered, the sergeant showed remarkable dexterity and quickness, fueled by adrenaline and terror, and snatched his feet from the stirrups to scramble atop the horse's left flank while the beast fell onto its right side. Miraculously the sergeant clung for dear life on the horse's body and did not allow any part of his own body to touch the cursed ground.

"*Very* quick thinking," Shaddor Rinn noted with an ugly grin. "But needless. You are safe for the moment. I only removed your man here, and your horse, from my protection. You are quite free to leave. I want you to spread the word that Shaddor Rinn is not a man to be trifled with.

"The rest of your men, on the other hand..." The mage aimed his crossbow at the soldiers out past his property line.

"*RUN!*" Sergeant Samuel yelled to his charges.

The five soldiers at the perimeter of the property had

been looking on, frozen with fear and indecision. Their sergeant's command spurred them into frantic action.

Unfortunately, Shaddor Rinn had loosed the first shot before they could turn their horses. The bolt hit a man high in his shoulder. By design it was not a killing blow. The force and pain of the impact sent the man falling from his mount just as another soldier was struck in the arm by a second blood-smeared bolt.

Their horses were running away by the time Shaddor had loaded and loosed the next befouled missile, but the soldiers were still in range, and a third man was struck in the thigh.

Sergeant Samuel took the red mage at his word and fled, running as fast as he could to get as far away from this cursed plot of land as fast as possible. He heard the thrum of the crossbow each time it was shot, and each report made him run that much faster.

The two undamaged riders were out of range of the blood arrows by that time, but sufficient damage had been done. Two of the three riders that were shot were still astride their mounts. They drew steel and heeled their mounts to run alongside the riders who had not been struck. The uninjured riders were taken completely be surprise when their companions drew their swords, leapt upon them and wrestled them from their mounts.

Before they had a chance to defend themselves, their bloodied squad members pummeled them into submission with the pommels of their swords. The first victim of the red mage's bolts joined the others as they dragged their unconscious fellow soldiers back into crossbow range. Shaddor Rinn casually shot the last two in their right shoulder. He them turned his attention to the fleeing sergeant, who had run around the curve of the building to take himself out of the line of fire.

Samuel, unfortunately, did not know about the spell cast on Shaddor's ammunition. The last thing he expected was for a crossbow bolt to curve around the building after him.

He was almost clear of Shaddor Rinn's property when he felt the bolt strike him in his right buttocks.

A shock of pain raced through his body, paralyzing his extremities and bringing him to the ground. A moment later he began to move again, completely against his will.

He rose to a standing position and turned back towards Shaddor Rinn's home. A moment later he was walking back around to the front of the house. He fought against the movements with all of his might, but all that did was send more pain arcing through him. Even his eye movements were not within his control. His gaze was forced to the red mage's little obsidian eyes, and then Shaddor Rinn's smug voice was in his ears.

"I changed my mind about you. I think I'll put you to use, after all. The beast blood used to spell my bolts was treated with substances that are poisonous to humans. There is no cure, but worry not. You will live for a day or so, more than long enough for my purposes. Now, come, join your men like a good little sergeant."

10.3

Raxe woke but refused to open his eyes. He was afraid of what he would see. When he felt the sudden exhaustion and the pain rage through his body he knew he had been poisoned. When he fell from that horse and everything went black, he knew he was dying, so the next thing he expected to see was hell.

Hell was not an unfamiliar sight to him. He had seen it countless times: first when he gave in to the magic of Demonsbane and then in his nightmares every night afterward. Even though he knew he was dreaming each time, he had no doubt that what he was seeing was real. Knowing he was hell-bound and having seen what his hell would be made him that much more terrified of his fate.

And then he *really* died. The Finder's dagger took his life and cast him down and, as if he needed the confirmation, Raxe learned first hand that what he saw in his dreams was indeed genuine.

The flames and the pain, the madness and misery had been all consuming. The faces of every person he had ever killed came back to him, screaming in terror or agony or rage. Searing skeletal hands clawed at his flesh. They shot him with the same guns he used to shoot them, stabbed or cut him with the same weapons he had used to stab and cut them. He gagged on his own blood the way his victims had when he fell upon them from the shadows and cut their throats.

He felt the terrible explosions of the planes he had shot down during his brief stint as a fighter pilot. He felt the impact of the pilots' bodies as their planes slammed to the earth or into the ocean.

This time, though, there was no heat or pain. There were no screams or explosions. There were no sounds at all.

He opened his eyes slowly and warily, fearing this was hell's idea of a joke, waiting for him to look before renewing its assault on him. What he saw was familiar, but thankfully, it was not hell.

Raxe found himself lying on top of the sheets in an unremarkable bed in an unremarkable room, surrounded by wood plank walls and flooring.

There was a chest of drawers opposite the bed. An east-facing window showed the slow but inexorable advance of nightfall. The suns' light still shone, albeit weakly, and the barest hint of three moons hovered low on the horizon.

He felt an almost nauseating sensation of *déjà vu* before he realized he had been in this room before. It was the same hotel room he awoke in when last he visited Southborough.

And just like that last time, a woman was there to greet him. Three years ago, the ancient sorceress Shanderah was standing over him smiling when he awoke. Now, a woman stood with her back to him, hands on her hips, looking out the window. A modest, long-sleeved sky blue dress was cinched at her slender waist with a length of thin rope. The frilly hem of the dress hovered a few inches over the ankles of her low-heeled, soft-soled leather riding boots.

She was turned away from him but Raxe could clearly tell she was far younger than Shanderah. Though the ancient sorceress was far spryer than she appeared, she had been bony and stooped, with severely wrinkled skin and long, wispy gray hair.

This woman had a thick head of dark brown hair parted neatly down the middle and flared out to the left and right, natural kinks and curls draping down to her shoulders. He could see the mahogany skin on her hands and the right side of her face. It was smooth and flawless.

And she was certainly not bony. She was lean but shapely. Raxe estimated her height at about five feet and five inches and her weight somewhere between one hundred twenty and one hundred twenty five pounds. Her back was turned to him so he could not estimate her top measurements, but beneath the dress she wore, he could see that her waist was a trim twenty-three inches; her hips a shapely thirty-seven. Nice.

She suddenly turned to him and said: "*Nice*, eh?"

"Um...what?" Raxe asked, knowing full well he had not said that aloud.

Her lips were a tad thin, her mouth a bit wide, her nose was a little long, but it all fit together to form an unconventionally pretty face. She pulled her shoulders back to emphasize her chest. "My 'cup' size, as you'd call it, would be thirty-two-C. Is that too small for you?"

"No. I'm more of an ass man."

"Not easily embarrassed, are you?" she asked. "Good. Neither am I."

"Who the hell are you?" Raxe demanded, a confused frown on his face. "How the hell did I get here?"

"You're as rude as ever, too. I thought perhaps you'd learned some manners since your first trip to Lorr, boy."

"Boy?" Raxe's confusion began to simmer to anger.

"Insulted, Raxe? Or do you prefer *Ryan* again?"

Simmering anger gave way to surprised recognition. The dress was probably a century newer than he remembered, the face and voice a century younger, but there was no mistaking her identity.

"Shanderah!" He shot out of the bed and rushed over to her. He stopped short of hugging her; uncertain of what he should do with this younger, attractive version of the crone he had grown to love like a favorite aunt during the time they spent together.

"You can hug me boy," Shanderah allowed. "Just keep your hands off my thirty-seven inch ass!"

Raxe laughed and wrapped her in a big bear hug, making certain not to move his hands below her lower back. She hugged him so hard that Raxe could feel it through his armor, which surprised him. He pulled away and held her at arm's length, his joy faded. He thought about his daughter and what was happening to her. And then he realized something else.

"Wait, Shandie. This means I'm dead, doesn't it?"

"No, you idiot," she answered.

"OK, now I *know* you're Shandie."

"Of course I am."

"But you're gone. I buried you. How can I see you and hold you if I'm not dead? And why do you look so young?"

"This is obviously not how *you* remember me, Raxe. This is how *I* remember me. The men thought I was quite fetching in my youth. This is the image of myself I put into your head before I died, along with the other information I put up here."

"So we're in…my head?"

"You are a slow one, aren't you? Yes, Raxe, we're in your head. You are indeed lying in that bed in this inn in the physical world, but the two of us are conversing in your subconscious."

Raxe's eyes narrowed. "Why am I getting the feeling that you put more than just information up here?"

"Ah, a rare flash of intelligence from the offworlder. My foresight revealed to me long ago that, for some ungodly reason, the Lord Ascendant has chosen to tie your fate to the fate of this world and yours. I twined a bit of my consciousness with yours to give you the help you'll so desperately need.

"A greater sacrifice I've never made, and I fear it still won't be enough. You're such a pitiful specimen. I've been here since my death, seeing everything you've seen, hearing everything you've heard." She paused to shudder. "I've seen it all. I've had to suffer through the whoring and the drinking… Honestly, Raxe, why in the seven hells would you drink from that man's wineskin, anyway?"

"*He* drank from it, so I thought it was safe. And I was damn thirsty."

"And you're a lush," Shanderah chided. "You could've drunk from your own *water* skin to sate your thirst."

"Alright, already," Raxe said, cutting her off. "I'm not dead. That means I can wake up and go get my daughter."

Shanderah shook her head. "No, I'm afraid you can't."

"Why?"

"Your body is healing," she said. "The enhancement gifted to you by Sabrina is working to repel the poison that would have killed any other human. But for now you are unable to move. You can't even gain consciousness yet."

DEMON OF LORR

Raxe flashed back to when the sea demon nearly killed him. The very thought of it made the pocked scars on his arms and legs from the demon's teeth begin to itch. This was further proof that Sabrina had not only saved his life. She also fortified him in ways he was still discovering. As thankful as he was, at that moment, it was not enough.

"Is there something you can do to speed up my healing?"

"What can I do? I was the most experienced conjurer in the Known Lands in life, as you well know. Here, though, I'm merely a remnant in your mind."

"Then tell me how I can do it, Shandie. Please, my daughter…"

"Would that I could," Shanderah said with genuine and completely uncharacteristic tenderness. "As I've said, I am but a remnant. What you see now, what you speak to now, is a part of you with just a shade of the great sorceress that graced your life for those few short weeks. I can do nothing save what you allow me to do."

"I'm allowing you now, woman," Raxe snapped.

"No Raxe, you are not. You only think you are."

"You're not making sense, Shanderah."

"I am making sense. You know I am. Do I really have to explain to you what, deep down inside, you already know?"

"Hell yeah you do."

Shanderah sighed. "I suppose I do. Listen closely now. The poison would not have killed you but those traitorous soldiers most certainly would have finished the job while you were unconscious and healing. I knew I had to get you away from them.

"The only reason I was able to save your life with the teleportation spell that brought you here was because you were more dead than alive. All of your being's conscious and subconscious effort turned to the task of combatting the poison. That allowed me to come to the fore to control your body and weave the spell. In fact, the only reason you and I can talk now is because you're in a coma and your body is still trying to heal itself.

"The subconscious constructs you've built to imprison me were weakened in your near-death state, but they grow stronger every moment as your body heals. They're keeping me from imparting any more of my knowledge of magic to you. Soon I will fade away completely."

"What *constructs* are you talking about?" Raxe asked. "I want this information. I need it!"

Shanderah shook her head slowly. "Do you remember how long it took you to accept Demonsbane? You never really embraced the enchanted battleaxe. You accepted it because you had to. But in your heart you still loathe its magic. You fear magic in general. You don't understand it and you're not confident you can control it.

"You're afraid of what it can do if it's not properly controlled, what it can do to you, and what it can do the few people you care about. You confronted your fear of flying years ago, and admirably, but the fear still exists. You merely push through it to achieve your goals.

"Magic is a different thing altogether, and you know it, so your subconscious has confined it, and me, to its deepest recesses. With the right triggers you may from time to time glean information from my memories, those that are not directly related to conjuring. As long as those constructs exist and thrive, you cannot mine my recollections for spells."

"Then what the hell good are they?"

"They helped you find WorldHopper's mountain, did they not?" Shanderah reminded him. "And perhaps, with the right triggers, they may yet assist you on this quest."

"So all I can do is wait…while those turncoat bastards are doing who-knows-what to my little girl."

"I doubt the soldiers still have her," Shanderah said.

Raxe blinked. "They were taking her to the red mage."

"I remember a minor conjurer named Shaddor Rinn residing in this area," Shanderah explained. "If no one has killed him yet, I'd be surprised if he's not still here. He's a self-important, territorial slug."

"What would he want with my daughter?"

DEMON OF LORR

"He may be attempting to delay your quest. He is not, as you would say, 'a fan' of the Head Mage. Rionn rebuffed his request to join the Conjurer's Alliance more than once and the little warlock has always been bitter about it. He'd just begun an apprenticeship with the Mad Wizard Drake when Rionn delivered Drake to WorldHopper for crimes against dragon kind. Drake was a powerful red mage.

"There were whispers that Shaddor went sniffing around the hem of Mar-dah's robes for apprenticeship and was rejected then, as well. He's the kind of tool the Dierglyorr would employ. The little coward would soil his breeches at the mere notion of working for a demon, but the Dierglyorr had a penchant for working through intermediaries. I would not be surprised if that was the case here."

"You know a lot about the Dierglyorr, huh?" Raxe noted.

Shanderah smiled the same sly smile he remembered, except this smile contained many more teeth.

"I know lots of things," she said.

"If this Shaddor is so irrelevant," Raxe wondered, "why would the demon bother with him?"

"Even the most seemingly insignificant threat can cause a significant amount of harm when underestimated or ignored. Think about a terrorist strapping an IED to a small child."

Raxe cocked his head. "Where would you have heard about improvised explosive devices?"

"It's strange," Shanderah said. "You look as though you're paying attention. You even respond the way a lucid person would, yet you keep asking stupid questions."

"Oh, yeah… You've literally been in my head for the last three years," Raxe remembered. "I guess that means you can see my memories, too."

"And the light bulb shines a tad bit brighter," Shanderah teased. "The surface memories, yes."

"Thanks for the head's up, Shandie. If Shaddor shows up, I'll be ready for him."

"What will you do if he has your daughter?"

"Make him wish he didn't."

"Will you kill him?"

"If you've been in my head as long as you say, you already know the answer to that."

Shanderah shook her head slowly. "I have to say, Raxe, I agree with Dan on this point. This 'no more killing' stance you've taken may not be the wisest path for you."

Raxe's strong jaw set stubbornly. "I swore an oath."

"To whom, Raxe? And why?"

"To myself...and to God...or the Lord Ascendant, if you prefer. You said they were the same entity."

"But why, Raxe?"

"You're in my head," Raxe mocked. "You see my memories. Why ask questions you know the answer to?"

"To make you ask them of yourself, Raxe, again and again, because apparently you need to. You've vowed not to kill in some desperate attempt to save your soul, I know. Do you understand that even if you go the rest of your life without taking another's, you will still be held accountable for the killing you've already done?"

"I don't understand what the hell I'm supposed to do, then," Raxe said. "Are you telling me it's OK to kill? Are you saying it doesn't matter what I do because I'm bound for hell regardless? What are you saying?"

"The same thing I told you as I lay dying in your arms: You should not do the right thing for the promise of reward or out of fear of punishment. You should do the right thing because it is right. When desire for reward or fear of punishment motivates you, your acts are not from the heart. The Lord Ascendant's concern is what is in your heart."

"So it's OK to kill if you do it for the right reasons?"

"There is never a 'right' reason to kill," Shanderah answered. "Some people kill to save themselves or others and are tortured by it for the rest of their days. Some kill because they enjoy it, or because of some psychological malfunction, a compulsion that they cannot control. Some kill as a means to an end and are completely indifferent to it. It's not a question of it being OK. It never is. It's a question of why you did it, how you feel about, and how you atone for it. That is what determines whether or not you can be forgiven."

"I've *been* trying to atone for it," Raxe argued.

"But Raxe, *why* have you been trying to atone for it? You've always been indifferent to killing. And we both know that you lusted to take the Finder's life. You would have reveled in it had you not been able to stop yourself.

"So I ask again. Why have you been trying to atone? Is it to keep from going to hell, or because you believe – not in a logical or legal sense, but really believe in your heart – that you've been wrong all of these years? If I could penetrate that part of your consciousness and give you an answer I would gladly do so. But that is an answer you must find for yourself, on your own."

Raxe stared at the young-old sorceress. An unfamiliar feeling of helplessness overcame him. It was a question for which he had no answer.

"Well," he finally said after his long pause. "Can you at least shed some light on why the Dierglyorr is sending his walking dead to Ridgeland? That's not directly related to conjuring, right?"

"Finally, an intelligent question," Shanderah said. "And I *could* shed some light on that subject if you weren't about to wake up from your healing stupor."

And then Shanderah was gone.

Raxe blinked. When he opened his eyes he was lying in the hotel bed looking at the ceiling. He sat up and looked at the east-facing window again. He saw someone standing there again, but it was definitely not Shanderah, young or old.

"It took you bloody long enough to wake up," The Ranger Elf Rell Kallen noted.

"How long have you been here?" Raxe asked.

The elf shrugged. "Not long."

"How did you find me?"

"I'm a Ranger Elf," Rell answered.

"I'm going to get my daughter back," Raxe said, his damaged, gravelly voice like ice scraping stone. "You can come with or go to hell."

10.4

It was full dark when they approached Shaddor Rinn's acre. The Ranger Elf had appropriated horses from somewhere and Raxe was glad of it. He felt Azh's presence the moment he regained consciousness. He was relieved to feel the echo of a heartbeat just barely out of synch with his and that whisper of her thoughts, but both were weaker than they should have been, indicating that she was in grave distress. Raxe knew she was roughly five miles away from the inn and was prepared to sprint the whole way if he had to. His body, however, was not quite ready.

When they mounted their steeds, Rell Kallen tried briefly to convince Raxe to abandon the girl, that the mission was more important. After all, the girl was virtually a stranger to him. He insisted they ride due south into the Demon's Spine to continue their search for the Hell Key.

Raxe ignored him and directed his horse to the southeast, where he knew his daughter was being held. Her aura was weak but it was still there. He was going to get her back and God help anyone who got in his way.

The autumn nights were getting colder. Instead of numbing his injured hand, the lower temperatures aggravated the pain. Chilled air crept under his cloak. Raxe barely noticed any of it. His enchanted armor absorbed most of the cold air. The pain in his hand only fueled his anger. Anger and adrenaline warmed the parts of his body that his armor did not cover.

The three moons frosted the landscape as they crept across the blue-black sky. Raxe could see the vapor of the horses' breath as they galloped along the grassy foothills. He knew how to ride horses, and that was all he knew about them, but he could tell these were good horses. They were strong and fast, but as they raced nearer to the red mage's land they began to slow. Raxe had to struggle with the reins to keep his horse from veering off to the left and right and he had to keep a heel in its flanks to keep in moving. Something was spooking both horses.

DEMON OF LORR

Raxe looked ahead to where the land flattened out and saw what the horses were sensing.

The offworlder had grown so accustomed by now to his visual perception of the natural magical energy rising from the earth as well as the plant and animal life that he rarely paid it any mind. The magic radiating from Shaddor Rinn's land was markedly different.

It was not the continuous spray of translucent, pale, white orbs that drifted several feet from its host before dissipating. The energy he spied here was a jaundiced yellow that rose sluggishly from the earth only a few inches and then lost its momentum and dropped unceremoniously back to the ground, where it oozed back into the earth that spawned it.

Rell Kallen could not sense magic the same way the horses or the offworlder could, but he did have some sensitivity to it. He could clearly sense something was amiss, and even if he could not, the growing unease of the horses would have alerted him to the presence of something sinister. The elf pulled up on the reins to stop his horse and hoped for the offworlder's sake that he would do the same before his horse stopped short and threw him.

Raxe reluctantly reined his steed in several yards away from the tainted magic. He dismounted and surveyed the dismal area, especially the foreboding bucket-shaped stone building. He had no idea what the magic would do to someone who stepped into it but he did not care. He had his enchanted armor and was determined to rescue his daughter.

Rell Kallen saw the intent in the offworlder's posture. Even in the moons' light, his keen elven eyes could also see the line in the earth where the grasses that were already beginning to yellow with the changing of the season faded slightly into an unnatural grayish brown. He knew it had to be foul magic in this place. When Raxe began to stride toward that line in the grass, the elf spoke up.

"The horses refuse to step foot on that blasted land, human. You would be wise to follow their lead."

"Probably," Raxe said as he stepped onto Shaddor Rinn's property.

*   *   *

The red mage was exhausted from burying the two dead guards and frustrated at having to get started with his *true* work later than he wanted. Those distractions, along with his fascination of the light blue blood pulsing through the two tubes protruding from the little girl's veins into the heavy stone basin etched with runes almost caused him to miss the disturbance to the spell form that warded his property.

His benefactor told him that the girl was the bastard child of Raxe and Sabrina, the Mistress of the Sea, so Shaddor knew she was special. He had absolutely no idea how special. Raxe might have been a Child of the Old Ones but he was many generations removed from his divine predecessors, and others had seen him bled in battle. His blood ran red, as a human's blood should.

Everyone assumed Sabrina was a powerful Elemental with a flair for the dramatic. If that were true, that would mean she was also a red-blooded human. But if this girl was any indication, her mother was anything but human. Not only did she have this strangely colored blood, she had gills on her neck that were nigh impossible to see without the closest of inspections. This girl Child *had* to be part faerie. Only a creature of faerie could mimic a human so closely yet be so different. That could only mean the Mistress of the Sea was indeed a full-blooded faerie.

With that discovery, Shaddor Rinn knew exactly what to do. The girl lay in a shallow iron coffin half filled with sand. The sand was not quite high enough to cover her ears. The coffin rested on a grate elevated over a low burning flame. The heated sand drew all the moisture out of the girl to keep her weak and barely conscious.

A red mage used blood to amplify the potency of his spells. Animal blood usually sufficed and was the most plentiful and readily available to Shaddor Rinn. Human blood was far more potent and was Shaddor's preference, but it was more difficult to acquire.

The Wizard Drake preferred the use of dragon blood, which boosted his raw power higher than any conjurer save

Mar-dah and the Head Mage himself, both wizard Children of the Old Ones. For Shaddor Rinn, dragon blood was completely unattainable, but he could only imagine what kind of power faerie blood would bestow upon him. He would not, however, have to imagine very much longer.

As a warlock, Shaddor Rinn did not have as strong a natural connection to magic as a wizard, but he had more sensitivity than a sorcerer. A sorcerer might not have felt the stirring of his magic when it activated on the spell form that warded his property. Shaddor did. He initially dismissed it, knowing any person or animal foolish enough to trespass on his land without permission would be dying by now, vomiting and crying and pissing and shitting blood, thus fortifying the ward.

After a few moments, though, he noticed that he could not feel the strengthening of the spell. That was what finally got his attention.

He turned to look at the spell form. The dried-blood drawing there in the cold basement was the twin to the drawing on the top floor in both form and function, so Shaddor knew what he expected to see if the magic worked as it was constructed to work. What he expected to see was a newly moistened spot of blood on the outer circle and a subsequent droplet running from that spot to the closest symbol between the circles as the trespasser died.

Instead, he saw a breaking of the symbol. It was if an invisible finger was rubbing down the form in a straight line, heading right to the representation of his front door. The symbols reformed in the line's wake though, like displaced sea water flowing back together after a ship's passing. Shaddor had never seen this before. He had an idea what it meant, though, and he did not like it. He did not like it at all.

He turned to where his six new thralls stood near the foot of the spiral staircase. The men stood as still as statues. Only their eyes moved, and to a man, their eyes were full of terror.

"Guard the entrance!" the red mage ordered.

The men followed his order involuntarily but instantly, their bodies exploding into motion, drawing their swords and sprinting up the stairs.

Shaddor knelt down and dipped his hands into the basin on the floor that was slowly filling with the half-faerie's blue blood. Her blood was thinner than a human's but clung to his skin just the same. A tingle ran through his hands that he had never felt with human or animal blood.

He then picked up his ever-present crossbow from a bench behind him and scrambled up the stairs. While ascending, he reached into one of the deep pockets in his robe to retrieve several more crossbow bolts.

A repeat of the same chant he used earlier to spell the crossbow bolts empowered them once more. Shaddor could feel the extra power radiating from the blood infused with the essence of both faerie and a Child of the Old Ones. By the time Shaddor arrived at the arrow slot in the north-facing wall of the second floor, he was ready to enthrall or kill his trespasser. He loaded the crossbow, stuck it through the slot and took aim. And then he gasped and almost whimpered with fear.

Shaddor made it a point to question the soldiers after he enthralled them. Under his spell, he knew, they were incapable of lying to him. The offworlder Raxe drank the poison and fell from his horse. There was no question about that. He should have been dead within seconds. Yet there he was. There was absolutely no mistaking the identity of the intruder striding toward his home.

The wind blew his cloak open as he walked, allowing the moons' light to glimmer sharply off of his gleaming silver armor. The open topped half-helm, more visor than helmet, was breathtaking in appearance but left a ridiculous amount of his head unprotected. Only thick strands of twisted hair sprouting from his scalp protected the top of his head. Everything beneath his nose to the his neck was uncovered.

His muscled cuirass and the single-leaf pauldrons at his shoulders looked to be molded directly from his body, yet most of his deltoids, all of his biceps and the tops of his forearms were completely exposed. Even his gauntlets were fingerless and his wrist coverings slotted. A codpiece, thigh armor and slotted boots protected his lower body only a bit better than his upper body.

The enchanted armor was certainly beautiful to look upon and Shaddor had no doubt that it was as impenetrable as every account indicated. However, with so many unprotected areas, the red mage had every confidence that his exponentially fortified crossbow bolts would make short work of the offworlder. His confidence boosted by so many potential targets presented on Raxe's body, he slid his loaded crossbow through the slit and let fly.

*   *   *

Raxe heard the thump of the crossbow firing but he could not see the bolt in the darkness. What he could see, and very clearly, was the spray of dingy yellow globules of magic spiraling from the approaching missile. At first it looked to be poorly aimed, and then its trajectory impossibly changed in midflight and it sped toward his right arm. It would have struck true if Raxe had not sent it spinning away with a flick of his battleaxe.

Another bolt came at him seconds later, this one streaking toward his face. Another flick of Demonsbane turned that one aside as well. The red mage shot the next one at his left arm, which was the side on which he carried the enchanted battleaxe, thinking it would be more awkward to deflect.

It would have worked, but at the last possible instant – too late for the arrow to change direction – Raxe shifted his body so that the bolt caromed off of his armored chest with a clang.

His attacker grew tired of sending crossbow bolts his way and sent men instead. The front door of the home flew open and six men came rushing out. Raxe recognized Sergeant Samuel and his men and smiled.

He was hoping to run into those sons of bitches again.

*   *   *

As soon as he saw his thralls engage the Child of the Old Ones, Shaddor Rinn knew the fight would not last long.

The warding spell was not a problem for his thralls. It

was designed to kill any trespasser crossing over from the outside of the outer perimeter, not exiting the house.

Raxe was their only problem.

Shaddor thought the armor's failure to cover so much of Raxe's body was a flaw. If anything, it was an advantage. Raxe's arms and legs had the freedom to move with almost inhuman speed and accuracy.

Shaddor Rinn did not care. Those men were expendable. All he needed them to do was buy time for him.

He hurried down the two flights of stairs to reenter the basement. More of the girl's blood had flowed into the basin. The red mage dropped to his knees and pressed his hands and forearms into the basin, coating his arms up to his elbows with the girl's blood. He stood up straight, closed his eyes, and uttered another spell.

He let the magic fill him with heat until it was nearly unbearable. Steam rose from his blood-soaked hands and arms and a thrill ran all through his body. The pain was euphoric. The energy within him was almost too much to contain. He had never felt this kind of power.

With renewed confidence and razor sharp focus, the red mage charged up the spiral staircase to the first floor.

*   *   *

Demonsbane broke their blades. Precise punches and kicks broke their bones. Raxe could see the same jaundiced aura that polluted the crossbow bolts and grounds radiating from the soldiers and knew they under the red mage's control. The soldiers would have had small chance of defeating Raxe under the best of circumstances. The spell that compelled them made them that much easier to dispatch.

Their movements were jerky and hesitant. Raxe could see the fear and reluctance in their eyes. Their enthrallment took most of the fun right out of the fight.

Raxe refused to kill them. The flat of Demonsbane's crescent blades was used against their flesh instead of its fatally sharp edges.

He stopped them with precise blows thrown with the

intent to maim and disable. It did not matter if they were being controlled. If their arms and legs did not work, or if they were unconscious, they simply could not fight.

Raxe spent an extra few seconds inflicting a little extra damage to Sergeant Samuel. The squad leader might have been under the red mage's control during the nighttime battle, but that was certainly not the case earlier that day when he poisoned Raxe and kidnapped his daughter.

Two broken arms, two broken ribs, and one broken leg later, Raxe was striding purposefully to the house again.

The little warlock stepped into the open doorway. His aura was almost blinding to Raxe's visual perception of magic. It was not pure white, but it was nowhere near as polluted as his victims and magically charged objects. It was familiar, as well. It was too familiar.

He felt his daughter's essence in that foul aura.

Raxe growled and charged the red mage, Demonsbane held high.

Shaddor Rinn thrust his arms out and screamed an unintelligible command, casting a spell he would never have been powerful enough to cast without the hybrid blood supplementing his magic.

Awesome whitefyre leapt from the earth between him and the attacking Child of the Old Ones.

The magical flames lit up the night as bright as day. The sudden intense light blinded everyone on or near the property. It hissed like a giant serpent as it burned the very air around it. The crackle of the blanched flames was like a continuous rumble of thunder, but with a higher pitch.

The red mage thrust his arms forward further still and sent the whitefyre rushing at the offworlder. To his mild surprise, Raxe made no effort to avoid the deadly all-consuming flames.

The flames quickly engulfed him. Raxe's scream of pain rang out even louder than the hiss and crackle of the whitefyre. It danced around him and on him until he could no longer be seen. The whitefyre started to fold in upon itself, shrinking slowly as black smoke plumed from its core. The enchanted armor might be impervious to the conflagration, Shaddor knew, but the exposed skin of the offworlder's body would fall prey to the ravenous flames.

The red mage watched with satisfaction and waited anxiously as the whitefyre faded and the chill wind carried the black smoke away. Soon it would carry away Raxe's ashes. Shaddor's only regret was that he would not be able use the offworlder's blood to further heighten his power. The armor, he thought, would make a fitting trophy.

The black, inky smoke wafted away, revealing a pile of dark ash and a large area of blackened earth.

"Yes!" Shaddor Rinn snarled. "I have felled a Child of the Old Ones!"

And then Raxe emerged from the pile, ash and soot sliding off of his armor like water. With a gravelly roar, he pointed Demonsbane forward and sent the red mage's whitefyre screaming back at him.

The flames quickly swept around Shaddor Rinn and began to close in. In his shock and panic, the diminutive conjurer barely managed to weave the spell to extinguish his own magical conflagration.

At first Shaddor was afraid it would not work. He feared the magic had been changed by the offworlder and he would not be able to control it. But it was still his. It was the exact same whitefyre he cast so it took only a few fearful seconds to douse the flames.

Once he did, he saw the offworlder virtually flying toward him with his right leg and armored boot extended. The next thing he saw was a flash of light. The next thing he felt was a flash of pain in his jaw, and then he did not see anything.

*   *   *

Until his eyes fluttered open and he found himself lying face down on the cold floor of his basement.

A furtive glance around the room revealed that Raxe had hacked a hole in the stone wall where the warding spell form had been drawn. The basement spell form was linked to its twin on the second floor, so its destruction effectively disabled the home's protection.

The fire beneath the iron coffin holding his daughter was extinguished but she had not been removed. The offworlder apparently knew enough about magic to not put his bare hands in the sand to extract her…or to even touch the coffin.

Raxe sat before him on the same bench where Shaddor's crossbow rested a few minutes earlier. The offworlder stared at the little warlock, and Shaddor could see murder and madness in his countenance. The candlelight and the glow from the fading embers beneath the iron coffin lent a pinpoint of red to the offworlder's pupils. Smoke wafted up from his left hand where it gripped Demonsbane's handle and Shaddor thought he could smell the barest hint of burned flesh. Raxe's right elbow rested on his armored thigh, and his deformed right hand twitched.

"You thought your little fire trick would stop me?" Raxe asked. "You got some bad intel."

Shaddor Rinn could feel his heart in his throat. His jaw throbbed with pain with each beat. He could not keep himself from shivering with fear.

"Are you…are you going to kill me?"

"Don't know yet," Raxe lied. "Depends on what you have to say. I have two questions: How do I safely remove her from this contraption? Who told you to kidnap her?"

The red mage was about to answer, and then something strange happened. The look in the offworlder's eyes all but assured him that he was dead man. That surety infused him with confidence and defiance that startled even him.

The offworlder eyed Shaddor Rinn as the warlock considered his response. Apparently he took a beat too long, because Raxe suddenly thrust Demonsbane's double crescent axe blades into the extinguished but still smoldering embers of the pyre that had been built to keep Azh's coffin warm. The movement sent a jolt of fear through Shaddor, but then he smiled that disgusting smile of his and scrambled to his hands and knees.

"You do not frighten me, offworlder," he snarled. "You righteous Children of the Old Ones are too altruistic to lower yourself to torture. If you are going to kill me, just kill – ” His challenge turned into a shrill scream when Raxe stomped down on his right hand. Shaddor Rinn looked down at his crushed hand and tried in vain to pull it free.

As he struggled, he saw the flat of the sliver axe blades flash horizontally through his field of vision and then he was rolling across the floor as his hand was suddenly released. When stopped rolling, he looked over at Raxe and saw his hand still under the offworlder's armored boot. He looked at his wrist and saw to his horror that it ended in a painful and smoking cauterized stump.

The red mage's eyes widened in pain and disbelief, almost bulging out of his skull. His left hand came up instinctively to clutch his arm just beneath the stump. He saw a flash of movement out of the corner of his eye and Demonsbane streaked through his field of vision again, vertically this time, and he saw the edge of the axe blades instead their flat sides. And then his left hand hit the floor with a wet thump. The red mage was looking at a cauterized stump at the end of his *left* wrist.

A gurgling cry of agony and shock exploded from his gaping mouth. As soon as it did, the sadistic offworlder shoved his misshapen claw-like right hand into the red mage's mouth and gripped his tongue painfully between pincer-like fingertips.

Shaddor tasted the cold metal coating Raxe's fingertips and the burnt flesh of the uncoated portions of his ruined hand and almost gagged. He somehow managed to hold down his bile, deathly afraid of vomiting on the Child of the Old One's hand and angering him even further.

“They say conjurers need their hands and mouth to cast spells,” Raxe mused. “Some of the more powerful wizards can use one or the other, and not necessarily both. I'm guessing both sorcerers and warlocks have to use both, but I don't know a lot about magic so I could be wrong. Answer my questions or I cut out your tongue just to be sure.”

Shaddor nodded frantically. Raxe released his tongue.

“Only I can touch the sand in the coffin safely, but if it's emptied from the coffin you'll be able to remove the girl without harm." His voice cracked and he had to continually snort back snot running from his nose as freely as the tears ran from his eyes. He kept talking. "The Head Mage of Cartha employed me to have your daughter abducted. I was not told why. They promised gold and all of the blood I would ever need for my spells."

Raxe looked closely at the red mage and asked another question: "Can you cast spells verbally, or do you have to use your hands and spoken words? If you lie to me, I'll know it."

"Both," Shaddor sputtered. "Though not necessarily at the same time. I can use my hands to lay the foundation for a spell and then speak a word to activate it later...or I can lay the foundation verbally and activate it later with a gesture."

"Do you have any more surprises set up for me?"

"No, offworlder, I swear it by the Old One Hargathall!"

Raxe was trained to spot lies. Besides, the agony and shock the little warlock was feeling would make it virtually impossible for him to lie. Raxe shoved his right hand into the other's mouth, breaking crooked rotting teeth in the effort, stretched his tongue as far as he could from the crying man's mouth and cut it off anyway.

The blade still held enough heat to cauterize the flesh, so at least the beleaguered warlock would not choke on his own blood. When the deed was done, Raxe knelt down near the sniveling man and dropped the severed tongue to the floor. When the offworlder spoke, his damaged, gravelly voice rumbled in Shaddor Rinn's ears like the growl of a demon.

"That was for fucking with my family."

Raxe spent the next few minutes freeing his daughter. He cut a large portion out of the coffin near Azh's feet to let the sand spill out. He used Demonsbane as a lever to tilt the coffin up to void the residual sand. Once all of that was done, he gently removed the tubes that were siphoning her blood.

Even though the half-water faerie-half-human girl was too weak and dazed to form coherent thoughts, Raxe's link to her as a Child of the Ones and his daughter was able to sense the one thing for which her very essence cried out from the moment he awoke from his healing stupor.

He slipped Demonsbane's handle through the metal ring of its axe frog, pulled a water skin from his cloak and poured the water onto her neck. The gills on either side of her neck pulsed frantically, sucking up most of the life-giving liquid. The small bit of water they missed soaked into her skin like water into a dry sponge. The puncture wounds from the tubes closed and healed as if they were never there.

Azhju'lestra's big beautiful eyes opened and found Raxe immediately. A weak smile formed on her lips.

"You came for me?" she asked.

"Damn right," Raxe assured. "You're my little girl. I'll always come for you."

He gathered her in his arms, lifted her from the empty coffin, and made his way to the spiral staircase. She spied the maimed warlock sitting on the floor, his back propped up against the wall. His blackened wrist stumps resting limply on the floor, his tongue-less mouth moving slowly with no sound escaping.

"Who is he?" Azh asked without a hint of unease.

"The man who was hurting you. I made it so he can never use magic to hurt anyone again."

Azh nodded and rested her head in the cradle of Raxe's taut biceps. "Good," she whispered as sleep claimed her.

Raxe carried his daughter from the oddly shaped building and across Shaddor Rinn's property. The contaminated aura was gone, replaced by the natural translucent white orbs of radiating magic that Raxe was accustomed to seeing.

He had guessed correctly. The spell form drawn in blood on the basement wall was the source of the spell that warded this property. When he destroyed the drawing he terminated the spell.

He noticed the fallen soldiers were beginning to stir. Those who were unconscious were waking up. Those who could stand were attempting to do so. Sergeant Samuel, with his shattered leg, could only sit upright.

"Is the warlock dead?" the squad leader asked, his voice hoarse with the pain of his broken bones.

"No," Raxe answered. "But I'm sure he wishes he was."

"After what he's done to us, we will make his wish come true soon enough," Samuel swore.

Raxe scoffed and walked on. "Karma's a bitch, ain't it?"

He met the Ranger Elf just outside the property line where he left him. The horses were grazing peacefully. Rell Kallen leaned casually against a tree, plucking seeds of some sort from a small pouch and popping them into his mouth. He looked up at Raxe with a slightly curious expression.

"I heard sounds of torture coming from the house," the elf observed. "Not very becoming for the great Raxe, Child of the Ones, dragon rider and demon slaying hero."

Raxe thought about the conversation he had earlier that evening with the younger incarnation of Shanderah. He had lost control a little, yet again. Was it right to torture and cripple the warlock? The honest answer was that, at least for the moment, he did not know if it was right.

But it damn sure *felt* right.

He looked at the elf. "Who the hell said I was a hero?" he rasped.

Chapter 11: Hargathall's Cleft

11.1

The offworlder, elf, and half-faerie arrived at Shaddiston an hour or so after dawn. Raxe was glad he had not lost his pack when the sky sleighs were brought down and doubly glad he had recovered it from the traitorous royal soldiers. Otherwise, they might have been forced to steal what they needed. If the elf carried money he was not about to admit it.

They paid a guide for directions to Hargathall's Cleft, and the price was certainly steep, but they could not pay anyone enough to accompany them. The people of Shaddiston felt much the same way about their kingdom as the people of Southborough. Very few people were willing to risk the treacherous mountain ranges. Of the few that were, no one was going to do it for the crown and a Child of the Old Ones.

The trio spent the rest of the day in Shaddiston resupplying their stores. At nightfall they found an inn with a proprietor who cared more about money than pride and politics. They tended to the horses and themselves and went to bed early so that they could rise at first light and continue their trek. The night passed without incident, to Raxe's delight, and they wasted no time continuing their journey.

The landscape at the southern edge of Shaddiston grew increasingly rougher as it elevated toward the Demon's Spine, so much so that the Ranger Elf decided it was too dangerous for the horses. Raxe wondered why the elf, being in such a hurry to find the Hell Key, cared about the loss of a couple of horses if it meant expediting their journey. He suspected the elf cared more about animals than humans.

So they walked. And Raxe quickly grew exhausted. He wondered if his half-faerie daughter and the elf felt the same. If they did they gave no indication of it. Azh seemed miraculously recovered from her trauma but it seemed to be just starting to catch up to Raxe. They had been walking nonstop for hours and their pace was as brisk as it had been when they set out. Neither the elf nor half-faerie complained. Neither of them seemed to be winded.

DEMON OF LORR

Not wanting to seem like the weak link in their small group, Raxe made an effort to not complain and tried his best to conceal his discomfort. All the while he wondered if his companions, with their superhuman perceptions, could tell how worn down he was.

Now the three of them trudged along the mountainside path that was supposed to take them to Hargathall's Cleft. Raxe exhaled in relief. His legs were sore and tired. The further they traveled, the more his injured right hand throbbed. Every step sent jolts of searing pain across the surface of his palm and fingers. The blood pulsing in his hand felt like acid coursing through his veins.

The suns' placement indicated that it was well past midday. The uneven and unyielding terrain only made the trek worse. They had encountered steep inclines and too many switchback paths to count. And somehow, the sun's light in the clear skies managed to shine bright enough to make him sweat despite cool autumn air and brisk mountain breezes that made the edges of his cloak flap behind him.

Raxe clutched with his left hand at the thick leather strap of the pack slung over his shoulder and grit his teeth against the damp, chill wind. He almost wished they were still in close proximity to the Forsaken Desert. Their destination currently led them east, away from the warm dry winds that buffeted them from the unnaturally warm desert region during that part of their trip.

Close proximity to the Forsaken Desert made the danger of encountering the demon-spawn sand creatures dwelling in and around the region worth the risk, though it was not a risk for Raxe. The creatures' presence sparked his magic. Having seen Rell Kallen in action against the *Ken d' Zanir*, he was fairly sure that the crafty and formidable Ranger Elf could hold his own against the four-tentacled sand creatures.

It was his daughter he was worried about. Raxe looked down at Azh and considered offering to carry her, but he was not sure she would accept the offer. As young as she was, he was surprised she was not already winded and had not asked to be carried. He would not hesitate if she asked but he feared she had not asked because she was still as uncertain about him as he was about her.

The only good thing about their travels had been his daughter. Azh's innocent and quietly pleasant demeanor was a welcome contrast to an otherwise monotonous trek and the tiresome standoffish attitude of the elf. If not for her, the trip would have been much less bearable. Anger warmed his right hand every time he thought about what the red mage had done to her and he had to struggle to contain his frustration.

Azh seemed more comfortable with him since he rescued her. The more time they spent together the more she opened up and endeared herself to him. She was not exactly talkative but eventually she began to ask direct, succinct questions about Raxe's home world and his past. Raxe soon found himself feeling a bit homesick as he talked continuously about Chicago, the United States, and other countries.

His time as an assassin for the organization was not a topic for discussion. He did speak briefly of his days as an Air Force pilot but even then he would not give any details about aerial combat.

At first Azh's inquisitive nature reminded Raxe of Quick. Three years earlier, Quick had bombarded him with similar questions. It quickly became evident that her curiosity dwarfed the changeling's. She asked follow up questions with a startling level of detail, demonstrating an uncanny ability to grasp concepts with impressive speed. He felt a growing sense of awe when he considered that this girl, who looked to be about six years old and sounded as intelligent as a ten year old, had only been alive for three years.

As the trip wore on she asked about all of the different types of technology in his world. Raxe was sorry he could not answer many of her technical questions in as much detail as he wanted. The only technical expertise Raxe had was in fighter jet flying and assassination. He had not been in a cockpit for so long that he wondered how outdated his knowledge was about even that.

It was early evening when they rounded a wide turn on the mountainside and Hargathall's Cleft swept into view.

DEMON OF LORR

All talking stopped.

Raxe had never seen anything like it. In his early twenties, his air force days, he had flown over the Karakoram and other mountain ranges of Pakistan. He once had to bail out over the Hindu Kush, an experience he was still trying to forget. In his brief career as a Cutter he led his team into a hidden installation in the Carpathians to extract a defecting scientist. In his late twenties he had performed hits, or "served pinked slips" as they called it, for the organization in both North American and South American mountain ranges.

In all of those harsh landscapes he had never seen a canyon or valley quite like Hargathall's Cleft. In, fact, from their elevated viewpoint it did not appear to be so much a naturally formed canyon as it did a clean, giant gash in the heart of the earth. The cleft stretched out over the southwestern horizon from the northeast in a smooth, soft arc. At just over a mile and a half at its widest point, it was nowhere near as far across as it was long.

They were at the location Bartok referenced: the northernmost point of the giant canyon. It also happened to be right where the cleft made a very brief southeastern turn and ended. They could see the rounded end of the canyon and Raxe estimated the distance around that curved edge to be more than four miles.

He was relieved that they could also see the small mountain pass Bartok told them to look for. The dwarf told them the best time of day to see the pass was at midday. It was closer to dusk than noon, but there was just enough light remaining for the keen-eyed elf to spot the pass. Raxe could also see it after Rell pointed it out to him.

Raxe turned his attention back to Hargathall's Cleft. The canyon walls were perfectly shear and fatally deep in some places. At other spots, it sloped steeply and was just barely traversable.

The shear walls were too perfectly straight to be natural. The sloping areas seemed to be where the less stable stretches of the earthen walls had crumbled away over time. The floor of the canyon was rocky in places but for the most part, what they could see of it was fairly level.

He whistled softly. "So the legend is that the Old One Hargathall cut this canyon into the ground with his colossal sword?"

"Possibly," Rell Kallen grunted. "But the legends have been translated by many different tongues over the course of millennia. Some speak of a giant sword. Some believe the mention of the sword is only a metaphor for a bolt of divine energy."

"And all of them say the cleft is cursed," Azh added casually. "Mother says the Old One Hargathall was one of the Leaders. He and the Old One Lorr destroyed each other in the battle, but not before Hargathall cursed this canyon for all of eternity."

"Indeed," Rell Kallen grunted distastefully. "It certainly reeks of old, stale death."

Raxe did not smell anything out of the ordinary but he knew better than to doubt the elf. He also remembered well what Rionn Lorr said about the canyon.

While it definitely looked strange, he could not detect anything sinister about it. He peered even more sharply at the canyon, paying particular attention to the shimmer of magic radiating from the cleft.

It was faint, no different than the rest of the rocky, windswept terrain, no different than the natural magical energies that radiated from every other landscape. But after hearing a little more about the story of the cleft's origins from his daughter, the Ranger Elf's condemning words about the smell of the place, and the Head Mage's warning before they set out on this mission, Raxe began to have doubts about crossing it.

"Maybe we should go around," he suggested.

Rell Kallen scoffed. "Don't be absurd. That would take far too much time."

"You're suddenly in a hurry again?" Raxe demanded. Annoyance made his already unnaturally raspy voice sound like two coarse rocks rubbed forcefully together. "We could've been here yesterday if you weren't so concerned about the death of a couple of horses. I suspect you cared more about them than us."

The Ranger Elf turned his sharply canted eyes on Raxe, his already thin lips pressed into a hard line. "Indeed I do, offworlder. But that isn't the only reason I left the horses behind. I don't know if you're familiar with wallowgrumps or rock badgers or mountain cats that, while not as large as tygras, still stand on all fours as tall or nearly as tall as an average human. These mountains are rife with them."

Raxe was all too familiar with wallowgrumps and rock badgers from his first visit to Lorr. A wallowgrump was one of the first creatures to greet him. Quick attacked him in the form of a rock badger.

"Any one of them would happily try to make a meal of us," the elf continued. "I've led us along a path to get us to this point as quickly as possible while allowing us to escape their notice. The scent of dead horseflesh would have attracted them to us like flies to dung.

"Going around the canyon might very well put us in the path of the very predators I seek to avoid. I cannot lose any more time or put us in greater danger because you fear old legends. You and your brat can go around the canyon if you choose. I'm going across."

Raxe had been wondering why they had not seen any animals in the mountain range. It made sense. The best way to avoid predators is to avoid their prey. Raxe had no doubt that the Ranger Elf could use his acute sight, hearing and sense of smell and likely years of tracking experience to do exactly what he said he had been doing.

Both mollified by the explanation and irritated by the elf's tone, he huffed. "I understand. But you don't have to be an asshole about it, man."

The elf, having no idea what the relevance of a hole in a beast of burden could be in this context, still knew he had been insulted. It was not, however, the reference to the animal that offended him. It was the last word of the offworlder's sentence.

"I am not a *man*," the elf said in an admonishing tone. "I

am far more than a weak human, and you would do well to remember that."

"Who's wasting time now, *elf?*" Raxe put as much sarcasm and derision as he could into that last word and still it did not rile the Ranger Elf as much as being called *man.* Raxe made a mental note of that.

Rell Kallen turned on his heels and stalked down the mountainside. Raxe stood watching, still debating whether or not he wanted to follow and trying to ignore the persistent and growing ache in his hand.

Azh, after watching the exchange curiously, looked at Raxe with her big curious eyes. "I thought you did not wish for Rell Kallen to find the Hell Key without you," she said.

"I don't," Raxe admitted. "Yeah, I guess we should get a move on. Hey, you want me to carry you? Your tiny little legs have to be tired after all of this walking."

"Not at all. You are the one who looks tired," Azh said matter-of-factly. "I was going to ask if you wanted *me* to carry *you.*"

Raxe raised an eyebrow at the Child less than half his size and wondered if she was joking. There was no hint of a smile on her face, only sincere concern. He wondered if she really could carry him. He started to ask if she was serious and then decided that he would rather not know.

"No thanks, Azh," he finally said. "I think I can make it. Let's go."

Azh turned and headed down the slope after the elf. She said over her shoulder as her father followed:

"Let me know if you change your mind."

Raxe chuckled and kept walking.

11.2

Within in a few minutes they were making their way down one of the sloping walls of the canyon. The vertical distance to the bottom was roughly a quarter of a mile, but the sloping path they had to take made the trip twice that long. When they finally reached the canyon floor they decided to take a brief pause to eat from their rations and drink from their water skins. Less than ten minutes passed before they were on the move once again.

The food and drink refreshed Raxe somewhat, but any relief he felt was soon swept away by a fresh wave of pain in his hand. His exertions with Shaddor Rinn aggravated the injured hand almost to the same level of agony he felt when he initially made the *gun* for Ethan. He started to wonder if the damage to the appendage had been necessary. There was no doubt in his mind at the time. Unfortunately, though, the conviction that spoke so strongly within him then had gone utterly silent.

Looking back, it seemed more than a little rash. As if the pain alone was not enough of a distraction, Raxe was right-handed. About the only things he *could* do well with his left hand were fight and shoot. He found himself torn between hoping Ethan never had to use the stave and hoping the youngster would have to use it often so that the sacrifice of his strong hand would not have been for nothing.

A Far Eastern breathing and meditation technique helped him cope with the pain that pulsed in time with his footsteps. It also helped to calm the frustration building within from second guessing himself. Before long, the pain that had been distracting him was relegated to a dull ache somewhere in the recesses of his consciousness. His doubts about his decision to forge the stave were pushed to distant memories. His internal focus excluded all but his breathing and footsteps.

His external focus on his daughter and the elf, both walking several yards ahead, made him only vaguely aware of the slow and deliberate movement of the two suns as they crept across the skies.

He barely took notice of the sharp wind that whipped across the bottom of the canyon and pressed his cloak against his muscled cuirass, or the warm rivulets of blood that started oozing from the painful seams between his crusted, healing flesh and the hardened Titan's Ore. Just over halfway across the canyon floor, the soft and sporadic patter of droplets of his blood on the ground joined the other muted sounds of their small procession.

Both suns had drifted down behind the wall of mountains to the west and Azh and Rell Kallen were already heading up the incline by the time Raxe made it to the far side of the cleft. His legs were aching in protest. Raxe prided himself on his conditioning but he had not walked this much since his last visit to Lorr.

Outdoor exercises of any kind, including walking or jogging, were not an option while he was on the run from the organization. He stayed indoors as much as possible to avoid the video cameras that seemed to be everywhere in his world. He also knew the organization had access to spy satellites that could take high definition pictures from space. He performed indoor exercises on a regular basis. He walked or jogged on treadmills and rode stationary bikes whenever he could. Even with all of his stretching and calisthenics, there was really nothing he could do to simulate the amount of walking on various terrains that he had done over the last several days.

Raxe was tempted to stop and sit on the ground for a brief respite before tackling the incline. He looked up at the half-faerie and Ranger elf sauntering up the incline and his ego decided him against it.

The decision saved his life. He would never have been able to get up in time when the dim, pale aura of magic radiating from the floor of Hargathall's Cleft flared into blinding luminescence.

The sudden change startled him into action and he immediately tried to leap the few remaining yards to the canyon wall. The attempt was in vain because his feet would not move. He looked down and was stunned to see that the rocky floor had risen above the bottom of his armored boots.

It was as if the rock had become liquid, crept up onto his feet, and hardened once more, rooting him to the spot. Only the rock was not liquid. It was solid, and it continued to inch up his feet while pulling him down at the same time.

The failed attempt to jump threw him completely off balance and he began to fall forward. He feared that if he tried to brace his fall with his hands, they would be snagged by the living stone as surely as his feet were. His arms windmilled as he fought to keep from toppling over but all that did was slow his inevitable fall.

"Offworlder!" Rell Kallen called.

Raxe looked up and saw that the elf, still a few yards up the sloping wall of the canyon, had removed his cloak. He flicked it out towards Raxe, who snatched it from the air with his left hand and held tight.

As much as Raxe wanted to feel relieved, he could not. Rell Kallen was immensely strong despite his slender frame yet he could not make any headway in his attempt to pull Raxe free. The stone floor continued to pull him down while creeping up along his feet toward his ankles. The stone did not only pull at him. It constricted, compressing with enough force for Raxe to actually feel the compression against his feet...*even through the enchanted metal of his invulnerable armored boots.*

Raxe was officially scared to freaking death. Other than Shanderah's dream-hug, he had never felt any external pressure through his armor. Even after falling from nearly a mile in the sky and while being chewed like a stick of gum by a giant fifth level sea demon, he did not feel so much as a twinge through the armored parts of his body. Now he had no doubt that no matter how the cleft was created, it was definitely created by an Old One. Only the magic of the gods could produce such force.

The foot of his armored boots terminated an inch above his ankle. From there, the boots were composed of three horizontally oriented rings of enchanted metal that protected his shins, each band just over an inch wide and a half inch thick, topped by a band wide enough to cover his calfs.

The rings and bands were spaced a few fingers' width apart and were held together by an inch-wide, vertically oriented rod of enchanted metal that ran down the front of his shins. It was attached to the foot of the boots by a nearly invisible hinge that allowed range of motion for Raxe's feet.

His fear was that once the cursed stone got above his ankles, it would thread through the spaces between the bands of his boots and pulverize the flesh and bone of his shins. His fear spiked when he heard and felt the fabric of Rell Kallen's cloak straining against the opposing forces of the elf's strength and the undeniable power of the cursed stone floor.

Raxe remembered Demonsbane. But he was holding onto the cloak with his good hand, so using that hand to pull the battleaxe free was not an option. At the angle he was being pulled he would slam to the ground the moment he released the cloak. The living stone would have his entire upper body.

With no choices left and the hungry stone edging closer to the top of his ankles, Raxe reached for Demonsbane with his ruined right hand. The hand was frozen with the fingers curled in a permanent clawing gesture, but the space between his curved thumb and his four fingertips and his palm were far too narrow for the battleaxe's handle.

Raxe slammed his damaged hand against the axe head with enough panic-enhanced strength to it snap painfully over the diamond-like jewel that held the large crescent blades where it rested atop the ring of his axe frog.

He did not even try to hold back his roar of agony when his damaged fingers were forced open, snapped back, and then constricted against the jewel. When he snatched Demonsbane from its frog, the smooth, sloping surface of the jewel allowed his hand to slide down to – and constrict around – the enchanted metal of the axe haft.

Acute pain, fear and adrenaline drove him to immediately hack down at the stone. Instead of biting into the earth as Raxe expected, the crescent blade rebounded with a loud toll.

The god-forged battleaxe with divinely keen edges barely nicked the canyon floor. Even more surprisingly, the blow brought a shrill, ear-splitting wail from somewhere deep beneath the cursed ground.

Raxe was heartened by the sound and the fact that the blow made the creeping stone hesitate in its pull. He hacked again and again at the living stone, letting his pain and panic power his assault. Each blow brought another cry of pain from him and another unearthly howl from below the earth. Both sounds were so loud that Raxe almost failed to notice the sound of the cloak finally ripping.

A new wave of fear surged through him as he raised Demonsbane for a final blow. Before he could bring the battleaxe down, the earth suddenly opened wide beneath him.

To Raxe's extremely good fortune the cloak had not completely torn free. It was intact enough for the sudden absence of the opposing force and the power of the Ranger Elf's pull to sling shot Raxe into the air. The fabric finally gave at the apex of Raxe's arc. The momentum sent him sailing a half dozen yards up the sloping canyon wall. There he landed face down, head pointing downslope, Demonsbane still clamped painfully in his right hand.

He took a moment to catch his breath and finally raised his head to look down at the spot where he had been stuck. It was now the roughly ten-foot wide termination point of a long, narrow wedge of blackness stretching perpendicularly away from the base of the canyon wall almost to the midpoint of the canyon floor.

He turned to Rell Kallen. "Thanks, ma-...elf."

"You're still useful to me," Rell Kallen snarled.

"Thanks anyway," Raxe returned. He inspected the new crevice again.

A sustained rumble like underground thunder rose from the bottom of the cleft. And then, as swiftly as it opened, the cavity slammed shut with a boom that shook the earth. The concussive wind that wafted past Raxe made him gag. Now he could smell what the Ranger Elf smelled when they first arrived at the cleft.

The air was so thick with the cloying stench of death and decay that Raxe could taste it.

He coughed until he had expelled any trace of the putrid wind and continued to stare where the wedged pit had been.

There was something about it that seemed familiar to him. It took a moment for him to realize that the wedge followed the exact same path the trio had taken across the bottom of the canyon. For some reason the wedge-shaped cavity ended, or started, a few feet past the the midpoint of the width of that part of the cleft…

…right where he started bleeding.

"I'll be damned," Raxe rasped.

"Why will you be damned?" Azh asked with concerned curiosity. She had eased silently over and was standing at his right shoulder.

"Just an expression," Raxe said, not wanting to verbalize the many reasons he likely would be. "I say that sometimes when I'm surprised."

"Why are you surprised?"

"I just realized why the Cleft tried to eat me," Raxe explained. "Once the sun went down my blood woke it up. That must've been a convenient little human disposal system for Mar-dah."

"It took this long for you to come to such an obvious conclusion?" Rell Kallen snapped as he stalked past.

Raxe got to his feet and stared after the elf. He chuckled coarsely and called after him.

"Stop bluffing, shorty! You know I figured it out first!"

The Ranger Elf did not spare the offworlder so much as a glance as he strode on.

"Why do you taunt the Ranger Elf?" Azh asked.

Raxe shrugged. He had not really thought about it. "I don't know. It's fun. I guess I just don't like him."

He gripped Demonsbane with his left hand and gave a powerful yank, snatching the battleaxe painfully from his clawed right hand.

"Shit!" he barked, the sudden agony too sharp to suppress the expletive. He looked guiltily at his daughter.

"That's just an expression, too, Azh. It's not for children to repeat. Understand?"

Azh smiled suddenly. It was a brief flash of teeth that reverted back to her usual serious and curious aspect.

"You are strange," she said, making it sound like a compliment.

11.3

LAS VEGAS

Dan was right. I hate *this damn plan.*

Lisa frowned in both concentration and irritation. Sitting on the king-sized bed and assembling the small, hard-plastic pistol, she focused on fitting the pieces together correctly and snapping them firmly into place. It took her days to get up the nerve to put the gun together and she was ashamed of that fact. Dan would have complained incessantly if he knew. And she would have deserved it.

This was her fourth night at the Las Vegas hotel. For the first three nights she tried to ignore the individual pieces of the pistol spread out among her three bags. The small cylinders, pins and cartridges were camouflaged as common items found in travelers' luggage and carry-on bags, including makeup kits, electric toothbrushes and personal computing and communication devices.

Four slender ammunition cartridges filled with explosive plastic bullets were hidden in the ridiculously high, blocky heels and soles of the wedge shoes she wore on the flight from Memphis. The bullets and soles were made of the same hard plastic alloy and compressed together so tightly that the airport baggage scanner read each sole as one solid piece.

She had almost forgotten some of the steps to putting the gun together that Dan had her memorize. When he first showed her how, it had taken her two days of monotonous assembly and disassembly to finally learn to put the gun together without his help. Tonight, after a couple of hesitant moments and backtracking, she eventually put the pistol together. It took just under an hour.

It looked like a toy. It felt like a toy. According to Dan, though, it was far from a toy. From what she saw of his modified shotgun/machine gun, she was inclined to believe him. That customized weapon looked every bit like a futuristic child's toy that shot water or pellets, but she watched Dan use it to blow a man's head almost completely from his shoulders.

DEMON OF LORR

Dan explained that her plastic gun was not as powerful as a standard handgun, but it was easily powerful enough to make its ammunition penetrate flesh, muscle, and bone at close range. The explosive rounds would do maximum internal damage once they did. Dan would have been pissed that she waited so long to assemble the pistol but he would have been proud that she was able to do it without him being there to look over her shoulder.

That was why she was irritated. Dan was not there. His plan consisted of him submitting a fake flight plan to Dallas to throw their pursuers off their trail temporarily while only flying as far as Meridian, Mississippi. He expertly landed the small stolen airplane on a desolate country road just outside of the city. From there, Dan managed to walk, with more than a little help from Lisa, to a nearby tavern where they called a cab.

He had the cab drive them to the airport where he suggested that they split up and fly to different cities, which Lisa thought was ludicrous. His rationale was that the demon and the organization were not looking for her. They had been after Raxe, Joel and Dan because they were Children of the Old Ones and therefore a threat to the Demon. Dan insisted that it was likely tracking them using not only organization resources but also by following Dan's magical aura. Lisa was safer on her own than with a crippled old man acting as a beacon for their pursuers.

Lisa argued vehemently at first. Dan was insistent, and the vehemence of his insistence was greater than her reluctance. He might have been flirtatious and flippant most of the time, but when he was resolute, he could be as immovable as a stubborn old bull elephant. She had seen him in action, too, so she knew he could be just as dangerous. She watched him, a man close to two hundred years old if not older, use one bare hand to kill a young would-be robber. She saw him perform feats of magic that were potentially fatal to his enemies. Lisa witnessed the serious side beneath his lighthearted façade and knew that side of his personality was not to be trifled with, so she finally relented.

Even though Dan thought she would be safer on her own, he still insisted she stay well under the radar. He produced four fake IDs and credit cards that he assured her were beyond detection and without limits respectively. And then there was the silent, plastic gun that was absolutely fatal within ten feet. When Lisa questioned why he gave her such a small gun with such limited range he explained that she was not a good enough shot to hit anything any further away. Even though that meant letting an assailant get dangerously close, it was better to save the bullets and make them count if she ever had to use them.

She wondered if she was assembling it now only because her paranoia had gotten the best of her. She had never left the hotel. She never had to. There were enough eateries in the palatial hotel/casino for her to enjoy a variety of cuisines. There was an exercise room with a pool if she wanted to work out. The credit cards Dan provided would allow her to get into any show taking place in the multiple theaters within the complex had she been inclined to see them.

If she had not been afraid of being spotted by spies or demons, this would have been an excellent vacation. Until the previous night she had not even left her room. The room service was great and her suite was luxurious.

Eventually, though, she began to feel claustrophobic, even in the spacious suite. She decided to check out one of the popular buffets on the lower floors.

The experience was horrible. The food was delicious but Lisa found herself looking around every corner and peeking behind every wide column she passed, expecting a "spook" of one type or another to jump out at her at any moment. The worst part was that she did notice someone paying a bit too much attention to her. She was disguised then as she was tonight, with a reddish brown wig of straight hair that spilled down over her shoulders with long bangs that ended in a straight line just above her eyes. She paid acute attention to Dan when he applied makeup and spirit gum to disguise both of them. As a result she did an excellent job of darkening her skin and widening the tip of her nose.

DEMON OF LORR

Dark green contacts hid her brown eyes and even those were shaded with non-prescription eyeglasses with a light-brown tint. She wore the same shoes that hid her ammunition, and with her form-fitting but surprisingly comfortable black jeans, a low-cut, burgundy silk tank-top, and a black leather blazer completing her disguise, Lisa knew that at the moment she looked nothing like the woman that the organization was searching for. She should not have had to worry about being spotted.

That assurance went out the window last night when she spied the intense gaze of a tall, pale skinned man with short, neatly cut, light brown hair eyeing her from his seat in the middle of the restaurant. He watched her while sitting across a small table from a pretty, long-legged and tanned blonde. The woman never made direct eye contact, but Lisa was sure she was watching her out of the corner of her eye.

After wolfing down her food she hurried back up to her room, locked the door, took off the wig, and rubbed her forehead furiously with both hands for several minutes before finally forcing herself to stop. She told herself that the man was just admiring her. Lisa knew men found her attractive. That would not have been the first time she was ogled by a man even while accompanied by a female companion.

She was able to calm herself down enough to turn on the television and flip through the channels. Her attention was momentarily arrested by the tail end of a braking news story concerning a sunken inland oil tanker. The tanker reportedly went down in the Gulf of Oman in southwest Asia. The governments of the surrounding Middle Eastern countries were not volunteering useful details, but stories steadily leaked to the press. The vessel had not yet been located and there was no spill visible in the gulf to indicate where it might have gone down.

The story that followed did not interest her so she started surfing again. She could not find anything else of interest but at least the activity was distracting.

A smile lifted the corners of her mouth when her channel surfing reminded her of the Head Mage Rionn Lorr. Before he took her husband away from this world into the Kingdom of Lorr, he had been fascinated by the television and raced through the channels the same way Lisa did that evening.

And then she gasped and dropped the remote control to the floor. It took her a moment to catch her breath when she saw herself, without a wig or disguising makeup, smiling back at her from the flat panel television resting in the polished oak armoire. It was a picture of her taken a few years earlier that her parents kept on their mantle.

"Oh, God," she whispered.

The anchorwoman was reporting Lisa's disappearance. Lisa was too stunned to make out all the words. All she could catch were scattered words like "successful veterinarian" and "her career on the rise" and "possibly kidnapped" and "she and her husband may have been in an automobile accident."

Lisa's mother and father appeared on screen, both tearful and anxious, and then Lisa felt hot tears running down her own cheeks.

Her mother held another picture, this one of Lisa and Joel at a dinner party taken the year before. She was begging the world to contact the authorities if they had any information that would help them find her "baby girl." Her father had to hold the trembling woman up to keep her from collapsing. Her father almost violently denied reports leaked by the organization about Lisa and Dan being wanted fugitives.

The big middle-aged man, not yet bowed by time, insisted that: "if she's with him at all, that old man took her against her will. And I pray that Joel is all right. He would never let anyone take Lisa away from him."

A sleepless night of weeping followed. All Lisa could think about was her parents' anguish. She wanted to call them but Dan had warned her about the danger of contacting anyone, be they family or friends.

The organization almost certainly had the phones and computers of everyone close to Lisa monitored. They had the resources to track her down "almost instantly," Dan told her. She might not have been their target, but Dan promised that they would not hesitate to use her to get to her husband, Dan, and Ryan if the opportunity presented itself. It was in everyone's best interest for her to be difficult to find.

The next day was spent in a numb fog. Lisa mechanically went through the motions of showering and ordering room service for breakfast and lunch. The entire time she could think about nothing but her parents and other family members that had to be worried sick about her and Joel.

At dawn, Lisa knew what she had to do. That was when she started assembling her pistol.

The television had not been turned on since she turned it off after the disturbing news report. The last thing she wanted to see was more footage of her disappearance. She finished putting the firearm together that evening and slid one of the slender cartridges into the grip. A loud snap confirmed its correct insertion. The sound startled her in the silent suite.

A nervous hand started for her forehead but she stopped it an inch away. Instead, she used the hand to support the pistol as she brought it up and aimed it at an invisible assailant. She visualized the tall, thin man from the buffet and the woman with whom he was sitting.

"I hope you two aren't looking for me," she whispered with as much bravado as she could muster.

"You won't like what you find."

She dropped the small pistol into her purse, slung the purse over her shoulder and walked out of the suite.

11.4

PORTLAND, OR

Dan lay flat on his back in the king-sized bed, looking up at the ceiling and listening to the slow winter rain drumming against the fifteenth floor window of the waterfront hotel in downtown Portland, OR. The gray sky outside his window reflected his mood.

He was tired…tired of that damned wheelchair he now had to use again, tired of hotels, tired of running. The incident with Nathaniel shook him more than he wanted to admit. Dan was sure he hid his despair from Lisa even though on the inside, the treachery made his pain and exhaustion that much tougher to bear. Nathaniel Sr. and his family had always been like Dan's own extended family. Nate Junior's betrayal was like a sucker punch to the gut.

What was worse was that Dan knew it should not have affected him so much. Back in his more active days he would have been prepared for that possibility. There was no point in denying that he was feeling his age. Child of the Old Ones or not, the weight of two hundred years, too many of them spent fighting and killing, had caught up with him.

There was no point in wasting any more time. It was time for Dan to confront the bastards chasing him and get this over with. He knew he would not have to wait very long. He could feel them or coming, or more accurately, he could feel *it* coming. That hungry, feral magic had been trailing him since he left Chicago.

Dan knew the organization was searching for him using conventional means that he could evade. He and Ryan had done it for years. The red-light camera upgrades in Indiana were a new twist but he could handle that. A little research revealed the existence of new thermal sensor technology that used heat signatures to tell the difference between human flesh and prosthetics like the spirit gum he used to alter their appearance. After a couple of phone calls he acquired a new kind of spirit gum, one with a chemical agent that reacted to human skin by warming to match body heat.

DEMON OF LORR

The magic that trailed him was a different story. Dan felt it following him. Whoever – or whatever – it was that tracked him moved relatively slow. There were times when it seemed to pause. Sometimes the pause would last for a few minutes and sometimes for a couple of hours. He noticed that the sensation seemed to fade when Dan traveled by air but would slowly, inexorably continue to move in his direction.

The magic was more than simple evil. It was positively *voracious*. An undercurrent of savage and ravenous hunger permeated the magic, and for the first time in a very long time Dan was truly afraid for his own safety.

He was tired of being afraid. That was why he sent Lisa away. He did not want her to face whatever it was that pursued him. Dan was afraid that he would be distracted worrying for Lisa's safety instead of fighting with all he had when the dread magic ran them down. And it would run them down eventually. Every time he shook the organization the magic kept coming, tracking him like a bloodhound. It obviously could not pinpoint his exact location, though. If it could the demon's organization resources would have had him and Lisa long before now. And because Dan was certain that he was the beacon for the demon and the organization, Lisa was safer now that she was alone.

He felt horrible about splitting up with her but he knew they could not run forever. As of yet the demon had not gotten personally involved. Dan actually wished the demon would. Its mere presence would ignite the divine power within him, making him physically powerful despite his withering muscles and brittle bones.

That power would also fortify the few spells Dan had at his command. He had a few tricks up his sleeve that just might do away with the demon. The problem was that the demon realized this, too, and it was not going to make things that easy for the oldest living Child of the Old Ones. It was content to let subordinate magic and the organization do its dirty work.

They both knew that Dan had less of a chance against the organization once they caught up with him. It was a good plan: use magic to run him down and then bullets to kill him.

In any event, Dan would be ready. He had been resting for the last few days, using Shanderah's revitalizing spell while recalling every other potentially useful spell she shared with him over the years through their ability to communicate across the WorldGate. Local contacts allowed him to compile a small arsenal of small arms and explosives.

He did not fool himself into thinking it would be enough to defeat them, but he would do as much damage as he could before they took him down. He hoped that when the organization was done with him they would no longer worry about Lisa. If not, at least he would have bought her some time. If she followed his simple instructions she could avoid the organization indefinitely. When Joel and Ryan came back, Dan knew Ryan would be able to find her.

A phone rang. Dan snapped to a sitting position and looked over at the duffle bag sitting on the floor at the foot of his bed. He knew immediately from the chime that it was not the room phone. Every phone in his duffle had a different ring tone. It was something he did on purpose so that he would know which phone was ringing and would therefore have a pretty good idea of who was calling. This particular ring tone was from one of the phones he hoped would never ring, even though he was not overly surprised.

By the fourth ring he had managed to scoot over to the edge of the bed, pull the duffle bag into his lap, and fish out the ringing phone.

"Who'd she contact?" Dan asked without preamble.

"C'mon, uncle Dan," came a familiar voice. "No 'hi nephew' or some other nicety?"

"I'm not your uncle," Dan grunted.

"Stop being a hard-ass, unc. You're my uncle's father-in-law. By my math that makes you my uncle."

"Math never was a strong suit of your family," Dan said. "And I'm your uncle's *ex* father-in-law. That bastard left my daughter."

"Yeah, yeah," the man on the other end said. "If you really held that against his whole family you wouldn't be talking to me now."

"You're useful, Oscar," Dan reminded in an even tone.

The voice on the other end chuckled. "He was the only one of us you disliked and you know it. If you want this info, be nice. When you called to ask this favor we barely spoke. It's the least you could do, knowing I could get into all kinds of trouble if the agency found out what I was doing for you."

Dan sighed and finally cracked a smile despite his impatience. He had known Oscar since he was in diapers and watched him grow up in the fifteen years Cynthia and Martin were married before Ryan was born. Dan and Cynthia really had been close to her husband's family.

Before then he and Cynthia only had each other. His ex son-in-law's family welcomed them with open arms making them feel like they had always been a part of the family.

It was too bad Martin could not learn to deal with the truth about Dan and his daughter's legacy. After Martin left Cynthia shortly following Ryan's birth, Dan stayed in touch with a few people in Martin's family. Oscar was one of them. And when Oscar eventually joined the CIA as a technical analyst, he became a valuable resource for Dan and Ryan.

"It's nice to talk you, Oscar, it really is. Sorry it's been so long. How's the family? And you know I don't wanna hear about Martin."

"They're fine," Oscar said. "Same old, same old. All three of the kids are in college now, so I'm broke."

Dan was gritting his teeth in an effort to control his waning patience. It would not have been fair to snap at Oscar. He agreed to help and asked no questions when Dan had not volunteered any details. Oscar was right. The least Dan could do was be nice.

"I'm sorry, Oscar," Dan began, "But I – "

"I know," Oscar said. "You're in a hurry. I didn't think you were still in the spy game, but since you obviously are, I'll stop lollygagging."

"Thanks for understanding," Dan said sincerely.

"She sent an email to her second cousin," Oscar explained, "using a new email address and fake name. It was sent from an all-night library in Vegas."

"If the email was new and it wasn't her name, how'd you know it was Lisa?" Dan questioned.

"The content of the message," Oscar snickered. "It was cute. The fake name she used was 'Sugar Brown.' On top of that, the content of the letter was something like, 'Tell Junior and Mae we're safe and having fun on vacation. We'll be back soon.' The 'Sugar Brown' name sounded like a nickname to me so I did some digging. I found her high-school yearbook."

"Her nickname in high school was, of course, Brown Sugar. A little more digging and I found out that Junior and Mae are her father's and mother's family nicknames respectively."

Dan shook his head slowly as he listened. "At least the girl tried."

"Yeah," Oscar agreed, "but if I found all this out in a couple of hours someone else can. I don't know what you're into, Uncle Dan, but I know it's not good. You're not on the CIA's radar right now but the FBI is looking for you. And for some strange reason I have a feeling they're not the only ones. You be careful."

"I will, Martin."

"Is Ryan safe?" Oscar asked.

"We're not in touch right now, but I'm pretty sure he's OK," Dan answered. He could still feel his grandson's aura. It was as faint as it always was when they were on different sides of the WorldGate, but Dan could feel it nonetheless. If nothing else, Ryan at least was alive.

"Just wondering," Oscar went on. "I don't know much about the outfit he worked for, which in itself scares the shit outta me."

"Watch your language," Dan chided.

"Watch your backside, unc."

"Mine and everyone else's, and that's a promise. Tell your mom and dad I said hello."

"I'll tell Uncle Martin, too."

"Not funny. Talk to you later."

"You better," Oscar said with a hint of worry.

Dan pressed the off button and dropped the cell phone on the bed.

"I told you not to contact anyone for any reason," Dan said as if Lisa was sitting right next to him. He could not really blame her, though. She was not accustomed to life on the run or in hiding. When Dan saw the news report about her disappearance he knew it would have the effect the organization intended.

Dan had asked Oscar to monitor the email accounts and phones – both wireless and land lines – of as many as Lisa's family and friends as they could identify because he knew the organization would do the same. He was proud of Lisa's effort but the fact that she was thoughtful enough to attempt to disguise the message was cold comfort. If the organization did not already know where she was they would find out in short order.

Now Dan had to find the next available flight to Las Vegas. His confrontation would have to be postponed.

Chapter 12: Flight

12.1

EASTEDGE

Joel and Dayna awoke with alarm at the loud clang of their cell door unlocking. Their chains did not give any slack, which was an immediate indication that they were not about to receive food. That meant one of two things, if not both: a beating for Joel...or worse for Dayna.

Joel looked at Dayna, his forehead lined with worry. She looked at him with equal concern. They looked back at the heavy door swinging open. The dim glow of the corridor torchlight was enough to hurt their eyes after so many hours of complete darkness. Joel's heart dropped when the shadow of Tauran's bulk filled the doorway again.

His silhouette resolved as he stepped slowly into the cell. He regarded Joel with a sneer that was meant to be intimidating. Joel was in too much pain to care. But then that wolfish leer that Joel had learned to hate spread across Tauran's bearded face as he turned to Dayna.

"My love," he taunted. "It has come to my attention that you made me kill Jessup for nothing."

Joel's eyes widened in fear and surprise.

"What are you prattling on about, Tauran?" Dayna complained. "I spoke true. Whoever says different is a liar."

"You hear that, Bartholomew?" Tauran called. "She calls you a liar!"

A look of murderous anger flashed across Dayna's face for less than a second before she could replace it with her cold, defiant glare.

"If Bartholomew told you that, he lied," Dayna assured.

Tauran gave a knowing grin. "Your exhaustion has worn you down. You can no longer mask your feelings."

"What false promise did the false Baron offer to make the coward Bartholomew tell such a lie?" Dayna demanded.

"That pretty face of yours puts the lie to your words," Tauran said. "That is good. That means you will no longer be able to contain your joy when we have our way with you."

Leesil walked into the room. A smug half-grin curved up one side of his mouth while his eyes glinted a hardness that made the hair on the back of Joel's neck stand on end.

A bitter scent filled Joel's nostrils. It came from the two men inside the cell and from more men outside. The smell triggered something in Joel's consciousness. It was not the smell of magic, of that he was sure.

Through the invisible but pungent cloud of alcohol wafting from their pores and the booze-soaked breath of the loud-talking baron, there was something that whispered to him of madness. There was a pent-up frenzy within them, along with cold and dark expectancy. And there was one more scent. It was the cloying odor of fear and despair.

Another prisoner?

Two of Tauran's brutes drug in a third man by his chain-bound hands and feet. The prisoner was a severely thin, long limbed man with dark brown skin. His face was drawn, his cheeks hollow and his full lips, where not caked with dark brown dried blood, were swollen and cracked and purple. His face was contorted in pain and fear. His eyes, one purple and swollen, were closed tightly.

All the hair was shaved from his near naked body. A loincloth was the only thing between him and complete nudity. His ashen skin was almost gray and riddled with bruises and cuts, some fresh but many more scabrous. The top of his shaven head bore bluish knots and abrasions, making Joel wonder how many concussions the poor man had suffered. But the strangest thing about the man was that he was soaking wet. And judging by the goose bumps covering the prisoner's skin from head to toe, the water had been ice cold.

Dayna gasped at the sight of the man. Tears instantly filled her eyes and she cast a pleading look at Tauran.

"Please," she begged. "No. Not in front of him."

Joel's breath caught in his throat. The fear in her eyes betrayed her love for the prisoner. He had seen the same look of fear in Lisa's eyes after he killed those men on that snow covered Illinois highway, and just before he crossed the WorldGate with Rionn Lorr and Raxe. This man was either her husband or someone she loved like one.

"C'mon, baron!" Joel pled. "You can't do this."

Tauran turned his dark glare on Joel. "You have no idea what I can do." He paused for the briefest of moments, as if reliving a dark memory. The pause gave Joel a chill.

The baron shook away the recollection and continued. "For instance, I can promise Bartholomew that I'll not slaughter his foolish rebels who think they wait unnoticed in the forests just outside of my stronghold. I can have a small detachment of the Darshayan army, loaned to me by the king himself, soak the forest with their blood!"

He spoke the last sentence loud enough to make sure everyone in Joel's cell and the surrounding cells heard it.

"Tauran!" Bartholomew bellowed. "You bastard!"

"You *fool*! Bartholomew!" barked Dayna.

"Silence!" roared Tauran.

The sudden blast of his baritone voice gave everyone a start. It resounded painfully in Joel's skull, which already throbbed from the constant pain of his wounds, his fear for Dayna, pity for the man she loved, and his own despair at having to witness such horror.

"Jessup was a good man," the baron went on. "Your treachery has made me lose respect for you. At our last encounter, I shared you only with my longest friend, Leesil." Leesil, over-dressed as usual, gave a mocking bow as Tauran continued. "But now I will share you with the men who labored to bring your husband here to witness the festivities."

"You are worst than your demon employer," Dayna snarled. "There will be a special place for you among the seven hells."

Tauran paused. Joel noticed how the big man stiffened at the mention of the words "demon employer" as if it had come as a surprise.

"What?" Dayna challenged. "You didn't know you were working for a demon? Do you think it will pay you for your service with anything other than a bad death?"

Tauran quickly composed himself and scoffed. "If I can help it, pretty one, I'll live long enough and grow powerful enough to reside in the seventh level of hell after I finally die of old age."

"If the Baron does not object," Leesil interjected in a respectful tone. "While I do so enjoy this banter, I am quite eager for another taste of this one. She was exquisite."

"By all means," Tauran said, mocking Leesil with an exaggerated bow and a more proper accent. "I'll even be so kind as to let you go first."

"I'll tell you what you want to know," cried the prisoner in a dry, cracked voice. He opened bloodshot, tired eyes glistening with tears. Pain and confusion and fear could all be heard in his plea. "Just, I beg you, do not touch my wife."

"Jon! No!" pled Dayna. "You cannot! Do you believe he will stick to his bargain? Did you not just hear how he honored his agreement with Bartholomew? These men will do as they please no matter what. How many will die if you tell them what they want to know?"

The man could barely contain a sob as he cast a guilty look at Dayna. "I am so sorry, my love," he groaned.

"Don't be sorry," Dayna implored. "Be silent, my husband. And be *angry*."

"That's enough," Tauran declared. "Leesil?"

Leesil's hawk-like face was split with a toothy grin as he stepped toward Dayna, loosening his weapons belt.

No. Joel thought to himself. He promised himself and Dayna that he would not let this happen to her again. Joel could tell she had a good heart. And although he did not know this strange captive from Adam, his innate ability to understand people told him that Jon was a good man, too. They did not deserve this fate.

Oh, but they do, came the mocking whisper, *the evil*. And it was not the demon, Joel realized to his horror.

He had convinced himself that it had been the Dierglyorr trying to tempt him all this time, to turn him. But the whisper that mocked him in his waking hours, the evil that pursued him in his dreams, it had always been himself.

They deserve it and you deserve to watch. You all deserve anything and everything you're too weak to prevent.

God no...please, Joel prayed. *The priests, the preachers, they all told me You would never give us a burden too heavy to bear. How on earth can they bear* this*?*

You still believe in God, Joel? After all of this, how in the hell can you still believe?

A minister once told Joel that the Lord always gave his children the tools they needed to overcome hardships, but he often left it up to them to use those tools.

Where can I find the strength to help Dayna the way I swore I would?

You can't. The holy men were full of shit. Your precious Bible is even worse. It never spoke of a WorldGate. It never spoke of Children of the Old Ones. You know why? It's all bullshit, that's why. There's nothing but the here and now, and what you make of it. Take some good advice for once, Joel. Give up. There's nothing for you here and now but death and madness. Embrace one or the other...or both

Dayna's words to her husband then echoed in Joel's head.

Be angry.

Joel ignored *the evil's* whisper and decided to take Dayna's advice.

It was easier than he expected. All he had to do was think of all of the things he had seen and gone through. From the encounter with the agents posing as gangsters on that Illinois highway to almost murdering his own wife while in the throes of a nightmare, to everything that had happened to him since he crossed the WorldGate. It did not take much to get past his despair and find a smoldering anger.

There was anger at the unfairness of his life. The thought of his pregnant wife running for her life with a two hundred year old man as her only protection filled him with fury.

He allowed the helplessness of his abduction and imprisonment, his torture and the torture of the unfortunate couple before him to bring forth a flow of rage that cleared the haze of pain and melancholy that had clouded his mind for so long. He knew what he had to do.

"What kind of cowards are you motherfuckers?" Joel wondered aloud. "Especially you, Leesil."

This stopped the well-dressed rapist in his tracks. His shirt was almost completely unbuttoned, revealing his lean chest and flat, hard stomach.

"Especially me?" he asked with humor.

"You can't fool me," Joel accused. "You're more eager than anyone else here, aren't you? I can *smell* it on you. Why is that?"

Leesil chuckled. "She is ever-so-pleasant on the eyes, is she not?" He turned a taunting look to Jon where he lay on the cell floor. "Even in this pitiful state. You can not even imagine how good she *feels*."

"That's not it, Leesil," Joel countered. "You're over-compensating. You know what that means? It means you don't really enjoy the act, but you don't want your boys to know that so you try too hard. Look at you. You play the ladies man. But that's all it is, right? Play?"

Tauran teased with a loud guffaw. "What is this, Leesil? What is it you don't want us to know?"

"This fool rambles on about nothing," Leesil said a little too quickly. He spoke with transparently forced indifference, almost defensively.

"He doesn't want you to know that what he really enjoys is *you* watching him," Joel said knowingly.

"Shut your mouth!" Leesil snapped, snatching up his rapier. "I'll shove this blade down your lying throat."

"Whoa, there!" Tauran laughed loudly. "It seems he's struck a nerve!"

"Leesil wants you to notice *him*, not her," Joel reiterated. "And I noticed the last time that he was watching you, baron, more than he watched her."

Leesil took hurried steps toward Joel with his rapier in hand. "Say not another word, you deceitful bastard!"

"Leesil," Tauran warned. "Don't be a fool."

"You imagined she was the baron when you were with her, didn't you? You imagined it was him bent over and taking you and loving it. And when you watch him with her, you pretend it's you in her place. Just admit it, man. You know what I think of pretenders like you?"

Joel quickly hawked and spit a thick gob of phlegm for good measure, striking Leesil with a splash that stained his face and shirt with both spittle and blood.

"SILENCE" Leesil howled before launching himself at Joel with his sword raised.

An outline of deep red suddenly rimmed the edges of Joel's vision. He thought briefly of the last nightmare he had about the monstrous, glowing red-eyed version of himself, *the evil*, and how he was able to deny his urge to kill. As the darkness rushed upon him, three words echoed in his head.

Do not kill.

12.2

An unreasonable and unexpected rage filled Leesil when he heard the offworlder's insults. How dare such a weak, pitiful man question *his* manhood? In front of his peers, no less! The offworlder hung there half conscious and emaciated, looking like nothing so much as a starved cur, yet had the gall to taunt his betters. Leesil would silence the fool's lies with one stroke of his rapier.

As he lunged at Joel, he noticed with cold dread that the offworlder's eyes had turned milky white. Common sense finally pushed aside his embarrassment and rage but it was far too late. Leesil had committed to the killing blow. His momentum carried him forward and his sword was more than halfway home.

With a mighty heave, Joel thrust his arms and legs forward. He yanked the braces on his shins from the wall, sending the long bolts that secured them to the stone bouncing away. A metallic clank reverberated through the walls as the hidden lock gave way. The thick chains attached to Joel's wrist manacles and threaded into the wall came flying out with violent speed. A length of the chains curled outward to knock Leesil's blade arm away and strike Leesil across the face, abruptly reversing his momentum and sending him crashing to the floor.

Dayna watched with breathless fascination. She had witnessed the change in his eyes before, but this time, his shoulders grew broader under his filthy, tattered shirt and his arms had grown freakishly longer without getting any thicker. Greenish blue veins popped out under his dull brown skin. His arms, which had looked bony and frail a moment earlier swelled freakishly at the joints.

Tauran hurtled Dayna's husband and hurried out of the cell as Joel whipped the heavy chains around again. This time, he caught Tauran's two underlings as they turned to follow their master. The thick chains slammed into their backs and threw them both across the cell and against the rocky wall.

Dayna's eyes never left the offworlder. After the last two men slid to the floor and went still, so did Joel. He sunk to his knees and stared at the floor. His arms shrank back to their normal length and his joints snapped back to normal before Dayna's wide eyes. He blinked for a few seconds and when he was done, the milky white film that filled his eyes was gone. He turned his tired brown eyes to Dayna.

"Are you back, offworlder?" she asked.

Joel then turned a worried glance to Leesil and the baron's other men. He scrambled to over to Leesil and checked his pulse.

Dayna frowned. "What are you doing?"

"Checking to see if they're dead," Joel answered, going from Leesil to the other men.

"Would you like to check any of them for keys?" Dayna suggested.

It finally dawned on Joel that he was actually free. He was seized with a moment of uncertainty similar to what he felt when he broke his bonds during the first few days of his imprisonment. What were the chances of escape? Where would he go?

And then he thought about what he had gone through since that time and the decision was easy. By the time Dayna barked his name again, Joel was already rifling through Leesil's pockets. He found a set of keys within moments. A few moments later he was free of his bonds and freeing Dayna, helping her to steady herself on her bare feet.

Dayna spared a moment to rub her aching wrists and enjoy her relative freedom before turning to the offworlder.

"So? Are they dead?" she asked.

"No," Joel said with relief.

"Good." Dayna stepped over Leesil and retrieved his rapier from the floor.

She gave the fallen jailer a long, hard look before spitting in his face. The action roused Leesil. His eyes opened and the first thing he saw was Dayna standing over him. Unchained.

Before he could say a word she swung the rapier.

Leesil's words were lost in a gurgle of the blood from his slit throat filling his newly opened windpipe.

"What the hell?" Joel started.

Dayna's fierce glare quieted him. "If we had more time," she snarled. "I would have castrated him first. I only wish both he *and* Tauran were lying here."

She looked over at her husband. He had managed to get to his hands and knees but he was too weak to stand. She knelt before him, set Leesil's rapier on the floor, gathered his bony frame in her arms and helped him to his feet. Joel could tell the man was close to six feet six inches tall and worried that Dayna would not be able to hold him. The look of worried surprise that fell across her face like a veil betrayed her concern for how light her husband was.

"We have to leave here, and quickly," she declared.

"How?" Joel asked.

"You need a distraction!" called Bartholomew. Both Joel and Dayna turned at the sound of his voice.

"Free us!" he continued. "We'll help you escape. Surely we will be able to occupy the men that the Baron will be sending straightaway."

Dayna's hazel-brown eyes turned angry and cold once more. "Come, Joel, support my husband."

Joel did as Dayna asked. He was not sure he would be strong enough to hold up the long, lanky man. However, the adrenaline pumping through him along with her husband's malnourished condition made the task of supporting the half conscious man easier than he expected. Once Joel was holding him securely Dayna snatched the keys from Joel's hand, scooped up the rapier and purposefully stalked out of the cell.

As she stepped through the open doorway and turned in the direction of Bartholomew's cell, Joel looked around his own filthy chamber. His eyes fell upon Leesil's dead body and remembered that Bartholomew had sold Dayna out. That was when he realized that she was probably not planning to actually free Bartholomew.

Holding the tall man carefully, Joel made his way as quickly as he could to the outer hall. He was just in time to see Dayna pressing the point of Leesil's rapier against the throat of a fair-skinned man with long, dirty, dark brown hair and a bushy, unkempt beard. The prisoner was chained the same way Joel and Dayna had been: his arms stretched above his head, his wrists manacled with chains trailing from the manacles through holes in the wall. His legs were splayed to the left and right and shackled. The chains were bolted firmly to the walls. Two other men, similarly bound, hung from the adjacent walls and worriedly eyed the woman with the sword to their cellmate's throat.

"Give me one reason not to kill you, you son of a whore."

Bartholomew's fearful eyes were riveted to the bloody blade tip. He tried to move his head back but it was already pressed painfully against the wall.

"I...I just d-did," he stammered. "We can distract the false baron's men as you make your escape."

"And why should I trust you?" she snarled, putting enough pressure behind the blade to draw a droplet of blood. "You've betrayed me once."

"I did that for my men," Bartholomew explained anxiously. "Tauran promised not to slaughter the rebels hiding in the forest if I reported your conversations to him. Wouldn't you have done the same?"

Dayna's answer was a snarl. She did not move the rapier point away from his throat but she did not press it any deeper.

"Uh...Dayna," Joel called from the doorway as he struggled to hold her husband. "I hope you don't kill him, but whatever you do, do it damn quick. Tauran's probably gonna send reinforcements down here."

With an exasperated sigh, Dayna pulled the sword away from Bartholomew's throat. She turned her back to him, strode quickly over to the cellmate on Bartholomew's left and hastily unlocked his shackles. When the man steadied himself on his feet, Dayna handed him the keys.

"Do what you want with Bartholomew, rebel," Dayna instructed. "Personally, I'd advise you to leave this dog chained."

She hurried to Joel and Jon and helped the offworlder support her husband's weight. The three of them stepped out into the long corridor and looked in both directions.

"Which way?" Joel asked.

"There are nothing but more cells around the corner at the far end of this hall," Bartholomew offered.

Joel frowned. "How are we going to get past Tauran and his men?"

Dayna gave Joel an incredulous glare. "With your power, offworlder, you ask such a question?"

"You know I can't control it," Joel reminded. "I was able to provoke Leesil into trying to kill me but Tauran will make sure his men don't make the same mistake."

Dayna's answer was a frustrated sigh. She knew Joel was right and she had no ideas of her own.

"So," Joel said. "How do you propose we get out of here?"

"Quickly," Jon said with a quivering voice.

12.3

"This is taking too bleeding long!" Tauran bellowed to Malvor, formerly his third – now his second – in command.

"Why the rush, baron?" T'Cheln asked in an almost mocking tone that irked Tauran. "There is no other way but this," he continued, jabbing a thumb at the locked heavy wooden double doors that barred the entrance to the cells. "They must come through here if they wish to escape."

"Leesil had a set of keys," Tauran reminded. "They could be freeing the others." He turned back to the nervous Malvor. "Where are the rest of the men?" he demanded. "The rebels will have *dug* their way out by the time those sorry bastards get here!"

Malvor, short and stocky, wearing an ill-fitting cloth tunic under a tight woolen vest and breeches so long that they had to be folded several times at the hem, cringed slightly under the baron's verbal onslaught and the hard gaze of the quietly intimidating *Ken d'Zanir* vassal towering over him, his muscular arms folded.

"There," Malvor said with relief. He pointed down the corridor to where heavily armed men were sprinting around the corner.

Tauran inspected the thirty men assembling before him, crowding the receiving area of the dungeons. He threw his black velvet, gold-trimmed cloak back, allowing his polished blood red armor to gleam in the torchlight of the chamber to give everyone a clear view of the fabled Dragon-fang broadsword that hung at his hip, hoping the display would either inspire or make them too frightened to fail. With a sneer of disgust he looked at their glazed, half-closed eyes and slumped, drunken postures and wondered if his attempts to hearten them would be enough.

He knew they would be more than enough as long as they were not foolish and went against his orders. If they did, though, he feared they would not be nearly enough. Jon would still be too weak to pose a serious threat, but from what Tauran was told and what he had seen with his own eyes, the offworlder was dangerous enough to easily slaughter them all if they were careless.

"I care not if you were sleeping like fat, drunken dogs with full bellies. It's time to earn your keep! When we go through those doors, you are to kill anyone not in chains. The only exceptions are Jon and the offworlder. Beat them to unconsciousness if you must, but take care NOT to kill them…under penalty of your own death."

The baron stepped to the double doors, raised the bar and threw them open. He immediately saw Dayna and the offworlder supporting Jon at the far end of the long corridor. All of the cell doors, numbering seventeen on each side, were still closed. The three would-be escapees looked up at him in fear. Their expressions delighted him.

"Go!" he roared.

With an assortment of feral battle cries, the guards streamed through the wide entrance four at a time. Dayna, wearing Leesil's weapons belt around her slender waist, pulled his rapier from the belt's sheath and leveled it as if she was ready to do battle with all thirty of them by herself. Tauran chuckled at the sight.

Joel's heart nearly beat out of his chest as he watched the horde of jailers charge down the forty-yard prison hall with their weapons raised. He took on Jon's full weight as Dayna stepped forward with Leesil's rapier held ready for battle.

Time seemed to slow as they came ever closer. Joel waited for – hoped for – the red-rimmed vision that signaled the onset of his power. He tried to will it forth. But nothing happened. He had expected as much but he had to try.

The attackers had closed to within twenty feet of the beleaguered trio when almost every cell door swung open. Prisoners, nearing seventy in total, both men and women, flooded the hall with fierce howls.

Only three of them had weapons. Dayna wielded Leesil's rapier while Bartholomew and one of his cellmates brandished the broadswords that belonged to the jailers who carried Jon into the dungeons.

But with the advantage of surprise the two men quickly brought down two of the jailers. Dayna, with quick and masterful slashes of the rapier, put another jailer down. Swarming prisoners immediately snatched up the fallen men's blades as they fell upon the baron's men.

Many of the prisoners, particularly the unarmed ones, went down quickly under the blade. Most of them, though, were so-called rebels or were otherwise jailed unjustly by the despotic baron. As a result, their anger, fear, and desperation drove them on despite the deaths of their fellow prisoners.

There were far fewer women than men among the prisoners, but because of the added humiliation of the abuse they had suffered during their imprisonment, they attacked with far more savagery than the men.

Soon the prisoners' overwhelming numbers began to overcome the baron's armed men. Many of the prisoners had recovered weapons from fallen jailers, allowing them to press their attack even more effectively.

Tauran watched the scene with utter repugnance. He was amazed by how fast the situation was disintegrating before his eyes. With a growl he snatched Dragon-fang from its sheath. The jagged end of the greatsword carved from a dragon's tooth attested to the fact that it was broken. The weapon, however, was so massive that even though it had been broken at almost its exact midpoint, the blade was still nearly as long as a normal broadsword.

Tauran turned to look up at his foreign vassal. "Guard this door, T'Cheln. Let no one pass. You would not accompany us for our further interrogation of the prisoners. Had you been there we would likely not be dealing with this fiasco. The least you can do is hold this exit."

The tall, chiseled man raised an eyebrow for the briefest moment as he regarded the baron with an otherwise expressionless face.

"Do you understand me, *Ken*?"

"Perfectly," T'Cheln answered icily.

Satisfied, Tauran grinned and lowered his crimson visor over his head and waded dangerously into the melee.

DEMON OF LORR

T'Cheln looked on as the baron hacked and jabbed with his broken but deadly greatsword. The *Ken d'Zanir* warrior looked on interestedly as the baron whipped ferocious kicks at the knees, hips, and groins of the armed and unarmed alike. T'Cheln appraised the balance and accuracy of Tauran's attacks and found them both sorely lacking. Even so, they were more than sufficient against opponents weakened from near starvation and torture, most of whom were unarmed.

Those who came against him armed were at nearly as great a disadvantage as the unarmed opponents. The weapons they recovered from fallen jailers were for the most part well crafted, but they had no chance of penetrating Tauran's full suit of arms. He wore the dwarf-forged armor crafted for the infamous Mar-dah's Legion Midnight. Sword tips slid easily aside when they struck his armor. War axes bounded harmlessly away while barely scratching the blood-red surface.

Giving Tauran yet another advantage was the blade Dragon-fang, which was well known for biting through mundane weaponry if wielded by someone with enough strength to drive it. Baron Tauran was physically powerful, if nothing else.

T'Cheln knew, though, that the baron would not have been strong enough to fight with an intact Dragon-fang. It would have been much too big and much too heavy. But broken, Tauran was able to flick the blade this way and that, almost as he had been taught yet too wanting in control and precision for T'Cheln's taste. Still, the jagged-edged blade tore easily through metal blades and wooden hafts to bite through flesh and bone.

The *Ken* wondered at how fate could smile so brightly on a man with so little honor as the false Baron. He deserved neither the armor he wore nor the blade with which he fought. T'Cheln had heard the blustering baron tell stories of how he was heavily recruited for the Legion Midnight. He had to listen to several versions of the tale of how he came to posess Dragon-fang:

The Finder relinquished to Tauran the broken Dragon-fang after he fell during the battle that ended with the two of them besting Raxe as well as Worldhopper, the King of the Dragons, in the dragon's very own lair. In each version, the dragon and the offworlder ended up fleeing for their lives.

T'Cheln knew they were all lies. The Legion Midnight took on anyone with sword arm and more greed than common sense. The *Ken* believed it was nothing but fool's luck, or more likely that the god S'Zan, as usual, had plans for them all that went beyond a mere mortal's understanding. He had no idea how the baron *actually* acquired Dragon-fang. What he did know was that Tauran was a liar. T'Cheln heard the reports of the Ranger Elf and Raxe besting some of their finest *Ken* warriors during their assassination attempt at Port Lorrian. Tauran was not even close to being a good enough fighter to accomplish the feats in his stories.

T'Cheln was the one who taught Tauran the small bit of true fighting skill he was demonstrating. Tauran was but a hulking brute with a violent temper when T'Cheln was assigned to train and protect him. Now he was a hulking brute with unique martial training. And truth be told, the idiot would have fought twice as well if he had any discipline.

Yet the overmatched prisoners fell one and two at a time before Tauran's assault. The victims' blood spatters were all but invisible on his crimson armor. Those who did not die from the severity of their initial wounds would die later from the infectious bite of Dragon-fang. The broken broadsword would cause wounds that would fester and rot until the victims' were poisoned by their own decay.

As the *Ken d'Zanir*, "Fist of the Gods" when translated to Lorrian, watched the baron tear through prisoners right down the middle of the hall on his way to intercept his prized captives, he saw something that made him grin.

Bartholomew, Dayna and a third prisoner fought their way up the left side of the hall, toward the exit, towards *him*. They were pressed tightly against the wall and cell doors, impressively forming a protective barrier of steel between the jailers and the offworlder, who was supporting Dayna's husband and helping him move up the hall.

Tauran, lost in bloodlust and too intent on moving straight ahead and cutting down anyone in his way, failed to notice the very people he hunted as they crept past him.

T'Cheln saw movement out of the corner of his right eye. Without even turning his head fully, he snatched out his sword-breaker dagger and caught between its teeth the blade of a sideswiping long sword. T'Cheln gave a powerful twist and pull, snapping the blade and pulling the attacker toward him. As the attacker pitched forward, T'Cheln swung the long, toothed dagger in a tight arc and nearly beheaded the frail man that was foolish enough to attack him.

Another male prisoner charged him with a war axe held high. Before he could bring the axe down, T'Cheln snapped a quick, powerful kick to the would-be attacker's chest. The sound of breaking ribs echoed above the din of battle as the prisoner flew into a crowd of struggling jailers and prisoners.

* * *

Joel's gaze never left Tauran and T'Cheln. When the baron broke away from the *Ken* warrior to enter the chaos of fighting, Joel was heartened. Perhaps T'Cheln would do the same and leave the doorway unprotected. The five of them took care to stay low so the baron would not see them as they fought their way to the exit. Dayna, Bartholomew and Aldon were doing a great job of protecting them from the jailers.

The jailers engaged Dayna and their two companions fiercely, but only struck at him with fists or reached for him with clutching hands. Those who did were quickly beat back and had to defend themselves from the others' blades.

The escapees were weak from torture, injury, and malnourishment but they were bolstered by their desperate desire for freedom, adrenaline-fueled anger, and a severe lust for retribution. The baron's men were hale and healthy. Unfortunately for them, though, their battle adrenaline was countered by intoxication and over-sated gluttony.

As well as the escapees were doing, Joel knew it could not last. Their adrenaline would eventually be spent and their abused bodies would soon be overcome by exhaustion. And as well as Dayna, Bartholomew and Aldon fared against their attackers, they would not fare nearly as well against the baron or the *Ken d'Zanir*. Both of them were unusually big, strong, and well-trained fighters. Both were sober.

It became obvious that the *Ken* was not leaving his post at the wide doorway and Joel's fear magnified. When the exotic warrior began dispatching attacking prisoners with relative ease, Joel was even more worried.

"What are we going to do about the *Ken*?" Joel asked over Dayna's shoulder.

"We'll cut him down like the rest of these dogs," she answered distractedly.

"I think not," Bartholomew said above the cacophony of clashing metal, angry shouts and painful screams. "Even now he battles multiple opponents and they are falling before him even more quickly than they are falling before Tauran and Dragon-fang."

Joel studied T'Cheln as the five escapees moved ever closer to the exit. The big warrior looked almost disinterested as he dispatched any and all who attacked him. Joel noticed, though, that the *Ken* never attacked. He only defended himself – albeit with deadly efficiency. T'Cheln even made eye contact with Joel on several occasions as the offworlder struggled down the hall with Jon. The few times their eyes met, T'Cheln's gaze was slightly curious and amused.

"We've no other choice but to cut down the *Ken*," Dayna said. "I doubt he will let us pass if we simply ask nicely."

"Asking nicely might not be a bad idea," Joel advised.

The statement finally evinced words from the otherwise silent Aldon. "Your torture has surely addled your brain, offworlder!" he cried between blocks, parries, and thrusts of his broadsword.

"Take my word for it," Joel said, knowing his protectors were entirely unconvinced. Worried that they might get themselves killed if they did not take him seriously, he added one more phrase.

He had no idea if it would mean anything to them. He did not know if it even meant anything to *him,* but it was the only thing he could think of.

"Take my word as a Child of the Old Ones."

After several slow, agonizing and violent minutes, they were a few feet away from the exit. T'Cheln stood there, waiting, with his large sword-breaker dagger in one hand and his short sword in the other. Dayna and Aldon converged on one jailer to strike him down while Bartholomew thrust his broadsword through the midsection of another and then T'Cheln was the only thing between them and the exit.

Dayna, Bartholomew, and Aldon held their weapons at the ready as they inched toward the *Ken* but they did not attack. They walked carefully around the towering warrior, expecting him to strike at any second, but T'Cheln, with an unreadable expression, only watched them leave.

Joel gave T'Cheln a slight nod of thanks as he carried Jon past. The tall warrior ignored the thanks and only continued to stare until the five escapees were through the doors of the receiving chamber.

"How did you know?" Bartholomew demanded as they hustled down the dark corridor to the underground stairway.

Joel shrugged. "Just a feeling."

"As he said," Dayna huffed as she helped Joel support her husband. "Joel is a Child of the Old Ones. We may not understand their abilities but we have to accept that they have them. Where do we go from here?"

Bartholomew smiled slyly. "As I told you when we first spoke, I am the former baron's nephew and the *real* baron's cousin. I know these halls as well as anyone, definitely better than Tauran. There are many obscure passageways that will lead us to the storerooms just one level above us, and I would imagine the guards would have been called down to the dungeons by now."

"How does that help us?" Dayna asked.

Bartholomew looked over his shoulder and gave Dayna a "trust me" smile as he led them onward.

"The storerooms are not near the high traffic areas," he explained. "Many of them provide passage to the outside of the castle. The room we seek is an old grain storeroom that has been converted to storage for gin and rum barrels."

"Gin and rum barrels?" Jon asked, suddenly more alert.

"Yes," Bartholomew confirmed. "Rot-gut quality at that, better suited to lighting lamps than drinking."

"Our favorite kind," Dayna said, glancing at Jon.

It took a few minutes for them to reach the storeroom. The sounds of battle and heavy footfalls carried to them from the lower level. Fortunately the dark hall outside of the storeroom was free of guards. All of the available swordsmen had left to provide reinforcements for the beleaguered jailers down in the dungeons. Bartholomew and Aldon were free to hack away at the lock on the wine cellar door until it finally gave. The smell of cedar and liquor nearly overwhelmed them as air from the storeroom rushed out at them.

The wall opposite was a large set of tightly fastened barn doors reinforced by a wrought iron gate offset just an inch or so away. The gate, like the barn door, was tightly fastened.

"I was afraid of this," Bartholomew said. "These doors are often left open because they are always hauling liquor in and out at all times of the day and night. The guards must have locked them before they went down to the dungeons."

"There's no key for these doors on Leesil's key ring?" Joel asked with alarm.

"No," Bartholomew said. "And *those* locks won't yield to broadswords. We'll have to find another way out. The next closest exit is along one of the main halls. We will surely pass some of Tauran's men on their way to the dungeons."

"This exit will do," Dayna assured. "I want the three of you to move two barrels each against those gates, and then join Jon and me back in this corridor."

Bartholomew balked. "I know what you're thinking, but there is no time. The baron will soon discover we're missing. We have to put more distance between us and the dungeons."

"Then do as the lady asks," Jon said tiredly, barely managing to lift his eyes to give Bartholomew an exhausted but grave stare.

Joel noticed how sincere the husband and wife were. He decided to trust their certainty and carefully extracted himself from beneath Jon's long, bony arm. When he was satisfied that Dayna was supporting him as comfortably as she could, he hurried into the storeroom.

He went to the barrel nearest to the door that did not have another barrel stacked on top of it. With a grunt, he tilted the heavy waist-high barrel and struggled as he slowly spun it closer to the gate.

Aldon started to follow Joel into room but Bartholomew stopped him with firm grasp of his shoulder.

"I'll not waste time here, Aldon."

"Then help the Child of the Old Ones before you go," Dayna advised.

"I haven't seen anything to make me believe he is who he says he is," Bartholomew argued.

"I have," Dayna declared. "We're free, are we not?"

"He could be a gifted lock-pick for all I know," Bartholomew returned. "Now follow me or be re-captured."

Dayna grinned. "I was about to say the same to you."

"Come, Aldon," Bartholomew ordered.

"I'm sorry, sir," Aldon said. "But I will be staying with the Child of the Old Ones."

"Damn it all," Bartholomew swore. "Then let us help the offworlder."

The three of them were able to stack two rows of three barrels in fairly short order. When they were done, they ran back to the hall to rejoin Dayna and Jon. Bartholomew leveled an impatient glare at Dayna.

"I suppose we use our swords to drill a hole in a barrel, pour a trail of liquor from the hall to the barrels stacked at the door, light it and just wait for the explosion? Or will we be waiting for the flame to die, or to be discovered by those bloodthirsty mercenaries masquerading as jailers?"

Dayna returned his impatient glare. "I suggest you close and bolt the door and then follow us to far end of the hall."

Aldon did not wait for Bartholomew to follow Dayna's order. He quickly closed and bolted the door. The five of them rushed to the end of the corridor. Bartholomew and Aldon looked expectantly at Joel and Dayna, but it was Jon who began to glow. A golden sheen glimmered ever-so-lightly over his dark, ashen skin.

He closed his eyes and snapped his fingers. A small, orange-red spark jumped from his fingertips and began to race down the hall.

Everyone except Jon and Dayna watched in wide-eyed amazement as the flame streaked towards the storeroom they had just left. With every foot it travelled, it grew in size and intensity. It curved impossibly and then ducked under the thin seam between the store room door and the floor. From there, they could all tell the flame grew even stronger from the bright golden glow that suddenly poured out from under the door.

The five of them ducked as a deafening DA-DOOM rocked the hall. The thick, bolted door burst from its hinges and slammed into the opposite wall. A few smaller explosions followed. Gouts of flame belched from the blasted doorway with each blast.

Aldon and Bartholomew turned to Jon as if seeing him for the very first time.

"You are the Jon the Firemaster," Aldon breathed.

"Yes," Dayna confirmed. "Now let us make haste!"

They went quickly to the flaming doorway and looked into the destroyed storeroom. The acrid stench of burning alcohol threatened to render them all unconscious. Joel's excitement turned to dread when nothing could be seen in the chamber but fire and smoke.

"How are we supposed to get through –?" Joel began. He hushed up when he noticed Jon glowing weakly once more.

The conflagration parted down the middle, revealing the gate, which was steaming and flung open wide, displaying the nighttime landscape of the grounds just outside the blasted barn doors.

"Firemaster," Joel reminded himself. "Dumb question."

Chapter 13: Second Encounters

13.1

Tauran struck down another prisoner as he fought his way back to T'Cheln's side. "What the hell was that?" he barked. "An explosion?"

T'Cheln nodded. "It would seem one of your prized prisoners has started to recover. He has been out of cold water for too long, apparently."

"And *you* let them pass," Tauran accused. "You let others pass, too. Nearly half of the prisoners have escaped!"

The baron waved at the grisly corridor behind him, where thirteen of the original thirty men milled about the three-dozen or so prisoners that had failed to escape the corridor. Whenever his remaining men found one moving, they put him or her to a violent death by blade or bludgeoning.

"Yes. Those who did not attack passed without incident. The rest lay dead or dying in these dungeons," T'Cheln pointed out. "Would you slay them all?"

"Each one of them represents at best an irritant and at worst a dangerous rival, so, yes!" Tauran yelled. "And what of it? You said you would stop anyone that tried to get out!"

"No," T'Cheln corrected. "I simply acknowledged that I understood your order. I never said I would it obey it. Must I remind you yet again that the *S'Zan Rho* have been paid for me to serve as your protector and trainer? I am not one of your thugs to be ordered about."

"Why didn't you protect me against these prisoners?"

"With your armor, that blade and the meager skill you've somehow managed to glean from me, we both know you needed no protection."

Tauran's beard twitched as he gritted his teeth in frustration. "Malvor!" he finally called. The shorter subordinate was there in an instant...much quicker, Tauran noted, than Leesil had ever responded.

"Yes, baron?" Malvor asked.

"What happened to the reinforcements? There should be more men down here."

"I don't know, sir. The man I sent never returned."

"Gather these men," Tauran ordered, gesturing to the men in the cell corridor. "There should be a decent archer or two among them. We hunt the offworlder. And just to be sure, have the retrievers sent after them."

Malvor gulped at the mention of the retrievers but did as he was told. In five minutes he had gathered the men and arranged for the release of the retrievers, which was almost five minutes too long for the impatient baron. When Malvor returned, Tauran led the men in the direction of the explosion at a near sprint. They did not know the hidden routes that Bartholomew had taken so they had to go the long way around the winding halls of the stronghold.

"Do you think we will catch them?" Malvor gasped as he ran alongside the larger men. They turned the corner onto the storeroom halls and saw the blasted door.

"They can't keep a fast pace," the baron said. "They are too weak. The Firemaster has surely depleted what little energy he managed to recover in order to blast their way out. Otherwise they would be attacking us instead of running from us. If they manage to make it beyond the castle perimeter the retrievers will bring them back in short order."

Malvor looked doubtful. "Do you think the retrievers can stop the offworlder?"

"Of course not," Tauran answered. "When they attack him he'll likely kill them. But if we're lucky the beasts will kill his companions first. Once the threat of the retrievers has passed, he will revert to normal and be as easy to subdue as he was before. Anyway, all of this is of no consequence. The king's men should already be surrounding the castle. He'll never get past them."

Tauran turned into the room, flanked by T'Cheln and Malvor, and saw the last person he expected to see.

"I do not believe my good fortune," Tauran growled with an ugly smile. "It's the Sureblade whelp his pet changeling!"

13.2

Ethan and Quick, surrounded by the David and a handful of his men, looked up in mild surprise. Quick's hand was raised in a gesture that Tauran recognized as a spell. An unnatural wind was dying down and had extinguished the flames in the storeroom. The surprised looks of the young Sureblade and changeling did not last long. They expected to find Tauran, just not quite this soon. David and his men, however, were still staring at Quick with surprise and suspicion. They had no idea he was conjurer.

"I'm afraid the king's men will not assist you this night," Ethan told Tauran. From what I understand, a wallowgrump infestation caused them to abandon their post."

"Trickery?" Tauran asked. So his reinforcements never reached the dungeons because they were occupied with the rebels. He quickly dismissed the fleeting concern about the loss of the crown's soldiers. He had more immediate concerns. "You and the changeling sent them away only to rush headlong to your deaths. Come, boy, let us finish what we started that night at Tohrfell's Valley."

"Indeed," Ethan said with a dark smile.

"Changeling?" David asked one of his men standing near him. The man shrugged. "Elbert is full of surprises."

Ethan snatched his new broadsword from its sheath. He left the stave strapped to his back, fearing that his lack of experience with it and his inability to invoke its magic would put him at too great a disadvantage.

Tauran and Ethan came together with a loud clang of Ethan's metal blade and Tauran's much harder dragon's tooth blade. Tauran immediately pressed the attack. The force and quickness of his blows drove the smaller Ethan quickly back toward the charred, gaping hole in the wide outer doors. Ethan managed to deflect every strike but the weight behind each one caused him to backpedal to keep from losing his footing completely. By the time the baron's and David's men reacted to the sudden explosion of fighting, Tauran and Ethan were outside of the building.

DEMON OF LORR

Tauran's group more than doubled the number of rebels so Quick transformed into a land dragon to attack any of the baron's men who got past the rebels in an attempt to aid the baron. He had heard of land dragons as a child, but having never seen one, he never had a frame of reference to be able to transform into one. But after experiencing them at Port Lorrian he realized how effective such an animal could be.

The land dragon's thick hide and hard scales provided ample protection against most normal blades. The creature was agile enough to move quickly and effectively within the storeroom.

He was careful not to kill any of the combatants but he had to inflict enough damage to make them unwilling or unable to continue. Arm and leg bones shattered between the land dragon's powerful jaws. Its claws popped joints and hyper-extended limbs. Many of the baron's men fled the room like a herd of deer fleeing a hungry tygra.

David looked over in awe when he had a brief respite from the fighting. When David met the changeling, David was too busy fighting to notice or even suspect the abilities of the youngster he had known only as "Elbert." Now that he saw the transformation with his own eyes, he knew he was fighting alongside Quick, the famed changeling agent of the Kingdom of Lorr. That knowledge, as well as the ample job Quick was doing of turning the odds in their favor, encouraged him and his men as their battle spilled outside of the castle.

* * *

The sportsman in T'Cheln made him wonder if he could kill the changeling land dragon. Of course he had trained them as mounts. He had also slain the beasts before, on the western coasts S'Zan, the very edge of the Known Lands. But his brief reminiscing was for naught. A sword-breaker dagger and a short sword were not enough for killing a land dragon. Neither were his assorted hidden daggers, especially for an enchanted being like a changeling with the power of any beast he chose and the cunning of a human.

429

His magic-squelching talisman would not help him, either. It would lock Quick into his land dragon form and keep him from transforming into any other creature, but the land dragon was more than formidable enough.

Instead, T'Cheln eased his way around the perimeter of the room. Staying low, he managed to avoid the gaze of the distracted changeling and crept to the corridor entrance and exited the storeroom. If the adjacent storerooms were similar to the one he had just exited, T'Cheln knew he could get through both the gate and the wide outer doors in short order.

13.3

Ethan fared no better against the false baron in Eastedge than he had back at Tohrfell's Valley. Tauran was just too big and too strong. Ethan was quicker, though, and that was the only thing that kept him alive. Tauran's fighting technique left no openings that Ethan could exploit, at least not without getting inside of Tauran's guard.

Under normal circumstances a move to get into his opponent's body would be a calculated risk Ethan would happily take in order to score a potentially fatal blow. These, however, were not normal circumstances. Such a move would have been foolish against Tauran's nigh impenetrable Legion Midnight armor. Ethan stayed well away, parrying, sidestepping, and sliding back further and further away from the castle.

Ethan hoped Tauran would soon tire, fairly confident that his stamina was greater than the older man's. That might have been so, but each deflection of Dragon-fang sapped more of Ethan's strength. He realized it took more energy to defend himself than it took Tauran to press the offense.

The taller man's longer stride and superior reach required fewer steps to attack while Ethan's shorter stride required more steps to retreat. The false baron displayed more patience than Ethan expected. Not a single motion was wasted.

The sounds of battle from inside the storeroom, as well as elsewhere on the estate where the rebels battled Tauran's men, soon faded away from Ethan's awareness. The only sounds he heard were the deep ringing of their clashing weapons, their heavy breathing and deep grunts. It was all Ethan could do to stay out the extensive range of Taruan's long blade and powerful kicks. He hoped the larger man would eventually tire.

That soon became a hollow wish. Ethan's anxiety doubled when the wide outer doors of another storeroom swung open and the *Ken d'Zanir* strode out into the night. Ethan started to seriously consider running.

He was having a difficult enough time with Tauran. There was no way he could defeat Tauran *and* the big man's fighting instructor. The young Sureblade wished that he, Arrowhead, and Hammer had stayed together as Arrowhead suggested but it was too late to lament his mistake.

Ethan wanted to breathe a sigh of relief when the towering warrior halted to merely observe the exchange, but it was too late for that, as well. All he had time to do was block, parry, duck, and dodge as Tauran continued to press the attack.

The heavy blows started to take their toll on both Ethan and his weapon. The blade of his broadsword was nicked deeply on the flat sides and large sections had been bitten away from both sharp edges. Ethan's hands began to tingle and his arms grew tired and painful. Every blow threatened to dislodge his broadsword.

He thought about his father. Meldrick Sureblade had died at the point of Dragon-fang when it was whole and wielded by the Finder. And now Meldrick Sureblade's son was about to fall to half of the dreaded blade while Tauran, an underling of the Finder, wielded it.

A man who was half the warrior the Finder was, Ethan thought with grim humor. He wondered if that meant that he was half the fighter his father had been.

A particularly savage two-handed sideswipe of Dragon-fang almost buckled Ethan's broadsword, nearly lifted him off his feet and sent him stumbling backward. Instead of regaining his footing and trying to continue the battle, Ethan decided on the more prudent course of action. He allowed his momentum to carry him backward, regained his balance, and spun to sprint away.

Tauran was having none of it. He dashed after Ethan as the teen stumbled, intent on ending the duel quickly so he could get back to the business of squashing the revolt. His long legs carried him to Ethan just as the teen turned to flee. He swung his broken greatsword in a horizontal arc with enough force to cleave the boy in two.

But Ethan turned enough so that instead of tasting flesh, Dragon-fang struck the silver-blue staff strapped to his back. Ethan felt the powerful blow reverberate all through his body and this time he did leave his feet. His body continued to vibrate as he sailed several feet through the air and then went down headfirst. He hit the ground, rolled head over heels and came to his feet perfectly balanced.

He was facing Tauran and holding the staff in a wide two-handed grip. The broadsword rested in the grass a few feet away. Ethan could not remember discarding his damaged broadsword and pulling the staff free.

Tauran left him no time to ponder it. The big warrior was on him again, swinging Dragon-fang in a tight, deadly arc. Ethan spun the staff to a vertical orientation to block the blow. Tauran expected the strike to cut the staff and Ethan in half, or at the very least, knock the boy off balance again so he could finish him off. But Dragon-fang rebounded from the surface of the staff.

Before Tauran's surprise could register, Ethan swung the bottom of the blade up and struck Tauran a powerful blow to the side of his head. The baron's helm protected him from injury but the blow rang in his ears and sent him staggering.

Ethan stood in a wide-legged stance, his knees slightly bent and his left shoulder turned toward Tauran. He was almost as surprised as Tauran but he managed to keep his face fixed in an angry sneer. He could still feel the vibration from Tauran's heavy blow to his back moving within him.

The inner tremor continued and Ethan noticed that it was not fading. It lingered for a long moment and was suddenly accompanied by strange warmth. The young Sureblade realized that the neither the vibration nor the warmth was a result of Tauran's attack.

It was the *gun*'s magic.

"Do you propose to fight me with a bloody stick, child?" Tauran taunted.

Ethan snarled, "No, false baron. I'm going to *kill* you with it."

Tauran roared and charged again.

Ethan charged back. Controlled but powerful and quick blows came at Ethan from different angles. Ethan expertly deflected every strike. He stayed on the balls of his feet and moved fluidly, almost as if he was dancing.

He redirected a powerful thrust and spun in the same motion while Tauran's inertia continued to carry him forward. Ethan ended the spin by bringing his staff around in a savagely quick roundhouse blow to the side of Tauran's helm. The strike, along with Tauran's own momentum, sent him stumbling past Ethan, who swung the staff at the baron's lower legs to trip him. Tauran fell clumsily to the ground and had to scramble to regain his footing.

Even though most of the baron's face was concealed behind his scarlet helm, his eyes were clearly visible when the moons' light shined directly on him. Ethan saw a shadow of confusion and worry flash in the bigger man's glare.

"Raxe has taught you a few of his tricks during the few weeks since we last fought," Tauran growled. "They'll do you little good. I've trained under the *Ken* for *years*. I'll take your head and your little stick and mount them on the wall of my trophy room."

"Then shut up and fight me, false baron," Ethan returned.

T'Cheln raised an eyebrow as Tauran and Ethan clashed once more. He noted with interest that the youngling's entire fighting style changed when he began to use the staff.

His footwork was better. He kept his center of gravity low and his work with the staff was much more precise and powerful than his work with the broadsword had been. He even demonstrated increased flexibility when he bent backward at the waist at a deep angle that would injure a person's back if they had not trained for years to accomplish such a feat, and the youngster did it while jabbing his staff at Tauran's helm for another ringing blow.

It was as if T'Cheln was watching a completely different fighter. He watched Ethan raise the staff horizontally over his head with both hands to block a downward swing of Dragon-fang that was so powerful it drove him to the ground.

But instead of buckling to his knees, Ethan descended into a smooth, easy split, his legs perfectly straight and splayed in different directions. Tauran raised his massive broken sword for yet another powerful blow, but Ethan swiftly whipped staff around and jabbed it beneath Tauran's helm. He could not keep the staff from screeching along the bottom edge of the helm and lessening its force, but the blow still found Tauran's chin and sent him staggering away.

Ethan drove the tip of his staff into the earth with one hand and used it to pull himself to his feet. Tauran was already coming back at the teen, Dragon-fang in mid-swing. Ethan spun the staff around with both hands to his left to stop the strike and then lifted his right foot to deftly knock away Tauran's left foot as the baron tried to snap a bone breaking kick to his right knee. The baron was caught by surprise and thrown completely off balance by the maneuver, which Ethan quickly followed up with two staff strikes to either side of Tauran's helm.

As the baron staggered away, Ethan took a swift stride forward, used both hands to plant the forward tip of his staff firmly into the ground, and then used the staff to vault himself into a perfect soaring kick that caught Tauran squarely in the middle of his helm. Tauran reelrd backward and his helm went flying. His arms flailed as he tried to regain his balance, and then he finally toppled to the ground.

Ethan reveled in the magic surging through him. It was nothing like he expected. He thought it would make a marionette out of him. To his delight and relief he had assumed incorrectly. He felt stronger and faster. The pain from battle, which had been slightly numbed from adrenaline, completely dissipated. He could sense the additional combat knowledge flooding his consciousness.

The knowledge did not feel new at all. It was as familiar to him as the more conventional skills he had learned from years of training with his father and at the military academy.

With a confident and victorious battle cry, Ethan rushed Tauran, holding his staff with both hands and pointing it forward so that he could jab it through the bastard's eye and into his brain, or into the bridge of his nose with enough force to drive bone fragments into his brain. Either way, Tauran was about to die.

As Ethan approached the false baron for the killing blow, he caught something big angling toward him with frightening speed. He turned just in time to bring his staff across his body and catch a monstrously powerful kick from the *Ken d'Zanir* warrior. The blow bore the full weight of the incredibly tall, incredibly muscular attacker and threw Ethan, who was nearly one hundred pounds lighter than T'Cheln, almost ten yards through the air. If the staff had not absorbed the blunt of the attack it would surely have caved in his chest.

Ethan struck the ground with enough force to drive all of the air out of his lungs but he managed to climb to his feet quickly and get into a fighting stance. T'Cheln crouched to charge and then glanced up at the three moons. After looking to the sky, he stood up straight and assumed a relaxed posture.

Tauran sat up and glared at his vassal. "What are you doing, fool? Kill the little bastard!"

T'Cheln ignored the baron and spoke to Ethan.

"Impressive, youngling," he began. "I've seen you fight more than once. I've heard the reports of your confrontation with my brothers at Port Lorrian. There has been no evidence of the skill you've displayed with that staff in hand. I wonder..." The warrior reached to his belt and opened the flap of a small pouch.

The warmth and the thrumming of the magic within Ethan disappeared as if it had never been there. Pain and exhaustion replaced the magic with a jolt that buckled his knees. He had to stab his staff into the ground and hold on tightly to keep from falling.

Tauran's eyebrows bunched together in angry realization.

"Magic!" he accused. "Ha! I knew there had to be a reason you gained the advantage." He struggled mightily to get back to feet. His unsteady posture betrayed the residual dizziness from Ethan's attack. He pointed a finger at Ethan.

"Kill him, T'Cheln! Without his magic, it will be the easiest kill you've ever made. Send him to join his father and the rest of his family."

Ethan gasped. "What have you done to my family?"

"I'll die before I tell you," Tauran taunted. "Or better yet, *you* will die before I tell you. It is enough to know that you will join them soon. I say again, T'Cheln, kill him."

T'Cheln cast a disinterested gaze at the baron.

"No," he said.

"NO?" Tauran barked. "You've been paid to protect me!"

T'Cheln pointed to the three moons. "Look at the sky, at the position of the moons."

Tauran's gaze followed the *Ken*'s finger. "It's just past midnight," he noticed. "What of it?"

"The duration of our agreement has expired," T'Cheln explained. "As of midnight tonight, I am no longer your protector or teacher. Thanks be to the Old One S'Zan."

"What kind of foolishness is this?" Tauran sputtered. "I have until sunrise, at least! You would dare dishonor your indenture?"

T'Cheln's countenance, usually an impassive mask, twisted into an angry snarl. "What do *you* know of honor? Your lack of honor sickens me. For any other indenture I would wait until sunrise as a mere courtesy, though it is not a requirement. But *you,* false baron?" T'Cheln spat on the ground. "I can suffer your idiocy no longer."

"Rkam Lonos will hear of – "

"Rkam Lonos is no more my superior than you," the *Ken* interrupted as he stepped deliberately over to Tauran. The baron tried unsuccessfully not to cower, knowing that he would not last one minute against his former mentor. T'Cheln, however, did not attack. He thrust a hand into Tauran's cloak and brought it out with a small wooden whistle clutched in his powerful fingers.

"That's mine!" Tauran complained. "It was given to *me* by the wizard to control the scythe wings. Where is the honor in such thievery?"

"You no longer need it, Tauran. You definitely do not deserve it. Consider this a small refund for the extra frustration you've caused."

"What are you talking about?" Tauran demanded.

"Your flippant tongue with the Desert Witch nearly got us both killed. I've watched you rape women and kill an infant. Speak to me of honor once more, you buffoon, and I will stab you in your black heart."

"Leave us, then," Tauran said with a dismissive wave. "I'll finish off the boy on my own."

T'Cheln had already started jogging away. Tauran was not worried about besting the young Sureblade. The ungrateful *Ken* left the pouch on his belt open and Tauran knew that he still had ample time to kill the boy before T'Cheln had taken his magic-extinguishing talisman far enough away for the boy's magic to return.

As if the foreign warrior was reading his thoughts, T'Cheln closed and fastened the pouch. To make matters worse, David and his surviving rebels had chased Tauran's men back into the castle, and the young Keeper's Hounds, the female archer and the big man who wielded the wicked war hammer, sprinted around the far corner of the castle.

Ethan smiled and beckoned.

"Come, false baron," he bade. "You said you would die before you tell me what's been done to my family. Let us test the truth of that."

Tauran turned and staggered back toward the castle. Ethan started to pursue him when Quick's voice called out.

"Ethan!" Quick yelled from the tree line of the wooded area just beyond the estate. "Come! And make haste!"

"Are you daft?" Ethan cried. "I'm finishing Tauran. I'll make him tell me of my family's fate with his dying breath!"

"He's lying," Arrowhead assured. "You have to know that. He said those things to distract you."

"That may be," Ethan allowed. "He still needs to die."

"Is vengeance more important than our mission?" Quick challenged. "I've found the offworlder's scent. He's in a carriage heading east."

"Then we have more than enough time to kill Tauran and then catch up to Joel," Ethan argued.

"Not before his pursuers run him down," Quick warned. "Retrievers have been sent after him."

Ethan frowned. "What are retrievers?"

"Trouble!" David said.

"Indeed," Quick confirmed. "Believe me, there is no time to explain."

"Take Hammer and Arrowhead with you, then," Ethan decided as he watched the baron approach his stronghold. "I'll go after Tauran."

"Don't be a fool," Arrowhead admonished. "He'll be back in the castle with his men in a moment. Our mission is to join with Raxe in pursuit of the Dierglyorr."

"We've won the day," David assured him. "My forces will deal with the *former* false baron and what few mercenaries remain. In the morning I'll send a carrier pigeon to Lorr to get confirmation of his lies about your family. A bird can get there faster than you could."

Still Ethan hesitated. He knew they were right but he did not care. Even if Tauran was lying about Ethan's family, Tauran had to die for his crimes, for working with the man who killed his father, and for wielding the fell weapon the Finder used to commit that murder.

"Eagle Eye," Arrowhead started, using his Keeper's Hound code name to remind him of his duty. "What would your father do?"

"Not this," Ethan answered with a sneer.

His hand moved with the quickness of a striking cobra as he snatched Arrowhead's loaded crossbow from her hand. Before anyone could stop him, he aimed and fired.

Tauran was almost back to the blasted barn door of the storeroom where several of his men were waiting for him. The big mercenary was already planning his next move when he cast one more defiant glare at the rebels and the interlopers from the Kingdom of Lorr. He did not get the chance to turn his head completely around.

The crossbow bolt smashed into his temple, through his skull, and into his brain. He crashed face down in the threshold of the storeroom entrance.

Arrowhead, Hammer, and Quick stood dumbfounded. Ethan watched as Tauran's men drug his unmoving body into the castle. The sounds of battle fell to barely-noticed background noise.

"You're right, Ethan," Quick said. "Meldrick would *never* have done that. He once stopped Raxe from killing a fleeing enemy."

Ethan turned to his best friend. "I'm fairly certain that enemy didn't cut an infant's throat to help a demon unleash a plague of walking dead."

Hammer shrugged his massive shoulders. "Good point."

Arrowhead narrowed her eyes at the young Sureblade. "Is that really why you did it, Ethan? Or were you exacting from Tauran the revenge you can never exact from the Finder, your father's *actual* killer?"

"I'm off to find Joel," Ethan declared. "Ride with me or don't." He turned to the true heir to the Eastedge Barony. "David, when you've confirmed my family's safety, you will send a message to Ridgeland."

"You have my vow," David promised.

The changeling and the Keeper's Hounds dashed off into the night.

13.4

Joel really wanted to sleep. The weird night sky, with its three moons and countless stars throwing pale light across a blanket of darkness, was strangely relaxing. The cool air buffeted him comfortingly and soothed the dull ache of his many burns, scars, and bruises. It also reminded him of early autumn in Chicago. Almost everything was perfect for a nice long and much-needed nap. Unfortunately, there were two rather significant problems with his attempt to sleep.

The first was the wagon he was riding in. It jostled madly along the rough trail. They were still in the forested foothills of Hell's Mountains and the way would only get rougher when they reached the air of the higher elevations.

The second was the sound of the snapping whip that startled him every few seconds, accompanied by Dayna's forceful voice shouting "Hyah! Hyah!" while she urged on the two draft horses pulling the wagon.

Dayna, with her thick hair pushed back by the strong breeze, yelled something to him over her shoulder. Joel could barely hear her above the din of thundering hooves, whistling wind, and the rattling wagon.

"How is Jon?" she asked a second time, louder than the first time to be sure Joel heard her.

Joel looked down at the man lying with his eyes closed.

"How are you, Jon?" Joel asked, not expecting a response. But he actually saw Jon's mouth move.

"Alive," Jon managed weakly.

"He's fine," Joel shouted to Dayna.

"Is he breathing?" Dayna asked.

Joel turned to Jon. "Are you breathing?"

"Yes."

"Yes!" Joel shouted.

Dayna nodded and cracked her whip again.

Joel stared at the night falling away behind him. The golden glow from the fires at the baron's castle had almost faded completely from view.

"So, Jon," Joel said, "what did Tauran want with you?"

"Much," Jon answered tiredly.

"I understand if you're not up to talking, now," assured Joel.

Jon lifted one of his long-fingered hands. "No," he said. "I need to tell you. Tauran didn't know it, but he was holding me for the demon. He spoke of a 'dark wizard' who kept his identity secret. If the dark wizard isn't the demon, he's an agent of the demon. It wants my speaking stone."

"Your *what*?"

"Speaking stone," Jon repeated. The mere utterance of the words seemed to buoy the exhausted, haggard elemental. "Speaking stones allow conjurers to communicate across vast distances with a minimal use of magic. It is the greatest honor the Conjurer's Alliance can bestow upon an uninitiated. It makes one an honorary member of the Alliance. It means they respect and trust me enough to fight by their side."

"Sounds like there are a few of those things out there," replied Joel. "What made yours so special? Why didn't Tauran pick another member of the Alliance?"

Jon went silent for a moment. Joel was still trying to determine whether Jon was reluctant to speak or just too tired when Jon finally continued.

"I'm not privy to their secrets, but I know more about them than anyone outside of the Alliance," the Firemaster explained. "One of the few things they did tell me was the potential danger of the speaking stones."

"Dangerous how?" Joel pressed, suddenly interested.

Jon went silent again. This time Joel knew why.

"I'm a Child of the Old Ones," reminded Joel, deciding to use the troubling fact to his advantage for a change. "I'm fighting against the demon, too. Whatever you say won't go any further. I promise."

Jon studied the offworlder for a long while. Joel could see the wheels turning behind the elemental's deep-set brown eyes. One eyebrow twitched as Jon apparently came to a decision.

"I suppose it's not difficult to guess if you think about it," Jon began. "The speaking stones provide a link between the majority of the most powerful magic wielders in the Known Lands. There's a bit of our essence in each of our speaking stones. That connection could be used as a deadly weapon against us. Our locations would never be secret, and as surely as we can send our thoughts through the bond of the stones, harmful magic could be sent through by a powerful and skilled enough conjurer."

"Why pick you out of all of the other wizards that carry them?" Joel asked again. "And why waste time with torture when they could just kill you and take it? Wait…you must have it hidden somewhere."

"Of course," Jon concurred. "I do not always carry it with me for several reasons. But when not in my possession, it is well hidden. The demon picked me because I'm *only* an honorary member of the Alliance.

"I'm an elemental whose sole power is the manipulation of fire. Official members are accomplished wizards and would be much more difficult to capture and break."

Jon saw the offworlder's confused expression. "The bond between the owner and his speaking stone has to be broken in order for another to use the stone's magic," he revealed. "I have to willingly relinquish the speaking stone to the next owner for them to be able to use it. Simply killing me would gain the demon nothing. I am without question the least powerful owner of a speaking stone. They assumed it would be easier to force me to relinquish mine that it would have been with the other wizards."

Jon's shoulders managed to slump even lower. He dropped his chin and looked at the floor of the wagon.

"And after seeing what was done to my Dayna," he said between deep, slow breaths, "I'm afraid they were right. I was prepared to give them what they wanted. If you had not intervened I would have jeopardized the lives of the entire Alliance. Thank you, Joel. Thank you."

Joel did not respond. He did not want Jon's appreciation. He had no desire to see Dayna raped again, or Jon killed, but deep down Joel knew that everything he did, he did to get home to Lisa. He would not be a hypocrite and accept undeserved gratitude.

"I only wonder why the demon did not confront me directly," Jon wondered aloud.

"I think it's trying to be very careful," elucidated Joel. "It's laying low, or hiding, as you would say. Based on what you just told me, I suppose if you had managed to conceal that stone on your person and the demon came around, a wizard as powerful as Rionn Lorr could probably use it to strike at the demon. I know for a fact that it doesn't want to fight any of the Children of the Old Ones directly, at least not without having some kind of clear advantage."

Jon tilted his head to the side. "You know this for a *fact*, you say?"

"You think Tauran's going to come after us?" Joel called to Dayna, ignoring Jon's question and chiding himself inwardly for saying more than he intended. For some reason, Joel felt he could trust Jon more than he could his fellow Children of the Old Ones, but he refused to let himself trust anyone too much. Besides, Dayna would eventually tell her husband about the Dierglyorr's visit.

"That bastard Tauran will be busy for a while yet with the attack on the castle," Dayna called back. "I suspect he'll try, but we will have covered too much ground. They'll never catch us before we get to Ridgeland."

Joel settled back down into a slightly less uncomfortable seated position. His body continued to painfully absorb all of the bumps and bucks of the speeding wagon. A glance at Jon revealed that the man had somehow managed to find sleep, or at least something that passed for it. Good. Joel was tired of conversation. This was the closest thing to peaceful calm that Joel could remember in a very long time.

But then he remembered something he overheard back when he was first captured.

"What are retrievers?" he asked Dayna.

Dayna shrugged. "Someone or something that retrieves, I suppose," she said distractedly. "I don't know if I understand the question."

"I don't know if *I* understand," Joel said. "I overheard Tauran and his men talking about sending their retrievers after me."

"Retrievers!" Jon echoed worriedly, eyes suddenly open wide. He forced himself to his hands and knees and crawled to the front of the wagon where Joel perched.

"Yeah," Joel confirmed. "Have you heard of them?"

"Beasts from the *Unknown* Lands, according to legend," Jon said. "Fierce changeling creatures banished after Heaven's War. Their initial form is that of a small canine, allowing them to move around populated areas without calling attention to themselves while they hunt.

"A skilled conjurer can manipulate them to transform into various lethal creatures to do their killing when they finally run down their prey. The demon must have provided them."

Joel looked into the trees flashing by and shrinking into the darkness. He caught the scent of magic, dark and unsettling magic. The hair on his arms and the back of neck stood on end. The horses whinnied, and even Joel, who knew nothing about horses, could hear their burgeoning panic.

"What kind of 'lethal creatures' do these things turn into?" Joel asked.

"Whatever the controlling mage wishes," Joel said.

"So I guess those aren't out of the question," Joel said, pointing.

Dayna looked over her shoulder into the dark forest. Jon managed to prop himself up on the side of the wagon to peer into the shadowy distance. Beams of moons' light cut through the dark forest canopy in random patterns and they could see large, darker shadows flitting through the pale shafts of illumination.

Huffing and snorting, the large horses thundered out of the darkness of the forest path, turned onto a much wider wagon trail and into the moon and starlight.

The wagon rocked forcefully as they turned, nearly throwing Joel and Jon free before settling back on all four wheels. They were not quite fifty yards down the trail when two massive wolves burst from the darkness like nightmares come to life.

They took to the trail behind the wagon and began to close the distance between them. Both wolves were nearly the size of the big draft horses pulling the wagon.

"Wraith wolves!" Jon breathed.

In the nocturnal light, the monstrous canines were nothing more than gray shadows moving so fluidly they might as well have been flying. Their gleaming yellow eyes and white, wickedly snapping teeth were the only things that made them appear to be of the corporeal world.

"Burn 'em or something!" Joel yelled frantically.

"Can't," Jon said. "Not strong enough yet."

The wraith wolves came closer with alarming speed. Joel scooted back against the front of the wagon where he doubled over in pain and grabbed his stomach. Jon heard him mumbling "no, no, no," and wondered if the offworlder was losing his mind from fear.

Jon was barely conscious during their flight from Tauran's dungeons. He knew Joel had been the key to their escape but had no idea of exactly what the stranger could do. Dismissing Joel as useless, Jon tried to call upon his fire to combat the gaining wraith wolves. It was no use. He had tapped the miniscule reserves of power he managed to replenish when he caused and controlled the explosion and resulting conflagration that allowed them to escape the castle. He felt as useless as Joel appeared.

Joel suddenly shot to his feet and yelled "NO!" at the top of his lungs.

Jon looked over at him and was shocked by the milky film clouding Joel's eyes. Despite the urgency and pain in his voice, his face was expressionless. And then, even more to Jon's shock, Joel took one long step and bolted from the back of the wagon. The lead wolf leapt to meet him. A wide-eyed

Jon watched Joel's skinny body disappear, engulfed within the wraith wolf's massive body.

In the moons' light he saw Joel and the wolf crumple to the ground and skid to the side of the trail. They disappeared into a ferocious tangle of shadows, limbs, pluming dirt and spraying blood.

"By the gods," Jon whispered, as fascinated by the sight as he was afraid of the second wraith wolf that continued to close on – and then leap for – the wagon.

13.5

Joel, his body aching and covered with foul smelling blood, rose unsteadily to his feet. He stood over the corpse of the torn wraith wolf to watch the remaining one vault into the air to overtake the rushing wagon. But just as the wraith wolf went beyond the apex of its leap and started downward, a larger shadow swept down out of the sky and seized it. It darted back into the sky and faded into the darkness.

"Guys!" Joel called. "You're forgetting somebody!"

It was no use. He knew the horses were spooked and would not be coming back any time soon. He turned his eyes skyward and looked for the retreating shadow. A thud and gust of wind from behind him made him turn. The second wraith wolf, broken and twisted, lay a few feet away.

Joel was knitting his eyebrows in confusion when a huge shadow fell over him. Before he could react, something slammed into his waist and snatched him skyward. He felt the horribly painful and familiar sensation of giant avian talons wrapped around his waist.

It was the scythe wings swarming him all over again. Panic overcame him and he tried madly to pry the massive talon loose. The appendage would not budge.

Somewhere in the back of his mind was the realization that this talon was much bigger than the ones that tore at him after he fell from the doomed sky sleigh what seemed to be so long ago. And this time, there was only one talon clutching him as opposed to the countless claws that tore at him during his abduction. There was only one pair of wings flapping above him instead of dozens flapping all around.

Joel finally looked up from the huge talon and saw that he was being carried by an avicaw, not a scythe wing. As the avicaw descended, Joel saw that the wagon had stopped and Jon still lay in the back. Dayna stood next to the wagon talking to someone, a kid, with blonde hair. The avicaw descended further and released him, dropping him clumsily to the ground.

He landed on his feet, but in his tired and disoriented state, he stumbled to his hands and knees. Dayna and the blonde kid helped him up.

"Ethan?" Joel asked when he saw the youngster's face.

"Finally!" Ethan said. "We've been searching for you for days."

"Days?" Joel asked. "Felt like weeks. What the hell took you so long?"

"I suppose it was closer to two weeks," Ethan conceded.

The shadow dropped from the sky again. Joel ducked but this time there was no reason.

The avicaw folded in on itself and began to shrink and shimmer, turning into a much smaller ball of shadow falling from the sky. It unfolded in the form of a lanky teen boy. Quick landed deftly on the ground beside him.

"A warning would've been nice, kid," Joel complained.

Quick grinned. "A vocal cry in my avicaw form would have frightened you more than the grab, my friend."

"Boys," Dayna cut in. "I sincerely thank you for your assistance, but Jon and I must be away. We were kidnapped from our home, making our town more vulnerable to attack. Ridgeland is in grave danger."

"More than you know," said Quick. "We've learned that Ridgeland is under siege by what is being called an army of walking dead."

Dayna's mouth opened slightly. "All the more reason for us to hurry," she finally said. "I wish you well on your mission." She turned to climb onto the wagon but Ethan called out to stop her.

"Wait, ma'am," Ethan began. "In Jon's condition, do you think it safe for you travel alone?"

"Are you offering to travel with us?" Dayna asked impatiently. And then her voice softened a bit. "We could use the extra sword." She looked incredulously at the staff strapped to Ethan's back. "Or stick?"

"But our mission," Quick reminded. "Raxe wants us to rejoin him in his search for the Hell Key."

"Raxe?" Jon muttered from the wagon. "Raxe is here?"

"He should be in the Demon's Spine by now," Quick explained. "He is searching for Mar-dah's keep."

"Help him," Jon said tiredly. "His must be the more important quest."

"But Jon," Dayna started to argue. Jon slowly lifted his hand to cut her off. "No, my husband," Dayna went on stubbornly. I will not agree with you in this. The offworlder is a Child of the Ones and better protected than we are."

"I'm sorry," Quick said. "Raxe is our commander. He's ordered us to find Joel and bring him to the Demon's Spine."

"I will accompany them," Ethan decided.

"What?" Quick asked.

"Of what use would I be if we faced the demon?" Ethan asked. "With you and the Ranger Elf, he does not need my tracking skills. The three of you, and Joel when his magic comes to bear, surely do not need my fighting skills. I fear I would be would be more of a distraction than an asset in a confrontation with the demon. I'll be of more use in the east."

"But Ethan," Quick started.

"I'm staying with the Firemaster and his wife," Ethan said with finality. "Raxe will understand."

Quick looked at his best friend for a moment and finally nodded. "I will take Joel to the Demon's Spine."

"But it will take at least a week for us to reach Ridgeland from here in a horse drawn wagon," Dayna said worriedly. "We have to get there sooner than that. Quick, is there *anything* you can do for us?"

The changeling paused, considering his options. He knew the importance of getting Joel to the Demon's Spine but he also knew that Jon, once recovered, would be a critical ally in the defense of Ridgeland.

Quick turned to Ethan. "Set the horses free. We'll use the reins to fashion an avicaw harness for the wagon. We do that while we wait for Arrowhead and Hammer to catch up with us. I'll fly you all to Ridgeland and then Joel and I to the Demon's Spine. You all will need your wounds treated and a change of clothing – "

Joel cleared his throat dramatically. "Don't I get a say in this? What if I don't want to go to the Demon's Spine?"

"You can come with us to face the walking dead," Dayna said hopefully. Apparently she had grown more confident in Joel's abilities than Joel had.

Joel looked at her as if she were crazy.

"Or you can see how well you fare on your own," Quick suggested, his usual expression of curious or happy excitement turned sullen and cold. "And you can end up back in the demon's possession when it sends someone or *something* else after you."

Joel thought about the absurd deal he had struck with the demon. The escape likely broke it already. The prospect of going it alone in this alien world, though, especially if – or more likely when – the Dierglyorr came after him again, was preposterous. He did not believe he could bear such captivity and torture again.

If he had known anything about wilderness survival his decision would have been different. In the end, he came to the conclusion that he should be where the most help was available when the next nightmare reared its ugly head.

"I guess I'm riding with you, Quick."

13.6

King Vergoth swept into the Carthan Head Mage's study. His long, burgundy, silken cloak clung to his right side while the left side flapped open, revealing the cloak's shimmering black lining and an ornamental straightsword resting in a bejeweled sheath at his hip. Four guards, all carrying spears and armed with scimitars hanging from their hips, flanked him. The queen strode into the room in the men's wake.

Head Mage Samuel Tilsworth and his First High Advisor, Mage Michael Roderick, were seated across from each other on low benches hunched over a low table. They looked up in surprise. The two wizards shared a quick, puzzled glance that turned to dismay when they looked back at the king and noticed the angry expression on his face. The king stood there for a moment, his scornful glare burning into the wizards and then taking in the small yellow bones scattered across the table. The wizards stood and inclined their heads in deference.

"To what do we owe this honor, your highness?" Tilsworth greeted with a respectful bow.

The king glared a moment longer before he spoke. "Where is the third stooge? I would speak to the three of you. Where is Glund?"

Mage Tilsworth blinked at the insult but managed to keep his tone respectful. "The Second High Advisor is in Lorr, as commanded, overseeing that part of our campaign."

Vergoth scoffed. "Overseeing. I wonder if he can see anything. I wonder the same about you. The two of you are playing children's games while you allow my schemes to crumble like dried cat dung."

"Children's games?" Tilsworth asked, offended. "I assure you, my king, that this is no child's game in which we are engaged. We are reading portents in the bones."

"Are they telling you fools how the offworlder and the elf yet live?" Vergoth challenged.

Mage Roderick spoke. "This, we already knew, sire. The bones, however, have told us –"

"I did not address you, underling," Vergoth interrupted. "I was talking to your superior. Although I fear 'superior' might be a grievous overstatement." He turned his attention back to the Carthan Head Mage. "You already knew this? And when did you intend to inform me."

Me. The queen thought. *He omits his wife and partner yet again.*

"My king," Tilsworth replied after shooting a chastising glance at his second. "I thought not to waste your time with information we knew you already possessed. It is public knowledge that the offworlder, his daughter and the elf have passed through Shaddiston and are now travelling to the Demon's Spine."

"When they should have been dead long ago," Vergoth reminded. "They should have died that night in Port Lorrian. They should have died when the sky sleighs were brought down. They should have died at Southborough. You have been given the simplest of tasks, more than enough resources to complete it successfully, and still find a way to fail!"

Queen Lairen smiled. This man was certainly *not* the Vergoth she knew and tolerated.

He had always had a temper but his acute sense of self-preservation usually stayed his tongue in the face of an obvious threat, and angering the two most powerful wizards in the Kingdom of Cartha definitely posed the most obvious of threats. But based on the information she had recently received from her independent sources, she should not have been surprised.

The Carthan Head Mage cleared his throat before continuing. "The bones indicate that the elf and the offworlder will *not* be successful in their quest. We know the *Ken d'Zanir* still track them. Their delay at Southborough has allowed the *Ken* to gain even more ground. The portents say clearly that their pursuers will overtake them. Surely that is what the bones are telling us. I would advise –"

The king's arm shot out with violent speed as he struck the older man with a backhanded slap. Tilsworth stumbled back several steps, his flowing robe fluttering. He would have fallen had the younger wizard not caught him.

The queen's eyes went wide. She knew the king was incensed at the unraveling of his plans. Now she was certain her husband had gone quite mad.

Or had he? Did he have reason not to fear the wizards?

"You will advise *nothing!*" Vergoth growled. "Because of you, I have been made to look the fool in the eyes of the other sovereigns of the Known Lands. You have lost my faith and favor and are hereby dismissed from service to the crown. You will leave this castle and this kingdom with all due haste, either on your own or with an escort of cold steel."

The wizard Tilsworth straightened. His brown-eyed gaze went as cold and hard as ice.

"It is *you* who have lost *our* faith and favor. You have refused intelligent counsel at every turn. King or no king, *no one* takes a violent hand to the High Wizard Samuel Tilsworth and lives. I do believe it is time for the Kingdom of Cartha to be rid of her idiot king."

With the speed of striking cobra, the old wizard lifted his hand and pointed a finger at King Vergoth. The guards gasped and stepped back in fearful anticipation of the wizard's wrath and…

Absolutely nothing happened.

It was the wizards' turn to gasp. Both Tilsworth and Roderick stared at the pointing outstretched hand as if it belonged to a stranger. The queen looked on, her expression unreadable. But the king smiled with the grim humor of a bird of prey.

"You dare to cast ill magic at your king?" Vergoth asked in a thin, even voice that sent a chill down the bewildered wizards' spines. The king swept back the right side of his cloak to reveal a fist-sized leather pouch with its flap opened. "Or should I say you dare to *try* to cast ill magic?"

Tilsworth saw the pouch. "It can't be," he whispered.

Roderick stared. "How did you get one of the talismans?"

"Do you think I would allow my pawns to use such a gift without saving one for myself?" Vergoth taunted. He snatched the straightsword from its sheath and plunged it into

Tilsworth's heart.

The magic-stealing talisman, the Queen thought. So, that was the source of his newfound confidence. He had it all this time and never said a word to her about it. He had been distancing himself from her from the moment the dark wizard came to him secretly to convince him to undertake this campaign.

This last bit of exclusion decided her.

The old wizard grit his teeth and glared defiantly at his murderer. "This makes you no less the idiot, Vergoth. This once-great kingdom will go to hell under your rule."

Vergoth twisted the blade, coaxing a pained cry and then a death rattle from the wizard. He snatched it free and watched the wizard Tilsworth crumple to the floor. He turned to his guards. "Kill the underling."

"But I did nothing, sire!" Roderick pled. "I was merely –"

Whatever words he planned to utter died with him as one of the guards jabbed a spear into his throat. As he coughed and gurgled and collapsed to his knees, another guard put him out of his misery with a spear thrust through the doomed wizard's heart. Still smiling, Vergoth knelt and cleaned his blade with Tilsworth's robe. He stood, sheathed the sword and turned to face his wife.

"And he called *me* an idiot," he said smugly.

"Do you think killing them was wise?" Queen Lairen asked. "They have provided faithful service over the years, and helpful counsel, second only to mine own."

"I've grown tired of suffering fools," Vergoth answered.

"Tilsworth was right," Lairen said. "You *are* an idiot. You've always been. But I had no idea you had grown to be such a bloodthirsty idiot."

The king's head jerked backward as if he had been slapped. His suspicious eyes darkened with anger.

"Have you gone insane, you lowborn whore?" Vergoth growled as he wrapped his hand around the grip of his sword again. Lairen looked in his crazed eyes and saw the bloodlust there as he continued. "Your flippant tongue has outweighed your usefulness for far too long. I think I will have your corpse left on the peasant streets where your parents failed to raise you suitably."

Lairen's reply was a cool, thin-lipped smile. The enraged king stepped forward, drawing his sword. Only half of it cleared the sheath before Vergoth stopped short. His crazed anger turned to fearful surprise when he looked down to see a bloody spearhead protruding from his stomach.

"Tilsworth was right about something else," the queen went on. "Cartha would surely go to hell under your rule."

"Who…" Vergoth sputtered as he fell to his knees, the spear still skewering him. "Who will rule, then? Cartha will not follow a woman…"

"Your guards did," she said seductively. The guard that thrust the spear through the king's back released the haft of the spear and stepped around the king to join the other guards at the queen's side.

Vergoth dropped to his hands, trying and failing to assume as defiant a posture as his Head Mage had during his last moments. Vergoth managed to lift his head, tearing his terrified eyes away from his own blood pouring onto the floor tiles of the wizards' study.

"You will nev…" he said breathlessly, "…never rule…"

"I suppose that's true, though it's a shame that the rest of our subjects aren't as bright as your guards," Lairen returned. "If they were, they could see how your schemes threaten to break the First Great Directive and bring down the Old Ones' wrath on all of the Known Lands.

"They would see you pushing this kingdom to the brink of a war with Lorr that we cannot win, at least not without allies. Our military is not even fully recovered from your ill-fated grab at the southern regions of Lorr, and you would assault them again?"

Vergoth's hands slipped in his pooling blood and he toppled over to his side. He looked up at his treacherous wife and guards, his fluttering eyelids grew heavy but he glared nonetheless. His lips fluttered as well, but no sound escaped.

"The Carthan citizenry *will* follow our son," Lairen promised. "He is as beloved as you and far more malleable.

DEMON OF LORR

"He endeared himself to the Lorrian people while attending their academy and will improve our relations, thus making it easier to betray them in the future, when we are much better prepared to defeat them.

"Yes, dead king, this lowborn whore will rule through our son and take this kingdom in the direction its highborn idiot of a king could never manage: the *right* direction."

The guard whose spear protruded from Vergoth bent to Lairen's ear. "My queen, should we find the last mage and send him to join these two?"

Lairen thought for a moment. "I think not," she answered as she stroked his square jaw softly. "I'll allow Mage Glund to complete his charge. There are too many gears in motion to stop now. My husband, with his customary impatience, did not stop to consider that his campaign might yet be successful. And if it is not, we will then kill the Second High Advisor to the Head Mage and lay the entire plot at the feet of the dead king and his wizards."

She turned to her husband with an implacable gaze. "As far as Vergoth the Second and the rest of the Carthan Kingdom are concerned, your wizards went rouge and killed you. Your guards managed to kill them and save my life. I will make our son believe it. He will, in turn, make Cartha believe it."

"No," Vergoth whispered. "Never..."

"Oh, yes," Queen Lairen insisted. "They will. I know they will. But there is one thing I do not know. Which is more foolish? Is it the fact that you would serve as a demon's pawn, or that you would serve as a demon's pawn without realizing it?"

The dying king's fluttering eyelids stopped fluttering. They bulged with shock, almost popping out of his head. And then they closed forever.

Chapter 14: Mar-Dah's Mountain

14.1

DEMON'S SPINE MOUNTAINS

The exhausted trio camped for the night just inside the cut of the concealed pass. Man, elf, and half-faerie were all so exhausted that the need for rest overcame their haste. They set out the next morning and had a blessedly uneventful trek through the pass. The high rock walls to either side hid them from most predators.

The few man-eating animals that discovered them, two mountain cats and a rock badger, were handled quickly with fatally accurate single shots from the Ranger Elf's longbow. In each case he made it a point to retrieve the fletched arrows. He cleaned them with a rough cloth coated with a dark resin and returned them to his quiver.

A full day had passed and dusk was approaching when they finally approached the end of the pass. It took longer than Raxe expected or hoped, but he was happy there were no other surprises. He was already plotting a return path that did not include crossing through Hargathall's Cleft again even though they did not seem to have much choice. Going around it would take too long and he doubted he could persuade the elf to use his phoenix stone to fly them over the treacherous canyon.

But there had to be another way. After almost being devoured by the cursed canyon floor, Raxe had no desire to tempt fate again. As averse as he was to using magic, his fear of Hargathall's Cleft made him wish he could pull the myst spell from Shanderah's memory. He would happily fly himself and Azh across and leave the Ranger Elf to his own devices.

They emerged from the pass and just as Bartok promised, Mar-dah's mountain loomed just before them, towering behind a line of much lower mounds that concealed its base.

DEMON OF LORR

There was nothing particularly distinguishable about the mountain itself, but one thing left no doubt in Raxe's mind that they had finally reached their destination.

There was a complete absence of magic. Raxe had become so used to the near-transparent shimmer of magic that radiated from every object in nature, both animate and inanimate, that unless he made an intentional effort to see it, he only noticed it on three occasions: when it was stronger than usual, as it was with objects or beings that were possessed of more magical energy than normal; when it was tainted the way Shaddor Rinn's subjects were tainted; and when it was missing altogether, as with Joel. This mountain was conspicuous to him because it was the only one that did not have a shimmer at all.

Raxe thought back to his first visit to the Kingdom of Lorr when he, old Shanderah, Meldrick Sureblade, and the other royal soldiers visited Infinity Isle. Raxe was taken underground, against his will, by massive humanoid creatures called Havoks so that he could claim the enchanted armor he now wore. Shanderah found him by looking for an *absence* of magic. She correctly assumed that was the only way Raxe's aura could completely escape her detection. Raxe now understood what she must have sensed.

It was like looking at a ghost of a mountain. Raxe had not noticed it until this moment, but his sensitivity to magic had become as much a part of his perception of the world as his sight, hearing, touch and taste. Seeing the mountain without seeing its magical aura was like watching a dog bark without actually hearing the sound, or hearing a disembodied voice with no physical being attached. It was weird, an unnatural anomaly that disturbed him more than Worldhopper, the King of the Dragons. And it was almost as scary.

Raxe looked over at Azhju'lestra. He was not sure how his daughter perceived magical auras, but from the uncomfortable and confused look on her face Raxe could tell she also realized that something was seriously amiss. A person with no sensitivity to magic would never notice anything out of the ordinary. To Raxe and his daughter, the sensation was akin to losing one of their five senses.

"I wish we did not have to go in there," Azh said worriedly. She was standing at his right hip, looking up at him with her wide and shimmering pale brown eyes. The needle-thin bands of light and dark streaks in her irises caught and reflected the dying light, intensifying the stark emotion in the young Child's countenance.

"So do I, Azh," Raxe said, absently placing a comforting hand on her tiny shoulder and drawing her closer.

Rell Kallen looked even more annoyed than usual. His deepening frown only added to the sharp lines of his angular features. He tugged softly at the tip of his long, light blonde braid as he gazed at the mountain.

"This place smells...wrong," the Ranger Elf growled. "Like death, both old and recent."

"Yeah," Raxe said. "Even I can smell it. Decomposing bodies."

Rell spat. "Let us find the Hell Key as quickly as possible and be gone from this accursed place."

This was one time Raxe was in complete agreement with Rell Kallen.

And then Raxe sighed angrily, noting that they faced yet another obstacle. They were just a few yards away from the edge of a deep ravine that cut a gash in the earth between them and Mar-dah's mountain.

This was not a sloping descent into a deep canyon like much of Hargathall's Cleft. It was a sheer drop on both sides that, in the half-light of dusk, was swallowed by shadow. The ravine stretched in either direction until it disappeared within the midst of the barren, rocky mountain range. Raxe gauged the distance between cliffs at roughly seventy feet.

"Not even *you* can jump that, can you?" Raxe asked Rell.

Rell Kallen ignored Raxe and peered into the distance. "It would have been nice if the dwarf had mentioned this." He peered down into the ravine, narrowing his canted eyes and breathing deeply through the flared nostrils of his long, thin nose. "There is water down there."

"Yes," Azh agreed. "There is a narrow river almost two miles down."

"There's gotta be a bridge," Raxe said. "Mar-dah may not have needed one with his magic, but how else could his men cross this?"

"Gryphons," Rell Kallen reminded in a condescending tone. "A sky sleigh, perhaps." He knelt and studied the rocky earth, his sharp eyes wide and intense. "There is scant evidence of a pack animal trail that has not been used in quite some time. There had to have been a bridge somewhere close at one point. If it isn't here anymore, we'll make one."

Raxe gave the elf an incredulous look. "What are you going to do, pull the building materials out of your ass?"

The Ranger Elf scowled. "What is this fixation you have with pack animals? Why do you speak of asses so often?"

"What?" Raxe asked. "Oh…yeah. I keep forgetting."

Azh giggled softly. "I know what you mean, father."

"I've no time for this foolishness," Rell Kallen grumbled.

Without another word, the elf bent his knees and sprung high into the air. He sailed at least fifteen feet high before landing lightly on a small outcropping of rock on the mountainside. He began to climb, finding hand and foot holds that Raxe could not even see. He scrambled quickly up another twenty feet or so to another ledge that was so small it looked to Raxe like the elf was clinging to the sheer face of the mountain like a bug.

After peering both east and west for a few moments, he leapt from his high perch, did a somersault, and landed at almost the exact place he stood a few seconds earlier.

"There's a bridge less than a half mile to the west of us. It's along this path."

Without another word, he stalked away in that direction.

14.2

It was past sundown when they made a sharp turn along the edge of a path parallel to the ravine and spotted the bridge. The three moons had not quite risen above the jagged peaks of the Demon's Spine, but all three of them must have been full because the night sky was tinted with pale silver light. Deep, ghostly shadows blanketed the mountainscape in random, sinister patterns all around them.

"Finally," Raxe said breathlessly. He was no longer willing or able to mask his exhaustion.

"Wait," Rell Kallen said, holding up a hand. "Quiet."

The Ranger Elf's sharply pointed ears twitched, his nostrils flared again, and he stared hard at the bridge.

"I hear nothing but the wind rushing through the mountains, I smell nothing but rocks and dirt and the familiar mountain creatures hiding from us and stalking us from the shadows…but there is something else."

Rell Kallen walked toward the bridge once more. This time, though, his pace was slower. His steps were even lighter than usual and he was more alert than ever. Raxe followed closely, holding Azh's hand protectively. Rell stopped again when they had come to within ten yards of the foot of the bridge.

The shadows crept back slowly as the moons rose higher in the eastern sky to reveal the bridge in more detail. It was a narrow, sagging structure made of thick ropes and short wooden planks. On the near side of the bridge sat two large rough-hewn boulders almost as tall as Raxe and three times as wide. They rested just beyond the outside of the waist-high rods that secured the rope handrails.

The boulders did not seem to be a part of the bridge architecture and were too coarse and uneven to be decorative. Raxe noticed how the monoliths reflected the moonlight with slightly more intensity than their surroundings. He moved closer and recognized the stones' dim glow as magical auras.

"There's magic in those boulders," he informed the others. "What do you think it could be?"

The Ranger Elf shrugged. "Perhaps Mar-dah infused them with some sort of magic to warn him of anyone's crossing."

Raxe turned to his daughter. "Any ideas, Azh?"

"I think they might be alive," she whispered.

"Living rocks?" Rell Kallen scoffed. "Alive with magic, no doubt. Mar-dah is long dead, so there's no one for the rocks to alert."

Raxe could tell the bridge was old and well used yet it looked like it was still sturdy. But the way it sagged and rocked in the sharp winds that whipped through the mountains worried the hell out of him. He had all but conquered his fear of heights and he was fairly certain that his armor would protect him from the impact of any fall, but he was still not keen on the idea of free falling two miles or more into a narrow mountain stream of unknown depth.

"No point of waiting," Raxe said. "That bridge ain't getting any lower or shorter." He turned to his daughter. "Wait here, Azh. I'll see how sturdy it is." He looked at Rell Kallen. "You coming?"

Instead of answering, the elf went to one knee and placed his right hand, long slender fingers spread wide, on the ground. He looked down at his hand as he did so and sniffed at the air once more. He finally rose to his feet and spoke.

"There's a pulse in the ground, faint and irregular," Rell Kallen muttered. "I'll stay here with the girl in case there are any unwelcome surprises."

Raxe's eyes narrowed as he regarded the Ranger Elf. His sudden concern for Azh or anyone or anything other than himself and his mission was out of character. Raxe held no illusions that the elf was starting to warm to them. He reached up to his right shoulder, to where his open-topped helmet ringed his bare deltoid where it emerged from his cuirass's short pauldron.

Never taking his eyes off of the mysterious elf, Raxe slid the helmet down and off his right arm. He winced briefly when the helmet tapped painfully against the sensitive flesh-and-metal-coated claw that was his ruined right hand.

He slipped the helmet on his head. If there were to be any surprises, either from the elf or some unknown threat, he would be ready. With his left hand clutching Demonsbane's handle, he covered half the distance between him and the bridge with slow, cautious steps. As he walked further, he gazed alternately at the bridge, the blackness of the ravine, the night sky, and over his shoulder at his daughter and the elf. Both of them watched him expectantly.

When he turned back toward the bridge the ground lurched violently beneath his feet.

The next thing he knew he was flipping backwards head over heels and landed flat on his stomach. He scrambled to his hands and knees and lifted his head just in time to glimpse a massive stone club hurtling toward his face. Battle-honed reflexes snapped him to his feet. Instead of striking his head, the club smashed into the stomach of his muscled cuirass with an ear-splitting clang.

The enchanted silver armor, made of the same Titan's ore as Demonsbane and the metal that sporadically coated his right hand, protected him from the blow. The force of it, however, still sent him tumbling uncontrollably through the air. He felt weightless as the star-and-moon-lit sky flashed before his eyes, followed quickly by the shadowy ground and then the sky again. With a monumental effort he regained his bearings and pulled his legs beneath him in time to land hard in a crouch a few feet behind Rell Kallen and Azh. He stood quickly, brandishing Demonsbane and looking at the bridge.

A giant arm, just longer than Raxe was tall, and seemingly covered with segmented plate armor carved from pale, grayish brown stone, protruded from one of two boulders at the foot of the bridge. The arm held in its gargantuan three-fingered grip the five-foot long, stone, blocky cudgel that had just knocked Raxe flying – as if an appendage so formidable even needed a weapon.

A similar appendage expanded from the other boulder with an explosive crack that shook the ground and echoed throughout the mountain range. It pulled up a chunk of the stony earth before it for its own cudgel.

DEMON OF LORR

The way the arm lifted the stone club from the ground was an indication to Raxe of what flipped him over so unexpectedly. The first creature must have pulled its weapon from right under his feet.

And then another arm broke free from both boulders as they began to shudder, sending tremors through the ground that were strong enough to make Raxe fear an avalanche. The trio watched in horror as both boulders unfolded with loud cracking and crumbling sounds. Broad legs that seemed relatively stubby compared to the arms, sheathed in the same stone armor, broke noisily away from both sides of both boulders. The legs ended in massive three-toed feet that slammed into the ground and gained purchase so firm that the feet seemed to merge with the rock. The huge arms and legs pushed down until the larger central parts of the boulders rose from the ground.

Smaller boulders, squat and rectangular and as large as Raxe's torso, swung down from the bottom of the boulders. The boulders pivoted and reshaped themselves until giant caricatures of beardless dwarves with dense stone armor rose from a crouching position to their full height of ten feet. The creatures' eyes were completely hidden within the shadow of their protruding ridged brows.

Two small, horizontal slits in the middle of their flat, nearly featureless faces served as nostrils. The closed mouths cut into their stony faces, grotesquely high and less than a human finger's width below their nostrils, were nothing but thin, barely visible fissures turned down on both ends into sullen scowls. The monoliths were nearly identical. The only noticeable difference between them was that one's face bore a more rounded chin.

"What the hell are those things?" Raxe rasped in a near panic. "And what kind of armor are they wearing?"

"Those are monsters that have no business in the Known Lands," Rell Kallen answered. "Their entire race was banished to the Unknown Lands at the end of Heaven's War for fighting on the side of the Leaders.

"They fought to dominate and subjugate the human, elf, and dwarf races. And they are not wearing armor. They are, in fact, naked."

A spark of recognition flashed in the recesses of Raxe's memories. They were not Shanderah's second-hand memories, either. He had never seen them before, but his mother and grandfather had described them vividly when they told him stories of the Kingdom of Lorr and of Heaven's War, stories that he had always believed were faerie tales until he crossed the WorldGate for the first time.

"Oh, shit," Raxe swore. "Rock trolls."

"It was their heartbeats I felt," Rell Kallen realized. He reached up to his neck and tugged at the string that secured his torn cloak, letting it drop to the dusty earth.

The two beasts cracked open their mouths impossibly wide with the sound of rending stone and roared. The bass echoing sound was like massive stones being ground together. The deep vibrations thumped Raxe's eardrums like giant hands clouting his ears.

The terrible sound sent tremors all the way to his bones. It felt as if the sonic resonance would disturb the rhythm of his heartbeat. The painful noise disoriented him for only a moment. When his head finally cleared, the trolls were charging with their clubs raised to strike.

Raxe spared the briefest moment to check on his daughter. She was gone. Fighting down a quick surge of panic, he looked up to see one of the monolithic creatures swinging his weapon again. The creatures were surprisingly nimble despite their cumbersome appearance. They were not very quick, but their height and monstrous wingspans allowed them to cover a great deal of space in a very short amount of time.

A dive to the right took Raxe out of the cudgel's deadly path. The swipe was so powerful that the wide edge of the blocky club threw a blast of wind that kept Raxe airborne longer than he had planned. By the time his feet touched down and he pivoted to face the troll, he had to dash forward in a deep crouch to avoid the downward-arcing cudgel.

DEMON OF LORR

The head of the cudgel hit the ground right behind him like an explosion. The concussion sent Raxe tumbling between the widespread columnar legs of the troll. He went into a controlled roll and came to his feet. The troll pivoted to its right, sweeping the deadly cudgel along the ground in the same direction, looking for its victim. Raxe ran in the direction of the pivot to stay out of the monster's field of vision. He darted to the troll's left leg and swung Demonsbane as hard as he could.

The crescent-shaped blades were curved so severely that they almost formed a complete circle, like a disk with a two-foot circumference. The diamond-hard, razor-sharp edge of the fore axe blade sliced smoothly into the rocky hide of the troll's left calf. The rear blade followed through just as easily. Unfortunately for Raxe, the troll's calf was more than twice as wide as Demonsbane's blades. The leg was cut deeply but was not completely severed.

Thick black blood with the consistency of syrup ran from the wound. The troll roared in what sounded to Raxe more like irritation than pain. But instead of reversing its pivot and wheeling back to its left to head off its target, the troll continued to sweep the cudgel around its back. Raxe saw the blow coming out of his peripheral vision and instantly knew he could not clear the wide breadth of the cudgel in time. He had just enough time to pivot, brace himself, and take the blow in the torso again.

Raxe wrapped his arms around the cudgel. The business end of the weapon was wider than Raxe but he managed to drive Demonsbane into one side of the stone club with his left hand. With his right hand, his agonizingly clawed fingers found secure purchase on the rough, pitted surface of the massive cudgel.

He held on with all of his might and fought back an agonized scream from the pain burning in his right hand as the cudgel whipped back in the other direction.

14.3

Rell Kallen was surprised when out of the corner of his eye he saw Azhju'lestra dive gracefully over the cliff and into the deep gorge. He also took note of the offworlder diving clumsily out of the way of an attack. The next moment he himself was leaping backward, easily avoiding the hammering blow of the other troll's cudgel. By the time his soft-soled, booted feet touched the ground again his bow was poised horizontally and knocked with two arrows.

He released the taught bowstring and let the arrows fly into the shadows beneath the troll's eye ridges. The troll stood up straight and threw its head back, bellowing in pain. It tried to pull the arrows from its eyes with its free hand but the wooden shafts were too small and its three fingers were too broad to get a hold of them.

It decided to attack where it had last seen the elf, sweeping its cudgel blindly to the right and left. But Rell Kallen was long gone from that area. He had swiftly and quietly dashed around behind the troll, shouldered his bow, and from his baldric he had drawn his long sword. The long sword was nearly five feet long, more than half as long as the width of the troll's massive skull. A strong jump took him to the troll's right shoulder. He wrapped his legs around the troll's wide neck and drove the blade of his long sword into the sliver of space in the fist-sized, stony lump that was the troll's right ear.

The ear hole was as narrow as the blade was wide. The elf had to use as much strength as he could muster to drive the sword in. Sparks poured from the dense metal and a high-pitched keening screech rang in the night until the hilt of the long sword finally halted the momentum of the blade.

The troll roared again. This time it dropped its cudgel and lifted its arms. Well before the monster could reach him, though, the Ranger Elf braced both feet against the side of the troll's head, gripped the long handle of his sword in two hands and pushed mightily with his legs.

DEMON OF LORR

The powerful shove pulled his blade free and flung him from the troll's shoulder just before the creature's giant groping hands could grasp him. He somersaulted and landed in a crouch. The troll turned slowly, unsteady on its feet, and sniffed weakly in search of its enemy.

*   *   *

The troll attacking Raxe was apparently accustomed to seeing something airborne after being struck. After its cudgel made contact, it took a moment to look for Raxe soaring off to the left. When nothing was seen, it sniffed and then pivoted its boulder head around and saw Raxe clinging to its weapon. With a rumbling growl, the troll swung the cudgel in a wide arc that slammed Raxe into the mountainside. Because of his armor, the blow did not even knock the wind from him, but he was growing dizzy from being whipped about as if he were the troll's toy.

When it noticed its victim still holding on, the troll raised the cudgel high to slam it to the ground. Raxe pushed up and away from the cudgel when it reached the top of its swing, using its momentum to throw him straight and high into the air behind the troll. The troll smashed the weapon into the earth hard enough to leave a crater. The creature cocked its head curiously when it noticed its would-be victim was gone. A moment later it heard Raxe landing behind its left leg.

Raxe took another powerful hack with his enchanted battleaxe to widen his first cut to twice its original length. But this time he could not turn in time to dodge or even catch the swinging cudgel. The stone bludgeon hit him in the back and the backside, launching him forward like a polo ball.

Unfortunately, Raxe was facing the ravine. As he soared over the edge, he found himself wishing the troll had hit him twice as hard. At least that way he would have flown clear to the ground on the far side of the ravine. Instead, he flew to nearly the mid point of the perilous drop and then fell straight down into the seemingly bottomless chasm.

14.4

Rell Kallen watched his attacker clutch its bleeding ear hole, wobble back and forth as if drunk, and then topple backward and crash to the earth like a fallen tree, or better yet, a fallen monolithic stone column. After flicking the thick black blood from his blade, the elf turned just in time to see the other troll bat the offworlder into the chasm.

"By Eleshay's emerald eyes!" the elf swore.

He knew Raxe would survive the fall even if no water ran through the bottom of the deep ravine. The properties of the offworlder's god-forged armor were no secret to him. But he also knew that it would take much more time than he could spare for Raxe to climb back out.

In any event, he had no real concern for the lives of the offworlder Child or his halfling daughter. The girl was useless, anyway.

Rell Kallen did not know why the foolish offworlder insisted on bringing her along. She obviously shared Raxe's power as a Child of the Old Ones, but that power was useless unless or until they confronted the demon or its magic.

There was something different about her, he knew, in addition to her divine heritage. But whatever that difference was had not proven of any use to them in their quest. He was relieved to see her lose her wits and dive over the edge rather than face the trolls, but he still had need of Raxe. He could use either of them to lead him to the Hell Key. Their connection to the talisman as Children of the Old Ones was interchangeable. Raxe, though, was at least somewhat useful in a fight. At the *very* least he could provide a distraction for the elf if the need arose.

His attention was suddenly pulled back to the surviving troll. It swiveled its head slowly to the left and then right with the sound of grinding sandstone. It sniffed loudly as it did so and then realized that there was another victim to attend to. Rell Kallen readied his bow and reached for two more arrows as the beast tried to turn, but the troll faltered.

DEMON OF LORR

Its left leg snapped cleanly away at Demonsbane's cut in its calf. With a loud pop that was a combination of wet, snapping bone and the breaking of dense stone, the black-bloodied leg stump struck the ground. The troll tottered clumsily to the left. Before it could right itself, it stumbled slowly over the ravine cliff.

"Well," Rell Kallen said aloud, "there's that, at least." He counted the seconds until he heard the fading echo of a splash so very far below. "One less troll to waste my time."

And then an unexpected noise drifted to his sensitive ears. It was the sound of rushing water coming from behind, causing him to turn and look out over the great chasm.

To his surprise, he saw the two Children of the Old Ones, father and daughter, resting atop a narrow geyser of water that held them suspended a few feet above the top of the ravine. The girl stood straight and stiff, her hair flowing out in every direction in defiance of the path of the blowing wind. Her back was to him and her arms were slightly raised, obviously steering the geyser east, in the direction of Mardah's mountain.

Raxe sat with his legs folded, facing Rell Kallen, smiling like an idiot and waving his uninjured hand.

"See you at the mountain, shorty!" Raxe taunted as they receded into the deepening shadows.

So, Rell thought, *the offworlder copulated with the Mistress of the Sea of Spirits.* He had not known or even cared about the identity of the girl's mother until that moment. The Elder's Council of the elven Kingdom of Thâlstrën had long ago informed the Ranger Elf that Sabrina, the Mistress of the Sea of Spirits was not a mere elemental, but actually a creature of faerie.

She was the last water faerie, in fact, until the birth of this little girl. Rell Kallen knew that faerie creatures were extremely powerful and unpredictable; their logic not easily understood by other races. He would have to watch that mixed-breed Child.

With an irritated grunt, the Ranger Elf sprinted to the bridge.

14.5

Raxe was surprised – even though by then he should not have been – when he saw Rell Kallen emerge from the shadows at a dead sprint. By Raxe's estimation, Azh had ferried them directly down the middle of the ravine for nearly a mile in less than two minutes, putting their speed at roughly thirty miles per hour. Even though the Ranger Elf had to cross the long and sagging bridge, he was still only thirty seconds behind them, and he was not even winded. Raxe expected the ill-tempered elf to voice displeasure at being left behind but Rell refused to give him the satisfaction. Instead, he stalked closer and looked at the same thing Raxe and his daughter was watching.

Rell Kallen could not sense magic the ways the Child of the Old Ones could, so he was not aware of its complete absence. However, he, like Raxe and Azh, knew *something* was there, some kind of barrier, a barrier very different from the barrier Shaddor Rinn used to ward his property. Even a human with absolutely no sensitivity to magic would know there was something there. The unmistakable stench of death, along with the grisly sights scattered about the ground just within and without the unseen barrier, clearly revealed its presence.

Along both edges of the barrier rested the remains of different species of animals, from amphibian wallowgrumps to massive rock badgers, from mountain cats to rams. Almost every carcass was headless. In a few cases only the tops of the animals' skulls were sheared away. In even more remote cases, the entire top half of beasts were missing.

In every case, the missing parts were cut away and cauterized in a neat line. The animal carcasses had even fallen in a definite pattern, in an irregular path parallel to the foot of the mountain.

"There aren't many fresh bodies," Raxe observed. "Most of them decayed a long time ago, but look at the few fresher ones."

"That is curious," Azh noted. "The poor animals' bodies on the outside of the barrier, the ones that are still rotting, have piles of dust on the other side where the missing parts of their bodies must have went through."

"That's not dust," Raxe corrected. "The barrier burned them to ash. The wind hasn't blown it all away yet. Some of the animals must have tried to go through with more momentum than others."

"Observe how they have been scavenged," Rell Kallen said, pointing to several of the newer corpses.

"Do you see how the parts of the bodies closest to the barrier are untouched? It appears the carrion eaters were smart enough not to venture too close to the barrier. Pity that their food was not."

"What kind of magic could create a barrier this powerful yet completely undetectable?" Raxe wondered aloud.

"The magic of the Old Ones," Rell Kallen reminded.

"OK," Raxe said. "Any ideas of how to get through it?"

"Step away," Rell Kallen commanded. He reached into the folds of his cloak and pulled out a small, shiny, dark green marble. "One of these stones penetrated the magical barrier surrounding Rionn Lorr's island. It should do the same here."

He failed to mention that the Head Mage was within arms reach of him seconds later. That was neither here nor there. The fact remained that the magic-infused marble given to him by the most talented elven wizards in Thâlstrën opened up the barrier long enough for the Ranger Elf to walk safely through.

He tossed the round stone at the barrier. The marble sailed right through where the barrier should have been and fell harmlessly to the ground on the other side. The elf frowned.

Raxe saw the frown. "I take it you were expecting something else. It must not be as similar to Rionn's barrier as you thought."

"Child," Rell Kallen snapped, "Why don't you put the mental energy you waste thinking up pointless and flippant blather to better use by coming up with an idea of your own."

"I can think and bother you at the same time, shorty," Raxe taunted. "And right now I'm drawing a blank."

"Of course you are," the elf grumbled.

"Let's sleep on it," Raxe suggested. He saw the look of disgust form on Rell Kallen's face. "We don't know what we're going to face when we get into that mountain, elf," Raxe continued before Rell Kallen could object. "I want to be rested and alert. You're free to find your way in without us. Then again, if you could do that you wouldn't need us."

"You take first watch," the Ranger Elf directed.

As the elf and half-faerie bedded down for the evening, Raxe's mind wandered. In this moment of calm he could not help but wonder what the others were going through.

Were his grandfather and Lisa safe? Had Quick and Ethan found Joel? How close was Rionn Lorr to finding a cure to the demon's plague of walking dead?

Was Annastace Sureblade thinking about him?

Chapter 15: Loose Ends

15.1

It took Louis five large mugs of strong ale to bolster the courage to finally go through with it. Every drop was drained before he slammed the mug to the tavern table. He resented the Sureblade woman, to be sure, but he had never killed anyone. Of course, the baron did not say Louis *had* to kill her, but Louis knew he could not assault a woman as well known as the Sureblade widow and leave her alive to tell the authorities.

Though he had never killed before, Louis was no stranger to rape...or at least the attempt. He was with Tauran fifteen years earlier when they tried to ravage a young serving woman at the military dining hall. Louis was a civilian employed there as a cook and Tauran, his friend, was a new recruit. As comely as the girl was, it did not take much prodding for Tauran to convince Louis to take part. Meldrick Sureblade walked in on them just in time to save the girl. He reported them both, which resulted in Tauran being kicked out of the military and Louis losing his job.

Louis did not harbor nearly as much resentment toward Meldrick as Tauran did. In fact, his resentment toward Annastace did not even directly involve her late husband. The resentment started because he loathed working for a woman. He only did so because she paid field laborers better wages than the other employers in that part of the kingdom. His biggest problem was her constant rejection of him and every other man who paid court to her, as if she was too good for any other man.

Beauty like hers was supposed to be shared with and protected by an able man. Louis once told her as much, and he promised her that he would not hesitate to leave his wife and four children for her. Her response was a snobbish look down her pretty little nose at him from the high seat on her carriage and a command to get back to work.

It was time for her to pay for that humiliation.

The three men seated at the table with him finished their ale. A chorus of belches rang out around the table. One of the men across the table from Louis, a laborer named Marwood, wiped his mouth and turned an amused gaze to Louis.

"Are you thoroughly fueled for tonight's adventure then, Louis?"

After another loud belch, Louis nodded. "And then some. Let's ride."

Gordon, also known as Weasel, was a short, wiry man with dark brown skin, coarse, short-cropped hair and wide, shifty eyes, was the first to shoot to his feet. He was the smallest of them but the biggest drinker, and he never seemed to get more than a bit tipsy. "Yes, yes," he agreed. "I've been wanting to pluck that bit of fruit for years."

"We all have," said Brandon, called the White Bull by his friends, as he stood. "The bitch is too uppity for her own good. I'll bet no one's skewered that fruit since the Finder skewered Meldrick. She needs a powerful sword like mine, and a powerful man like me to drive it home."

The White Bull was of average height. That was the only thing average about him. His skin was so pale he very nearly was pure white. His hair was carrot red, the same color as the freckles that dusted his broad face. He was so disproportionately wide that from a distance he appeared to be dwarfish, and not a bit of his girth was fat. His temper matched the animal for which he had been nicknamed and it only got worse when he drank. He was tossed out of the military for fighting and made his living on the Tyne as a ship loader for riverboats.

Marwood came to his feet. He was a hair taller than Louis, lean and raven-haired. He was called Crow for his black hair and black eyes and long beak of a nose. His widow's peak and ponytail pulled back tightly against his scalp made him look even more birdlike. He was fair-skinned, though not nearly as blanched as Brandon. He had a sly humor that hid a sadistic nature to everyone save those who knew him well.

"Do you need help to stand, Louis?" he taunted.

DEMON OF LORR

"Hells no," Louis snapped. He stood too fast and had to put a hand on the table when the room began to spin. When the spinning stopped, the euphoria of intoxication settled in and he knew he was ready to go through with it this time.

He had started the trip to Annastace's home almost every night since his return from Eastedge, only to stop and turn back. He had done many unsavory things in his life, but always on impulse. There was something about the premeditation of tonight's endeavor that had been giving him pause. Too much forward planning left too much time for common sense and fear of repercussion to stop him.

Every night he turned back he knew he was risking his own life. There was no doubt that Tauran's threat was genuine. The *Ken* assassin could come for him at any moment if he did not do as he was ordered. When his paranoia finally overcame his trepidation, he knew just what he needed to carry out this deed. Liquor and partners.

It was a short ride from the tavern to the Sureblade home. Louis was sweating despite the cool autumn night and was thankful that the ride was a short one. If it had been any longer he feared he would lose his nerve. He was also thankful that the home was relatively solitary. It sat at the end of a curved cobblestone path that cut through a stand of pine trees and brambles for twenty yards or so, at the center of a half-acre of cleared land and a neatly manicured lawn. The house was flanked by a large barn and small horse stable.

The half-acre was surrounded by forest. Good. The only ears that would hear them belonged to a few goats, chickens, and horses.

The cottage was dark and quiet. No candles or lamps burned within and the shutters were drawn. Louis had never been inside the home but he was familiar with the general layout of cottages such as these. The bedrooms would be around back. The home was fairly large, so a careful entry from the front was not likely to be heard. Even though it was a big home, it was still a one-story cottage and a relatively modest dwelling considering Meldrick had been a prosperous knight and landowner.

"The righteous Sureblade clan," Crow sneered when the cottage came into view. "They live in a hovel when they can easily afford a manse, but the oh-so-altruistic Meldrick Sureblade happily sacrificed his own self-indulgence in order to pay a larger wage to his employees."

"What's worse," the Bull added, "is that it's all for show. You know the bastard was only angling for the king's favor. He wanted a lordship like any other man would. His widow is no different."

Weasel chuckled evilly. "I hate false modesty. All the more reason to do 'er and have done with 'er, eh?"

"And the brats," Louis said, the ire of his companions strengthening his resolve. "And as soon as the oldest boy, the Keeper's Hound, comes sniffing around hunting for vengeance, we'll send him to join the rest of his family."

Louis reined his horse to a halt and signaled for the others to do the same. "We walk from here, and quietly."

As they all dismounted and hobbled their horses, the Bull looked around nervously and whispered, "No dogs running about, eh? Sureblade seemed the type to keep dogs." He eased his dirk out of the sheath hanging from his sword belt.

"If so, I think we'd have heard them by now," Crow whispered back.

"No guards either," Weasel observed. "Seems the royal guard she had protecting 'er that last day of the harvest didn't extend t' home."

Louis licked his lips. "All the better for us."

"I get first taste," Weasel declared.

"You'll stick to the plan," Louis snapped in a hushed tone. "Quiet now, and wait for the signal. Let's not muck this up with clucking like bloody roosters."

All but Crow shot Louis irritated looks, resenting his haughty and authoritative tone. Crow only smiled. But they all fell silent as they crept up to the cottage.

When they reached the cottage, Weasel bent low and went around to the back. The Bull and Crow eased their way to either side of the cottage while Louis tipped up the two stairs of the front porch.

DEMON OF LORR

At the back of the house, Weasel approached a window with the shutters cracked an inch. Someone preferred it nice and cold while they slept. Two young but tall oak trees sprouted from each side of the window a few feet from the wall, their braches twining a few feet above the roof edge. He inched into the shadow of the nearest oak and then to the edge of the window to peek through the thin opening just under the hinge of the shutter. The thin silver shaft of moons' light that shone through the cracked shutters was just enough to reveal young Arielle Sureblade fast asleep in her bed.

She was approaching her teens, Weasel knew, and she had her mother's alluring looks. In the dim light of the moons and stars he could not make out her features clearly but he had seen the girl before by the light of day on more than one occasion. He knew exactly how pretty she was. Her smooth brown skin and full lips with those big blue eyes gave her an exotic aspect. And even though she likely had not flowered yet, she was already developing in ways that hinted that she would be as buxom as her mother.

Weasel smiled and cautiously pulled the shutter toward him to open it further, holding his breath and hoping the hinge did not creak or squeal. When it did not, he pulled his longsword out an inch from its sheath to make sure it was clear and then let it slide quietly back into its scabbard. The windowsill was level with the bottom of his chest. It would be an easy climb through the window. He smiled even wider when he thought about what he would do to the pretty little brown haired girl before he killed her.

He stepped over to the front of the window and then yelped in surprise and confusion when he heard a snap, felt a painful grip on his left ankle, and was flipped over and snatched into the air.

*　*　*

Arielle's eyes popped open at the sound of the snap and she was on her feet by the time she heard the yelp.

She moved to the window in a flash and looked out and up to see a near panicked man bobbing upside down, held fast by his ankle from a taut rope suspended from a branch of one of the trees outside her window.

"Damn it!" he snapped. "Cut me down from here!"

She set that trap for her twin brother. The two of them always played games like this. They set non-lethal traps for one another to see who could come up with the best snares. They took turns tracking each other in the woods and tried to spy on one another without the other one knowing. They competed against each other in archery, reading sign, javelin throwing and the like. Ethan used to play with them before he went off to the Royal Military Academy. Arielle never dreamed her trap would catch anyone other than August.

Their eyes met. The surprise, fear and then anger she saw in the skinny man's eyes frightened her. Before either of them could speak again, she heard another yelp from outside, somewhere around the corner on the west side of the cottage. And then a loud crash sounded from inside the home, from the direction of her mother's room.

No, she thought in a near panic. She gave the stranger a last fearful look, turned and rushed away from the window.

"Wait," Weasel called in harsh whisper. "Get me down you little…"

Arielle was gone before she heard the name he called her.

* * *

The White Bull had his back pressed to the wall just outside of August Sureblade's window when he heard Weasel's cry. That was definitely not the signal, so he did not move right away. But then, as he listened to that fool Weasel curse the young girl loudly enough to wake the dead, he also heard the boy moving inside his room.

He unsheathed his dirk to smash open the shutters and rush the pre-teen, but when he moved to the front of the closed window and raised his weapon, the ground beneath him gave way. He gave a yelp as tumbled into a deep pit.

The unexpected fall sent him head over heels. He lost the dirk in the fall, and found it again the moment after he struck the bottom of the pit backside first, and he found it in the worst way.

The dirk landed point down, right through his thigh. His roar of pain echoed within the deep pit just as a loud crash rang out.

*   *   *

Annastace was reaching for her rapier where it lay beneath her bed when she heard the man outside cursing her daughter. She had it to hand when she heard the other voice, deeper than the first one, cry out in a surprised yelp from somewhere further away outside. She was halfway to her bedroom door when her window came crashing in.

She turned to see a tall, slender man with jet-black hair scrambling carefully through the broken window. Had she not feared for her children she would have rushed back to the window and run him through as he entered. The twins came first, though, so she turned back and rushed out of the room, turned left and sprinted down the hall toward her children's rooms. She cried out and almost ran herself through as another tall man with his sword held out before him stepped into the corridor from an adjacent hall.

Annastace danced nimbly to the left to narrowly avoid the point of the shadow man's longsword. He moved quickly to keep her from continuing down the hall, forcing her back in the direction from which he had just come. He followed her, thrusting his sword at her again and again to force her backward and into the adjoining corridor.

Annastace had to hold her rapier with both hands to bat away the heavier longsword as she backed into the parlor at the far end of the hall. The attacker stepped into a shaft of moons' light shining through the parlor window.

"I see Meldrick gave you some sword lessons before he died," the intruder observed. "But not enough."

"Louis," Annastace breathed. "Louis, please...I implore you, go home to your family."

"You don't have the king's men to guard you, now," Louis said, ignoring her pleas. "And you cannot hope to outfight me."

Her fear for her children was turning into outrage at Louis's brazenness.

"Is that why you brought the others, you craven bastard? How many men does it take to steal coin from one woman?"

She wondered where those other men were. Her worry for her children grew.

Louis smiled an ugly smile and leered at her in a way that made her want to wretch. The loose shift she wore could not completely conceal the curves of her ample bosom and hips. Louis took it all in greedily.

"It's not your *coin* I want, woman. Now, save us both some trouble and put the sword down. This will go much easier for you if you do."

"For what you want, Louis, you'll have to kill me first."

A voice floated to them from down the hall and around the corner. "Do we *really* have to kill you, Anna?" Crow walked into the far side of the hall. He had a handful of her son's curly hair in his left hand and with his right held the edge of his short sword to August's throat.

Annastace's heart dropped. "Please don't hurt my son," she begged, her outrage quickly souring to despair. "Where is my daughter?"

They all heard the White Bull's moaning.

"I'm sure Arielle is otherwise occupied," Louis taunted. "You can end all of this, Anna. All you have to do is put down your sword."

Annastace knew none of them would be left alive. "Let my son go," she insisted. "Bring my daughter. *Then* I will put down my sword."

Crow shook his head in mock apology. "I'm sorry, but you have no leverage here. We'll bring you your whelps after you've put down your –" He was silenced by an arrowhead suddenly jutting from his throat.

August looked up, gasped, and then moved. He snatched Crow's short sword and spun out of his grasp as the tall raven-haired man crumpled to the ground. When he fell, Annastace, August and Louis saw Arielle standing at the end of the hall brandishing a bow half as long as she was tall. A quiver filled with arrows was strapped to her thigh.

DEMON OF LORR

Annastace's heart broke at the fear and regret she saw in her daughter's aspect from what she had just done. However, Annastace also saw Meldrick's calm resolve in his daughter's wide brown eyes as she kept them locked on Louis and reached for another arrow.

* * *

Weasel was sawing feverishly at the tough hempen rope with his longsword when the sounds of fighting from inside the cottage went silent. He could still hear the Bull's moaning around the corner, though the sound had changed. It had gotten weaker. The cries were less from pain and more from fear. Brandon started whimpering, and that was a sound Weasel never thought he'd hear from the White Bull.

Weasel had no idea why theBull was blubbering the way he was. The only words he could make out were "help" and "bleeding bad" and "get me out" before the sounds turned incoherent. Whatever it was, Weasel knew it was nothing good, and that made him saw at the rope with renewed vigor.

The hush that had fallen within the home was just as puzzling. Weasel did not know if it meant Louis and Crow had silenced the boy and were having their way with the females or if they had simply killed them all. If they had killed the Sureblades, surely they would have come looking for him and the Bull by now.

On the other hand, if they were doing the mother and daughter there would have been screams. Well, not if they gagged the wenches, Weasel realized. It would have been just like those tall, arrogant bastards to get the first tastes before bothering to find out what was taking their accomplices so long to join the festivities.

Weasel was pondering the silence within the house and the Bull's moaning outside so deeply that he was taken unaware when the rope finally gave. It was all he could do to turn his body to keep from falling on the top of his head and breaking his neck. He landed on his back and the pain rushed in as all of the air in his lungs exploded out. Several seconds passed before he could make himself rise.

He contemplated going in through the window but there was something unsettling about the silence. Instead of going in there by himself, he ran around the house to check on the Bull.

By the time he rounded the corner in a wary but rushed jog, Bull had fallen silent. The shadows were so deep on that side of the house that he almost missed the hole beneath the bedroom window. He came to a stumbling halt that caused his feet to slip from under him. A painful fall to his backside and a slide upon the grass and fallen leaves left his legs dangling over the edge of the pit.

"Bull," he whispered as he peeked down into the dark hole. Weasel could see the darker silhouette of the Bull's stocky body in the darkness of the hole, but his friend was not moving.

The silence inside and outside of the cottage became too much to bear. Weasel scrambled to his feet and took off in a sprint toward the front of the house. As he cleared the front wall, he was startled to the point of nearly stumbling when Louis burst through the front door at a dead run.

Louis ran in a zigzagging pattern, and before Weasel had a chance to wonder why, he caught sight of an arrow zipping past the taller man's shoulder. Weasel quickened his pace and instinctively mimicked his accomplice, and it was a good thing he did. A searing pain cut through his right buttocks and hip as an arrow whizzed by *him*.

The two survivors managed to make it to the cover of the trees without catching a fatal shot. They both shunned the cobblestone path and weaved among the pines and brush on either side. Both men gasped with exhaustion and relief when they reached their horses where they were hobbled a few yards from the road within the stand of trees.

They quickly mounted and snapped the reins, leading their horses back onto the road. Their relief turned instantly to horror when they saw that they were surrounded by a dozen mounted and armed men bearing the colors and badges of the Port Lorrian City Guard.

Four of the guards raised loaded crossbows at them while the other eight drew their steel.

"Drop your weapons and dismount," their leader ordered. "The two of you are now captives of the City Guard."

"Dragon piss," Louis cursed as they did as commanded.

Just as their feet touched the ground, Annastace, Arielle, and August Sureblade emerged from the cobblestone path riding Thundergait, Wisp, and Zephyr respectively, mother and children all dressed in nightclothes and cloaks against the cool autumn night. The beautiful horses came to a quick halt at the urging of their riders. Annastace had her rapier to hand, August clutched Crow's short sword, and Arielle had her bow slung over one shoulder and a sheathed dirk at her hip.

The mother of the little Sureblade clan surveyed the situation and smiled a big, beautiful, icy smile that made Louis want to throttle and ravage her at the same time.

"It seems you've robbed us of our sport tonight, Dennis," She said to the team leader.

"We received word from your eldest son, by way of the new baron of Eastedge, that the previous baron, Tauran, sent some malefactors to assault you and your children."

Annastace visibly bristled at the mention of the mercenary and traitor to his kingdom, and lackey to the murderer of her husband.

"These would be they," she informed.

Dennis chuckled. "Only two?" he asked. "A smarter man would have sent more for the Sureblade clan."

"You'll find two more back at the cottage," Annastace said matter-of-factly. "One in the parlor and another in a hole on the east side of the house. Neither will be going anywhere until their bodies are hauled away."

"Was there any other word from Ethan?" Arielle and August asked at the same time, and in nearly the same voice, Annastace noted. August's voice had grown a tad deeper.

"Yes," Dennis said. "He did for Tauran and is bound for Ridgeland."

Annastace was pleased to hear her son was well but distressed that he was going east. She knew full well what horrors awaited him at Ridgeland.

The boy was so much like his father. Too much, she feared, though there was nothing to be done about it.

"Is there any word of the offworlder Raxe?" she asked. "Ethan was travelling with him and the Keeper's Hounds."

Dennis shook his head. "His message didn't reference the Child of the Old Ones, milady. He only spoke of himself and this would-be threat."

"Oh, well," Annastace said, resigning herself to more worrying about her son and Raxe. "These two idiots are quite lucky you caught them before we did. Please be so kind as to get them the hell out of my sight, and the bodies of their friends from my home."

"By all means," Dennis said respectfully. "Catherine Lorr instructed us to provide safe passage for you and your children to the palace should any danger befall you. I'll admit you seem quite capable, but…"

Annastace smiled again, warmly this time, at the thought of her good friend's concern. "If the Head Mage's wife makes such a request, I suppose I can ill afford to refuse."

She took pride her self-reliance but she was no fool. Tauran would never have been able to recruit Louis if Louis had not already harbored animosity toward her. There could be other rejected suitors or disgruntled employees wishing to do harm to her and her children.

There was nothing she could do to protect her firstborn while he was adventuring, but she would be damned if she did not do everything she could to keep her twins safe.

15.2

A large crow perched atop the Stratosphere Tower and looked down at Las Vegas as if it owned the bustling metropolis. And why should it not? Las Vegas was a kindred spirit. She was a predator that lured her prey with seductive promises of fortunes won of fantasies fulfilled. Any passion, no matter how mundane or perverted, could be sated in this city. The price, however, was extremely high for the weak or unwary, for they were the easiest prey.

The strong, or at least those who thought themselves strong, were by far the most delectable prey. Nothing in this or any world was as sweet as newly corrupted innocence.

In the end, the city's victims left Las Vegas diminished, and usually in more ways than one. Some of her victims never left at all.

All of this danger was hidden beneath a façade of slick newer attractions designed to promote a family-friendly atmosphere. Indeed, Las Vegas used multiple identities as bait for her prey. She could be anything to anyone. She could be a false Eden or an all-too-real Sodom and Gomorrah. What city could possibly be a better tribute to the Dierglyorr?

The midnight-black demon bird, as large as it was, was all but invisible against the night sky, all but the marble-sized orbs of its intense, glowing, blood-red eyes that took in everything that happened in the streets almost a quarter of a mile below.

She is here, the Dierglyorr croaked. *She is close.*

And she was alone.

The call the foolish girl made saved the Dierglyorr the trouble of using magic to find her. She and Dan had been diligent in removing physical traces of themselves during their travels. It was physically impossible to conceal *every* trace, of course. The merest spore, the barest mote of a skin cell floating on the air as a speck of dust, was more than enough for a being as learned and powerful as the Dierglyorr to craft a highly functional tracking spell. But finding that mote and crafting a tracking spell would take time.

It was just as well. The Dierglyorr had been many different things before the Leader gods fused them to create a sixth level demon. It had been a human sorcerer and politician, a changeling, and a dierglii.

Before they became extinct, dierglii were vicious predators and the most fearsome hunters in existence. To this point the Dierglyorr had employed magic and manipulative talent to use humans like chess pieces. It had not had many opportunities to allow its skill and instincts as a predator to dominate its actions. Now it could bring those abilities to bear to hunt the girl. The demon knew it would not take long to find her scent and pinpoint her exact location.

Dan must have realized *all* of the ways he was being tracked. The demon had anticipated that Dan would be able to feel the retriever's magic as it followed him on his meandering and utterly useless trek across the continent. Dan and his pursuers were near the northwestern coast, but Lisa had been traced to Las Vegas, which meant that Dan had sent her away with the foolish belief that she would be safer without him.

The Dierglyorr would not face the old man directly if it could be avoided. Dan might have been bowed by time and the frailty of human physiology, but his mind was sharp and filled with two centuries of knowledge. And he was a Child of the Old Ones, a direct descendant of the Gatekeeper. That meant his magic would make him formidable if the demon confronted him directly. But the retriever would have no such difficulty. The Dierglyorr had made certain of that.

The girl, however, was a different story. It was true that the woman had not been a real concern. That changed when the deal was struck with Joel, an agreement that Joel wasted no time in breaking. By helping Jon the Firemaster and his wife escape the baron's stronghold, the offworlder helped the Dierglyorr's enemies. As a fire elemental, Jon's magic would make him a powerful ally to the Head Mage. And Jon's speaking stone would have made it that much easier to cripple the Head Mage from a distance, as well as the rest of the Conjurer's Alliance.

DEMON OF LORR

Their escape would be short-lived, the demon knew, but Joel had nonetheless violated his part of their agreement. It was time for the Dierglyorr to exact its payment. It did not have very much time to spare for such sport, but then again, it would not need very much time. What it did to the dancer, Synn, was nothing compared to what it had in store for Joel's wife.

The demon spread its crow's wings and dived, wondering what form it would take when it raped, tortured, and devoured Lisa Harvey.

15.3

The tall blonde guy trailed Lisa as she ducked and dodged through the throngs of people on the Las Vegas strip. She knew he was there and tried her best to lose him. She was steadily increasing the distance between them but she was never quite able to shake him. Lisa regretted having the taxi drop her off at the five and dime store near the end of the strip. The store was a short walk from her hotel. She thought she would pick up some snacks to eat that night so she would not have to come out of the room again, or even risk ordering room service, before checking out of the hotel. She planned to move on to another city, possibly Los Angeles, first thing in the morning.

But that five and dime was where the man from the buffet found her. Lisa spotted him across the street shortly after she exited the store. She did not see the blonde woman with him. He started over when he noticed her. Her first instinct was not to go to her room and continue to a casino to try to lose him in the crowd, but she was sure that by now both he and his tall lady friend knew she was holing up in the hotel where they first saw her. Even if she lost them, all they had to do was stake out the hotel and wait for her to return.

So she decided to take the direct route. She would rush to her room, find a security guard on the way and tell him she was being harassed, grab her bag and rush back out. And she would not leave alone. She reached nervously into her purse, intending to call the police to report the couple as stalkers. Perhaps the police could occupy them long enough for her to get away. Her hand brushed against the cool barrel of her plastic gun but she did not feel her cell phone. The moment she glanced down into her purse someone bumped into her forcefully.

Lisa stumbled sideways and spun halfway around, causing her purse to swing around to her side. She quickly righted herself, snatched her purse back to her chest, and looked up at who bumped into her. It was the tall, pretty blonde woman.

"You can't do anything to me with all these people around," Lisa warned.

The blonde favored her with a beautiful smile beaming with perfect white teeth. Her pale blonde eyebrows, perfectly arched over crystal blue eyes, creased with a hint of guilt.

"I'm sorry," she said, slowly lifting a slender hand with impeccably manicured fingertips. "I didn't mean to give you the wrong idea. My friend Bjørn and I, we saw you the other night and thought you might be someone who would want to party with us."

Lisa took an involuntary step back. She looked over her shoulder to see the blonde man approaching at a casual pace. She turned a suspicious glare to the blonde.

"What do you mean *party*?" Lisa demanded.

The other woman's fair cheeks flushed. "I am *so* embarrassed," she began. "We thought you were a, you know…"

"A 'party girl'?" Lisa asked incredulously. "No, I'm not. But I *am* in a hurry." Lisa did not believe the woman's story for a moment. She brushed past her and continued on before the man could reach them. She changed her mind about going to her room.

After looking over her shoulder three times, she could no longer see the attractive couple. Suddenly she was afraid that they would head her off, that she would be cornered, trapped, if she went to her room. Instead, she reached for her cell phone again with her right hand.

And someone bumped into her again. It was a man this time, with dark, dirty hair and a fearful but desperate look in his bloodshot eyes. He reeked of alcohol and urine. The sight and suffocating smell startled her, and so did the knife that she saw less than an inch away from her ribs. No one on the bustling thoroughfare noticed. He grabbed her left arm.

"Say something and you're dead," he hissed.

Lisa was frozen with terror. All she could do was stare breathlessly for what seemed like forever. Before she knew it, her assailant managed to hustle her into a dark alcove between buildings.

He shoved her roughly against the wall a few feet behind her. The sounds of the strip were only yards away but they seemed distant and muffled in the shadows with the skinny, sickly looking man wearing a torn jean jacket, filthy work slacks, and bare feet standing between her and freedom.

"Drop the purse and run, bitch," he snarled.

Lisa started to do just that when she once again became aware of the cold, smooth plastic surface of her pistol. The touch reminded her with a jolt that she was not helpless. She might have been afraid, but she was definitely not helpless.

She was annoyed at herself for constantly jumping at shadows. She was tired of being intimidated.

She snatched the pistol out and pointed it at her assailant.

"Drop the *knife* and run, bitch," she snarled back. To her, though, it sounded more fearful than forceful.

And it apparently sounded the same way to her assailant. He smiled, showing off two or three brown, broken teeth.

"You gonna shoot me with a toy gun?" he croaked, just before he stepped toward her.

Lisa pulled the trigger without thinking. The pistol made a muffled pop and the edge of the mugger's left shoulder exploded in a spray of blood. A small chunk of stone exploded from the wall just behind him, making more noise than the gunshot. The man cried out in surprise and pain as the blow spun him around. Putting his right hand against the wall to support himself, he staggered out of the alley.

Lisa aimed at his back and her finger tightened on the trigger again. A cold logic in the back of her mind, in a voice suspiciously similar to Dan's, told her to eliminate him as a future threat. He might come back with junkie friends to attack her and finish the job.

But she could not bring herself to pull the trigger a second time. Instead, she watched him struggle out of the alley, moaning like a wounded animal. And then her adrenaline rush faded, leaving only terror in its place. Lisa slumped back into the wall and slid slowly to her backside on the ground, crying from both fear and frustration.

I shot someone…I fucking shot *someone.*

DEMON OF LORR

The only reason she did not rub her forehead raw was because she could not make her right hand loosen its grip on the pistol, nor could she make her left hand unclench the strap of her purse. She rocked back and forth and almost shrieked when her phone began to ring.

The ring blessedly distracted her after initially terrifying her. Her trembling right hand finally dropped the pistol back into the purse as she retrieved the phone. She knew it was Dan. All four throwaway cell phones in her purse were from Dan. No one else had the numbers. Just knowing he was calling helped to calm her fear a bit, but only a bit.

"Dan," she exhaled after clicking the talk button.

"Are you ok?" Dan asked worriedly.

"Yeah. I'm just scared to damned death."

"What happened?"

"I just *shot someone,*" Lisa said, fighting panic again.

"Breathe, Lisa," Dan reminded. "You're ok. Just remember that. Now calm down and tell me what happened."

"I think the organization found me," Lisa said. "A man and a woman, they looked like models or something, have been trailing me. I was running from the man and bumped into the woman and she fed me some crap about wanting to party. The street was crowded so she couldn't make a move and I managed to lose them but then some homeless dope fiend or something dragged me into an alley to rob me and I shot him. I fucking *shot* him, Dan!"

"Slow down," Dan said in the calmest voice he could manage. "Where is the mugger now?"

"He ran," Lisa answered. "What do I do?"

"Get the hell out of Vegas. And no more libraries."

"I never told you I was in Vegas," Lisa realized. "Or the library!"

"Exactly. And if I know, the organization will, too."

"So it *was* them?" Lisa asked fearfully.

"Probably not," Dan said. "If it was, you'd already be captured or worse. The mugger sounds like a junkie looking for money for a fix. From the way you describe the blonde couple they were too conspicuous to be agents.

"Either they really wanted to party or were running some other scam. You said the lady 'bumped' into you. Check your purse to see if anything's missing."

Lisa searched for a few seconds. Her eyes widened.

"The key card for my room is gone!"

"I thought it'd be something like that," Dan said. "They're planning to rob you. Or they're waiting in your room to have that party with you...whether you want it or not. Either way, you don't want to go back to that room."

"So what do I do?" Lisa asked again.

"I just told you. Get the hell outta Vegas. And don't send any more damn emails!"

"How did you..." Lisa gasped. "The email?"

"I'm just one old man with a few connections. So you better believe that the organization's gonna find you if they haven't already. Just because you're not a primary target doesn't mean they won't snatch you up if you put yourself on the radar. You're making it easy for them."

"So where do I go?" Lisa asked. "There's nothing at the hotel that I have to have. I've got all my credit cards and ID's in my purse. I can leave from here."

"Good," Dan said, a hint of approval finally in his tone. "Get to the bus station and take the next bus to Reno. I'll meet you there. Hopefully the organization will concentrate their focus on the strip and the library. They know by now we're not together. They may underestimate you, think you'll be careless enough to stick around Vegas longer you should.

"If you're disguised, and you damn well *better* be, you should be able to slip by them at the bus station. Pad your bra, and if you can, find something to pad your stomach. And remember to change your gait. That's another way they could recognize you. Shorten or lengthen your normal stride, maybe put a rock in your shoe, but don't walk crazy enough to call more attention to yourself than necessary."

"Ok, Dan, I will. What do I do when I get to Reno?"

"Wait for me."

15.4

A beautiful couple stepped off of the elevator on the sixteenth floor. The passengers remaining on the elevator gawked at both the man and the woman in something like awe. They were perfect, both of them tall, fair-skinned, blonde. The woman wore a form-fitting white dress that terminated well north of her knees and the man an exquisitely tailored, double-breasted navy blazer over a white cotton shirt that was tucked neatly into slim fitting white slacks. Both of them were slender and fit and moved with smooth athletic grace.

Hand in hand, Bjørn and Danica glided to the door at the far end of the hall. Bjørn slipped the key card into its slot and smiled when the little green light flashed. He pushed the door open and led Danica into the darkened room. Danica turned to Bjørn's as he ushered her into the suite.

"Do you think she will come back here this evening, darling?" she asked hopefully.

"I certainly hope so," Bjørn answered with a wolfish grin. "She's hot. That honey-brown skin must taste as sweet as it looks. I *know* we could convince her to party with us."

"But if she realized we took her key card..." Danica began.

Bjørn closed the door and grabbed Danica's pleasantly curved hips and swept her down the short hall. "Don't worry," he assured. "She won't suspect us. She'll just think she lost it and then she'll get another from the front desk. We've done this before, love. You know how well I pick them. Why so nervous?"

"It's been a while since we've been with a *sister*," Danica said with a lusty smile. "I'm anxious to see if she's a natural redhead. I don't want to miss out."

Bjørn waved his hand dismissively. "You worry far too – *Herregud*!" he swore. Danica yelped.

Soft illumination from the city lights seeped through the closed curtains to reveal a figure sitting across the room.

The recliner was filled with the bulk of a huge man with skin so dark-brown it was almost black. He was bulging with overdeveloped muscles and sported a shaved head.

"No," boomed his heavy baritone voice in perfect Norwegian. "Not even close to your God."

"Who the hell are you?" Bjørn demanded in his native tongue. "Are you the boyfriend?"

The stranger stood up slowly and it seemed to Danica that he would never stop rising. By the time he was completely vertical, he stood over a foot taller than Bjørn. He seemed to grow wider as well. His massive shoulders spread wider than the backrest of the big recliner. The couple took a frightened step away.

The bald giant smiled, revealing big white teeth, including evilly pointed canines.

"I was hoping to be the boyfriend," he answered, his bass voice rumbling like muffled thunder. "Even if only for an ecstasy-filled brief moment in time."

A crimson glow started to bleed from his dark eyes. Unintelligible words oozed thickly from the demon's black lips before it spoke to them again in their language.

"If only I was not in such a hurry," he lamented. "We would all wait together for Lisa's return. I could do oh so many delectable things to the two of you while we waited. But alas, I have precious little time to spare, so many obligations. I suppose the two of you will have to do."

Bjørn tried to reach for the small pistol he kept tucked beneath his blazer in the small of his back. He found to his dismay that he could not move. Danica tried to scream and bolt but no sound would escape her lips and her body could not move, either.

The demon's smile grew wider, so wide that its ears crept higher up on its head to accommodate the rictus that was slowly filing with dripping ivory daggers.

EPILOGUE

Almost three hours had passed since Lisa spoke to Dan on her cell phone at half-past eleven. That was more than enough time for her to catch the midnight bus to Reno and become thoroughly bored watching the local station playing from the television gated high in the corner of the bus terminal. The local news was being re-played. When she was not scanning the terminal for potential agents Lisa kept her eyes focused on the TV in order to keep them away from the haggard transients scattered about the terminal. She made it a point to avoid eye contact to keep any of them from mistaking it for an invitation to panhandle.

A breaking story interrupted the news replay. A petite brunette, pretty despite her tired eyes, stood before a police barricade of wooden horses, police tape, and uniformed officers. Firemen, paramedics, and police were rushing in and out of frame behind her while multi-colored lights flashed from somewhere off camera.

> *"I'm here in Las Vegas on the north end of the strip where an explosion has rocked the plush high-rise hotel and casino behind me.*
>
> *"The explosion blew apart the northwest corner of the 16th floor and did serious damage to the adjacent floors. The fire has now been contained. The dead and injured are being removed from the wreckage, including two victims who, by the damage done to the bodies, are believed to have been in the suite that firefighters have determined to be the origin of the blast. No identifications have been made at this point."*

Lisa realized she was holding her breath. She had been staying at that very hotel, *in* the corner room. Her hotel window provided her a beautiful view of the Yucca Mountains in the distance.

"Coincidence?" whispered a familiar voice.

Lisa jumped at a strong and very familiar hand on her shoulder. She turned quickly and then reached into her purse for her gun when she saw an entirely unfamiliar elderly man's face under a dusty dark gray fedora.

But the voice and the gleam in the brown eyes were unmistakable.

"You scared the hell outta me, old man," she hissed.

"You should've saw me coming, girl," Dan chastised. "I saw you scoping the terminal but you just glanced over us – shall we say – less fortunate-looking people. You understand that's another way they could come at you, don't you?"

Lisa grudgingly agreed with a guilty nod. Dan was disguised as a handicapped homeless man, from the coarse and ragged gray whiskers effectively concealing the lower half of his face to the dark ashen skin, from his ratty shoes to his foul smell. He had even managed to sneak up on her in a wheelchair. His long duffle was strapped vertically to the back of the chair and a quad cane lay across his lap. She decided not to ask how he accomplished the smell and just accepted that the old guy took his disguises *very* seriously.

"And for the record, that was no coincidence," Dan continued. "*That* was the organization, almost certainly under the direction of the demon posing as one of their high-ranking executives. They used a similar move on me a few years ago at my assisted-living apartment. The police will never trace it back to them."

"Of course they won't," Lisa said.

Dan looked her up and down. "I like the look," he said flirtatiously. "It took me a half-second to spot you."

"How *did* you spot me?" Lisa asked.

"The walk. It's distinctive. It's nice but distinctive. I told you, you have to work on that."

"Yes sir," Lisa said sarcastically. "So, where to now?"

Dan smiled. "The last place they'll expect us to go, sweetheart. I got us two tickets to Chicago."

END

www.ingramcontent.com/pod-product-compliance
Lightning Source LLC
Chambersburg PA
CBHW071628260626
47170CB00001B/9